Sterlin

TITAN

STERLING NIXON

The final approval for this literary material is granted by the author.

First printing

ISBN: 978-1-951780-03-6 (trade paperback)

Printed in the United States of America

Dedicated to Colleen Nixon, Elizabeth Thompson, Robin Hamblin,
Sterling T. Nixon and my wonderful wife, Julia

ONE

Bracks stepped slowly, his footfalls echoing in the long, metallic hall. The room had circular, metal pillars that slanted in at an angle until they joined a domed roof far above. This massive room was unique amongst starships, but this was the fleet's flagship, and it dwarfed every vessel that was assigned to the Earth providence.

Pincers that sprouted from Bracks' elbows clicked menacingly against the serrated blades that ran along his forearms. These primitive appendages were once the pride of the Decamont. In those vicious days, the power of each warrior was recognized by the length and use of their pincers. But now they were forgotten except in the most savage of battles.

Bracks' grey exoskeleton was lined with scars, evidence of the fierce battles he had endured. War had worn him down, but never broken him, earning him the moniker "The Wall." In one battle, after his commander had been slain, as his oozing black blood had nearly completely dyed his grey armor, it was his skill alone that kept the enemy at bay. He had been raised three Links because of his efforts, a feat that was unheard of near the Capital, but more common on the Fringe. It was that feat that had earned him the rank of Revelator and had placed him in charge of several human cities, including Acadia. Unfortunately, for him, two days later, Acadia was in open rebellion.

His armor was bulky and lined with yellow stripes—the sign of the Unborn, those who had passed the Three Trials. Each line that traversed his chest was a badge of honor, a symbol of his triumphs in the Trials. That would do little for him here, on the Fringe of the Decamont Empire, under the rule of a Crine.

Their society had once been governed by many voices, but now they had consolidated their authority to only a few. A Crine on the Fringe was essentially a god in the sight of the Decamont. Their decisions were unquestioned. Their rule, absolute.

Bracks lowered his eyes as he approached a series of steps that led to the seat of the Crine. The Crine poignantly ignored Bracks' approach, his eyes elevated to the tops of the columns above. His chair was massive, large enough to seat three or four Decamont, but this Crine filled it well. It was, after all, this Crine who had been elected to oversee Earth, an honor that had no parallel among the Decamont.

Bracks did not know the actual name of the Crine. Names were rarely used unless someone of the same position was present. Like many titles of the Decamont, this one became his name. His title became his sole identity.

Bracks began to climb the long, exaggerated steps to the throne. Each step was more of a platform than anything else. As a Revelator, he was allowed to climb seven of the nine steps. When he reached his destination, he bowed low, his fist held fast against his chest. He would be in this position until his presence was acknowledged. He had never seen or spoken to the Crine before, but he had heard rumors that he might be in this position for hours before he was acknowledged.

For good or ill, this proved false.

"Hail the ArCrine," the Crine said, his tone flat.

"Hail the ArCrine," Bracks echoed.

The Crine stood, his size somehow diminishing the massive chair behind him. The Decamont clicked his pincers menacingly, sending an ominous echo through the hall. When he finally spoke, his voice was a low growl. "Three."

Bracks kept his eyes to the floor, his features flat. He hesitated between asking a question and remaining silent. Thankfully, the Crine spoke first.

The Crine's pincers snapped shut. "Iberia, Armean, and now, Acadia. Three. That's how many cities we've lost to rebellion these last two hundred years—and until recently, none of them were during my tenure. Out of three thousand seven hundred and forty-one, only three have rebelled. The first two rebellions were easily crushed with only one Division each, but neither city had electricity. But they tell me this rebellion is different."

"It is, my Crine," Bracks said.

"Explain."

"A Numberless by the name of Titan severed the connection between us and them," Bracks answered.

"How did he even know how to do that?"

"I do not know—"

Bracks' words were interrupted as his body was seized upon by an incredible force. His instincts kicked in and he fought back, flailing his pincers at the attacker. His actions were in vain, however; he had moved too slowly. He was now prey in the hands of a predator.

"Do you know what I did to your—" the Crine began but was interrupted as he received a quick, decisive blow to the chest. He stumbled back, releasing Bracks from his grasp. The Crine looked first to his pincers and then to Bracks, a smile now on his face.

Bracks stood to his full height, a trail of black blood dripped down from his neck, right where the Crine had held him fast.

"So, you are truly a student of the Sanctuary—not just a shell with yellow stripes on your armor."

Bracks nodded. "I am Unborn. I have passed the Three Trials."

The Crine repositioned himself, his pincers flared in the ancient style of Kamory. "That means little here on the Fringe. I have defeated your kind." With this, the large Decamont rushed forward, attacking with all the speed and ferocity as before. This time Bracks was prepared and ducked under the onslaught, returning an attack aimed at the Crine's side. It was blocked, but just barely.

The two stepped back, momentarily gauging each other. The Crine's smile had turned into a sadistic grin. To him, this was just a game. They clashed again, locked in fierce combat, the echoes of their struggle spreading throughout the empty hall. The Crine hit Bracks once in the cheek, twice more in each of his arms. The blows were powerful, numbing attacks that made his fingers tingle.

Bracks frowned. The Crine was talented, of that there was no doubt. He had a speed that defied his large stature. At first glance, he had no weakness, but this went against every doctrine Bracks had learned in the Sanctuary. So, he studied his opponent, biding his time as the battle intensified. And then Bracks found it. In each series of attacks, the Crine's first several blows were with precision, but his technique fell apart the more he persisted.

This had always been Bracks' talent. To watch. To understand. And finally, to anticipate. Then something shifted in the conflict. The Crine no longer could drive his much smaller opponent back. His attacks no longer reached their target. It was as if the Crine was facing someone different entirely.

Then the Crine was struck hard, a solid blow to the side of his neck. It had been the first time Bracks had struck him with all his power, but it had been enough. The Crine crumpled to the ground, his legs becoming useless. To his credit, he tried to stand, but his efforts only shifted him to the opposite side. Guards appeared from behind the throne, each one dressed in silver armor. Within moments, several of them had trained their Blazers on Bracks while others rushed forward with drawn Arc Blades. The Crine waved them off, and the guards' charge stalled before it finally stopped.

Bracks offered a hand to the Crine, a gesture of goodwill, but the Crine only looked at it as if it were a trick. He finally forced himself to a knee. It was a minute longer before he could stand.

The Crine's eyes were filled with an unquenchable fury. But instead of turning them to Bracks, he focused his attention on the guards. "Did I call for the Asminian Guard?"

The warriors looked towards their commanding officer, their faces marked with confusion.

The lead guard sheathed his sword and took a knee. "I'm sorry, my Crine. I thought you were in need of assistance—" His words stopped short as head was removed from body, spraying the grey throne with black blood. The head fell to the ground, bouncing twice on the stairs before it circled across the court, leaving a curved line of blood.

It seemed the guards had been somewhat used to this brutal display, and they departed quickly, exiting where they had entered. Only Bracks seemed surprised by the sudden decapitation. Once again, Bracks and the Crine were alone, save for the headless body that remained on the steps.

"Someone had to die," the Crine said, "the Capital would've demanded it. It would have been you," he nodded to Bracks, "or him. And I don't think I'm ready to get rid of you just yet."

"The Capital would have called for blood?" Bracks asked. He had not been to the Capital planet since he was a boy. He had fond memories of the Capital—which had always been a place of learning and tolerance, not one that would demand the death of a loyal Decamont. *Could things have changed that much?*

As the Crine matched eyes with the Revelator, the little patience he had regained now seemed to wane once again. "Yes, the Capital. You've been on the battlefield these last few decades, and so you may not have noticed, but ruling has become a bloody affair. But that's not our concern. We have lost control of a city. Worse, that city seems to have functioning power still."

"Give me command, and I will take it back," Bracks said, his words taking on a bitter edge. "Give me a chance to earn your favor, my Crine. Give me command, and I will salt the ground of Acadia with their dead."

The Crine narrowed his eyes, his expression stuck between a look of annoyance and disgust. "How many Divisions do you require?"

"Four," Bracks replied evenly.

"Four?" the Crine answered. "When the other two cities rebelled, they were able to destroy them with only one."

"Acadia still has its shields," Bracks answered. "With it, we won't be able to soften their ranks with long-range fire."

"Well, anyone can take the city with four Divisions," the Crine said. "There's no honor in a one-sided battle."

"Grant me three Divisions, my Crine, and I will crush the rebel city tonight."

"The issue is not so much what you need; it is more of an issue of what we have. Supplies have been running thin and all excess warriors have been pulled away from the Fringe. We only have a single Division in reserve."

"We can siphon Roaches from the existing Divisions around other cities," Bracks answered.

"How much time will that take?" the Crine growled.

"I could get it done in four months," Bracks answered. "I'll have to organize, transport, and coordinate the troop movements, but I'm confident I can complete it by then."

The Crine looked appraisingly at Bracks, as if seeing him for the first time. Bracks met his black eyes, something that was against custom but seemed appropriate in the moment. Finally, the Crine spoke, his voice becoming law as soon as the words left his mouth. "Your fate is tied to the success of this campaign. Fail me, and I will not only execute you; I will execute all those who ever called you friend."

Bracks took another step up the stairs towards the Crine, again defying tradition. "Worry no more, my Crine. I will crush Acadia."

TWO

Cojax focused on a single point in the flames, his entire body as still as the massive building behind him. The fire spread quickly, completely enveloping the flesh in seconds. The heat came next, hitting Cojax in waves around the parts of his body that were not protected by Static Armor—the neck, face, just above the knees, and hands. His armor adjusted, cooling down his core. It was an odd sensation: both hot and cold, both the sweat on his brow and the chills around his chest.

Titan lay before him, his body slowly being taken as flecks of ash began to rise. He was the last of those on the Infinite Council—the last of those who had ruled the city. The rest had either died in battle or had fled, leaving a void in the new city of Titan. The forum where they now stood had been cleaned. The dead removed. The conflict from the night before now seemed more of a nightmare than a reality. The only remnants of battle were the charred marks along the building from the Blazers. As the fire progressed, warriors studied their surroundings, as if looking for direction.

A Validated stepped forward into the view of the HoverCams. She was clearly a First Tier, as evidenced by the sheen of her perfectly crafted armor. She removed her helmet, her head bowed low. She saluted to the crowd, who responded in kind. She was a remarkably beautiful individual: her long flowing black hair, her rounded chin, her sharp cheekbones that seemed crafted from marble rather than flesh. Cojax recognized her. She was an Omega, the highest commanding officer on the battlefield. She was one of the most talented warriors ever to grace the CityScreens, having risen quickly through the Tiers from the time of her Crossing. Out of a city of ten million, she alone carried the highest Score at the time the Numberless fell. She was not the biggest warrior, but she certainly commanded attention.

"I am Abria, Omega in the Armstrong Faction. We are Titans, as my young friend has stated, and we shall not falter. Some of you may doubt or even question the actions of what took place last night. Some of you may question the validity of this revolution. I wish to speak to those now. I spent the greater part of this morning looking through the Numberless Information Network. I want to add my voice to those that already have spoken, that indeed, the Numberless deceived us, they lied to us, they manipulated us. And so now, we start anew, as a people born again. We shall form a new government, one selected by Faction leaders that will be best suited to our needs. This is not a time for discontent; this is not a time for contention. Go about your day as you always have before. You are still Validated—you are still defenders of this great city."

Cojax lost interest in Abria's words almost as soon as she started to spill them. His focus was on his father's body and the flames that embraced him. Others spoke but Cojax did not heed them. It was not until Marcus' hand rested on his shoulder that his concentration broke. The two brothers stared at each other, their expressions solemn, their bodies rigid.

Marcus finally spoke. "I want to speak to you in private." He gave a poignant nod towards the Trinity.

Cojax followed, his features unreadable. Each step he took away from his father's body felt like a hammer against his chest. Marcus led the way inside. The Trinity was as impressive as ever, its grand entrance inviting and yet somehow foreboding. The walls were smooth, the floors polished. Some of the fiercest fighting last night took place in the area where Cojax now stood, but all blood and debris had disappeared. Marcus led him down a hallway and through a door before they reached a small but functional room that was lined with rows of shelves topped with storage boxes.

Marcus shut the door and turned, facing his brother with a solemn expression. A reverent silence settled between the two of them. Finally, Marcus spoke. "Are you alright?"

Cojax slowly raised his chin. "I can't believe he's gone. I barely knew him. He wasn't just part of the system; I thought he *represented* the system. And yet, in a moment, he gave it all up. In a moment, he turned his back on the world he knew, the world that respected him. He chose to rebel—to fight against the Decamont."

"Bis vivit qui bene vivit," Marcus said. He stepped forward, putting a thick hand on Cojax's shoulders. "He lives twice who lives well: for he has the joy of his life, and he lives again in our memories long after he is gone."

"He gave his life so the Aberration might live," Cojax said in a whisper.

"He gave his life for all of us."

The room fell silent for several moments before Cojax spoke. "Do you remember our mother?"

"Of course."

"Just before she was Released into the Killing Field," Cojax said. "She grabbed us both in a desperate, long embrace, one that was most certainly illegal. I can still remember her stoic, soft features; her confident, calm disposition. Titan did not move to break the embrace, as his duty required, but, instead, he waited patiently for it to end. I can remember with perfect clarity the intensity of his gaze. No words of grief or regret escaped his lips—only those of duty—but you could see his countenance change, as if he was a shell of his former self. That was who he was—who he would have been had Acadia not folded him to its will. Do you remember?"

"Yes."

"I wish I could have known *that* man."

Marcus nodded, his words low and solemn. "The best we can do now is to take the city in the same direction that Titan would have wanted."

"We pushed Titan in this direction; he didn't choose it. I can't help but feel that it was a mistake."

"What do you mean?"

Cojax stepped back, examining the lines on his palm. "If Titan did not aid us, the Acadia System, the computers, our electrical power would have been crippled by the Decamont. They would have shut down our water, our food supply, our ability to function. If Titan had not severed that connection, our revolution would have ended before it even began."

"But he did."

"And what other pitfalls are waiting for us?" Cojax asked. "What other traps are waiting just underfoot? We cannot afford to make mistakes—each one could cost lives. Titan was one of the first to fall, but there will be more to follow."

Marcus nodded, soaking in each word with a nod. "Well said.

We might be in a different situation, but we are of the same mind. We've won our first victory, and if we don't act quickly enough, it will be our last. But, we don't have to go it alone. *You* don't have to go it alone. Why don't we stand together?"

Cojax nodded, his expression sad but stoic. "We need—"

Just then, Marcus and Cojax's ArmGuards simultaneously chirped.

Cojax looked at the device, studying it in earnest. "It's Adriana. She wants us to meet her in one of the small control rooms."

"I just got the same message," Marcus replied.

"I'm sure she's already come up with some elaborate scheme to protect the city."

"Perhaps," Marcus answered, "but let me ask you something: Do you trust her?"

"She's in the same situation we are," Cojax answered. "She needs us as much as we need her."

"And when she's not in the same situation as us anymore, what then?"

"What do you mean?" Cojax asked.

"I know her only by what you've told me," Marcus said, "and what you've told me is that she has a gift of manipulating all those around her. What she did in the Mahghetto—how she controlled the Disciples—is something that should not even be possible under the strict rules of the Acadian Code. Now that there's no AC, who's to say what she's capable of."

Cojax smiled. "Good thing I've got my big brother to watch over me then."

Marcus frowned. "I'm serious."

"I know you are."

Marcus sighed before continuing. "If you don't listen to anything else I say, listen to me now. Don't trust anyone more than you have to—especially her."

THREE

The small control room had an oval table with hard, black chairs that circled it. The seating was not so much for comfort as it was for function. Cojax found a seat next to Jessica, who gifted him a warm smile. Adriana seemed disappointed at Jessica's presence, as if it had not been her idea to invite her. The room already had several individuals inside and most had opted to stand. Cojax knew most of these faces, but a few were unfamiliar. He found himself studying the newcomers with a hard, intense gaze. Most were of the BloodBorne Faction, but that did not mean he trusted them.

Cojax nodded a greeting to Orch, Ion, and Finn, who had positioned themselves in chairs next to Adriana. Finn looked especially eager to get as close as possible to the beautiful vixen, who was now stealing the attention in the room. Once enough people entered, Adriana began in her typical smooth and sultry voice. The room fell silent as she used her ArmGuard to activate a video. Cojax's face appeared on the screen, his stance stoic. "This city will no longer be called Acadia—that was its name in slavery—but it shall be known as Titan, after the noble man who died for our freedom. And now, my friends, the Decamont have controlled us for so long, they think we will crack under the pressure they'll most surely set upon us. They will come at us with their armies and try to place us back into bondage. They think we are but mere mortals. But they're wrong, my brothers and sisters, for we are Titans."

She ended the video, nodding curtly to Ion, who switched the screen off. She turned first to Cojax and then to Finn.

"That was amazing," Jessica whispered.

Finn wore a grin so wide it threatened to split his ears. "Cojax just flicked the AC away, as if it were nothing more than a fly in his soup."

"It's done," Marcus said, his words solemn but strong. "Alea iacta est—the die is cast. The AC has been broken. No one can reverse that now; it's already in everyone's head."

Finn was still smiling as he spoke. "We ended the war and the AC in one day—one day! They're going to make statues of us—life-size ones, although they might have to fabricate Jessica's height a little so she's not dwarfed by the rest of us."

"Tombstones," Adriana said from behind, "more likely."

Jessica recognized the word, but several others did not.

Adriana rolled her eyes and sauntered forward, her perfect curves demanding Finn's gaze. "Tombstones were once used to mark someone's grave when they died. They'll make tombstones for us if we aren't careful—not statues."

Finn looked up, like a child whose ice cream had just rolled through the dirt. "What are you talking about? We're liberators."

"We're unpredictable," she replied, "and that means we threaten all those in the Top Tiers."

"Sounds like someone likes to see the cup as half empty," Finn teased.

Adriana looked at Finn, annoyance apparent in her features.

"Oh, come on," Finn said. "We won."

"Why do you say that, Adriana?" Cojax asked.

"We have won, yes," Adriana answered, "and the AC is abolished along with the Tiers, but that does not mean it will stay that way."

"Who wouldn't want the AC gone?" Cojax asked.

"You can't be that naïve," Adriana said, "how come all the cute ones are so clueless? Jessica, I'd think twice before your relationship gets much more serious."

Jessica tensed but did not answer.

"Alright," Adriana said, "I'll break it down the best I can." She turned her attention to Ion, who had been a rapt listener to the conversation. "Ion, can you pull up the video file of everyone in the forum at the time of Cojax's announcement?"

"Yes," Ion said.

"I'm not done," she said with a sexy smile, "I also need you to run an emotional recognition meter. Can you draw it into an index file and link it to a graph? Pictures are so much better for this crowd."

"He doesn't know how to do that—" Finn said.

"Done," Ion answered.

"Can you bring it up three-dimensionally?"

"Yes, ma'am."

Jessica felt a hint of jealousy at Ion's reactions. Before when she tried to get Ion to broadcast her signal last night, he was full of questions; for Adriana, however, he seemed to provide nothing but solutions. *She's the mean one and I'm the one that has to ask twice to get things done.*

Adriana nodded to Ion. "Play the video in real-time but be sure to turn down the volume; I don't want Jessica to become so entranced with the voice that she loses focus on everything else." The video played, showing Cojax's ash-covered face in a perfect three-dimensional image. At the bottom of the video were several lines in different colors. They peaked at some points and troughed in others. When Cojax spoke of the AC being abolished, there was an explosion of color.

"Alright," Adriana said.

"How did you even know the Acadian System was capable of doing this?" Finn asked.

"My mother worked in the Main Control Room before her head was taken by a Damnattii," she said with no hesitation. "This type of analysis was done every time they made a major announcement. It was one of the ways they gauged the city's temperament. Unfortunately, the CityScreens are the only platforms that are capable of recording and analyzing; so, we only get a slice of a much bigger picture. This will give us a decent sampling size, however. Ion, can I get this divided into Tiers?"

"Done."

Adriana took a few seconds to interpret the chart before she spoke. "The blue represents joy, relief, excitement—all positive emotions. You can see that those in Tiers Ten through Five have an average emotional response that is much more positive. They welcomed the news. And of course they did; they were mediocre and then suddenly they were not. Those that were in the Tenth Tier experienced the greatest positive feedback because they were on the verge of being Rifted—this makes sense. As each Tier ascends, however, the positive emotions are replaced with orange, brown, or even red, which is anger or disgust. By the time you get to the Third Tier, the average blue score is much lower, and the red one is positively bleeding. It's pretty safe to say, Cojax, that there are some out there in the Top Tiers who would put a dagger in your heart if given a chance."

"You know," Finn said, "on second thought, I don't want my own statue."

"Can't they see that they're better off?" Cojax whispered.

Adriana sighed. "Not for some of them. You did the right thing. You seized the moment, shattering the AC. Until that moment, our course was uncertain, but you clearly placed us on the path of rebellion. In a moment of confusion, you took control and rewrote the script."

"Why didn't the First Tiers oppose him?" Finn asked. "Why didn't they try killing him as he made the announcement?"

"Because, my handsome friend, perception determines reality. When Cojax announced the end of the AC, people shouted for joy. They cheered. They celebrated. Those that were against it did not know if they were alone—and so, they stayed quiet until they could figure out if others agreed with them. The human psyche is not too difficult to figure out: we are much more willing to go along with something if everyone believes it is what the group wants. If tonight was the last time we had to deal with all these people, it would have been a solid move, one that was so unexpected and dynamic that it could not have been prevented."

"But…," Jessica prodded.

"…but we do have to live with these people," Adriana said with a groan, "and so, they will do what any group does when they suffer a defeat: retreat…regroup…reassess, and attack."

Finn nodded to Cojax. "I really thought that the last one was going to be another 'r' word."

"I guess I could've said reengage," Adriana said, sparing a wink for Finn. "So, as soon as they figure out that other people feel the same way they do, they'll try to take power for themselves, and they'll cite their authority and superior experience over yours."

"She's right," Finn said.

"She's kind of right," Cojax answered.

Adriana folded her arms. "Explain."

"The people won't be put back into ignorance. Once the truth has been released, it can't be unlearned."

"True, but they'll move to take control—to institute their own system of government," Adriana said. "Did you hear Abria? She did not say the government would be chosen by the people; she said a form of government would be selected by 'Faction leaders' that will be best suited to our needs."

Marcus stood. "They've already started to consolidate their power."

"Who?" Orch asked. "And how do you know that?"

"The First Tiers have been communicating amongst each other through their ArmGuards," Marcus replied. "There're only ten-thousand First Tiers, and so there're far fewer opinions."

"Let them hash it out," Finn said. "Who cares what government we end up electing."

"What if they get it wrong?" Cojax asked. "What if they put us back in the chains we just broke from?"

"There's a group gaining some popularity called the Restorationists," Marcus supplied, "that wants to do just that. They want to revert back to the Tiers; revert back to the things that they know."

"They can't be serious," Cojax said, his voice taking on new venom.

"And so, some of the sheep want back into the pen," Orch said with a handsome grin. "What other groups are there?"

Marcus looked at his ArmGuard in earnest. "These are the most popular ones: First Tiers, who want to set up a kind of Oligarchy with former First Tiers in power—Abria is leading that movement; then the Unbroken, a group that wants a man named Onar to rule as a Dictator; the Statesmen want to formulate each Faction into an independent State; and The Republic, which wants to operate by elected officials."

"That's rot," Cojax said. "The First Tiers are making all of the decisions. That's the very thing we were fighting against."

"Where were the First Tiers when we were raiding the Trinity?" Jessica asked. "Where were they when we were sacrificing our blood and bodies so that everyone in the city could know the truth? They were the ones fighting against us—and now they think they should rule. They were the ones doing the bidding of the Numberless."

Marcus shrugged. "I honestly don't know any better way to do it. If we involved too many people, the process becomes too complicated; too few, we invite corruption. At least there's some semblance of order. One of the rules that the First Tiers have established early on is that only political parties backed by at least one Faction get any say. That has helped to keep the conversation down to a manageable level."

Jessica stood, her fists slamming into the table. "They're going to prioritize all the benefits to the Top Tiers! We're simply replacing the Numberless for First Tiers. We aren't changing how the system works. We fought to liberate the disenfranchised, not give them false hope and then force them back into the same situation as before."

"If we put in a government that is *just* and fair," Marcus replied, "then those disenfranchised will get a voice in our new system. They'll be better off than they were before—all of us will be."

"And who decides what a *just* government is!" Jessica was now screaming with rage, her small frame shaking from the noise. "We don't even know who's leading these movements. They could be agents of the Numberless, hell-bent on pitching us back into Acadia."

"I'm one of the leaders," Marcus replied, his voice matching Jessica's intensity.

"What?" Cojax asked with surprise.

Marcus refused to look at his brother as he answered the question. "I was the first to contact all First Tiers. We need a clear ruling body, and I wanted to make sure that there was a just, concise process to that aim. If I had not started the conversation, someone else would have, and they might not have set the right tone. Right now, we have an opportunity to make something new; right now, we have a chance to form a government that is *fair* for all."

Orch leaned back and folded his arms. "What government are you suggesting?"

"The Republic," Marcus replied evenly. "It's the only way we can ensure equitable treatment of everyone from the First to the Tenth Tier."

"What about the Rifters?" Jessica asked.

"And the Rifters," Marcus added. The large man let his words sink in. He leaned back, meeting the eyes of everyone in the room in turn. "And I need all of your help. Cojax and Jessica started this movement. They have tremendous influence among the Bottom Tiers. The people also see Titan as a hero. And Cojax and I are the last surviving sons of that hero. If you join my cause, if you throw your support behind The Republic, we can beat all the other parties."

"How would the Republic function?" Orch asked.

"We hold elections for positions of importance," Marcus answered. "We elect a body that makes laws, another one that enforces them, and a third that interprets them. We'll have a comprehensive system of checks and balances that ensures the greatest equity for all."

"I still don't like the idea that the government is being formed by First Tiers," Jessica added.

"What other options are there?" Marcus asked.

"A mass election," Jessica responded.

"In a city of ten million people," Marcus answered, "you'd be left with ten million different ideas of how to rule. I don't even know how you could logistically organize something of that scale."

"Marcus is right," Adriana replied. "A mass election would be a foolish endeavor. People would end up voting for people they don't even know."

Jessica's face turned red.

"But," Adriana replied, her voice taking on a thin edge, "I don't think that letting the First Tiers choose how to govern us is a good idea. They're used to being the elite, the untouchable, the ones elevated in society. Any power structure they chisel out will favor the Top Tiers."

"Not if we set it up in such a way that it doesn't," Marcus said. He then turned to his brother, his voice slightly pleading. "Will you help me? Brother, we can do this together, as our father would have wanted it. Will you back The Republic?"

Cojax slowly stood, his face expressionless. He looked down before his gaze slowly drifted up. "None of this matters now—whether we have a just or an unjust government. We're in the midst of a war. The Decamont are going to come in with everything they've got, and we need to be ready for them when they do. They come to wipe us from the map. We don't have time for any of this."

"What are you saying?" Marcus asked.

"Every Republic of the past failed or succeeded because of one principle: they take time to accomplish anything. The leaders of a Republic might be corrupt, but because it takes so blazing long to get anything done, much of that corruption is abated. A Republic is the last sort of government we can afford to have."

Marcus shook his head. "What do you suggest?"

"We need one individual to rule," Cojax answered. "In a city of ten million, we need one voice that can be heard above all else."

"You want a tyrant?" Marcus asked.

"We need a monarch," Cojax answered.

"And who do you suggest we put in?" Marcus said. "Onar the Slayer is already calling himself a King. Do you want to put him in power? Before we crushed the AC, he was about to be appointed to the position of a Numberless. Would you have him rule?"

Cojax choked on his words, his hesitation highlighting his indecision. He finally spoke. "I don't know anything about him."

"Exactly," Marcus answered.

"It doesn't change the fact that we need someone that can move us to action," Cojax replied. "Even during the Roman Republic in times of crisis, the people sometimes elected a King. Remember that one…Cincinite or something. He gave up his power as soon as he defeated the enemy."

"Cincinnatus," Marcus corrected.

"Marcus, we are in a crisis," Cojax said.

Marcus frowned. "This is true, brother. But be careful you don't become the very thing you just defeated. Remember, it was the Numberless that used the 'crisis' of the invading Roach armies to justify how little freedom they gave all of us." The large man leaned back, pushing off the table with his stumped arm. He looked around the room, a warm light in his eyes. "This is something that each of us needs to consider, to contemplate, to figure out for ourselves individually. I pray that you will take the next few days to come to a decision. You know where I stand—I hope you stand with me." With this, he turned, his movement slow as he left the room. Ion stood as well; his eyes downcast as he too retreated out the door.

FOUR

"Well," Finn said, "I'm just going to say it. That was awkward."

Marcus' absence left a heavy weight in the room—even Adriana seemed unnerved by it. The remaining individuals looked at each other, unsure if they should continue. The tension had been rising by degrees, and now that Marcus left, that tension turned into unease.

Adriana finally spoke. "Well, that's unfortunate."

"He's just stubborn," Cojax answered.

"Or we are," Orch said.

"It's already begun," Adriana said, "and we're falling behind."

Finn leaned forward. "What has?"

"The shift in power," Adriana replied. "We have an advantage, but if we want to keep it, we have to move quickly."

"What advantage is that?" Finn asked.

"The Rifters," Adriana answered, "and the Bottom Tiers. They'll be less than excited to hear that the First Tiers are deciding how we are to be governed. We need to be seen as being separate from the First Tiers by making ourselves appear as champions of the people. We have the numbers. There are over seven million people that are in or below the sixth Tier."

"I'll start developing a message we can put out through our ArmGuards," Cojax said.

"We better do it quickly," Jessica said, "before the First Tiers try to eliminate our ability to communicate with those in the city."

"They can't cut us out completely," Finn replied.

"The Aberration is right," Adriana said, her face shifting into a foul grimace. "That's the first thing they'll try to do—eliminate our ability to communicate with the Bottom Tiers."

"Call me Aberration one more time," Jessica said, "and you won't be communicating with anyone."

Adriana smirked.

Cojax turned to Orch. "Can you work on that? Can you make

sure they don't cut us out of the Acadian System?"

Orch frowned. "I'm good with the Blazer, remember? Not preventing people from being cut out of the Acadian System. But, I can ask around and see who might be."

"We've got to reveal the First Tiers' little secret game to the city before they have a chance to cut us out," Cojax said.

"It will give us leverage," Adriana answered. "If we can rally support and form a coalition, we'll have a voice in how we are governed. If we represent the Bottom Tiers, they'll *have* to include us in the conversation."

"So, we can free the Rifters, right?" Jessica said. "That's the whole point of us forming a coalition, so we can protect the Bottom Tiers, not just use them to carve out a piece of power, right?"

"Of course," Adriana answered. "But as it is right now, unless we consolidate our influence, the First Tiers will cut us out completely."

"When do we plan on freeing the rest of the Rifters then?" Jessica asked, her voice now taking on a skeptical tone. "We've freed all those that followed us, but the vast majority of Rifters are still living as slaves. We have to tell them that they're free now."

Adriana bit her lip. "That might complicate things."

"Complicate things?" Jessica's eyes became accusatory slits. "We were fighting for their freedom as much as ours."

"The Rifters are in charge of food growth, preparation, and delivery along with a dozen other critical tasks," Adriana replied simply. "If we freed them right now, how will that affect the system? Who will do those jobs? Who will stay behind and train others to do those jobs?"

Silence fell over the room as Adriana's words were being considered. Finally, Jessica spoke, her chin portraying her disgust. "Wait. What? What are you suggesting?"

Adriana did not meet eyes with Jessica as she answered. "We will free them—I promise you. That's what we fought for, but if we do it prematurely, we risk destroying the very thing that's keeping us from chaos—continuity. Who would go down there, in the belly of the city, to work in the dirt? Who among us would be willing to enter the Rift every day and receive very little food in return?"

Jessica was on her feet, her jaw so tight it threatened to crack her teeth. "I can't believe what I'm hearing. We need to free those in the Rift regardless of what effect it will have. It is morally wrong to keep them as slaves."

Adriana rolled her eyes. "Please don't make this about morality. Yes, I agree with you. Keeping them as slaves is not ideal, but what are the logistics of letting them go right now? What if you told the Rifters they were free to go where they pleased, to eat what they pleased? Our food stores would be depleted within months; our farmers would disappear. We don't even have adequate housing for them above ground. Where will they stay? What will happen to the food delivery system?"

"We will have to offer some form of wage or currency for the Rifters' service," Cojax answered.

"Yes, that will have to be the long-term solution," Adriana agreed, "but we can't even agree on what sort of government structure we want to establish, much less on any consideration for currency. Our society is so different from anything in the past that we are pretty much starting from zero. The data Ion released to the city about the Rift only contained basic information. The Validated might know where it is located now, but *we* know how the Rift operates. We know how to find our way down there; we know how to control the Rifters; we know the different Tiers that exist and how they function. I doubt any of the First Tiers know or care about any of that. That means we can control them, and if we control them, we can regulate the supplies that run through the city."

"How long do you propose keeping them as slaves?" Orch asked.

Adriana met eyes with Orch, it was warm and inviting. "I don't have any idea. It depends on how long it takes our city to establish a government. Could be weeks; could be months."

"As long as it isn't forever," Orch said.

Jessica turned her attention to Orch. "You've been down there. You know how the people live—how the Hoarders are close to starvation. How can you condemn them to another day of that hell? How can you even consider keeping them in the Rift?"

Orch looked down, his usual arrogant smile gone. "I agree with you, Jessica. It is wrong, but I agree with Adriana that it is necessary. By design, the food they produced is exactly what is needed. If those in the Rift consumed more, or even if they demanded more for their work, we would all soon starve."

Jessica turned to Cojax for support. "And what do you think of all this?"

Cojax sighed and stood. "I think we should consider all of our options before committing to any of them."

"That sounds like such a safe answer," Adriana replied.

"In the meantime," Cojax continued, "we need to consolidate as much influence as possible. We need to organize the Bottom Tiers into a group that we can communicate with—much like the First Tiers did amongst themselves." Cojax nodded to Finn. "Can you help me with that?"

"Me?" Finn responded indignantly. "What makes you think that I would want to spend my time putting together some trite propaganda? I'm not the best at…umm…putting words together."

"As evidenced by your last sentence," Orch replied, his arms folding in front of his chest. "Cojax is not talking about putting words together, but developing a unified, cohesive message that's not only short and punchy but also poignant." He unfolded his arms, beginning to pace the room. "If the Bottom Tiers are going to throw their lot in with us, they need to feel that they will be better off for doing it. It can't just be a single-dimensional message that we push on a generic group of people, but a personalized mantra that appeals to a myriad of perspectives." Orch stopped, cocking his head towards Cojax. "And I just volunteered myself for the position, didn't I?"

"I do believe you just did," Cojax replied.

"Alright," Orch said, "But before we work together, I want to make sure we understand each other: I'm in charge of the message."

Cojax shrugged indifferently. "Sure."

Orch nodded and winked towards Adriana. "Don't worry about a thing, darling."

Adriana rolled her eyes and folded her arms.

"We also need someone to organize those in the Rift," Cojax said, careful not to make eye contact with Jessica as he said it. "The First Tiers might not know how they're organized, but it won't be long before they do. We need to make sure we are in control of the Rift."

"I can—," Jessica began but she was abruptly cut off by Adriana.

"—I already have."

All heads turned to Adriana.

Finn's eyes went between Jessica and Adriana, carefully gauging the intensity of the stares between the two girls.

"You did what?" Jessica said.

"It needed to be done, and most of you were otherwise occupied," Adriana said simply.

"When?" Cojax asked.

"It doesn't matter," Adriana replied. "It's done."

"Who's in charge of the Rift?" Orch asked.

"I've handled it," Adriana replied. "Things will continue as they always have. We don't have to worry about food shortages."

"Who's in charge of the Rift?" Jessica growled.

"I've taken care of it," Adriana replied, not bothering to hide the annoyance in her voice.

"You seem to be doing a lot without letting the rest of us know," Jessica accused.

"I'm not going to second guess myself just so Jessica can feel good about my decisions," Adriana replied.

"If you plan on working with us," Cojax retorted, "then you will. We need to be unified—now more than ever."

Adriana bit her lower lip. It appeared she wanted to say something else but decided not to.

"…But it was the right move," Cojax said, his voice falling to a low whisper.

"We also need someone to make contact with the Damnattii outside the wall," Orch said. "They might have a better idea of what we're facing and how we can defend ourselves."

"Eeh," Finn said. "Who would want to volunteer to climb down into a slimy Roach den?"

"I saw my father deal with them before I came to Titan," Jessica stated. "I don't remember much about it, but maybe it will be useful. I'll go talk to them."

"I'll go with you," Cojax said.

"Cojax, I need you to help out with our message," Orch stated. "You're the one who stood in front of the camera and abolished the AC. So, anything we send out, you've got to be part of it."

"Well, someone has to go with her," Cojax said.

Everyone looked around, and most eyes rested on Finn, who

suddenly became very interested in his Armguard. The collective weight of the silence bored into Finn's chest.

"Oh, come on," Finn protested. "It reeks down there in the Roach dens. Plus, we were mortal enemies with the Roaches just a few days ago."

"I'll talk to Aias," Orch said, a smile spreading across his face. "We'll get you an escort of a few dozen armored Rifters."

"Alright," Finn said, his voice becoming serious, "but before we take an expedition down there, I want everyone to understand one thing: I am in charge."

"That's not going to happen," Orch replied.

"Not even a possibility," Adriana added.

"Maybe next time," Cojax assuaged.

Finn nodded again. "Okay, alright, I can respect that, but a simple 'no' would have sufficed. No need to sugar coat it. But at least give me the title of Ambassador."

"No," Orch said.

"Actually," Finn said, "that sounds even more harsh. Do you mind going back and trying to sugarcoat it a bit?"

FIVE

"Wait up," Cojax said to Jessica's back. "Where are you going?" She had left the meeting in a rush, her eyes focused on some point in the distance.

Jessica did not respond, and so Cojax tried again. "Wait, can I talk to you? Are you heading for the Roach den right now? If so, we better get an escort before—"

Jessica turned to Cojax, her face flushed with rage. "—That beast—that bloody Rifter. I would love to beat the rot from her smiling face."

"Who are you talking about?" Cojax asked.

Jessica continued walking, her words becoming so bitter that it made Cojax cringe. "Adriana. How did she convince everyone to keep the Rifters as slaves? We were slaves just like them not twenty-four hours ago, and yet we keep them in chains. That manipulative Rifter."

"Where are you going?"

"To the Rift, Cojax," Jessica replied. "*She* put someone in charge of it. That means she's controlling it."

Cojax nodded. "Relax. She's not going to do something that will jeopardize our alliance. She needs us as much as we need her."

"There's no telling what sort of twisted plan she has for the Rifters," Jessica replied. "They might have been better off under the AC rather than under Adriana's control."

Cojax held a door open for Jessica, who barreled inside. The two quickly descended a series of stairs, walked into a maintenance closet, and slid open a grate, revealing a tunnel that led down to the Rift. This was one of the many tunnels that Orch had cut with an Arc Blade.

Cojax grabbed Jessica's arm. "Wait, please don't do anything rash."

Jessica turned towards Cojax, their eyes meeting for a few tense moments. Her face was alive with passion, her chin set with determination. Despite the low light, Cojax could not help but notice how beautiful she was. He leaned forward, his lips pursed.

Jessica stepped back. "Were you going to kiss me just now?"

Cojax pulled back, his face flushing red. "Maybe."

She rolled her eyes.

He shrugged, "We were in a dark room; you were looking right at me."

She smiled and winked, "You're cute." Without another word, she placed her helmet on and rushed into the tunnel. Cojax followed closely behind, sighing as he did. They reached the Rift not long after. Jessica's steps became more urgent the closer they were to the makeshift city that lay below Titan.

Much of the Rift was wide and open, broken up only by pillars or long walls. But the heart of the Rift was located at what would be the edge of the Wall had they been on the surface. There the Eleventh through Nineteenth Tiers had built rooms, farms, labs, and everything else they needed to facilitate the demands of those in the city above them.

The first thing Jessica noticed was the lack of Twentieth Tiers or Hoarders as they called themselves. Even though the Hoarders typically grouped together, there were usually a few stragglers that preferred the solace of being alone versus the convenience of living in a group. Now, however, the Rift seemed devoid of any life—even the small creatures known as Riftlings seemed to have disappeared.

Jessica could not help but put her hand on the sword at her side. The Rift was never welcoming, but it had never been this desolate either. This was Cojax's first time in the Rift, so he had no idea what to expect. But he could tell that Jessica was becoming more cautious with each step that she took.

"What do you think?" Cojax asked.

Jessica slowed her pace and glanced around before answering. "It's changed. We should have run into some Hoarders by now. Something must have scared them off."

"Should we go back and get more Validated?" Cojax asked.

"As much as she annoys me," Jessica replied, "I think you're right about Adriana. I don't think she would risk harming you—you're too valuable for that. Plus, we both have Static Armor. There's almost nothing the Rifters could do to us even if they wanted to. Come on."

They continued in silence until they reached the food distribution area. This was the same place where Jessica first ran into Brutus when she lived in the Rift. It, too, seemed devoid of life. Jessica started moving forward, but Cojax grabbed her by the shoulder.

"Guards," Cojax said. "Two of them on the far left."

Jessica had been so focused on where she was going that she had not even seen them. As she panned her helmet around, it picked up on the heat signatures. She zoomed in with the helmet, allowing her to see the hefty Blazer in each of the warriors' hands.

"What are they doing here?" Jessica asked.

"Only one way to find out," Cojax said. He took a direct path towards the two warriors, while Jessica took a circuitous one. It was not long before they caught sight of Cojax, their Blazers being raised to their shoulders.

"Not another step," one of them said.

Cojax took two more steps.

"Stop," the second warrior growled.

This time Cojax obeyed, his hands raised in a friendly gesture.

"No need to be rude, my sparks," Cojax said, "Adriana sent me down here." As he spoke, he studied the warriors. They had Static Armor and it was charged, but he could tell it had not been well maintained. These were Rifters, not Validated standing guard. Judging by their voices, they were young and likely had been Rifted sometime during their Mahghetto. They were holding their Blazers wrong too, much too low to be very effective.

"We don't know any Adriana," the first warrior stated.

Cojax frowned. He had initially thought that since Adriana was so hesitant to mention who was in charge, that it was likely that she had put herself in charge. But that would not have made sense. She had never even been to the Rift, much less known how to operate it.

"I'm here to speak to your leader," Cojax said as he shuffled forward.

"Not another step," the second warrior called out, "or we'll rip your Rifting limbs from your body one at a time."

Cojax was starting to become annoyed. This whole charade seemed to be a pointless gesture. He could draw his sword and slice both of them down before they could get three shots off. He was pretty sure he could cleave them both with a single pulse of his blade.

"We're on strict orders: no one comes in, and no one goes out—"

In a flash, both of the Rifter's Blazers laid on the ground, their weapons each cut in two. They looked first at each other, and then at the unseen threat that was walking up to them.

Jessica sheathed her sword and removed her helmet, her long blond hair giving pause to the two guards. "Well then," Jessica said, "now that you know we're serious, it's probably best you just do what you're told."

One soldier hesitated, the other did not. Soon they were both in a sprint towards a far door.

Cojax removed his helmet, squinting in the dim light. "Nicely done."

Jessica nodded. "Be careful. We have no idea who Adriana put in charge down here."

"You judge her too harshly," Cojax replied. "She's our friend, not our enemy. She helped us take this city."

"Just because our goals were aligned for an instant does not mean our motives were," Jessica replied. "Who knows why she helped us."

"She gained just as much as we did."

"I don't think she's interested in having just as much as anyone," Jessica replied. "I don't trust her."

They did not have to wait long before a towering figure appeared, flanked by four warriors in complete Static Armor. These ones were armed with Arc Spears and Repulse Shields rather than Blazers.

The lead figure stepped forward, his arms spread wide as if to hug the room. He suddenly clapped his hands together. "Why if it isn't my two favorite people in the world. And here I thought it would be weeks before I saw you again."

"Is this a joke?" Cojax asked. "Brutus, what are you doing down here?"

"I was Rifted," Brutus answered coldly, "I belong down here. The better question would be, why do I choose to remain down here."

Cojax did not answer.

Jessica placed her helmet on her head and drew her sword. "You are sorely mistaken if you think we will let you run the Rift like your own little kingdom."

"Who did you expect? Who else would want to come down here in this darkness? To live off the scraps of the Validated?" Brutus replied. "The position was vacant, and to my amazement, no one else was applying for the job. You were too busy planning Titan's funeral."

Cojax put on his helmet. "His name does not belong in your mouth."

"My deepest apologies," Brutus replied. "Now sheathe your weapons or we'll cut you down. We outnumber you."

"I'll be sure to remove your head before I fall," Cojax answered, "and after that, nothing else will matter to either of us."

"Perhaps," Brutus replied, "but that wouldn't benefit either of us. Come now, let's be honest with each other. Did you come down here to fight or to talk? I haven't even drawn my sword."

Cojax looked to Jessica and then back to Brutus.

"Listen, Cojax," Brutus replied. "Let me be honest with you as you were once honest with me. I want to kill you. But I can't, just as you can't kill me. You see, by force of circumstance, you and I are now allies. Adriana pointed us in this direction, but a mutual need will keep us on the course. I can't kill you—you're now the face of the rebellion. If I end your life, I'm very much limiting my ability to do anything."

"Why do I need you?" Cojax asked.

"Because," Brutus laughed, "I know how the Rift works. I know the systems, the food production, the organization. I, after all, have lived among the Rifters."

"So did I," Jessica supplied.

"You were a Hoarder," Brutus answered. "You merely collected weapons from the dead. You were the Bottom Tier, as you were in the city above. The only thing you learned about the system was where to collect your food. I, on the other hand, was in food distribution. I was exposed to a little bit of everything. There's much more to the system than you know. And if I had not stepped in when I did, it would have fallen apart. The Numberless were the only ones that knew about the Rift—they were the only ones that performed the system checks. Now, there wasn't much for them to do, it mainly ran itself, but they did provide guidance to the Eleventh Tiers. The Eleventh Tiers were like the governing body of the Rift, but they did so with the leave of the Numberless. And then, one day, you cut the

Numberless down. Who else would the Eleventh Tiers look to for guidance? Who was there to ensure that our food production did not fall apart?"

"It's only been a day," Jessica sighed.

"Yes," Brutus answered, "but what would've happened if the Eleventh Tiers figured out that the Numberless were no longer in control? How much food would they have eaten had they realized that they were no longer slaves? Would they have left the Rift, leaving vital systems unattended? Would they have taken control of the Rift, seizing all the food stores and refusing to send anything more to the surface? Chaos, even for a day, can lead to devastating results."

"I understand it's necessary," Cojax said, "but I don't like the idea that you took control of the Rift without anyone else deciding on it."

"What do you propose?" Brutus answered. "A vote? A committee decision? You already have too much confusion on the surface. The way Adriana explained it to me, no one has any idea how the city is to govern itself. At least this one decision is decided."

"How can we know you're treating the Rifters fairly?" Jessica added.

"These are my people," Brutus answered. "They might have been born as Acadians, but the city above rejected them. They're my brothers and sisters now, and I will see to their protection."

"I demand to see them," Jessica said.

"Adriana said you would," Brutus answered.

"They can't be killed or tortured," Jessica said, her voice pleading. "You can't cage them as animals. We fought for their freedom just as much as ours."

"Yes," Brutus replied. "But, just as you can't give a large meal to a starving man since he'll most likely overeat and kill himself. We can't give them absolute freedom. It will come in degrees and will be measured. Remember, we need them just as much as they need us."

"Let us see them," Cojax said.

"No," Brutus answered.

"I wasn't asking for permission," Cojax replied, his grip tightening on his sword.

"They've seen too many changes already," Brutus replied. "I don't want two people wandering around here like a set of dimmed tourists. It would be odd—out of place. Perhaps, I will arrange for a few of you to come down to check on conditions much later, but not now."

Cojax's fist worked the handle of his sword while his mind debated the issue. A part of him wanted to call Brutus' bluff and cut through the guards. But a larger part of him knew that Brutus was right. Neither Jessica nor Cojax had any idea how the Rift functioned. Finally, Cojax slowly sheathed his sword. "This conversation is not finished." He turned around, heading for the door.

Brutus' face split into an ugly grin. "Enjoy your time on the surface, Cojax."

Cojax passed Jessica, who still held her sword in hand. She too sheathed her blade, but she did not turn away. "Make sure you treat them well, Brutus, or I will carve each and every one of their names into your body." Finally, Jessica turned and left.

Brutus watched their frames disappear into the darkness. He was getting better at hiding his emotions. He turned his head slightly to the soldiers behind him. "Double the guard. I don't want those two wandering back over here again."

SIX

Marcus stirred in his chair, his face restless but stoic. To his right sat Sejanus, a warrior who was just as skilled with the sword as he was with his rhetoric. They had first met each other in the pits of the Mahghetto, where weaker men and women had been broken like glass. By force of circumstance, they were competitors then, but now they were the greatest of friends. They processed information much the same way, viewing it through the eyes of the ancient philosophers. But, while Marcus retained the information better, Sejanus was able to translate their thoughts into his own, somehow elevating them to greater significance. To his left was Ion, a loyal friend, who, although not very articulate, understood computers better than anyone Marcus knew.

The room was only partially filled, which both encouraged and disappointed Marcus. His words had been well received through the chats on the ArmGuard by many of the First Tiers, but now, it seemed that few had actually been driven to action. But, at least the room was not empty.

They waited for another five minutes after the appointed meeting time. Sejanus made it look like they started late because they were busy attending to important tasks, but in reality, it was in hopes that more First Tiers would arrive. No more did.

Sejanus took to the floor, as he and Marcus had planned. He was a tall man with a face made rough with hardship. He was thinner than most, his muscles more toned than broad, but the room fell silent as he stood.

Marcus and Sejanus had spent much of the night before discussing who should address the crowd—who should be the face of the Republic. Each one insisted that the other was the person for the position. Eventually, ironically, Sejanus was so convincing in his argument, so eloquent in his words, that he proved he was far more suited to the position. When Marcus pointed this out, Sejanus finally acquiesced. Sejanus would be the face of the Populi. He would be the one that they rallied behind.

Sejanus looked around the room, locking eyes with all those who would return his gaze. The crowd was hopeful but also skeptical. "I'm glad all of you are here," Sejanus began. "This is the first meeting of many where we hope to change what Acadia once was, into something much better. As you all know, we have a void in our government that must be filled. And already there are those that cry for a king, others who wish to return to the meritocracy of Acadia, and still others that would break us up into States and different governing bodies. But we just removed the shackles of slavery, and so I will not endure us to be ruled by a king—I will not have us revert back to the very thing we fought against. Marcus and I have brought you together to form a government of representation. The purpose of this meeting is to establish the First Republic of Titan." The room filled with scattered applause.

"We are few," Sejanus continued, "but we seek after equality, fraternity, and freedom. We seek to raise the disenfranchised, to bring voice to the mute, to lift up the cripple, to protect and preserve without sacrificing liberty. Because of this, we shall continue to grow. For our cause is not only the logical one, it is the right one. Our greatest virtue, our greatest gift we have to give, is the freedom to choose. With the Numberless, we were denied this essential right, but now, our people will be empowered by it." More cheers followed. "Now, let's do more than exchange words and instead organize ourselves into a body of action."

Sejanus turned to Marcus, giving a slight nod. Without hesitating for a moment, Marcus stood and called for a vote, first on the name of their party, which was to be called the Populi and then on their mission. Positions were proposed, sustained, and organized—Marcus leading the discussion for each one. This had been the plan between Sejanus and Marcus: Sejanus was to embody the lofty, high-minded principles of a republic, while Marcus would offer a more practical and pragmatic approach. This two-pronged strategy allowed them to appeal to a wide array of personalities in the crowd.

Marcus was called to be the Supreme Judge—Sejanus made sure of that. It was Marcus' job to arbitrate in all disagreements. Ion was sustained as the General Secretary. For the rest of the meeting, it was Ion who kept the minutes of the proceedings.

A Senate was soon formed, followed by the much more numerous House of Prolits. The Senate was placed in charge of all matters of warfare, while the Prolits were placed in command of the general wellbeing of the people. In order for a new law to be made, it could only be proposed by either the Senate or the Prolits in official proceedings. The law would have to pass a majority ruling by both houses before it came into being. As the day continued, heated arguments erupted. But each time this happened, it was Marcus, the Supreme Judge, that defused the conflict and restored order.

"I say we elect a president," said an older man. He was tall with deep-set eyes that magnified the intensity of his gaze. He was a great warrior in his day, his body too stubborn to be claimed by war. Marcus had only met him once, but he remembered his name almost instantly—Segundus. Segundus continued in his low, bellowing tone. "We need one person to represent us. If we hope to get any traction among the Bottom Tiers, they will need the leadership of a single person."

"But Presidents eventually become tyrants," a man named Hagnon said. "Executive orders eventually lead to Supreme Dictates."

"A Consul then," Marcus suggested, "or rather, two Consuls, as it was with the Romans. Where the authority of one can cancel out the other."

"I second that motion," Ion echoed.

"Perhaps we need to open the floor to debate?" added a voice.

"Let's vote on it first," Marcus called. "Just to see where we stand."

The idea of electing two consuls was unanimously supported as well as term limits. Next qualifications for the Consul was set forth—the first being that only someone who has obtained the First Tier could be voted into office. That left a bitter taste in Marcus' mouth, but his rebuttal was quickly shot down by Hagnon. Marcus made a motion to remove the qualification anyway, but he was easily outvoted. More qualifications were put into practice: the Consul had to be older than twenty-five, they had to have been in good standing in the Tiers, they had to be a skilled warrior, they had to have held the command of at least a Phalanx in the past. This then led to an argument about the qualifications of Senators and Prolits. It quickly became law that only those of the First Tier could be elected to serve in the Senate or the House of Prolits. Again, Marcus protested, stating that this is the very elitism that they were fighting against. Again, he was outvoted.

Someone called for possible candidates for the two Consuls. Sejanus was quickly suggested, much to Marcus' relief. A few times during this meeting, things had taken a different turn than expected, and it did not quite sit well with him, but the whole plan had been to make Sejanus one of the leaders of the party. More candidates appeared, each one presenting their qualifications as best they could. After several heated debates, a vote was called. Sejanus won, but just barely. As the voting commenced for the second Consulship, Segundus was called to make his case for the position. The only thing he did was to stand up, point at Sejanus and simply say, "I will keep that man in check."

Marcus almost openly mocked the terse speech. Up to that point, the only thing Segundus had done in the conversation was to take the opposite position of Sejanus on almost every issue. When it came to the vote, Marcus would have wagered everything he owned that the only vote that Segundus would get would be the one he cast for himself.

For the third time that day, Marcus was astounded by the results of the voting. Not only did Segundus win, he won by a large margin. Marcus looked at all the candidates in turn, trying to figure out how in the world Segundus was voted into office. Marcus came to the conclusion that Segundus won simply because he was not Sejanus. He won because he adamantly *opposed* Sejanus. Somehow, Sejanus had appeared too powerful. His rich rhetoric got him elected, but it also set him up as a threat. These results made Marcus reassess his whole approach to the situation. *We have to be passionate but not appear too powerful. We have to provide solutions but not be so convincing that it seems they're being forced into it.*

The conversation evolved, growing more complex as time progressed. Smaller, more functional duties were given to certain members of the party, granting some of them powers, others balances to those powers. A small guard unit was formed to protect the Consuls.

For a while, Marcus was lost in his thoughts. He had studied Democracy all his life, but it was something different entirely to see it in action. It was not until the conversation shifted from the organization of the party and into political strategy that Marcus found himself listening again.

"What's the boy's name?" Segundus shouted. "What's the boy's name that abolished the AC? That's who we need to guard ourselves against. With no consensus from the people, he irrevocably changed our laws. That's who we need to criticize publicly. We have to show the people that under no circumstances can one person dictate how the rest are to live."

"But he was the one that liberated us," said a voice.

"He liberated us, yes," Segundus answered, "but it should have stopped there. He should not have abolished the AC like that. Decisions of that magnitude need to be weighed and measured. We do things with order and with reason. Our best strategy is to discredit the boy before he changes something else that has dire consequences."

"He means little now," someone said. "Now that the AC has already been undone."

"No," Segundus said with a chiding tone, "he still represents the disenfranchised. He still holds sway with the Bottom Tiers. Our most powerful argument is one that Sejanus already made—that we are the champions of the oppressed. For them to follow us, we need to give them another option besides Cojax."

Marcus was surprised by the mention of his brother's name. He had known, of course, who Segundus was referring to, but Segundus had, for some reason, initially pretended that he did not know Cojax's name. It was then that Marcus realized that Segundus was not as simple or as straightforward as he pretended.

"What do you propose?" Sejanus asked.

"We destroy the boy's reputation," Segundus replied simply.

This was met with tumultuous applause. Many of the First Tiers secretly resented the fact that a Tenth Tier had abolished the AC, even if he had been the one to liberate them. Now that Segundus stoked the flames of this resentment, it began to grow.

"He's a boy," Sejanus answered.

"That overthrew the Numberless and abolished the AC," Segundus offered. "If we don't deal with him, he'll soon be our king."

This statement was answered with a ripple of consent.

Sejanus looked to Marcus, his eyes asking for help. Segundus was quickly winning the crowd to his side, and Sejanus could not push the issue much longer without looking weak.

Marcus stood, his eyes becoming alive for the first time since the meeting started. "If this is your plan, I'm afraid it is destined to fall short."

Segundus did not take the bait, and so Sejanus finally asked, "How so?"

Marcus walked forward to Segundus, squaring off with the man. "Unifying people by bringing a scapegoat to bear will provide a quick result, but not a long-lasting one. Dirtying my brother's name may be effective initially…" Marcus paused for effect, "but we will soon become known as the group of old men who blame the world's woes on a boy." Marcus turned around, seemingly pulling out the support from all those that met eyes with him. "We need a message—something powerful and poignant. We need people to come to us because they believe in our cause, not because we've destroyed their belief in every other cause. Freedom. That is what we offer. We offer a government that allows people to choose. That is what will win the hearts of the people."

"I was going to suggest that before you interrupted me," Segundus said.

Marcus whipped back around to Segundus, "Well, you didn't. I say we call a vote." Sejanus seconded the motion and Marcus continued. "All those in favor of us presenting our case by carrying the cause of freedom, raise your hand."

The vote was unanimous—even Segundus voted in favor after seeing he was outnumbered.

"I would also like to call a vote," Segundus said. "All those in favor of attacking the reputation of the Cojax son of Titan, raise your hand."

The motion was seconded and voted upon. Marcus' hand was the only one in the room that was not raised.

SEVEN

Cojax stirred and stretched—his body ached from sleeping on the floor. He laid back down, his right hand slowly rising up and down with his chest. Then his eyes found the helmet of Titan—the one he wore the day he died. Cojax had kept it. It was still bloody and tarnished from battle. As he studied the helmet, thoughts, unbidden and unwelcome, invaded his mind. *He died protecting her. He died protecting the supposed Aberration. He was only pretending to be who he was.* This thought filled him with a mixture of comfort as well as trepidation. He was glad to know his father was not entirely the monster he had appeared, but it left a pit in his heart knowing that he would never know who his father really was.

Cojax reached over, slowly picking up the helmet. It was large and well made. He raised it until his eyes were even with the armor. He then flipped it around and placed it on his head. It was too big for him, but it adjusted. Even with the adjustments, it still felt loose. Then the helmet flashed red as it scanned his eyes.

"Not authorized user," the helmet said.

Cojax ripped off the helmet, a sudden wave of claustrophobia overcoming him. Helmets were not typically linked to only one user, so it was surprising when it denied him access. He pushed the helmet away and fell back to his pillow.

Jessica's armor had recorded Titan's last words, and he could have requested Ion to bring up the footage, but he hesitated. If he listened to it, it was done—all the possibilities of what he could have said were finished. *I need to listen to it. I need to hear his last words.* Even as he thought it, he knew he probably would not go through with it. The wound was still too fresh, and so he would put it off until tomorrow.

As he looked up, he thought he heard a voice from another room. Jessica had taken Titan's room while Cojax and Finn had slept in Cojax's room. It once was lined with bunk beds, evidence of the large family that had lived there, but now it only had one small bed.

Finn now occupied it. Cojax slept on the floor. Finn refused it at first, but Cojax would not accept anything less. Neither friend found sleep quickly, and so they spent much of the night in conversation. When sleep finally found them, it was intermittent and broken at best.

Even before the sun rose, Cojax stirred awake. He laid there, half expecting his ArmGuard to chime with an alarm, but it never did. He did not have a schedule on his ArmGuard anymore—that disappeared soon after Ion had control of the Acadian Systems. He suddenly sat up and headed for the shower, making as little noise as possible so as not to wake Finn.

Cojax let out a long sigh. It had been three days since the start of the rebellion. He had slept so little since then that it reminded him of the early days of the Mahghetto. But, with one significant difference: in the Mahghetto, they never had to worry about what they needed to do, they always had direction; now, it felt as if there were no objectives. Cojax smiled to himself as he thought of the warm shower he was going to take. It would not be a thirty-second shower or even a minute. He would take as long as he liked. He would let the steam fog the mirror and fill the room. He would let his body soak in the heat. He felt wicked with the thought, as if this crime would dishonor his Faction for generations to come.

When he slid his hand over the Implant Reader in the shower, however, no water exited the showerhead. Instead, a loud noise traveled up the pipes until it reached the nozzle above. He tried the Reader again. This time, water began to trickle out. It was cold and biting. He first rinsed himself and then applied soap, his former training kicking in and allowing him to accomplish the task quickly. He was only able to rinse half of his body before the water stopped completely.

He sourly dried himself with a towel and exited the bathroom. Finn sat up as he walked in, a smile spread across his face. "How was it?"

"If you're referring to the hot shower, not what I expected."

"Better?"

Cojax pulled a tunic on. "The water came out in a trickle, and if it were any colder, it would be in the form of ice."

"What?"

"There's no system in place," Cojax replied. "No reason anyone would limit their shower now and, unfortunately, I was not the first one to think of that."

"The showers have always worked before," Finn replied. "You sure you swiped the Implant Reader, right?"

"You're welcome to try, but I do believe that whatever reserve of water and energy was allocated for shower use has been expended. I'm sure it will fill back up eventually, but it will most likely be used just as quickly."

Finn fell back into his bed, his head hitting the wall with a hollow thud. "I guess freedom comes at a high price indeed."

Cojax pulled on his boots, followed by his greaves.

"Why are you putting on your armor?"

Cojax looked at his friend with half a smile. "Did you forget about the Decamont or the fact that half the First Tiers wouldn't mind removing our heads from our bodies because we upset the AC?"

"Fair point," Finn said. "It's a little disappointing, though, wearing it now even though we don't have to."

There was a knock at the front door.

"Who's that?" Finn asked.

"No idea," Cojax replied. "No one has knocked at my door since the last time the Comms were down."

Cojax pulled on his breastplate, followed by his ArmGuards. He attached a sword to his waist and an Arc Lance onto his back. He contemplated taking his shield, but then decided against it. He headed for the door, one hand resting gingerly on the hilt of his blade.

"You plan on fighting whoever's at the door?" Finn asked.

Cojax did not answer. He opened the bedroom door to find Jessica exiting Titan's room at the same time. She also wore her armor, and a blade at her side, but had opted for a Blazer instead of an Arc Lance on her back.

"Who is it?" Jessica asked.

"No idea," Cojax answered. Jessica walked first down the hallway, closely flanked by Cojax. She stopped in the living room, while Cojax approached the door, swiping his palm over the Implant Reader. The door slid open, revealing not one individual, but several.

Cojax recognized the man in the front. "Byron?"

The man nodded. "How are you, my boy?"

The tone was so relaxed, Cojax did not know how to answer.

Byron was an Omega, one of the few that held the position without also holding the title of Numberless. He had straight hair that flowed around his ears and mixed with his beard. It was thick, but well maintained, making him look more like a sage than a great warrior. But to be fair, he had a reputation for being both. He was in the First Tier and one of the Tier Setters among the BloodBorne. The only reason Cojax had even met the talented warrior was because he had stopped by to speak with Titan several times before. Cojax did not think Titan had any close friends, but if he did, he knew Byron would be considered one of them.

"What can I do for you?" Cojax asked.

"Mind if we come in, lad," said another one of the Validated.

Cojax swallowed hard, debating with himself whether allowing them in was a good idea. Byron was as close as one could be to becoming a Numberless without ever reaching the title. He alone could finish Cojax off in short order, not to mention the other large warriors that flanked him.

One of the other warriors finally leaned forward. "Oh, we're not going to kill you—if that's what you're thinking."

Cojax suddenly realized that the Validated in front of him really did not need Cojax's permission to enter. They could have easily forced their way in if they had wanted. Cojax suddenly nodded, gesturing the group inside. There were nine in total, all from the BloodBorne Faction and all from the First Tier. Jessica's body tensed as they poured in. She recognized four of them—either from the CityScreens or from BloodBorne announcement videos.

"Is this the—" Cojax began.

"—The BloodBorne High Council," Byron completed. "Yes, it is. Each Faction is responsible for creating their own leadership, and in the BloodBorne, we are subject to the BloodBorne High Council of Twelve."

"I only count nine," Cojax said.

A taller, thinner man with thick, harry arms shook his head. "Are we sure about this, boy? I think we might revisit—"

"Quiet, Cato," Byron said. "We've been at this all night, and we came to our conclusion. We've voted, and now we're here."

"Voted on what?" Jessica asked.

For the first time since the encounter began, the BloodBorne leaders cast scrutinizing looks towards Jessica. Two, in particular, did not seem to care much for what they saw.

Byron continued in his low, comforting voice. "Sit down—both of you."

No one knew exactly when it happened, but in the shuffle for chairs, Finn had appeared.

"What about him?" asked one of the Validated.

"He can stay," Byron replied. "He's one of the revolutionaries after all."

"What's this all about?" Cojax asked, his curiosity getting the better of him.

"First, we'll start with introductions," Byron said. "I'm Byron, but you've already met me. But to my left is Cato, Parmenion, and Decima. To my right is Thaddaeus, Rasta, Damon, Miltiades, and Doriana."

Cojax, Finn, and Jessica saluted, bowing low as they did.

"It's an honor," Cojax said. "How can we serve you?"

The BloodBorne leaders looked at each other. Finally, Byron stood and walked over to an Arc Blade that hung by the door. It was a massive blade that was a full hand wide. It seemed more apt at butchering opponents than just defeating them. It was Titan's sword but Cojax had only seen his father handle it a few times.

"This was the Arc Blade Titan was wielding the day he died," Byron said. "I'm glad it found its way back here after the battle. I know it by its true name—the Archaic. Do you know the purpose of this blade? It's not meant for striking down Reevers—it's far too powerful for that. It was not constructed for cutting through Razer Backs, Diggers, or even SataniKahns. This blade is for felling gods—this blade is for killing a Numberless. I saw a duel once between Numberless, and it was as if I were watching the collision of two storms. Their blades command so much more energy than our pathetic weapons. That's when I realized that we are nothing like them. They are so much more than the common Validated.

"But it's odd, don't you think, that he kept the Archaic by the door. Every other weapon Titan owns is in his room at the Trinity. I thought it so odd, in fact, that one day I pushed aside all protocol and asked him why he kept his Arc Blade here. Do you know what he told me?"

Cojax shook his head.

"He said it was to guard against the true enemy," Byron said. "I must admit, at the time, I did not know what it meant." He turned away from the blade, meeting eyes with Cojax. "But now I do. The Numberless were the true enemy. For all his titles and rank, Titan was a prisoner in Acadia as much as any of us. And, I don't think he much cared for it. And so, he kept this blade by the door, ready for use at all times—ready to use it against any Numberless that opposed him." Byron's voice trailed off as he looked at the ceiling, his eyes focusing on some distant memory.

Cojax looked to Jessica and Finn before finally speaking. "What does that have to do with me?"

Byron walked closer to Cojax. One of the BloodBorne leaders stood, allowing Byron to take the chair next to the young man.

"Titan went along with the Numberless," Byron said, "because, I believe, he saw no other way. At least, no other way that would have a pleasant outcome. But that doesn't mean he didn't consider other options, as evidenced by the Archaic being placed next to your front door. Titan was different than most of the Numberless. He took the time to get to know me as well as the others here. I knew him well. I considered him a mentor, a teacher, a leader. I considered him more than someone I would just follow into battle. Perhaps I can explain it best by using the old Latin phrase, 'Cedo Mayori.' Do you know what that means?"

"I yield to someone greater," Cojax answered.

"Yes," Byron said. "That phrase has guided me through this life. That if someone can do something better than I, I gladly yield to them in their area of expertise. I will gladly learn from them until I can do it just as well, or I always revere their judgment if I can never do it better. And this is important for one major reason: Titan has named you as his heir."

"His heir?" Finn asked.

"Not just of his possessions, but more importantly, of his position," Byron said. "He was the Numberless assigned to the BloodBorne Faction. He was the one that commanded it, that controlled it, that governed it. And so, we are here to honor that man's last will and testament."

"What do you mean?" Cojax asked.

"Titan could not have been more clear in his instructions," Byron said. "He must have recorded it sometime before the battle—I imagine when he first discovered what you and your friends were planning on doing. Titan has named you as the leader of the BloodBorne Faction. You are to govern the BloodBorne. The members of the High Council have been tasked to assist you in this endeavor."

"What about Marcus?" Cojax asked. "He's my older brother, and in the First Tier."

"He did not name Marcus as his heir," Byron replied.

Cojax stood up, rubbing his hands over his face. He walked to the wall, his mind lost in thought. His vision eventually fell on The Archaic. He turned around, carefully judging each face in the crowded room. "Why just the BloodBorne Faction? Why would he only want to assert control over them?"

"I don't know," Byron replied. "Perhaps he tried, but no other Faction heeded his instructions. Or perhaps, he did not even attempt to control the other Factions. We received the message the next morning after the AC fell, just before Titan's funeral. He must have made it so it delivered automatically."

"Why are we just hearing about this now?" Jessica asked.

Byron looked to his companions, searching for answers. Then he nodded towards Cojax. "It took a while to process the information."

"You mean to debate it," Jessica said.

"Yes, partially," Byron replied. He let out a long breath of air. "It was a big decision—and it was important that at least the majority of the Twelve of the BloodBorne High Council came to a consensus.

"Perhaps I'm not the greatest at math," Finn said, "but I only count nine of you."

"Not everyone agreed," Byron answered. "But, fortunately, the other three on the Council withdrew to another Faction, instead of dividing us any further."

"Who?" Cojax asked.

"Sejanus, he's a friend of your brother," Bryon said. "The other two, I don't think you would know."

"What does this mean?" Cojax asked.

Byron looked to Cato, who took over the conversation. Cato looked at Cojax appraisingly. He had sharp eyes and a pointed chin. He kept his back straight and his gaze level. In his eyes, he held all the pride of his Tier. "It means that your voice becomes law among the BloodBorne. If, however, at least seven of the BloodBorne High Councilors oppose you on a specific law or regulation, they may overturn it."

"We need to appoint three more to the Council," Cojax said.

"We will work on that, but as for—" Cato began.

"—I want Adriana and Orch on the Council," Cojax said quickly. "And I want to appoint Jessica and Finn as my Chief Advisors. If I'm not present, their word is my will."

Byron looked at the faces around him, judging their expressions. "That's one thing you can't dictate. New members of the Council are only selected after a unanimous vote during a Council meeting."

Cojax nodded, "Fair enough. Then let's have our first Council now."

Byron shook his head. "That's not how things work."

Cojax leaned forward. "With all due respect, all of this is uncharted territory. You're moving to sustain a leader over the BloodBorne, which, as far as I know, has never been done before. We can't be concerned with how things have been done in the past. You have to understand one important thing: I don't know any of you, and you don't know me, at least not that well. The only link we have is that all of us knew Titan. I need people that know me on the Council."

Cato shook his head. "No."

"Why not?" Cojax asked.

"Titan only had a few rules, and one of those was that the Council elects its own members," Cato replied. "There would be no check to your power if you were allowed to put in individuals who would agree with everything you said."

"That's fine moving forward, but we need to fill those positions, and I need people I know and trust," Cojax said, instantly regretting his use of the word "trust."

"Trust is it?" Cato replied, his voice rising slightly. "We're the ones putting a great deal of trust in you. You can at least return the favor and put some faith in us."

"I trust you," Cojax replied, "but I trust these four more. No offense intended, but I've gone through a lot with them, and I just met you."

Cato's eyes narrowed, but before he could speak, Byron cut him off, "Let's think this through. Cojax, the Council of Twelve has always consisted of First Tiers of the BloodBorne Faction. Its members are selected by existing members. Those who live in this Faction know this, and when they see your friends are on the Council, it won't look good. What little tradition we have, you'd be breaking."

"Well, find someone else to rule then," Cojax said. "I can't imagine anyone would want to surround themselves with counselors that they hardly knew. How do I know which one of you is impetuous or has sound advice or has the wrong motivations? I don't know you—any of you."

"Cojax," Byron said, exhaustion evident in his voice, "be reasonable. You don't know us now, but you will. Each of us has decided to serve you—to support you."

"I just need you to put someone I know on the Council," Cojax replied. "That's it."

Byron looked to the other BloodBorne leaders, sighed, and then looked back to Cojax. "Alright, fine. We'll put Orch and…who else did you say…Adriana on the Council. Orch shouldn't be too hard for the people to accept—he's Second Tier after all. What of Adriana?"

"She's not from the Second Tier," Cojax answered.

"Third?" Byron suggested.

"The whole point of this revolution," Cojax said, "is to show that our Score does not define us—that we can have abilities and talents that aren't limited by the AC. You say that the people will not accept it if someone less than a Top Tier is on the Council; I would argue that people would be more accepting of the Council if not everyone on it was from the First Tier."

"She's from the Tenth Tier, isn't she?" Cato proclaimed.

After a long pause, Cato opened his mouth in protest, but Byron cut him off, "A valid point, Cojax."

"What about the third position available?" Cojax asked.

"We will elect someone," Byron asserted.

"Alright, then," Cojax said.

"Cojax," Jessica whispered, "we don't even know if this is the best move we can make."

Cojax turned to her, meeting her deep blue eyes with his

piercing black ones. "What do you mean? This is what we were working for."

"We represent the Bottom Tiers," Jessica replied. "We were the ones that gave voice to the downtrodden—that's what gave life to this rebellion. We have already gained much of their support with the messages that you and Orch have put out. If you set yourself up to be a king, you undo much of the message we are trying to craft. Now it looks as if the rebellion was not to liberate them, but to elevate you."

Cojax turned his back to Jessica and looked at the ceiling. He bounced different ideas back and forth in his head, trying to evaluate the various outcomes.

"She has a point," Finn said, "plus, I don't know if I can ever get used to the idea of calling you my King."

"He's not our king," Cato said with a hiss. "We will refer to him as Lord High Councilor."

"Oh," Finn said, "my apologies. I didn't realize there was a distinction between someone who held the title of King and made all the rules, and someone who made all the rules but that you didn't call a king."

Cato's body stiffened.

"This is certainly a shift from how we originally started," Cojax replied.

"I think we might be better off on our own," Jessica said, "no offense. This rebellion came from the bottom up, not the other way around. What I believe gave Cojax the power to abolish the AC was that he was a Tenth Tier. He represented the vast majority of those who are on the fringe of society. If we put him in this position, and surround him with a Council of First Tiers, it'll be hard for the Bottom Tiers to believe he's genuine. Perhaps it would be better if we worked in concert with the BloodBorne Council, not integrate with it. We already have a say in the government. Perhaps the better move is for us to appear to be two separate political bodies who have an unwritten alliance.

Byron nodded, a small smile spreading across his face. "Wise words and well-spoken. But there's a reason we're here now and not a moment later. You've already been cut out of the governing body."

"What?" Jessica asked.

"The First Tiers are meeting today in a group called the First

Assembly," Byron said, "to discuss and form political parties. If you did not get the invitation by now, it means that you were not invited. A few hours before the meeting, they plan on releasing a recording on all the CityScreens in the city that explains how the new government will be formed, as well as allowing the people to show their support for political parties through their ArmGuards."

"After all that work we did," Finn said with indignation.

"How?" Cojax asked. "We knew about the First Tiers communicating with each other, but how can they just cut us out and assume we'd be fine with it."

"Because all of the First Tiers are in agreement," Byron replied. "They plan on broadcasting the proceedings of the First Assembly. And ultimately, the type of government we establish will be based on the support of the Validated. The sixty-percent rule has been established. The governing political party will need at least sixty percent of the city's support."

"Well," Jessica said, "the other Tiers could form their own meetings. Why should we submit to the First Tiers?"

"Would they have Abria or Onar or Sejanus or Nicodema?" Cato asked. "These are the heroes of our age. They already have notoriety thanks to the battlefield. They are the Omegas and Invictors and the Gammas. Just because Cojax abolished the AC, does not mean those titles will go away. Take, for example, our BloodBorne High Council. We've been putting out messages to the BloodBorne Faction, and all of them have been well received. Those in the BloodBorne still see us as their leaders."

"I haven't been receiving your messages," Finn said.

"You haven't, but everyone Seventh Tier and above has," Byron replied. "We wanted to make sure there would be support for Cojax as our Lord High Councilor, and so far, we haven't received any opposition."

"They already know I'm the Lord High Councilor?" Cojax asked.

"No," Byron replied, "but they do know that Titan selected someone for us to follow. We put this idea out as if it were already decided and the people took it as if it were doctrine. So, if you make your meetings with other Tiers in an attempt to rally enough support to form your own political party, I think you will be sadly disappointed with the results."

"Orch was going to make sure we were not locked out of the Acadian Computer System," Jessica said with desperation. "We can still put out a message to all the Bottom Tiers."

"The First Tiers now control all of the Acadian Systems," Byron said calmly. "No system or program formerly utilized under the AC can be used without the express permission of the First Tiers. They've already set up a system to keep people out."

Jessica turned red with anger. "I bet that's Ion's doing."

Byron opened his hands in a welcoming gesture. "You've already done good work by consolidating the support of some of the Bottom Tiers. Becoming the Lord High Councilor of the BloodBorne will not take away from that, but will add one thing that you lack."

"And what is that?" Cojax asked.

"Legitimacy," Byron answered. "Without the backing of a major Faction, even if you rally support from the Bottom Tiers, you will lack legitimacy. You may hold some sway, but it won't be long before your Comms are completely cut off from the Bottom Tiers. It won't be long before you are edged out completely. The longer you wait to align yourself with a major political party, the more fragile your influence will become. Until one day, you will be irrelevant."

Cojax turned back to Byron. "How can any of you trust that I will effectively lead the BloodBorne? None of you know me."

"Cedo Mayori," Byron answered. "Titan believed in you, and I believed in him. I yield to the judgment of someone greater. So, Cojax, son of Titan, will you accept the position of Lord High Councilor? Will you serve as the leader of the BloodBorne?"

Cojax met eyes with Jessica. They were silent for a time before she finally nodded. He returned the nod, his face grim with duty. "I accept."

Byron stood, patting Cojax on the shoulder. "That is well. This isn't the first time I've taken this oath, but it is the first time I'm not swearing it to a Numberless." He looked to the other BloodBorne leaders, and in turn, they stood up, drawing their swords as they did. When the last blade was unsheathed, they kneeled on the ground, jabbing the tips of the blades into the floor. One by one, they repeated the same oath, starting with Byron.

"I swear to serve Cojax son of Titan, of the BloodBorne

Faction. I swear unwavering loyalty and faith; I swear to yield my own will and to take up his; I swear to give my time, talents, and life, if necessary, to further the will of Cojax, The Lord High Councilor of the BloodBorne."

EIGHT

"What am I doing here again?" Orch asked.

"You're now part of BloodBorne High Council," Cojax answered.

"Only First Tiers can be part of the Twelve," Orch said.

"And you…and Adriana," Cojax said.

"It warms my heart that you're so eager to watch out for my interests," Orch whispered.

"I needed somebody I could trust," Cojax defended, "I'm just glad you agreed."

"I agreed that I would excel at the position. I didn't agree to actually do it."

Despite having arrived early, Cojax quickly discovered the room was filled with First Tiers, almost all of whom were engaged in deep conversation or spirited debate. It was a massive space, more colosseum than room. It was shaped in a large oval, having a sandy pit in the middle and being surrounded by comfortable stadium seats that gradually grew in height the further they progressed from the center. It could easily have seated ten thousand comfortably, but it did not seem adequate to accommodate all of the Validated that were vying for seats.

Byron, his back straight and his gaze steady, was already seated. He waved a hand towards Cojax and Orch.

Cojax led the procession, followed by six Validated from various Tiers. They wore long, red capes marked with the symbol of the BloodBorne. Even though Cojax did not know their names, he could tell by their command presence that they were powerful men and women. They were his new retinue of bodyguards. Cojax did not much like the idea, but Byron had insisted. It was not so much a precaution, as it was for a show of strength and unity. Outside the assembly, Cojax was not required to have his bodyguards accompany him.

Cojax and Orch had also received more lavish sets of armor.

Despite the armor adjusting to his size as he put it on, it still felt uncomfortable to wear. This Static Armor had been reserved for First Tiers, and he was technically still in the Tenth Tier. He felt self-conscious as he walked to his seat, acutely aware of all the eyes that bore into him. Clearly, he was the youngest in the room by a large margin.

Cojax approached a seat of benches that had been reserved for the BloodBorne. Orch did not hesitate for a second; he sat down before Byron had even offered.

"Glad to see you're adjusting to your new title so quickly," Byron said.

Orch looked up at Byron, a cocky grin spread across his face. "Are you here to take our order? Can we get a pitcher of stock?"

Byron visibly tensed but ignored the comment. "I hear you're pretty good with the Blazer."

Orch nodded. "Depends on who you're comparing me to."

Byron nodded. "Fair enough."

"If you're comparing me to anyone else alive," Orch continued, "I'm excellent."

Byron nodded politely to the comment as he turned his attention to Cojax, his voice falling to a whisper. "I imagine you've already seen your brother."

Cojax had not, but it did not take long before he did. His brother was wearing a simple toga wrapped in a blue sash. To his left was Ion. To his right was a man Cojax had never met.

"Do you see the tall man next to your brother?" Byron asked.

Cojax nodded and Byron continued. "Until yesterday, that man was on the BloodBorne High Council. The man's name is Sejanus, and he didn't much care for Titan's idea. Now he's one of the two Consuls in the Populi Party. He's a powerful orator and well-liked—a dangerous combination."

"And who is the other Consul?"

"Not your brother, if that's what you're asking," Byron said. "His name is Segundus. I don't know him. He's from the Temmian Faction, which is one of the main supporters of the Populi. He's stern but well respected."

Cojax studied the Populi. Unlike him and his escorts, the Populi Party had selected garb that was more functional than ornate. Most of them were wearing simple but well-kept togas with blue sashes. The only thing they wore that had any semblance of power were the Arc Blades around their waists, which seemed to send a clear message. They were a large group, occupying a good portion of the arena next to the entrance, and they distinguished themselves with blue bands tied around their right arms.

"Next to them are the Statesmen," Byron said. "They've taken to wearing metal crowns on their heads, to symbolize that they are each empowered."

"How do they want to set up the government?"

"Each Faction governs how they like, and then the leader of each Faction forms the Council of Statesmen. They seem fond of browbeating their opponents rather than using reason—much like our friend, Orch. Really, it's just an oligarchy, but they're putting it in the context of empowering each Faction, or State, as they call them. They have an iron-clad rule that you may join another State at will. This, they reason, will enable the best government to form in one of the States because all the other Faction members will join it. They assert that one State will eventually become the strongest and will transform into the governing body. It's sort of an evolution of government."

"It sounds like a recipe for civil war," Orch said.

"On this, you and I agree," Byron replied.

"They don't seem to have many members," Cojax said.

"Actually, they have the most support of any party," Bryon answered.

"They seem full of dimmed Dependents," Orch asserted.

Byron sighed. "Each of their 'States' only sends as many representatives as they want. In the BlackHearts Faction, you can see there are only five individuals—I imagine one leader and four assistants. But then in the Screamers Faction, you have about twenty—I think they operate more like a Republic. So, it may appear they have less support, but they have the most. Forming the government along the lines of Factions is a rather enticing option for several reasons."

"It just allows more kings to rule in their little kingdoms," Orch said. "Pathetic pieces of rot—probably all have to compensate by carrying larger than average swords."

"Let me ask you something," Byron said, turning to Orch, "You're not planning on speaking during these proceedings, are you?"

"Maybe," Orch replied.

"Don't," Byron said, "First Tiers will not respond well to that kind of Bottom Tier language you seem fond of. They see themselves above your station, and any insult from you would greatly hinder any chance of gaining more influence."

"So," Orch said, "who do you plan on speaking for the group—the boy?"

"He's the Lord High Councilor," Byron answered. "And no, I think any speech he gives needs to be calculated and well thought out. I've already prepared something, so I'll explain who we are and what we represent. I don't want them to form any sort of opinion of us until we have a solid strategy in place. Right now, I think it's best to hold a prominent position, but a more silent one. Let's let the others compete for the floor; let's let others ruffle feathers and make enemies. We hold a position of power as long as we don't make any enemies."

"I have no intention of speaking," Cojax said. "I already feel out of place."

"And you, supposed Master of the Blazer?" Byron asked.

"I agree," Orch said. "The boy shouldn't make any speeches."

"What about you?" Byron asked.

"What about me?" Orch replied.

Bryon let out a prolonged sigh. "Will you be giving any surprise soliloquies to our esteemed group of friends here?"

"No," Orch replied. "I'd rather have dinner with a Roach than sit around and address these arrogant, hypocrites."

"These are the most powerful men of Titan," Byron said, "and many of them could be potential allies. Remember that before you judge them too harshly."

"This is a meeting of First Tiers that have purposely cut out all other Tiers during the formation of a new government," Orch replied. "It's hypocritical for First Tiers to be arranging all of this when they had nothing to do with the revolution. It was Rifters that rose up and uprooted the Numberless, and most of the Validated in this room fought against that."

"It's ironic," Byron corrected.

"What?" Orch asked.

"You said it was 'hypocritical,' but I believe you should have said 'ironic.'"

Orch took a deep breath, his lips opening to form a rebuke, but Cojax cut him off quickly. "Don't worry about Orch. He'll only speak if and when necessary. Tell me about the political party next to the Statesmen."

"Those are the Restorationists, as evidenced by the numbers written in on their breastplate Placards. They have actually set to etching their old Score in their Placards as a sign of their party. They only hold a minority of three Factions, and they barely have enough members to form a political party, but they're rigid and formal, acting as if they are still under the scrutiny of the AC."

"They want to restore the AC?" Cojax asked.

"Not exactly like it was, but pretty close," Byron answered. "They want to keep the Tier System, but lessen the punishment for Riftings."

"Lessen the punishment?"

"They want to put the people into servitude, but not slavery. They also say the elderly will be immune to Riftings—if they made it through the Mahghetto."

"Why would they want to bring back any form of Riftings?"

"Surprisingly, that's not the thing that most people don't like about the Faction," Byron said. "It's the fact that some of them have been talking about seeing if we can make amends with the Decamont. Perhaps we can be brought back into the fold."

"That's insane."

"It's not a popular idea, even among the Restorationists, but they have an easy argument to make—at least for restoring the meritocracy. People already know what it was like under the AC. Compare that to how blazing uncertain everything is now, and it becomes more of an attractive option."

"What's the next political party?"

"There are a lot of smaller parties, most of them almost too small to exist," Byron said. "For them to survive, they'll have to ally with a larger party and soon. But the next largest party is the FirstBorne. Many of the others here refer to them as the First Tiers, because their government focuses on selecting only a few of the best Validated to lead. Not surprisingly, it has a lot of draw for those who had the highest Score at the moment that the AC was absolved. The first, second, and third highest Validated Score holders all belong to the FirstBorne. All of them are arrogant and self-interested."

"How come you can call them arrogant?" Orch asked.

"It wasn't crass to call them arrogant," Byron retorted, "it was crass when you ridiculed the size of their swords."

"How can that party gain support from the Bottom Tiers?" Cojax asked.

"It'll be tough for them," Byron said, "but they might not have to. Already, even though they're a smaller party, they're one of the most powerful, having won over many of the Second and Third Tiers. They don't have the numbers, but they do have the skill."

"What I want to know," Orch said, "is who is the big guy sitting just opposite us?"

Bryon nodded. "Yes, certainly a formidable foe."

Cojax looked to where Orch gestured, locking eyes with a fierce-looking warrior with long, wavy hair. He appeared more savage than man. He wore no armor or shirt, exposing his chest to the light. Despite the fact the man was sitting down, he looked large and foreboding, his body occupying twice the space of anyone around him. He was covered in black, tribal tattoos, each one received after obtaining some victory in battle. Circling his eyes was a smear of black, war paint that complemented his features. The practice of wearing war paint was rare, but not unknown in the city, and it was primarily practiced by the Saken Faction. Along his lap, was a large two-handed weapon, much like the one Titan carried before he died.

"That's a Numberless blade," Cojax said.

"Yes, it is," Bryon agreed. "The man who carries it is Onar, son of Cleinias. He didn't steal it; he earned it. He's the only person I know that legitimately does not have a Score in this city. He had been accepted into the order of the Infinite Council just before the AC fell. In fact, the Numberless were performing the ceremony of Onar's indoctrination when you and your friends brought down the AC. Had that ceremony continued, he would have been made a Numberless."

"How come he didn't fight with the Numberless when we rebelled?"

Byron shook his head. "No one seems to know."

"I've seen him before," Orch said. "He's a brutal warrior who uses his sheer size to dominate anything he faces."

"He's a Nova," Byron added. "Besides you, Cojax, and your

brother Marcus, he's the only Nova that I'm aware of in the city right now. Onar and his followers call themselves the Unbroken."

Despite himself, Cojax found himself looking away from the intense gaze of Onar. Unlike any other political party present, Onar's followers were utterly silent, as if all of this was beneath them. The result had a chilling effect that seemed to draw attention to that side of the room. Cojax steered his gaze to the others surrounding Onar. He almost lost his composure when he realized that those around the giant warrior were also shirtless, including the females. Such an immodest display of flesh had been unprecedented, but now, it seemed to have the desired effect. Onar and his followers would not be subjected to the rules of anyone.

"And what government can we expect from him?" Orch asked. "One that favors shirtless Fridays?"

"He's a King."

"You mean he wants to be a King," Orch said.

"No, I mean he has already proclaimed himself King," Byron insisted.

"What? Of who?" Orch said. "Of all of us?"

"Yes," Byron said.

"Well, I didn't vote for him," Orch replied.

Byron studied his ArmGuard, pulling up a chart. "He has mixed support from the Bottom and Mid Tiers. Despite his high Score, I don't think there's another First, Second, or Third Tier in his political party."

"Any other party I should know about?" Cojax asked.

"Those are the ones that have any significant support," Byron said. "After today, the rest will likely be assimilated into one of these major parties."

Cato then entered the room, surveying it with the deference one pays an insect. He approached Byron and saluted. When he saluted Cojax next, it was hastily and carelessly done. He sat next to Byron, speaking in a low tone. "Everyone now knows that Cojax is to be our High Councilor, and the support is almost unanimous. Although, that may change when they discover exactly what Tier Cojax was when the AC fell. I think the boy's anonymity actually helped him in this case. No one knew him well enough to say anything negative."

"I believe you forgot to use his full title," Orch lectured. "He is the Lord High Councilor of the BloodBorne Party."

Cato was about to ask Orch who he was and what business did he have here when Byron cut him off. "He's right. You need to refer to Cojax as the Lord High Councilor, and this is Orch…I mean Orchulli, a self-proclaimed Master of the Blazer."

"So," Cato said. "This is the one that is to replace Sejanus. Stories of your self-promotion and bragging have spread far and wide, Orch. Even I've heard about some of your feats. Tell me, are any of them true?"

"You got me," Orch said with a smile. "All lies. Now I have a question for you: if I throw a stick, will you go away?"

Cato swallowed hard, his eyes narrowing at the comment. He was so unaccustomed to being spoken to in this manner, he did not know how to respond.

"I'm sorry," Orch said. "Turns out, now that the AC doesn't monitor everything we say anymore, I can tell you First Tiers what I really think about you."

Byron put a hand on Cato's shoulder before the warrior could react. "Easy, my friend. We need to appear united. We'll talk later."

"But he's only in the Second Tier," Cato replied. "He can't—"

"—Listen," Orch said. "I'm easy to get along with. If you respect me, I'll only slightly disrespect you."

"Be quiet both of you," Byron said. "One of the Arbiters is about to speak."

Cato looked insulted, first by Orch and then by Byron. Byron's persistence won over, and eventually, the hot-tempered man turned his attention to the center of the room.

An older man stood before them, his hands open in a gesture of peace. "I am Meloch, son of Zebder, who was slain after obtaining the First Tier. I am one of three Arbiters that you have elected to act as judges for this deciding body.

"The other Arbiters and I will not vote, argue, dispute, or participate directly in any proceedings. Any conflict with established rules will be settled by myself and the two other judges. Each party will be given a vote, and the weight of that vote will depend on how many individuals directly support your political party. The purpose of this body will be twofold: first, to vote on, discuss, and deliberate over pressing matters and logistics in how to run Acadia, or I mean Titan, as we are now calling it. The second goal is to discuss, persuade, and eventually elect how our city is governed. All of these proceedings are being recorded and broadcast across the CityScreens, and any individual within the city, using their ArmGuard, can change their support from one party to another. A Validated can change their allegiance a maximum of three times a day. When sixty-percent of the Validated support a single party, that party will become the undisputed governing body of Titan.

"The other two Arbiters and I are in the process of developing a system that would allow political parties to acquire advertisement time on CityScreens that will be broadcast out to the entire city. This will be done in order to foster transparency as well as allow each political party exposure so they can be judged by their merits.

"Once a political party obtains at least three percent of the support from the Validated, they will be considered a viable political party. Once they're considered viable, they will be given certain rights, to include a vote in the First Assembly. The power of their vote, however, will be determined by the amount of Validated who support that particular political party. A viable political party will also be granted a room within the Trinity that can be utilized as a base of operations for that political party.

"Now, creating a new and effective government is no easy task since the events that led us here were unseen and, consequently, could not be prepared for. We have the unique and important responsibility now to decide how we are to be governed. This is no light matter, as it will likely affect us the rest of our lives and the lives of generations to come. I will turn the time over to Melina, who will detail the rules that are to be abided by during these proceedings. If there are any disputations with the rules, we will call for a discussion, then a vote, and then establish a new rule or make changes to an old one."

Melina stood up, her appearance much like the man that proceeded her. Her voice was monotone and flavorless, and the more she spoke, the more Cojax stirred in his seat. The rules were simple at first but soon became more complicated as she discussed complex and unlikely voting scenarios. The voting process was discussed as well as procedures that were to be undertaken in the event of a tie; fundamental rights were mentioned as well as punishments for those that spoke out of turn.

Cojax tapped his fingers against the arm of his chair with every word that Melina spoke. It felt like the woman spoke for days before she finally sat down again. A woman named Mitra stood up, stating that she was the final judge who would be taking part in these proceedings. She was pretty but stern and wasted no time in pleasantries.

"To understand the situation better," Mitra said, "we will now hear from the spokesmen of each political party directly. You will have the floor for ten minutes, but be careful not to speak longer than your allotted time. Otherwise, the strength of your vote will be weakened in the next voting session, as previously mentioned. The order of this selection was random. First, we will begin with the Populi."

Sejanus stood, garbed in a white toga, addressing the crowd as if he was some ancient Greek philosopher. He started with some Latin and then transitioned into a series of points about freedom and how it empowers all those who wield it. His speech was good, but it seemed rushed towards the end. Cojax was impressed at how fluidly the man spoke, almost as if the words were liquid, and he was simply pouring them into the room.

Next, the Restorationists were called to speak, much to everyone's trepidation. The speaker, a First Tier named Deo, was rigid and formal. He spent much of his time condemning many of the actions of the revolutionaries and of the Populi. Somehow, Cojax maintained his composure during the verbal assault despite his hands tensing every time the speaker looked at him directly.

"Now we will hear from the BloodBorne Party, who, I'm told would like to elect a—"

"Lord High Councilor," Orch said, his voice easily carrying through the room. "And I know what you must be thinking, that I would be best for the position."

Byron did his best not to show his surprise at Orch's words, but, despite himself, his eyes bulged ever so slightly as he looked at the man who was now speaking.

Orch continued with his cocky, yet humorous tone. "But you'd be wrong. This man, who will speak to you shortly, was the one that worked with Titan to remove the chains of our bondage. While all of us, including myself, were content to live in slavery, he discovered the truth. The Populi Party talks of liberty, but it is this man who brought it to us. May I present to you, Cojax, son of Titan, our Liberator and Lord High Councilor of the BloodBorne."

NINE

Cojax slowly stood, hoping that his delayed movement was mistaken as being stoic instead of nervous. He looked around the room, not focusing on anyone in particular. When he reached the part of the room where Onar sat, he skipped it altogether.

Finally, someone from the Statesmen Party shouted. "Sit down—we don't need a longwinded speech from you."

Melina, the Arbiter, was quick to reprimand, pronouncing a punishment to the Statesmen Party for the outburst.

As the judge spoke, dealing out punishment, Cojax felt his anger rising, not at the judge, but at the stupidity of their situation. These First Tiers had wasted so much time already. Cojax's anger burned hot, turning his face red. His father was killed not days before, not by an enemy he understood, but by an agent of the Decamont. A race so powerful that they had deceived them for over two hundred years.

He clenched his fingers into fists. "I should sit down—that man is right. There should be no longwinded speeches by any of us. For there is no time. *They* are coming. When will they be here? A month? A week? A day? How will we fight them when they arrive? With our words that we've sharpened in this room? Or would we be better off sharpening our swords? How little all of this means if we are wiped from off the face of the earth and our city is set ablaze.

"While we talk, the Decamont plan. While we debate, the Decamont prepare. While we get fat off the blood of our new found freedom, the Decamont are forging new chains to make us slaves once again." Cojax's voice carried through the room, demanding silence from all those that heard him. "I will not let my father's sacrifice be in vain. I did not witness the life leave the eyes of so many brave Validated so that we can argue over who is in charge of what. What I offer is decisiveness. Let us focus on the true fight before us."

Cojax stared at the crowd around him one last time before

sitting down. The speech was so short that the judge was not ready to stand up. She finally stood, stumbling on her words as she spoke. "Next, we will have the Statesmen Party."

Cojax's ears burned. It was insanity. He just spent his time talking about this threat, a threat that everyone in the room was not only aware of but of whom they all feared, and they continued on with their proceedings as if it had no effect on them. Now, instead of tapping his fingers against his armrest, Cojax flexed his hands open and closed, pushing the blood from them, trying to calm the anger running through his veins.

Byron leaned forward. "That was not the plan, Lord High Councilor."

"It was better," Orch said.

"It had to be said," Cojax replied.

The speeches continued with each party. Some were long, others short, but from then on, all of them either directly or indirectly referenced Cojax's speech. Some spoke about the Decamont as if it was such a formidable foe that only their political party knew the way to defeat them. Others spoke of the Decamont as an old enemy who had weaknesses that could be discovered and exploited. At first, Cojax thought, his words meant nothing to this crowd, but the more the other party leaders spoke, the more he realized that because of his words, the entire conversation had shifted. Almost every leader now addressed how they would defeat the Decamont while still setting up the best system of government.

Then the debating and voting began. The Populi Party made a motion to prohibit any use of the Acadian Computer System, such as facial recognition analysis, GPS location data, and access to the live feed of a Validated's Static Armor camera. The Statesmen Party seconded the motion with impassioned interest. During the debate, Marcus made a forceful treatise on the importance of protecting every Validated's privacy. The motion was carried by a significant majority, the only dissenting votes coming from the Restorationists.

The Populi Party, encouraged by their early success, made a motion to establish a form of currency. This currency was to be based on everyone's Score prior to the fall of the AC. The motion was seconded by the representative from the Statesmen Political Party.

Marcus stood up, meeting eyes with Cojax for a brief moment

before speaking. "The Populi proposes that the currency be called Tines and that one Tine shall be given for every point a Validated previously possessed. For each Tier that one had obtained, we assert that an individual's Score should be multiplied by 10,000. For example, if someone obtained the Ninth Tier, their score would be multiplied by 20,000 and so on…." Marcus continued to speak, laying out the finer details of how they proposed to implement the creation of new currency.

Cojax could not believe what he was hearing. A financial system based in that way would impoverish the Lower Tiers while enriching all in the Top Tiers. Cojax did some quick calculations in his head: his Score was 9,898, and he was in the Tenth Tier. While his brother's Score was somewhere around 3,500 points, except he was in the First Tier, giving him a potential value of 35 million. In a heartbeat, all those in this room would be elevated to another class completely.

"How could he even suggest such an idea?" Cojax whispered to Byron. "He supposedly represents those of the Bottom Tiers. Does he know exactly how much that will separate the Tiers? He's a fool."

"Your brother is no fool," Byron said. "I'm sure he considered all outcomes to his proposal."

"The Bottom Tiers will not stand for this," Cojax whispered. "They'll not be forced into slavery."

"No," Byron said, "they won't, which makes me believe this is some sort of ploy. We should—"

Cojax tried to stand, but Byron caught his arm. "Let's see how this plays out. Remember, even though this proposal is political suicide, we are still in a room surrounded by First Tiers, who will benefit the most from this system. If you are attacking the proposal, they might see it as an attack on them."

Cojax clenched his teeth until it hurt. This proposal was madness. *How can we do nothing while these First Tiers vote themselves wealthy?* He felt a wave of anger spreading throughout his chest. His palms turned into fists, and before Byron could anchor him to his seat again, he stood up, his face flushed red.

"I've never heard such rot before!" Cojax shouted.

"It's not your turn to speak," replied Meloch, the Arbiter. "The Delegate from the Populi Party is still laying out the details of his plan."

Cojax was only encouraged by this rebuke. "I will not sit still, among you First Tiers, who seem fond of standing on those who you deem beneath you. This legislation goes beyond the mark, landing somewhere between absolute arrogance and ignorance. You are not better than them! Those in the Bottom Tiers bleed as much as you; they have fears, like you; they have made, and will continue to make sacrifices as you—"

"—Delegate from the BloodBorne Party," Meloch said, "you will be silent."

"Silent is something I will not be as long as that proposal is up for debate—"

"—Begging your pardon," Marcus suddenly said. "I would like to make a quick revision of my proposal. In my haste, I accidentally said that for each Tier a Validated obtained, their Score would be multiplied by 10,000. What I meant to say, and what we are proposing, is that for each Tier obtained before the fall of the AC that they receive an additional 10,000 added to their Score. But in any case, I apologize, Cojax, Lord High Councilor, for interrupting you. Please go on. I didn't quite understand your point, so please continue."

All eyes turned to Cojax, who stood still, his mouth slightly open. Marcus' correction had changed the entire proposal. Now it was an idea that seemed perfectly reasonable.

"The Delegate from the Populi Party," Meloch the Arbiter said, "has turned the time over to the Delegate of the BloodBorne Party. Please continue."

But Cojax had nothing to say. All the momentum, all the ire that was building up in him, had just been swept away as Marcus changed the proposal. Now instead of looking like a defender of the Bottom Tiers, he had been cast as an irrational, unreasonable fool who lost his temper the moment things did not go his way. He stood there, completely speechless, completely disarmed. He had been outmaneuvered so skillfully that he had not even seen it coming.

"Cede your time to the floor," Byron whispered.

Cojax swallowed.

"Cede your time to the floor," Byron hissed.

"I cede my time to the floor," Cojax said.

The room filled with scattered laughter as Cojax retrieved his seat.

"I have reviewed the written proposal from the Populi," an

Arbiter said, "and I concur. Marcus did previously misspeak. The written proposal submitted to me before this meeting states that for each subsequent Tier someone had obtained prior to the fall of the AC, their Score will be added to by 10,000. So that would mean, anyone in the First Tier would take their Score and add 100,000 to it, while those in the second Tier would take their Score and add 90,000 to it and so forth. Is that correct?"

Marcus nodded appreciatively.

The Arbiter continued to speak. "Marcus, do you wish to finish your proposal?"

Marcus stood, his face stoic, and continued right where he left off. This time, he seemed so much more reasonable and in control than his brother. He went on to explain how each political party should have the right to tax their followers as they deem fit. He also spoke about how every Validated would be given a monthly wage so they could support themselves.

"Wow," Orch said. "He just made you look the fool."

Cojax looked straight ahead, a vein near his temple bulging at the pace of his quickened pulse.

"Passion is good," Byron whispered. "I think we won points with the crowd with your speech this morning, but any ground we gained is now lost. Let's just keep our heads down for this meeting, and we'll come up with a comprehensive strategy after. Agreed?"

Cojax nodded ever so slightly. "Agreed."

TEN

Finn entered the HoverBucket slowly, as if he was going to his death. He brushed his hand across the hilt of his Arc Blade, confirming that it was still at his side. He always thought Cojax would end up getting him killed, but today, that might be something Jessica could be blamed for. No one had ever attempted what they were about to do, and Jessica, despite her small frame, did not seem the least bit worried.

"So," Finn said, trying to make his voice sound light, "what's the plan if they don't want to meet with us."

"They will," Jessica said.

"And if they don't?" Finn asked.

The question was lost in the drum of the engine as they shot up into the sky. Finn had armed himself well, two Arc Blades, an Arc Spear, a Repulse Shield, and a Blazer. The Roaches might have stopped attacking, but that did not mean they were friends.

As the engines became more constant, and the sound faded, Jessica scooted closer to Finn. "We'll be fine."

Finn nodded. "Maybe we should wait until our new government sanctions this trip to the Roach encampment."

"We could, but who knows how long that will take. Besides, they're just as likely to declare war as they are to declare peace. We have to strengthen our connection with the Damnattii if we are to survive."

"I'm just saying," Finn said, "we don't want any of the Validated blaming us for starting a war."

"I'm not part of any political party," Jessica replied. "I was Rifted, remember? All of us here were—except you, of course. So, they can't blame anything we do on the BloodBorne."

"I'm still part of the BloodBorne," Finn said.

"One BloodBorne won't make any difference," Jessica said.

The HoverBucket was full of Rifters, all armed much like Finn. Jessica had fought alongside these very same men and women when they took down the AC. All of them still blackened one side of their helmets with an 'X,' a sign of respect and loyalty to her. They were traveling with three other craft, each carrying twenty-five Rifters.

Jessica found it odd that the Rifters still marked themselves with the sign of the Aberration. She studied them carefully, feeling a pang of guilt. These Rifters had bled and died fighting for the same freedom Jessica now enjoyed. But unlike her, they still felt like outcasts, unable to walk among the other Validated without wearing their helmets. They had won their freedom but had not regained their confidence. While wearing their helmets, every single one moved, spoke, and acted as a model soldier. When the helmets were removed, and the crisscross scars revealed, that confidence disappeared as quickly as water down a drain. Most had even been too ashamed to try and contact old family members or friends.

Jessica turned to Aias, "Where are they all living?"

Aias leaned closer to Jessica, "In the Mahghetto. Since the fall of the AC, the Disciples who were there were released early, leaving plenty of beds and rooms behind."

Jessica hesitated before asking the next question. "How many are left?"

"We lost twelve thousand in the battle for the Trinity," Aias replied. "We have eight thousand who I consider Validated, another ten-thousand who have no experience with the Blazer or the Arc Blade."

"What about food?" Jessica asked.

"We've made a few connections with the other Rifters who run the food distribution," Aias replied. "They can't give us much, but it will sustain us."

"Do you know who is now running the Rift?"

"That boy that fought alongside you," Aias said. "What's his name, Brutus?"

"What do you think of him?"

Aias shrugged his shoulders. "It's not a job that many people would do, much less be good at. It's dark and damp down there—no natural light."

"Aias," Jessica said, turning to him in earnest, "I don't trust Brutus or Adriana. Both of them tried to destroy Cojax and me in the Mahghetto."

"That's different," Aias replied. "There are things you have to do in the Mahghetto to survive."

"Just the same," Jessica said, "Brutus still harbors a deep resentment towards Cojax. Can you keep an eye on him? Can you make sure he doesn't abuse his authority?"

Aias nodded, "Yes, but I don't really see why. If it ever comes to the point where we need to remove him, we can always do it by force. The little group of thugs he's managed to surround himself with have little training. I can't imagine that he has more than a hundred Rifters running around as his little police squad. And he can't expand his enforcement group because it costs him workers in food production and distribution."

"Please," Jessica said.

Aias saluted and bowed. "I will."

"And I'll try to get more food for your warriors," Jessica said. "How many Hoarders are left?"

"In the Rift?" Aias asked.

"Yes."

"There has to be a hundred thousand or so."

"We need them," Jessica said. "Is there enough space for them in the Mahghetto?"

"Yes…possibly…but I don't know how we can possibly feed them."

"I'll worry about that. Hoarders make their food by trading in the fallen equipment lost on the battlefield. Now that there's a ceasefire with the Roaches, the rest of the Hoarders will starve. I can't imagine a worse fate for someone than to die by starvation after they just won their freedom."

"What should we tell them?"

"I would just tell them the truth," Jessica said. "And then I would train them."

"Train them?"

"Cojax is meeting with several political parties today to discuss a new government—they're calling it the First Assembly," Jessica said. "And despite it being us who won our freedom, it's the First Tiers who are deciding how we should use it. Every other Tier has been completely cut out of the process, despite our best efforts. The only reason we have any say in this matter is because Cojax has been proclaimed the Lord High Councilor of the BloodBorne. But if things aren't going our way, we need to be able to defend ourselves either from the Decamont who invade us, or the First Tiers who try to rule over us."

"That will be a monumental effort."

"We'll do it together," Jessica said. "Let me know what you need, and I'll see to it that you get it. You have the support of the entire BloodBorne Faction and many in the Bottom Tiers. I can suggest to Cojax to have members of the BloodBorne skip a few meals a week so we have enough to provide to your new recruits."

"Then we will get it done," Aias replied.

Jessica nodded.

They rode on in silence for the rest of the trip. When the HoverBuckets landed, Jessica led the way out the side door, flanked by several Rifters who had their weapons drawn. Jessica gestured for them to sheathe their weapons. She looked around but only saw the desolate landscape. She had communicated with the Damnattii through the Numberless Comm channels, and they had agreed to meet her at these specific coordinates.

Finn walked up to Jessica, "I don't like the look of this."

Jessica nodded and turned to Aias. "What do you think? A trap?"

Aias did not answer the question directly. Instead, he turned to his commanding Alpha and barked out orders. "Set up a perimeter around the HoverBuckets. Assign ten warriors to protect Jessica—she lives, no matter the cost."

Jessica blushed at the words.

"What do you want to do?" Finn asked.

"We're early," Jessica replied, "we'll wait. We'll need their support in the coming war if we have any hope to survive."

Ten minutes went by and still nothing. Finn's usually light and casual manner disappeared completely as time passed.

After thirty minutes, Aias approached Jessica, "We better leave. No sense in waiting out here any longer than we have to."

Jessica frowned. She had felt confident that this meeting would be the first of several meetings to come; she had felt sure that this would come together with no complications.

Then something moved. Finn was the first to spot it—it was

as if a mound of dirt had suddenly shifted in one particular spot. Once he pointed it out, all the ground around them began to move.

"Lock shields!" Aias ordered.

Jessica took a step back, her throat closing. Within seconds, they were surrounded by SataniKahns. The creatures had been there the whole time, pretending to be part of the landscape, their backs covered in dirt, rocks, and branches.

Jessica looked to her ArmGuard, "Why were they not picked up on our scanners?"

"We better get out of here," Finn said.

"They haven't attacked yet," Jessica replied.

"If they had," Finn said, "we'd be dead. So, I suggest that before they do attack, we leave. They obviously don't have any intention of honoring their original agreement."

Jessica considered the situation for a moment longer. Then she sheathed her sword and walked past the surrounding Rifters.

"Jessica!" Aias shouted. "What are you doing?"

"I have to try," she replied. She turned her attention back to the massive creatures, which were only twenty-five yards away. Their bodies were full of movement, from the dozens of blade-like legs to the gigantic six pincers on their heads. Their bodies swelled with breath and shook as they flexed and relaxed each muscle in turn.

"I am Jessica of Claymont, a city not far from here. I am the daughter of James Halworth, the Great Warrior who slew the White Wolf, who was the son of Emily Halworth. We were friends with your people long before I came to this city. I come as an emissary of peace. We came here in good faith to discuss the future of our two nations."

One SataniKahn bellowed, shaking the ground with its powerful voice. Jessica did not react.

From behind the SataniKahn, a Damnattii appeared, his body dressed for war. He had four arms, all of which held weapons. "Jessica of Claymont. I come from the Gildead, who was born and raised of the Son's honor. He is one who has never been diluted. He speaks with the mouths of thousands, where he has been given one."

"Where is Qualix?"

The Damnattii ignored the question. "My name is TrasiniX. I will take you to the Gildead."

"What are your intentions?" Jessica asked. "We want no

trouble; we can just as easily leave now and go our separate ways."

"As long as you follow Damnattii law," TrasiniX answered, "then you will not be harmed."

"We don't know Damnattii law."

"Do not hurt our people, and you will not be hurt," TrasiniX answered. "You may take your weapons, but not all of your warriors."

Jessica swallowed. "Fine." She returned to Finn and Aias, speaking in a low voice. "Finn, you stay with the HoverBuckets."

"Rift that," Finn replied. "I'm coming with you."

"Me too," Aias said.

"Well, someone has to guard the HoverBuckets," Jessica replied.

Aias turned to his second in command, giving the order.

Ten of them set off, Finn in the lead. When they reached TrasiniX, he turned and led the way. They walked a short distance before entering a long, slimy tunnel. Finn glanced back at Jessica, and if his helmet did not mask his face, his expression would have very accurately conveyed his disgust.

They passed underground, the light dimming but not disappearing. The tunnel led to a series of tunnels. TrasiniX took one of the paths to the left. As they walked, their party grew. From the shadows, more Damnattii joined them, walking alongside as if they had been there from the beginning. Soon, there were just as many Damnattii as Rifters. Another hundred yards and the amount of Damnattii had doubled. TrasiniX led them to a subterranean vehicle that ran on a wide track. The vehicle had seats, but none of the Rifters sat down—they were too busy eyeing their hosts to be concerned with their comfort. All the Rifters, with the exception of Aias, wore their helmets, allowing them to study the creatures all around them discretely.

Most of the Damnattii had three arms—two that were situated at the shoulders and a smaller one that sprouted from the rib cage. The shorter arm seemed to be the one used for all fine motor skills, while the other two were designed for war. The only exception was TrasiniX, who had four arms, each one toned and graceful. Finn had first assumed it looked more natural than the rest but then realized the opposite must be true. The bodies of the Damnattii with three arms were bulky, and rough, much like their limbs. TrasiniX's appendages, on the other hand, seemed far too sophisticated to have been created by natural evolution.

The vehicle began to glide so smoothly that it took a while to figure out that they were even moving. Beams of light flashed as they continued on, blurring their vision. The vehicle must have moved quickly because it was not long before it stopped, the side doors silently sliding open.

Finn was the closest to the door, but he hesitated to exit. What he saw before him was a city of stone and concrete, not a slimy Roach tunnel. With a nudge from Jessica, Finn stepped out into the open air, his chest expanding with a deep breath. In front of him was an enormous, half-moon forum, lined with square columns of granite. The granite was not polished, but it was smooth. At first, Finn and Jessica both thought they were looking at houses, but it quickly became apparent that they were in a market. The market did not open up to the sky but, instead, appeared to be lit by glowing stones that were craftily placed at various intervals along the path.

TrasiniX took the lead, directing the party into the crowded square. Jessica's senses came alive with the smells and sounds. There was a group of merchants selling mechanical devices on the right, a Damnattii selling a mix of odd-looking meat on the left, a group of small children playing near a fountain. Jessica slowed her pace to study them—she had never seen Damnattii children, even when she lived in her village. Their features were larger, more pronounced.

"Keep up," TrasiniX said over his shoulder.

Jessica obeyed and turned, glancing back only once at the children before continuing on. The market was lively and disorderly as individuals bustled past each other, sometimes tripping over the wares of the shop owners. Despite the throng of Damnattii, they gave the newcomers a wide berth. Jessica first assumed this was out of fear, but as some of them began to bow, it seemed more like a sign of respect.

The Damnattii seemed fond of the color yellow, as it was used in almost every sign and with every piece of clothing. Their structures were not run down, but they were not new, as evidenced by the cracks in the granite, the uneven paths, and the lights that sometimes flashed off and on from above.

Finn focused his attention on the shops. Everything from the odd slabs of meat to the weaponry to the electrical gadgets were so foreign to him. The smells were far more varied and richer than anything he had sensed before—for good and bad.

The market narrowed into a large hallway. TrasiniX led them down to another vehicle, which promptly transported them to an entirely different place. When they exited, their surroundings were more austere and functional. Granite gave way to concrete, and the glowing stones became ordinary light fixtures.

TrasiniX led them to a large circular room. It was cold and dimly lit, except for a throne that was elevated by three steps. On top sat a large, four-armed Damnattii, crowned with what appeared to be a twist of thorns.

TrasiniX turned to the newcomers, his voice amplified. "May I present the Gildead: Lord TanereX, Speaker of Thousands, Defender of the Order of the Numberless."

Jessica stepped forward, unsure if she should kneel or bow. She saluted instead. TanereX crisply returned the salute.

Jessica began to speak, but she was cut off by another Damnattii who was armed as if he was about to head off to war. "You cannot speak directly to the Gildead unless you are a Numberless."

Jessica started again, this time referring her comments to the soldier instead of the Lord. "We are from the city of Acadia, which we now call Titan. We bring a message of peace."

The soldier then repeated the words to the Lord.

Lord TanereX nodded ever so slightly. "You say you bring a message of peace, but you have brought us war."

"War?" Jessica asked.

A Damnattii warrior stepped forward. "You do not speak to the Gildead directly unless you are among the Numberless."

Jessica turned to the warrior, "What does he mean by war?"

The soldier relayed the message.

TanereX took some time to respond. "Few people among the Damnattii knew of the Decamont. It was the Numberless that we served. But now that you've eliminated their control, my hand was forced to share with my people the truth of the Decamont. You've started a war you can't possibly hope to win."

"We've ended a war—" Jessica began.

"You do not speak to the Lord—" The Damnattii soldier began to say.

"—Enough," Jessica yelled. "By my hand, Atlas—a Numberless of the Infinite Council—died. I will not speak through one of your warriors as if my words can't reach you. There's no time for formality and tradition. The Decamont are coming to claim this land, and they will not honor any of our traditions when they arrive."

Awkward silence filled the hall. TanereX straightened up in his chair, as if he had just been scolded for slouching. Jessica locked eyes with the Lord, refusing to look away. TanereX finally yielded, gesturing to the warrior at Jessica's side. The Lord stood up, his steps slow and methodical. He descended the steps until he was on even ground with Jessica.

"You want to speak," TanereX said, "then speak."

Jessica nodded. "We are no longer at war with you or your people. For the first time in two hundred years, the Killing Fields aren't black and red with our shared blood. The enemy, the true enemy which we both once served, is who we need to fight."

TanereX shook his head. "It is hard to believe that they sent the Aberration, of all the Validated, to this place to speak with me. To negotiate terms of peace and cooperation."

Jessica swallowed.

"Yes," TanereX replied. "I know who you are. Atlas himself spoke of you, venting much of his frustration to me. He couldn't kill you, as it would have jeopardized his own life and position—Titan made sure of that—but that did not stop him from cursing your name every chance he got. We are not much different than you. We speak the same language, we served the same masters, we engage in the same pastimes. Acadia was being forged into a sword, and we were the anvil and hammer that was used to beat it into submission. But that's where our similarities end. We did not rise up; we did not rebel."

"What do you mean?" Jessica asked.

"You're right," TanereX said. "The Decamont are coming. Have you ever heard of Armean?"

Jessica hesitated before speaking. "No."

"What about Iberia?"

"I've never heard of either of those places."

"That's because, Jessica, they don't exist anymore. In their stead, you will find the earth blackened and charred. Plants and animals will not be able to approach those locations for at least a thousand years. Not a soul survived. Despite all of their technology, and their skill, and their determination, that is all that is left of them."

"Why does that matter?"

TanereX turned to Jessica, his eyes adding emphasis to his words. "Those cities were free once, as yours is now. Now, they are nothing but ash. And so, when I see you, I think of them. Your story is not unique."

"If everyone was slaughtered, how do you know about them?" Jessica asked.

"That's a perfectly reasonable question," TanereX said, "and the answer to it will define our relationship. Those cities were surrounded by the Roach armies as well. In both cases, by the time the Decamont arrived, some of the Damnattii had fled, fearing that they would be among those destroyed. After the cities were burned to the ground, do you know what the Decamont did with the Damnattii that fled?"

"Hunted them down?"

"No," TanereX replied. "They ignored them. And that's how I know about these two cities—from the Damnattii who survived. We are nothing to the Decamont. We are a tool that, once broken, can easily be replaced. The Decamont are coming, this is true, but they are not coming for me—they are coming for you. You and everyone in that city."

"If we stand together," Jessica said, her voice becoming tense. "We have a chance."

"In one city—I believe it was Armean—they attempted just that. They used the Roaches to surround the city, creating a moat of claw and carapace, and then they released the most volatile pollens we have in store—"

"Pollen?"

"That's how we control them, Aberration. That's how we work them up into a frenzy or pacify them."

"By releasing pollens?"

"Yes. The Decamont first destroyed the Roaches, then the Damnattii, and then all those in the city. It made no difference."

"Why would they care if one city rebelled?" Jessica asked. "And why would they utterly destroy it?"

"Does it matter?"

"Yes, it does," Jessica said in earnest. "That means that they weren't worried about one city rebelling. Don't you see? They're not afraid of the people rebelling, but the idea of a rebellion spreading. They fear us. They fear what we can do if we stand together—"

"No," TanereX said, his voice rising. "You cannot use my armies as a wall to protect your people."

Aias stepped forward. "What will you do instead?"

TanereX let out a long breath. "We will leave and join those who have left before. If you are wise, your people will do the same. Run from this place or be buried by it. Then pray that they will not hunt you down. That is the only wise decision you can now make."

Jessica did not know how to respond. Of all the potential outcomes of this conversation, she had not expected this one. She had assumed that the Decamont would be open to the idea of a treaty, as long as they were able to dictate how the war was fought. It was a while before Jessica spoke again. "And all of your people support you in this? Where is Qualix? He helped us end this war. Why is he not here?"

"He has been dealt with," TanereX replied.

"Dealt with?"

Finn stepped forward, speaking for the first time, his hand on the hilt of his blade. "What do you mean by that?"

TanereX smiled at this, his eyes coming alight. "So, is he a friend of yours?"

"He helped us end the war," Finn said. "He should be hailed as a hero among your people."

"Your definition of hero and mine are vastly different," TanereX replied. "We were living a stable life. Damnattii died, but most of them lived. Whole generations were born, lived, and found purpose here. Now, that has all changed. Now, we have to uproot our families and leave before all is lost."

"You were slaves," Finn said.

"We were warriors," TanereX replied. "Now, we are as sheep waiting to be slaughtered when the true master returns."

"Where is Qualix?" Jessica insisted.

TanereX returned to his seat, gesturing to the guards as he went. He then sat down, his body landing hard on the throne.

"Where—," Jessica began.

"—Patience," TanereX responded, a hint of his real demeanor

flaring up.

It was not long before Qualix was brought to the room, his body was black with blood and bruises. He only had two arms left; the others had been ripped off and then carelessly cauterized. From the pits of where the arms once were, black blood had collected and dried.

"Why?" Finn asked.

"Because of him, we might lose everything," TanereX growled. "Because of him, I have to take an unused path and ask those I lead to follow me into an uncertain future. His actions were not sanctioned. He made a decision that impacts us all, but he did so without first discussing it with his superiors. He did it without discussing it with me!"

"Release him to us," Finn said. "It does no good to butcher him here."

"Where is the justice in that?" TanereX replied.

"What orders did he violate?" Finn asked. "If he didn't even know the Decamont existed, how can he possibly be responsible for angering them? He simply saw that this war between the Damnattii and the Acadians was pointless. He was trying to save lives, and you tortured him for it."

"He will die for what he did," TanereX said.

Jessica stepped forward, her voice soft but stern. "If you do not release him to us, then we will take him from you."

TanereX laughed. "Before you could take another two steps, my warriors would cut you down."

"Then you've already declared war with my people," Jessica said. "And since the Decamont are not here yet, my people will focus everything they have on you. Just a few days ago, you were our mortal enemies. It wouldn't take much to convince the Validated that you are our enemy once again. What's more, now that we're here, they will know where your main forces are located. They will know how to expose your weaknesses. And they will use those weaknesses to make your escape impossible."

TanereX threw up his hands. "His life means nothing to me."

"Then let us have him," Finn said.

TanereX looked to one of his counselors, who in turn, nodded. He turned his attention back to Jessica. "Fine, take him. But know this. Until our people leave this land, I will treat every Validated found past the Killing Fields as an enemy." The large Damnattii turned to the warriors holding Qualix. "Release the traitor and escort the rest to their ships."

Qualix's energy cufflink fell heavy to the ground as he was released. The newly freed Damnattii looked cautiously back at his captors, as if asking for permission to leave.

"Come on, Qualix," Jessica said. "You'll not only be welcome among our people, but you'll be seen as a hero."

Qualix took one step forward, but it turned out to be his last. One of the Damnattii slid an Arc Blade through Qualix's chest before he could take another. The Damnattii fell to his knees and then to the floor.

Jessica unsheathed her Arc Blade, which set off a chain reaction with everyone else in the room. The only person that remained unarmed was the dominating Gildead, who seemed just as bored as before.

"You said he could be released to us," Finn yelled.

"And so, he is," the Gildead replied. "I said I'd release him—I never said he'd be alive when I did."

Jessica shook her head. "You would butcher your own just to prove a point?"

"I would butcher your entire city," the Gildead replied with a chilling tone, "if it meant I could get back into the good graces of the Decamont. Now, leave me before I decide to do just that, starting with all of you."

Jessica shook her head. "We might not be at war, but if you so much as threaten our city again, we will come visit your people with such destruction that no one will be left to tell about it."

"Save your empty threats for the Decamont," the Gildead replied. He turned to his guards. "Escort them out of here."

ELEVEN

Cojax knocked on the door, an old gesture that had been replaced by their advanced communication system. He would have typically hailed his brother on the Comm, requesting his location and a time to meet with him. But he decided against it. Instead, he chose to visit his brother; instead, he chose to knock. His body was a mix of emotions: half of him wanted Marcus to be absent, the other half wanted him to be there.

For a full hour after the First Assembly meeting, Cojax was flushed red with anger. Marcus had used his knowledge of Cojax to set a very clever trap. And Cojax had fallen right into it, almost too willingly. Cojax was reminded once again how much more superior his brother was to him. But then, Jessica arrived, explaining in detail her encounter with the Roaches. The conversation left him feeling vulnerable and alone. Now he needed Marcus more than ever.

Cojax was about to turn away when the door opened.

Marcus, still in his toga, draped in a blue sash, was the picture of stoicism. He stepped back, allowing his brother to pass. Marcus disappeared to the kitchen, returning with some glassware not long after. "I debated not letting you in."

"I debated not coming at all," Cojax answered.

Marcus nodded. "I won't apologize for what I did at the First Assembly."

"I don't expect you to," Cojax answered. "I was your opponent, and you did what you believed you had to do."

"You are not just an opponent, but *the* opponent," Marcus replied. "The BloodBorne is one of the largest Factions. Other political parties are much more vocal, but the BloodBorne has proven to be more loyal."

"We were the biggest political party until the first meeting," Cojax answered.

"Your numbers have not decreased."

"They haven't grown either," Cojax retorted. "While your own Populi has had a seven percent increase—the most of any political party."

"Democracy has always appealed to the masses."

"That it does," Cojax replied, "and perhaps it is the best eventual path."

"Still not convinced, eh?" Marcus asked. "If you can't be convinced by me, then study your history."

"What should I study first," Cojax answered, "the fall of the Republic of Rome or the fall of the Republic of America. Each one has unique qualities, but each one met with the same end."

"We now know what pitfalls consumed them," Marcus replied, "and we won't repeat them."

"No founding father or mother ever sets about making a system of government that will eventually fall by the wayside. You might be thinking you've ironed it out, but if history has shown us one thing, it's that time erodes them all."

"A dictatorship sooner than most," Marcus added.

"A king, a dictator, a tyrant," Cojax replied, "is what we need now. We can't have the majority vote us into victory. We need the decisiveness of only one ruler. Right now, I'd rather bend a knee to a tyrant than have a voice in a government that lasts only months before it is destroyed by the Decamont."

"Nihil pulchrae absque certamen," Marcus replied. "Nothing beautiful is without struggle."

"How long was the First Assembly meeting?"

"Not counting breaks, maybe six hours."

"Six hours, brother, and so little was accomplished," Cojax replied. "You'll see, as time progresses, how much we need to do and how little we've done."

"You want some stock?" Marcus said as he pulled a bottle out from the kitchen.

"Stock?" Cojax replied. "I thought you could only get that from the Red District."

"You can, and I did."

"And they let you take it?"

"For a price," Marcus said. "After the First Assembly meeting, the monetary system was quickly established, granting Tines to all

Validated. Shortly after that, I found myself in the Red District. And so, using my newfound money, I bought some stock. They didn't have any idea how to price it, so they practically gave it away. Not long after, word got out, and they had more customers than they knew what to do with. The price slowly ticked up, but it was too late. I'm told that the entire Red District sold out by the end of the day."

"And who keeps the profits?" Cojax asked.

"That's another one of those questions that no one seems to have the answers to," Marcus replied. "Right now, I believe the profits are being transferred directly to the business—and then portioned out equally to the workers. It won't work in the long run, as some hardworking and enterprising individuals will want more of a share of the profits, but it will work for now. Long story even longer, I got a great deal on this pitcher. I wish I had bought more."

"What does it taste like?"

"You've never had stock?" Marcus asked, a genuine smile spreading across his face.

"No," Cojax said. "I'm only a few months out of the Mahghetto and wouldn't have dared to visit the Red District just in case our father found out."

"Let's drink to his memory."

"I'm not sure what he would say if he knew we were drinking stock to his memory."

"You know," Marcus said, "until a few months ago, I would've said that if he saw us here, wasting our time in pedantic conversation, he'd come over, box both of our ears, and smash the pitcher of stock onto the floor."

"And you don't think he would do that now?"

Marcus poured Cojax a glass. "No, I don't." He put down the pitcher and picked up his own drink with the same hand. He put his stump onto the table, gesturing to it with the glass in his good hand. "When I lost this, I didn't think that Titan cared—he certainly acted like he didn't for the first several weeks. But then one day, he showed up, unannounced, a chest in his hand. Of course, I let him right in, saluting as best as I could. My place was not dirty, but it was far from clean. I thought I was about to get an ear full—perhaps he would even dock my Score. He came in, his eyes non-judgmental. He sat at the table, opened the chest, and inside, would you believe it, was a pitcher of stock. And in an act that was very different from anything I've ever seen from him, we shared a drink just as we are doing now. We hardly spoke, and when we did, it was mostly about nothing."

Cojax eyed his glass.

"Go ahead," Marcus prompted.

"Was that the first time you had tried stock?"

Marcus nodded. "I think he was trying to tell me something. I think he was trying to tell me that it would be all right if I did not succeed. All judgment was gone; all pressure and pretense had disappeared."

Cojax brought the drink to his lips, allowing his nose a moment to process the smell. He swished it around before taking a sip. The mixture instantly overwhelmed his senses, burning his tongue and his throat on the way down. He blinked twice, forcing tears out of the corner of his eyes.

Marcus slapped Cojax on the back, grinning widely as he did. "Got a bit of a bite to it, eh?"

Cojax leaned forward and coughed, wiping his mouth. "Wow…."

Marcus winked, taking a long sip of his own drink.

Cojax took another drink. When he placed the cup back on the table, Marcus topped it off again. "You'll get used to it."

They drank in silence, Marcus taking large swigs, Cojax only taking small sips. The silence ended with light conversation—mostly about their childhood, the time before Marcus had entered the Mahghetto. Cojax was skeptical about the stock at first, but the more he drank it, the more appeal it seemed to have. It put him at ease, relaxing his muscles and releasing the tension from his eyes. For a few precious moments, he was able to forget the world around him. Forget that he and his brother were now at odds with each other.

Finally, when they had both drunk their fill, Marcus looked up, his face wide with a smile. "So, if you didn't come here to try and convince me to join your political party, and if you're not willing to join my political party, then what—besides drinking my good stock—brings you here exactly?"

Cojax took another drink. The liquid still burned the same, but either his throat was getting numb, or he was getting used to the sensation. "I wanted to find out if you really planned on wearing togas during every meeting with the First Assembly or if that was a one-time event."

Marcus let out a good-natured laugh. "Believe me, it was not my idea. I like to quote the ancients, not dress like them. But, unfortunately, I believe it is something that's going to stick. But seriously, what really brings you here?"

Cojax studied his drink for a second before answering. "Just because our political parties are opposed to each other doesn't mean that we can't work together."

"Hmmm...," Marcus replied. "What do you propose?"

"We share information. I can't trust your political party, but I do trust you. And, if we can work together, I think it will be for the best."

"You want me to spy on my political party?"

Cojax laughed. "When did you become so blunt? No, nothing like that. What I think we should discuss are things that could hurt or help our real fight against the Decamont. For example, we've made contact with the Roaches."

"What do you mean?"

Cojax nodded towards the Killing Fields that were far in the distance. "When the First Assembly was meeting, the BloodBorne dispatched an embassy to meet with the Damnattii."

Marcus pulled back, his smile replaced by a deep frown. "You can't act without leave from the First Assembly."

"If I didn't, there would be no action," Cojax answered.

"Disbanding the AC was one thing, but entreating a potential ally on your own is completely different. This is something you should have presented to the Assembly."

"Blood and bile, for the sake of the Trinity, Marcus," Cojax answered, "the First Assembly was too busy assigning everyone from the First Tier lengthy and important titles. They were too busy deciding how much more money they should be allotted as compared to those of the Bottom Tiers. It would be weeks before they would have acted—if they would've acted at all."

"And what if you would've started a war with the Roaches? What if, in the collective wisdom of the First Assembly, they decided it would be unwise to approach them? You personally made a decision that could potentially affect all of us."

"You did too when you decided to overthrow the AC with me."

"That was different."

Cojax shook his head. "No, it wasn't. We did something we believed was right, despite opposition by our leaders. Marcus, we have to hold on to what we believe is right and fight for it, regardless of the criticism of all those around us."

"Not this way," Marcus answered. "If this information was to leak out, that you were making decisions that affected all of us, I don't think there is anything I could do to protect you."

"Protect me?" Cojax asked. "From who? The First Assembly? They aren't the real threat."

Marcus shook his head, poured himself another shot of stock, and drank it all in one swallow. He wiped his mouth with the back of his forearm and took a deep breath, relaxing his muscles. Then he nodded—once, twice, three times. "None of us have forgotten about the Decamont, Cojax, despite how you feel. But I do agree with you. I think it is best if you and I keep an open and honest dialogue. I apologize for losing my temper. The last thing I want to do is create bad blood between you and me."

Cojax let out a long breath, but he did not relax. "Alright, what we share with each other, can't be shared with others. Agreed?"

Marcus nodded. "Yes, agreed."

Cojax looked long and hard at his brother, waiting for him to share something in return.

Marcus suddenly winked. "I guess you're expecting some information in return. I hadn't really been planning on this conversation, but I do have something of interest that could affect our defenses of Titan. The Populi Party is in control of all the power generated in the city."

"How?"

"Well, in the repairs that followed the overthrow of the Numberless, it was discovered that all power flows from a structure that's located beneath the Vixor Faction building."

"And the Vixor Faction is a major supporter of the Populi Party."

"Exactly."

"Can they control which part of the city gets power and which doesn't?"

"Not yet," Marcus replied, "but I wouldn't be surprised if they eventually can."

"Blood and bile," Cojax swore. "And who signed off on that? One Faction controls all the power? How is that fair?"

"It's not," Marcus said, "and I opposed exploiting it. They aren't going to use it to leverage votes—at least not now. It's the Populi's wild card, if you will."

"That's blackmail." Even as Cojax said these words, he felt a ping of guilt in his chest. This was the very thing that his own party had done to the food production and distribution of the city. Initially, he had planned to share this information with Marcus as well, but something about his brother's previous reaction made him hesitate.

Marcus shook his head. "I don't think it will come to that. I don't think they'll ever use their control of the power to leverage political favor."

Just then, Cojax's ArmGuard vibrated. He looked down at it, noting that someone was trying to contact him. He paid it no attention at first, that is, until his fuzzy vision honed in on the name of the person calling him. It was from Titan of the BloodBorne Faction. Cojax swallowed, his face losing all color.

"Who's contacting you? You look like you've just squared off with a tenth level SataniKahn."

Cojax grabbed his helmet. "It's urgent. Thank you for the drink." With that, he exited the front door before his brother could say another word.

TWELVE

Cojax's heart pounded against his chest, threatening to crack a rib if it pumped any faster. Once out of Marcus' apartment, he put on his helmet, expecting someone's voice to patch through to him any second. Instead, a message popped up. It did not contain words, just GPS coordinates. Using his ArmGuard, he was able to pull up the coordinates. A moment later, a flashing dot appeared on the interface that overlaid his vision. It was coming from the Trinity—from an area that had previously been controlled by the Numberless.

Cojax shook his head, logic and reason leaving him. For a brief moment, he let his mind come to the conclusion that his father was still alive—that he had not died—but had simply been placed in stasis. His mind began to spin with the possibility. *Perhaps he had injected himself with something that slowed his heart. Maybe his armor somehow kept him alive.* More possibilities entered his mind, even the unlikely. After receiving this message, all of it seemed plausible. The Trinity had Stasis Chambers that could preserve life, even if only moments away from death. *Perhaps, someone had put him in there. Maybe, the Stasis Chamber healed him.*

Before he knew what he was doing, Cojax was running towards the nearest rooftop. Not long after, he jumped onto a HoverBucket that was taking off. The HoverBucket was not exactly going the right direction, and when it deviated from the trajectory of the Trinity, Cojax leaped from the vessel, landing hard and cracking the roof of a building below. This was an illegal action—at least before the AC was disbanded, but now, no one was around to reprimand him. He did get stares from a few other Validated in the area, but none of them addressed the infraction with him directly. Cojax ignored it all. He would gladly lose all of his points if it meant he could see his father again.

He then ran and leaped off the building, this time making sure no one was below when he landed. The concrete cracked beneath his feet, but he barely noticed it. He picked up speed as his armor synchronized with his implants, allowing him to go at a terrific pace.

The closer he drew to the Trinity, the more certain Cojax became that his father was in that building. That he was alive. That he would know how to lead the city of Titan. *He will have the answers that this city desperately needs.*

Cojax was so upbeat that not even the guards at the front entrance to the Trinity, who almost did not let him in, could lower his spirits. Once Cojax reached the floor where the coordinates were located, his movement slowed as doubt began to set in. *I set his body on fire. I saw him burn with my own eyes. There's nothing that could bring him back.*

Still, he pushed on, forcing doubt to the side. He passed a large conference room, followed by a dining hall. The amenities for the Numberless were nothing short of extravagant. Until the fall of the Numberless, no one else had been allowed to enter this section of the Trinity. Whether out of some sort of reverence or fear, even now, no one seemed fond of using this area. The hallways in the Trinity lit up as he walked, revealing the vastness of each room. Cojax stopped short of the next room. The coordinates were just inside. His hand hovered near the implant reader, not quite activating it. He retracted his hand and removed his helmet, straightening his hair with the other hand.

The door hissed open, revealing a room that was already well lit. This had been the very room where the two forces of the Numberless had clashed, Titan leading one side, Atlas the other. The signs of battle had been cleaned and cleared, almost as if it never happened. Since the walls and floor here were protected by a shield, they were devoid of the scorch marks that still appeared on other parts of the Trinity. The only real sign that a battle had occurred here was the area around the stairs that had been cut open to form another doorway. This part of the room was not shielded, and Atlas had used it as an improvised passageway to lead his forces through.

But Cojax was not concerned with any of that. Instead, his eyes were fixed on a broad figure on the other side of the room. His armor was a brilliant display of black, silver, and gold that was so ornately crafted it could have only belonged to a Numberless. On his back was an ax as wide as a person's arm and as thick as two thumbs. A cape hung from his shoulders, worn in the fashion of the BloodBorne, with two clasps on the chest.

The figure turned, facing Cojax. It was not Titan. But it was a Numberless. The door shut, leaving the two warriors alone in the room. Cojax took a step back, bumping into the door. It did not open again. He moved his hand over the Implant Reader. It beeped, but still, the door did not open.

"It's rude to leave so soon after you just got here," the Numberless said. "Why don't you stay awhile?"

Cojax's mind was reeling, trying to recognize the figure before him. It was more than possible that one of Atlas' Numberless survived the battle. Or, there could have been a Numberless that did not even participate in the battle and was waiting for the right moment to strike. Cojax was pretty sure he could recognize all of the members that were currently on the Infinite Council, but this face he did not.

This Numberless was as tall as Cojax, but his chest was thicker and his arms more muscular. His entire body seemed unmovable, like a boulder made flesh. From his chin dripped a grizzled beard, a unique feature among the Numberless. His body posture seemed apathetic, but his eyes were earnest. And they scanned Cojax as if seeing a new creature for the first time.

Cojax unsheathed his sword.

The Numberless laughed. "And what are you going to do with that toothpick?"

"Defend myself."

The Numberless laughed again, shifting his beard into a new form of disarray. "Boy, if I wanted to, there isn't anything you could do to stop me from ending you."

"And that's why I have my blade out," Cojax answered.

"I expected more than this," the Numberless said. "I expected to see the son of Titan, but you seem a far cry from the man I knew." The man stepped forward, his arms spread wide in a gesture of peace.

Cojax raised his blade. "Why did you summon me?"

"To measure your value." The Numberless removed the ax from his back and took two steps forward.

Cojax took a step to the side, deciding that having his back against the wall would not be doing him any tactical favors. "I've fought a Numberless before, and I held my own."

The Numberless frowned. "If that was true, then you weren't fighting a Numberless—that, or he was taking it easy on you."

With this, Cojax donned his helmet and pulsed with his Arc Blade, sending a beam of light through it. He attacked high, then low, an odd combination but also effective against a stronger opponent. The Numberless blocked, sidestepped and swung his ax wide, leaving a trail of light behind it. Despite Cojax being the aggressor, he was immediately put on the defensive. He was forced to block attack after attack. The Numberless soon overwhelmed him, seemingly attacking from all angles.

Cojax adjusted, off lined, refocused, and then charged in, surging energy into his sword. He stayed ahead of the Numberless for a few moments, almost nicking one of his shins, but the giant broke through Cojax's defenses, hitting him so hard he sailed through the air, colliding into a far wall twenty feet away.

The shielded wall buzzed, leaving splattered light for a split second where Cojax hit. The Numberless grinned, his face almost as bright as his armor. "I thought you were a Nova? Where is your power?"

Cojax stood, forcing the fear from his body. He raised his Arc Blade in a dueling stance and with a scream, charged again.

The Numberless nodded, falling back into a combat stance, his ax sweeping for Cojax's legs. Cojax jumped over the thick blade, sailing straight for his opponent's face, but before he could plunge his sword into his eye, the Numberless ducked, and Cojax flew on by. The Numberless then moved with incredible speed, sending the broad side of his ax right into Cojax's back. The attack increased Cojax's momentum and he was sent rolling across the floor. He caught his feet and turned, his body sliding a few inches before it stopped. Sword raised, he rushed in again, but at the last moment, he pulled back, dodging the Numberless' ax. Cojax capitalized on the opening, dashing in and striking the Numberless on the leg. The ax came for him then, but Cojax ducked, barely dodging the thick blade and stabbed upwards, hitting the Numberless in the chest.

The broad man stumbled backwards, a new grin on his face. "Now that's more like it, boyou." With this, the Numberless charged, spinning his ax so quickly, Cojax was forced to take several steps back to avoid being completely overwhelmed. Then the beating began. Cojax ducked under one blow but was punched in the head. He blocked another attack but was hit twice more. Sparks spilled from his armor with each terrific collision, lighting up even the darkest parts of the room.

Cojax tried to regain the initiative, attacking again and again, using every technique he ever learned in the Mahghetto or fighting against the Roaches. At first, the idea of facing a Numberless thrilled him, but as his shields began to drain, his thoughts drifted to survival. His boldness gave way to panic. His breath came in choppy gasps, mostly out of fear. Never had he been more sure he was going to die than at that very moment. The thought both thrilled and terrified him.

He kept losing his concentration. He could not focus on anything beyond his own death. Cojax's thoughts flashed to an image of his father. Then Hadrian. In his mind, he saw more bodies fall, each one had been significant to him in some way or another. And now he would lie among them, slain by some unknown Numberless.

He shook his head, forcing the fear down and allowing anger to rise up. At the very least, he would die on his feet as a true Validated. But a final blow swept Cojax to the floor, completely draining his armor of energy. He was a beetle on his back, harmless and helpless. *At least,* Cojax thought with some solace, *I still have my sword.* As if reading the youth's thoughts, the Numberless kicked the blade from the boy's grip.

The Numberless stood over Cojax, holding his ax just above his throat. "You lean too much on your energy signature. You are a Nova, yes, and you have a tremendously powerful attack that will overwhelm those you might fight out there, but it's just showy and unnecessary against a Numberless. Don't they still teach dueling in the Mahghetto?"

Cojax did not answer, thinking the question was rhetorical. It was not. "Yes," Cojax finally said, his voice sounding more like a question.

"Well, you'll need to learn more," the Numberless replied.

"I'll keep that in mind."

"Yes…," the Numberless stroked his beard. "You'll have to learn much more."

"Does that mean you're not going to kill me?"

The Numberless reached out an armored hand, pulling Cojax up. "My name is Horace. I'm an old friend of your father. So no, I'm not going to kill you just yet."

***

Cojax was sitting in an ornate chair, his face still pale and sweaty from combat. Horace's face, on the other hand, was flushed red as he consumed the food and stock laid out before him on an ornate table. They were in another, smaller room not far from where they fought. It was a kitchen of sorts, having all the expected amenities, albeit this was much larger than the average kitchen.

Initially, Cojax thought that the food was set out buffet style, but after Horace began swallowing whole chicken breasts in only a few bites, he realized it was all for one man.

Cojax stirred in his seat, feeling small compared to the broad man with the considerable appetite. His defeat had been no great surprise, but he was consoled by how long he lasted. *Of course,* Cojax reasoned, *he could have just been toying with me the whole time.*

"You fought well," Horace said through a leg of chicken. "But I've trained in single combat longer than you've been alive. What are you, twenty?"

"Seventeen."

Horace tried to hide his surprise but, despite himself, he choked on a piece of meat and gave himself away.

Cojax decided to be direct with the Numberless. "I haven't been out of the Mahghetto long, maybe six months. When I Crossed, I was only Middle Tier, and before the AC was abolished, I was in the Tenth Tier."

"And in that time, you've managed to turn the Numberless against each other, send the city into chaos, and abolish the AC."

Cojax felt each accusation as a flick to one of his ears. "Well, those things sort of happened all at once, but if you separate them like you did, it sounds a lot worse."

Horace took a swig from a pitcher that most people would use to pour into smaller cups. "I could've killed you, you know. Killed you and started waking some of the Numberless and restoring order to the city. Then, perhaps, I could convince the Decamont the rebellion is over. I bet if I delivered them your head with an apology note attached, reinstituted the Infinite Council, found a new lady with whom I could make a baby, they'd most likely call me a hero."

Awkward silence fell over the room.

"But…," Cojax prompted.

"Hmmm…," Horace said, turning to face Cojax, a large piece of meat caught in his beard. "But what? That's all I had to say."

Cojax was still unsure of what sort of person he was talking to. He was a Numberless, yes, but unlike any he had ever seen. He was crass and callow, his beard in disarray. The food disappeared faster than it should have, leaving behind a fantastic mess.

Soon, what should have been a meal for four, was consumed by one. Horace slapped Cojax on the back, giving him a wink, "You better hope your appetite comes back; you'll need your strength." He licked his fingers, relishing each digit. "You know, lad. They say that stasis does not affect the body, but I gotta be honest with you, I can't feel my left foot. Do you mind looking at it?"

Cojax frowned, placing his cup on the table. "Your left foot?" He kneeled, his armor still sluggish from losing its charge. At first glance, the appendage looked fine, but the more he studied it, the more he realized that it was not natural. A boot obscured the foot, but the calf, although skin-colored, was definitely not flesh. Cojax pulled closer, studying the strange mechanical limb. Suddenly, Horace broke wind, startling Cojax so bad he hit his head against the bottom of the table.

Cojax shot up from under the table, his face red. "Alright, I'm done here. Unless you start telling me why in the Rift I'm here, I'm gone."

"Sit, boyou," Horace said. "Ask me your questions."

Cojax had not counted on his outburst working, so it took him a while to formulate a question. Finally, he asked, "Tell me what happened to your leg."

"Really, that's the first question you want answered?"

Cojax shrugged.

"I lost it fighting for you," Horace replied. "I liked that leg—it was my favorite—always taking me everywhere I wanted to go. Now, I've got to take this metal appendage off every night so the synapses don't fuse together. And every day I wake up, I have to reprocess the fact that I don't have a leg—because it's not there. It's not there because

I lost this leg fighting alongside your dad when you took over the Trinity."

"You survived?"

"Most of me," Horace replied. "This was not the only wound, but it was the most pressing. But, yes, I survived."

"Why did you fight?"

Horace shrugged. "I believed in the AC—it's dirty, yes, but it will have an end. And when it does, humans will be stronger for it. But more than that, I believed in your father. He and I talked before about rebellion, even spent a few nights drowning ourselves in stock and planning it out. But those were words, cheap and ineffectual. When your father woke me from stasis, something in me came alive. I thought he was doing what no other dared before. So, I followed. But it wasn't his plan I was following, was it? It was yours. So, I recovered, found a new leg, and hailed you on the Comm. With bated breath, I waited to see the son of Titan, the leader of the rebellion, the one who led the raid against the Trinity and abolished the AC. I waited to meet this Validated who was so talented he could persuade ol' boy Titan to change sides. And you showed up."

Cojax swallowed.

"How did you persuade Titan to rebel?"

Cojax rubbed his hands together. "Honestly, I thought I was going to have to fight him."

Horace laughed. "Hah, well, I think we both know how that would've turned out for you."

Cojax slowly nodded. "Yes."

"Tell me what happened from the beginning—I'm still not convinced that killing you and re-establishing the Infinite Council is not a bad idea."

Cojax began the tale in detail, explaining how Jessica appeared and her origins; how she and Cojax met and how they protected each other in the Mahghetto. He explained how they brought down the AC, the conversation with Titan, and how the city is now struggling with leadership.

Horace listened well, only interrupting once. He drank more stock during the boring details, but for the most part, he seemed interested. By the end of it, either from the tale being over or the fact he was full of stock, Horace seemed to be in a better mood.

Cojax felt encouraged in the change of the Numberless' demeanor. "Can you help us?"

"I always thought it would be one of the other cities that rebelled—not us," Horace replied.

"You've been to the other cities?"

Horace ignored the question. "I'm still undecided whether I should kill you or not," Horace said. "I'll have to think it over."

After a long while, Cojax stood and nodded. "Well…I'll leave you to your thoughts then."

"Probably for the best," Horace agreed.

Cojax nodded again, assuming the conversation was over. He approached the main door, and this time, it opened. Before Cojax could disappear completely, Horace had one more thing to add. "Whether I kill you or not, you'll have to become better with the Arc Blade. I will teach you."

Cojax frowned, unsure how to react. "And if I say no?"

"Don't push me, boyou," Horace replied.

Cojax nodded in reply.

"When I call, you must come," Horace said. "If you are late, you'll find an enemy instead of a friend. I know you have a busy schedule, but I'm aware of it. I still hold the privileges of a Numberless after all. I won't call you when you're occupied, but you won't tell anyone else about me. And when you arrive, I expect you to take the role of a student and me the teacher. Do I make myself clear?"

Cojax saluted by pounding his chest. "Yes, sir." He bowed low to the Numberless before him and left the room.

THIRTEEN

Marcus was the last to exit the HoverBucket. He scanned the crowd, his eyes looking for any potential threats. He did not expect any trouble, especially in the Vixor Quarter, which was among the Populi's largest supporting Factions, but he never could be too sure. With greater popularity came greater dangers—something that he was having to continually remind Sejanus. Their party was growing each day—but not as much as he had hoped. It would still be months before they gained a majority. He was convinced more now than ever that his political party would win—just not as quickly as he would have liked.

Marcus turned the corner of the next street, running headlong into a large CityScreen. Cojax's face was prominently displayed, a message just below it read, "The Boy Who Would Rule You." Sejanus' voice narrated as it went into a long and lengthy explanation of how Cojax cheated his way through the Mahghetto. Marcus shook his head. He had vehemently opposed the commercials, but he had swiftly been outvoted.

Sejanus came up from behind, wrapping an arm around his friend. "It's necessary."

"I don't agree now, just as I didn't before," Marcus replied. "The BloodBorne won't want to work with us after we've smeared Cojax. These sorts of attacks divide us, and that's the last thing we need."

"It won't matter if they don't work with us," Sejanus replied. "It will only matter if *other* people will. Cojax represents an opportunity for our party. Through sheer dumb luck, the boy has somehow abolished the AC and led a revolt against the Trinity. And somehow, he consolidated the power of many of those in the Bottom Tiers and the BloodBorne, one of the largest Factions. But despite all of that, he is extremely vulnerable. He was in the Tenth Tier when the AC was abolished—so, none of the Top Tiers will stand for him leading us now. He won popularity, but because of his illegitimate claim to it, he won't be able to hold onto it. If we can persuade others he's good but misguided, then we can persuade them to follow us."

Marcus shrugged Sejanus' arm off his shoulder, turning towards his friend with a sharp eye. "I agreed to follow you, but you have to promise me that you will be better than this."

"We've run through this," Sejanus replied. "We can't just have a strong message. The people also need something they can hate, somewhere they can place blame. Nothing drives people closer together than having a mutual enemy."

"And you think my brother makes a good target?"

"He's the only target," Sejanus said. "Who else abolished the AC? Who else raised the city to rebellion? Who else has a face that everyone in the city of Titan recognizes? Everyone knows who he is by now, and they will follow him just because he's familiar. But that does not mean they should follow him."

"It's dirty," Marcus replied. "And they won't just take it, trust me. They'll have their reply, and you can expect it will be with the same animosity."

"And as long as several of the Senators of the Populi Party share time on the CityScreens, they won't know which one of us to attack. Therein lies the inherent flaw with the BloodBorne. They have invested all of their time in the success of one individual, and if he falls, so will the party. We, however, are not a single individual, but a movement. No single individual in our party matters."

"That doesn't mean we shouldn't be cautious," Marcus replied.

Sejanus shook his head. "Not this again. Come on, the people around us are Validated, not savages. If we show fear, then we show weakness."

"I still think we should have more bodyguards to protect some of the higher officials."

"And what message would that send?" Sejanus asked.

"That we are serious about keeping you safe."

"I am not the party, the people are the party," Sejanus replied. "Besides, the people of Titan are warriors, not assassins."

"The only difference between a warrior and an assassin is that one kills during the day, and the other at night. It wouldn't take much to transition one's skill set from the Arc Blade to the dagger."

"Don't be afraid, my large friend. Trust in the people. Not only will they select the best governing body, but they will protect me as well as you."

They arrived at a stage that had been hastily built from metallic boxes. Marcus looked up, locking hands with Sejanus. "Just promise me one thing. That when this is all over, we build a government centered on liberty and justice—not convenient targets."

"I promise," Sejanus said with a solemn smile. "Now tell these people who we are and what we represent."

Marcus took to the stage, greeted by a host of cheers from the gathered crowd. He raised his stumped hand, as was his fashion, a reminder that even those who had fallen during the AC were now welcome within the city.

Marcus took his time with his speech, gauging his audience by their emotional reactions. This particular crowd did not need much convincing. Most of them already wore the blue bands on their arms, the sign of the Populi Party. All he had to do now was push them on even further so that they were not only convinced, but inspired to persuade others.

"My friends—my family," Marcus began. "Our pursuit is not one of convenience or one of luxury. We, like those who have loved liberty throughout all generations, do not seek recognition or fame, but for a system that guarantees equality among all people. What we fight for is for the unalienable right to pursue our passions, the ability to feed our children, to work for the cause of liberty, to have a voice in how we will govern ourselves." The crowd cheered.

"We are one of the few political parties that holds rallies like these—among the people, in the streets of Titan. Do you know why? Because the others fear the people. They fear that if they give you too much voice, you will use it to usurp their power. But we do not fear the people in the Populi Party, because we are the people!" Again, the crowd cheered.

Marcus went on, his speech gaining momentum. Usually, after the first part of the address, he lost steam, or the crowd seemed to lose interest. But either from the anger of seeing his brother smeared on the CityScreens, or because the passion in the crowd was infectious, Marcus kept his vigor. So, instead of turning the platform over to Sejanus, he kept at it, speaking from his heart. He spoke of their ancestors, how they had to sacrifice life and limb to have the very government that the Populi sought after now. He spoke of how governments, whether it be an oligarchy, a kingship, or even Communism, will always end up alienating and disfranchising a large portion of the people. By the time Marcus finished, his head was beaded with sweat. He dabbed at it, surprised that it was there.

Sejanus pulled him into an embrace. "Where did that come from? Sometimes I believe it should be you who leads this party."

Marcus laughed. "I was just warming them up for the main event." Sejanus returned the laugh and took the stage, raising both arms in the air to a chorus of cheers. The people were enthralled to see Sejanus, and they let their voices be heard for several long moments before he could speak.

Sejanus kept the fervor going but, admittedly, it was not his best speech. He pulled from other lectures in the past but had a hard time connecting some of the more disjointed points. Regardless, the crowd cheered, their voices carried several street blocks away. Clips from the rally would be featured on the CityScreens later that night, and their message would spread.

Marcus smiled. His party would win.

FOURTEEN

"The Populi Party is gaining momentum," Byron said. "We need to either attack them directly or ally ourselves with one of their greater enemies. At this rate, we won't have much say in a few weeks."

"How many BloodBorne have left our ranks and joined their party?" Cojax asked.

"Five," Byron replied.

"That's hardly a threat," Finn said.

"No," Byron replied, "and I'm not worried about our ranks leaving and joining them—what worries me is the number of followers they're gaining on a daily basis from the other political parties. At this rate, it will not matter if we lose any BloodBorne to them because they will have so much support from everyone else. Our vote will become inconsequential."

Cojax, Jessica, Finn, Orch, Adriana, and the BloodBorne High Councilors were once again gathered in Titan's old apartment, an event that was becoming a daily occurrence. As a recognized political party by the First Assembly, the BloodBorne had been allocated a large conference room and several smaller rooms in the Trinity. But Cojax opted to meet here, at least for now. It was cramped but infinitely more private.

Adriana had quickly taken to her role on the BloodBorne High Council, much to Jessica's disappointment. Still, even she had to admit that as soon as Adriana had become involved in their strategy, they began to have more success.

Adriana studied the other BloodBorne High Councilors, gauging their body language. "Marcus is a passionate speaker. And worse, he believes the garbage that he spouts."

"How do you know?" Cato asked.

"I have my sources," Adriana replied.

"Sources?" Jessica asked. "What do you mean—like spies?"

Adriana completely ignored Jessica's comment and instead

changed the subject. "We need to garner support from a demographic none of the others have even tried to reach yet."

"What do you mean?" Cato asked. "Every Validated has been accounted for, and their vote is being monitored."

"Except for those in the Rift," Adriana stated. "When Cojax abolished the AC, he legitimized their vote. Logically, they must now be part of the voting process."

"No one in the First Assembly will support that," Cato said.

"No," Adriana said, her face curving into a wicked smile. "Not unless we have the support of a larger party."

"Which party?" Cato asked. "Ever since Cojax put his foot in his mouth during the first meeting, everyone has kept us at arm's length. None of the other five large parties will back us if we submit a proposal like that."

"There's one party that supposedly represents the downtrodden, the people who are without a voice, the rights of the Bottom Tiers," Jessica said, stealing some of Adriana's momentum.

Adriana rolled her eyes, annoyed by the interruption, "The Populi Party are the supposed champions of the people. So, if Cojax can frame the conversations right, they'll either have to support our cause to validate those in the Rift, or they'll damage their own rhetoric."

"Well," Cato replied, "that's a big *if.* If he can't sell this to the Populi, then we might as well start supporting another party."

"Easy, Cato," Finn said, his chest swelling up defensively. "It was Cojax's voice that destroyed the AC by simply saying it was abolished. I doubt anyone else in this room would have been able to do the same."

"It was just the right time," Cato replied. "Everyone was confused and without direction. By the time the confusion cleared, it was too late to reestablish the AC. So, I don't think it had anything to do with Cojax or his no-name lackey who follows him around like a dog."

Finn frowned, his face turning red. "And what have you brought to the table? What contributions have you made since all of this started? The only thing that ever comes from your lips is how you think we should support another party. Well, there's the door; if you want out, I think you can manage to find it."

Cojax placed his hand on Finn's shoulder, easing the tension in the room. He faced Cato, his eyes firm. "That may be a course of action we eventually choose, but we'll lose much of our voice if we side with them now. Let's focus on creating solutions and not more problems. Adriana, I like your plan. Prepare some notes on how we can frame it. We need more ideas. Who else?"

"We need to spend more on advertising," said Parmenion. Until now, Cojax had rarely heard Parmenion speak, let alone contribute ideas. Ever since the BloodBorne High Councilors swore their allegiance to Cojax, it had been an awkward process defining precisely what that meant. Some of the BloodBorne treated Cojax as a king; others saw him as the brat son of Titan who was next in line. Most of the time, the BloodBorne High Councilors spoke little and contributed even less, as if they were doing this more out of obligation to Titan than anything else. Cojax felt that it was a good sign that Parmenion was starting to contribute.

Cojax turned to Byron, who had been the unofficial treasurer of the group. "How are we financially?"

"Strong," Byron replied. "We set a heavy tax on the BloodBorne from the beginning, and since no one had any idea what currency was or how it functioned, they never got used to the idea of making more. Apart from that, besides some basic armor maintenance, light payments to bodyguards, and a little advertisement, we haven't spent much."

"We need to double our advertisement," Parmenion said, "if we want to at least compete with the Populi Party message."

"No," Adriana said, "we need more than that."

"More than double?" Byron asked skeptically.

"Much more," Adriana said, "half of our currency needs to be funneled to advertisement, and maybe more."

"That's not sustainable," Byron said, his voice sounding like a father scolding a child. "If we spend our money brashly, we won't have enough for unforeseen expenditures."

"We need to save some in reserve for events," said Amphis, who was a stocky but sure-footed Validated. Amphis had been a recent addition to the BloodBorne High Council.

"What events?"

Cato scooted forward in his seat. "The Council has been

talking. If we want to make any headway with the other First Tiers, we need to start hosting events that will attract them."

"You were talking about this without Cojax?" Jessica asked.

Byron sighed in exasperation. "It was just a conversation in passing, nothing official."

"And all of you were present except Cojax?" Jessica pressed.

Byron straightened up, eyeing Jessica hard. "We've come to the conclusion that if we are to have success, we need to impress the other First Tiers. If we host a series of grand events, we might be able to find some common ground. They're all giving us the cold shoulder during the meetings of the First Assembly. Many of us feel that to defrost those feelings, we need to interact with them face-to-face."

"And you're going to do this by hosting a party where only First Tiers are invited?" Jessica asked.

"Not just First Tiers," Cato stated. "Cojax would be invited too."

Jessica rolled her eyes. "And what about Finn or Orch. What about me? Do you think our names will be on the guest list?"

Cato's lips tightened, his mouth on the verge of a cutting remark. But Byron interrupted before he had the chance. "It was just an idea—one that we have not presented to everyone because it had not been fully thought out—"

"—I like it," Cojax interrupted. "We can set the tone of the gatherings and only invite those who are on the fence. In that sort of environment, we might be able to bring some over to our side. I think most of us want the same thing; we are just going about it in different ways. If we are to maintain any sort of position of significance in the First Assembly, we need to make some allies among the First Tiers."

"But they won't be impressed by something that's poorly planned and executed," Cato said, his voice holding a cutting tone. "We need to do this right, and for that, we will need to spend some money. If we can't appeal to their logic, then let's appeal to their appetite."

"Yes," Cojax said, "but that isn't a complete strategy." He turned to Adriana. "What sort of advertisements did you have in mind?"

Adriana shifted in her seat, surprised the conversation turned back her direction. "Well, we could start with an emotional appeal, telling everyone how the AC was toppled from the Bottom Tiers up."

"That divides us," Jessica noted. "It implies that the Bottom Tiers were the true heroes and that the First Tiers are not much different than the Numberless."

"They are," Adriana hissed. "But you didn't let me finish. We need to appeal to the Bottom Tiers first—they represent the greatest numbers as well as the most likely to join our cause. We then need to transition our message to the Middle Tiers by focusing on new titles and achievements that can be made in our government. We could highlight a few individuals who have received great honors among the BloodBorne, but who were from Middle Tiers."

"I don't think we'll have sufficient money to accomplish both of these tasks and do them well," Cato added with condescension.

"The more people we win to our side," Cojax said, "the more revenue we generate. We must spend money to earn followers. This not only earns us votes in the First Assembly, but it also generates revenue."

"There's still something to be said about exercising caution," Byron replied. "If we bankrupt ourselves, we'll have little to no say among the First Tiers. May I suggest we do both of these ideas but keep a third of our revenue in reserve?"

Adriana nodded a head towards Cojax. "He's right. It will not matter how much money we have if we don't attract followers. Already, many of the other groups have had their numbers bolstered. We're falling behind. Not only that, but I also don't believe the other political parties know how effective advertisement can be. Right now, to buy time during peak hours does not cost nearly as much as one would think."

"Who's to say it will be effective at all," Cato said. "Validated are not mindless drones. Hardly anyone listens when the Populi Party drones on for hours about the cause of freedom."

"We could play recorded footage of epic battles to draw everyone's attention to the CityScreens," Adriana added. "Once we have their attention, we can slip in the occasional political message. If we create a balance of content and messaging, I think we will have better results than the constant lectures of the Populi Party. A good clip to start with will be the one when Cojax charges headlong into the biggest SataniKahn most have seen on a CityScreen."

"What will all of that do?" Cato asked, failing to hide the scorn in his voice. "We need people to believe in our cause, not be entertained by it. You seriously want to spend a massive amount of our funds on entertaining Validated?"

"Perception," Cojax said as he gave Adriana a knowing look, "determines reality. If the BloodBorne Party appears to be in control of the CityScreens, then people will believe we are in charge of the city."

"Perhaps," Byron said.

"That's what we will do," Cojax said.

"I call a vote," Cato said.

"Are you challenging my authority?" Cojax asked.

"As is my right," Cato replied.

"A vote has been called," Byron said. "All opposed to Cojax's plan, raise your hand."

The room filled with scattered hands.

"It appears the room stands nine against and three that support the proposal," Byron surmised. "By the rule of the BloodBorne, Cojax's proposal has been rejected. I move, however, to make the same proposal, except we keep in reserve a third of our assets."

This time, the room was unanimous in support of the initiative. The message was clear. Cojax was in charge, as long as he did what those on the Council wanted.

"Well," Jessica said, easing the tension with her soft voice. "If we aren't going to spend as much on advertisement, I suggest we push a singular message instead of trying to appeal to multiple demographics."

Cojax turned to Jessica. "What do you suggest?"

"That the Decamont are coming," Jessica replied. "That they will wipe us out if we can't come together as a people."

"That won't drive people to our party," Cato said. "And everyone already knows the Decamont are coming."

"She has a point," Cojax said. "If people really knew that already, why are they still fighting amongst each other for power? Why haven't we come together? They need to be reminded of the real threat, the one that will wipe us out if we are not united."

Adriana nodded. She was not willing to agree with the idea if it came from Jessica, but now that Cojax reiterated it, she backed it wholeheartedly. "Cojax is right. We need to remind everyone of the real threat."

"Alright," Byron said. "Do we need to vote on this new proposal?"

Cato nodded. "I think we should."

Cojax clenched his jaw while the vote was called and counted. He tried to push down the anger rising in his chest, but Cato seemed to personify the very issue he was fighting against.

The motion was carried, but only by a small margin. The meeting addressed other concerns that required additional votes and decisions. Finally, Cojax called the meeting to be adjourned.

FIFTEEN

Cojax stared out among the city, studying the lights as he did when he was a child. He never tired of this view, but right now, he felt annoyed by it. The city reflected the orderly society it always had been. There were no signs of the pending Decamont invasion, no panic that ran wild in the streets. HoverBuckets moved placidly throughout the city, carrying Validated as if their imminent doom was not only months away. He grabbed the side of the building, tightening his fingers on the ledge. Light pulsed down his arms, concentrating around his fingers. He could have crumbled the concrete, smashed it as if it were nothing more than sandstone in a vice. Such destruction would have lost him points under the AC—now there was little consequence. Even if someone saw him, what would they do? *Why does no one seem to care about the Decamont?*

A pair of hands wrapped around his waist, embracing him from behind. Despite his mood, Cojax smiled.

Jessica joined Cojax's side, grabbing his hand as she did. "What's on your mind?"

"Look at the city, Jessica," Cojax said, his voice falling to a whisper. "No one seems to care. Sometimes I think it's best if we just cut our losses, take anyone who wants to join us, and leave the city."

"Why don't we?"

"Maybe we should."

Jessica squeezed his hand. "You and I started this whole thing. These are your people, and now they are mine. Even if we left, where would we go? The Decamont would not allow the cancer to spread—they would have to cut it out. At least, that's what the Damnattii believe."

"What will happen to the Damnattii?"

"They'll be forgotten—left to their own devices. It will be difficult for them, forced from their homes, carrying with them little food and supplies. They'll have to grow their food in areas where little vegetation can survive. If they draw too much attention, they'll be wiped out. Too little, and they might not have enough infrastructure to maintain their society. They'll eventually fracture, split along political lines, and each group will compete with each other for the best location. Supplies will be limited, food scarce. The strong will take from the weak. They'll turn against each other, becoming thieves, stealing from their own to survive. Order will give way to conflict."

"We would be no better than them if we left this city."

"Plus, we'd still be hunted by the Decamont," Jessica replied.

Cojax turned to Jessica, pulling her closer. "So, are you saying it's not just about surviving, but also making sure you don't lose yourself in the process?"

Jessica looked up, soaking in his sharp features. "Exactly. We need to finish this together, as a people."

Cojax nodded. "I might have an idea about how we can turn the tide in our favor. I met someone the other day, someone I think you've met already. Do you know a Numberless named Horace?"

Jessica's eyes suddenly went wide. "A Numberless? Here in the city? Did he somehow wake from stasis?"

"No, but that's something that we need to consider."

"Waking them up?"

Cojax nodded. "We don't stand a chance without them. And even *if* they follow us, we'll still need more. We need the support of other cities. There has to be a way we can free them from their ignorance. We've started a fire of rebellion here, but unless it spreads, I don't think it will last long."

"Wait," Jessica said. "First, tell me about this Numberless you met. You're jumping all over the place."

Cojax complied, explaining in detail how he was summoned, how he first thought it was his father's call. He told her how Horace helped in the fight against Atlas and how he now demanded that Cojax train with him. "And," Cojax added, "I'm pretty sure he'd kill me if he knew I was telling you this."

"And so, you're telling me anyway?"

Cojax shrugged. "If I can't trust you, then the rest of it doesn't matter. But, I think he might be the key to the Numberless."

"What do you mean?"

"Well," Cojax said, "if I can convince Horace to join us, then maybe he can convince the rest to follow. With the Numberless on our side, who could stand against us?"

"I don't think anyone on the First Assembly would agree to that—or anyone in this city for that matter."

"Jessica, you told me how powerful the Numberless were when you faced them alongside Titan. Somehow, I thought you might have been exaggerating, but you're right. After facing Horace, I now know that a common Validated is nothing compared to them. If we are to stand a chance, we have to have them on our side."

"Your father hand-selected a group of Numberless to fight against Titan," Jessica answered, carefully gauging her words. "Out of ten thousand, he only seemed to be able to find thirty that were willing to fight alongside him."

"That doesn't mean that others won't."

"I don't know. He took his time picking out the ones that would follow him. He even seemed to have second thoughts on a few of the ones he picked."

"He only selected the ones that would follow him without much convincing," Cojax replied. "That doesn't mean that others can't be convinced over time."

"But you said it yourself. Horace isn't sure if he's going to help you or not. He's still thinking about killing you—and he's one of the ones that Titan selected."

"That's just bravado," Cojax replied. "If he was going to kill me, he had his opportunity. Regardless, we need to start freeing other cities, and waking the Numberless if we are to have a chance at surviving."

"How do you propose we free other cities?"

"I don't know," Cojax replied. "But we won't stand a chance if we don't. Maybe we can start a rebellion in other cities the same way we did in Acadia. Start an uprising among the Rifters, take their Trinity, and broadcast the Numberless' lies to the public."

"I doubt it will work twice," Jessica replied. "I'm sure the Decamont have figured out what happened here, and they'd be fools not to take measures in other cities to prevent it. Besides, we'd first have to infiltrate one of those cities somehow. But you're right: we need the support of more cities. But I don't think this is something you should share with the BloodBorne High Council—their support for you seems thin already. If you started talking about waking the Numberless and initiating uprisings in other cities, they could see you as reckless."

"I agree."

"And give it time with Horace," Jessica said. "He knows the Numberless better than anyone in this city; perhaps he knows the best way to approach them with our new situation. If we can win him to our side, maybe we can start waking a few of the Numberless." She then shook her head, as if reconsidering her words. "But…if only one of them turns against us, there's no telling the damage they could do."

Cojax sighed, his shoulders slumped with unseen weight. "I didn't think it would be like this."

"What do you mean?"

"I thought there would be some disagreement, of course, but this is insane. We've got dozens of political parties, six major ones that are all pulling in different directions."

Jessica pulled in closer, kissing Cojax. He reciprocated in kind, enjoying the taste of her lips. Time slowed, the thousands of lights throughout the city adjusting behind them. Of all the things happening in the city that were wrong, this was the one thing that both of them felt was right.

SIXTEEN

Cojax arrived early, allowing him time to study the leaders of other political parties as they entered. Most made a great show as they did, their faces energetic as they spoke to others in their own party. At one point, a Statesmen looked up at Cojax, a smile slowly fading from his face. Cojax kept his face expressionless, not daring to blink. Finally, the Statesman turned, heading towards his seat. Orch leaned forward, his voice soft. "Looks like the new advertisements are starting to frighten the Statesmen. I swear if there was any more burning hate in those eyes, he would've caught the room on fire."

"Our support hasn't increased too much," Cojax responded.

"But the potential is there," Orch replied. "You're different than all of them—you don't have their pride or vanity. They can predict the actions of most of the First Tiers, but not those of someone so different from them. You're starting to push back, and it scares them."

The room was not nearly as crowded as it had been during the first several meetings. All that remained were the six large political parties.

Cojax watched the entrance as three giant warriors entered the room, their armor so polished that it appeared to be a source of light. Cojax knew their names well, even before the AC fell. Abria, a powerful warrior who was the number one Validated when the AC fell; Bacis, a large man with an even larger appetite; and Cineas, a quiet but shrewd individual who put title above all else. The three put on a show, waving to members in the crowd with the greatest of earnestness.

"The First Tiers are losing support," Byron said.

"Have their numbers changed so much?"

"No," Byron replied, "but they will soon. They started with a small tax on their followers—much less than all the other political parties had imposed, which allowed them to expand quickly, but now their growth has stagnated. They host the best and most elite gatherings to be sure, but they can't sustain their spending. They can either do one of two things: raise their taxes or decrease their lavish spending."

"Is that where Cato got the idea of hosting social events?" Cojax asked.

"Yes," Byron said. "And as the First Tiers' ability to spend decreases, they will have a hard time holding onto their followers. And that's when we can win them over."

"Do we really want to win people over that need to be catered to?" Orch scoffed.

"The First Tiers are small in numbers, but they have some of the best Validated in their ranks," Byron replied. "They don't have a good political structure or proposal for government. Right now, it seems they intend to rule as an oligarchy that focuses on celebrating the things Validated have always been deprived of. But, their political party has the most talented individuals, both physically and intellectually—and with that designation comes some legitimacy."

"So, how can we win them over?" Cojax asked.

Orch leaned in, "Bunch of shiny Tier Setters—think they're better than the rest of us cause they 'killed a few more Roaches in their day.' They don't care for unity, as much as they do their own vanity."

"Then we can play to their vanity," Cojax said.

"If we can host a few well-planned events," Byron suggested. "They might be interested in what we have to say."

Next came members of the Populi Party, their right arms wrapped in blue bands. They were energetic and mostly young, a mix of smiles and well-intentioned jests. They took their seats, ignoring all those around them, as if none of this truly mattered. Since the AC had fallen, their party had nearly doubled, as well as their political representatives in the First Assembly. If their party kept up this pace, they would soon be the dominant political party in a matter of weeks. It would not be much longer after that before they would win enough support to implement their government. Cojax, however, did notice one thing that seemed odd: Despite the dogma that their political party treated all people equally, their party representatives were almost all First Tiers.

Orch seemed to pick up on this at almost the same moment. He leaned forward, a smirk on his face. "Do you see who leads our Populi Party? Almost all First Tiers."

Byron leaned forward. "Astute observation. Even with best intentions, it seems the Populi Party does not want to let go of their elitist control. Cojax, do you have your speech ready?"

"I don't think I'll need it," Cojax replied.

Byron leaned in closer, "What you do you mean? We spent days drafting that, and several more practicing it."

"I could always take his place," Orch said, "if he gets stage fright."

"Please, don't," Byron replied.

Orch winked. "Don't worry B-ron, I wouldn't waste my words on this crowd anyway."

"I have the speech," Cojax said, "but I'm not going to present it unless I have to."

Byron frowned ever so slightly. "We need the support of the Rifters if we hope to sustain our advertising campaign."

Cojax was about to answer, but one of the Arbiters of the First Assembly took to the center of the room, his voice amplified by a microphone. "Let's bring this assembly to order. We'll start by reviewing the bullet points from the last meeting." The next fifteen minutes were spent listening to another Validated as she recounted several items from the last meeting.

Byron did not ask Cojax about the speech again, but he now seemed visibly nervous. He kept shifting his weight from side-to-side, wiping his brow every few seconds.

When the minutes were finished, each party was able to open with a speech. Most gave quick monologues, highlighting their most popular ideas. Cojax did the same, repeating, once again, that the real threat was the Decamont. Then it was Onar's turn, the self-proclaimed King of Acadia. Without saying a word, Onar stood up, dragging a piece of iron behind him. When he reached the balcony, he lifted the bar, showing the waiting crowd. And then he bent it in half. An audible gasp spread throughout the room. Such a feat would not be impressive had Onar been wearing Static Armor, but since he was shirtless, he had done it by his own natural strength. Even with the sensory implants channeling his energy to his arms, such power had seemed impossible. Onar threw the bar into the sandy center and returned to his seat.

Somewhat awkwardly, one of the Arbiters picked up the bar and attempted to straighten it. Despite being a wide-set man with a muscular chest, he could not even get the bar to move an inch.

"I want that guy on our team," Orch said.

"Since when does a king bow to anyone but his own crown?" Byron said. "He won't join us—I don't even think he could if he wanted to."

"What do you mean?" Cojax said.

"Well," Byron replied, "Onar's claim to the throne is all based on power. He believes since he is the greatest warrior, he should be in the greatest position of power. If he were to join a party, he would essentially be undermining his own argument. He would, in essence, be saying that he is governed by someone weaker than himself."

"So, then, perhaps he would follow someone greater than him," Cojax suggested.

"Undoubtedly," Byron said. "However, in this city, there is no one greater than him in skill."

"Oh," Orch said, "I don't think he looks that tough."

"Then why don't you challenge him to a duel," Byron suggested, a slight smile on his face.

Orch frowned. "I would, but then he would want me to be the king instead of Cojax. And what sort of advisor would I be if I were more respected than the person I advised. No, it's the humble road for me."

Byron scoffed as Orch mentioned the word "humble."

Byron shook his head. "Anyone who challenged Onar to combat would be brave but very foolish. He'd destroy them, leaving nothing but a grease spot behind."

"He's not a god," Cojax said.

"I don't think he'd let any challenger live. He would cut their limbs off as easily as other people whittle a stick," Byron proclaimed. "Then he'd claim their head, raising it on his sword like a giant olive and parade it throughout the city. We'd be lucky if we found enough of the challenger to bury."

"When do you think they serve lunch?" Orch asked.

"We just barely started," Byron replied.

"You're the one talking about olives being paraded around," Orch retorted.

Byron shook his head. "They serve lunch at lunchtime."

Cojax's focus drifted, and he could barely hear Orch's witty comeback. *There has to be a way to win some of these First Tiers to our side.*

The meeting transitioned into various proposals. The First Tiers made a proposal for name creation. Individuals in Titan had traditionally only used a first name and the name of their Faction as identification. They never needed more than that because their Score was their true identity. Now that Scores had disappeared, names, especially those that were much more common, were becoming a problem. A proposal of last names was put forth, discussed, and voted into law. Names would be randomly assigned, with the exception of the First Tiers, who would have 24 hours to select their new name.

Cojax was tempted to oppose the exception to the rule, but Byron grabbed his shoulder before he could stand.

Then Onar the King proposed the institution of a public policing force. Onar did not make the proposal personally, but instead, it was made by a young boy no older than seventeen. This action earned some hard stares from some of the other parties, but Onar ignored them all. Instead he spent his time polishing the grand sword that laid across his lap. At first, Cojax was confused by the proposal—he would have thought that Onar's political party would be the very last party to want a police force to protect the weak. After all, they were the party that put its greatest emphasis on strength and power. But then as the youth continued his explanation, he suggested that Onar's forces would be the ideal police unit.

None of the other parties seemed keen on giving that sort of power to any party, especially not to Onar, the man who had proclaimed himself a king. Before the youth could even finish, he was shouted down to silence by the Restorationists and then booed until he sat down by the Statesmen. Both parties were punished for this, but they took the punishment in stride. The Statesmen proposed that each party formulate their own policing force to protect their people. The Populi seconded the motion, and it was later passed into law.

The Statesmen then opened a discussion on who was controlling the media, and who was receiving money from the ads that were purchased. One of the Arbiters of the First Assembly answered that it was being transferred into an account associated with the Trinity and was being used for the public good. There was some discussion on how to make the sharing of airtime on the CityScreens more equitable, and eventually, the First Assembly voted to create a group of Validated that consisted of members from all political parties to ensure equal treatment. Advertisements could be purchased throughout the day, and the price would be determined by demand.

Other minor laws were proposed, discussed, and voted upon before Sejanus of the Populi Party requested the floor to make another proposal.

"Now, I come before you," Sejanus began in dramatic fashion, "with a proposal most urgent. We are no longer individuals separated by Score but are now united by a collective purpose. However, our new ideas do not reflect our current reality. We were brought from slavery and ignorance by a group of Rifters, who until this point, have participated in the rewards of freedom in name only. Despite them having as much freedom as I, they still do not have a vote—"

With this, the Restorationist Party went manic, standing, screaming, cursing the Populi Party and everyone that belonged to it. Some in the Populi stood in their defense, matching the screams of the opposing party. Insults were exchanged, individuals called out, combat seemed imminent. By some miracle, the Arbiters were able to regain control of the Assembly just before the two sides started an all-out brawl.

"How did you do it?" Byron asked, his voice betraying a trace of awe. "How did you get the Populi Party to propose legitimizing the Rifter's vote?"

"The Populi have been holding political rallies in the streets," Cojax said. "And at the end, they open the floor up for questions. I didn't get them to do anything. I just had someone ask the right question. Repeat the question enough times and it makes it appear like it's a real concern among the other Validated."

"How did you know it would work?" Byron asked.

"Adriana has at least one high-level spy among their ranks," Cojax replied. "An idea I did not like at first, but one that I have been coming around to."

"How did she manage that?"

"They are the party of transparency and inclusion," Cojax replied. "It wasn't that difficult, or so she tells me. She still won't tell me who her source is, but she tells me he is reliable. I think we are seeing the proof of that today."

"Brilliant," Byron said. "I really thought that you were going to…." His voice trailed off.

"…to mess this up," Orch suggested.

Byron blushed slightly and brought his hands together. "Those aren't my words."

"But that doesn't mean they weren't your thoughts," Orch said.

Cojax shook his head. "It doesn't matter. The Populi Party is fighting our battle for us.

"And a good thing too," Orch said. "It seems like the Restorationists are willing to go to war over the very idea of giving Rifters an equal vote."

Cojax looked back to the Restorationist Party and thought that if anything, Orch's sentiments were an understatement. The Restorationists were livid, their faces contorted with rage.

As with all proposals that were heavily contested, the Arbiters arranged a debate on the issue. All the parties were willing to add to the discussion except for the BloodBorne. Cojax held back, allowing the other political parties to use his allotted time.

"I'm not sure if giving up our time is always the best strategy," Byron said. "We need to be seen as leaders, not followers. This is a monumental vote, and we need to win it."

"As soon as we weigh-in," Cojax said, "we lock ourselves into a position. And we appear to, like everyone else, get caught up in the conflict."

"We already have a position," Byron said. "Blood and bile, we were the ones that were supposed to propose the position."

"I think I get what he's trying to do," Orch said. "If this comes down to a close vote, then the only vote that really matters is the last one that's cast."

"Exactly," Cojax said.

Byron dabbed his forehead. "Blazing boy, I feel more anxiety around you than when I'm heading to battle."

The debate continued, the Populi and the Restorationists taking center stage. Occasionally, other political parties weighed in, but neither side seemed to make much headway. Then Onar, the self-proclaimed King, spoke for the first time during a debate. Despite his trend of depending on his strength, he was surprisingly articulate with his words. He did not seem to use the superfluous language that the Populi Party was so fond of, nor did he drift in and out of the conversation with crass humor, as did the Statesmen. His words were blunt and forceful, demanding attention. Onar proposed that the Rifted should receive a vote, but since they had lost their first estate, their vote should only be worth a tenth of a regular Validated.

This proposal changed the debate completely. Instead of discussing whether or not the Rifted should be given a vote, the discussion became about how much of a vote should be given. The Populi argued to give the Rifters the same vote as any Validated. While the Restorationists asserted that each Rifter vote should be worth a twentieth of a Validated vote. The Restorationists argued that since Rifters had proved themselves inadequate warriors, or as possessing subpar intelligence, that they could not be counted on to make rational decisions.

For the first time since the First Assembly began, the Populi Party was being outvoted and out argued, even by the Statesmen who tended to vote along the same lines. As it stood, it seemed that most of the political party were settling on what Onar originally proposed, giving each Rifter one-tenth of a vote. If this proposal was carried, it would do little to bolster support for Cojax.

All the political parties had laid out their arguments and counterarguments. All except the BloodBorne. They sat in silence, listening but never contributing. All the while, Byron encouraged Cojax to stand, to make his position known, to add his support to the Populi Party. But Cojax did not. Instead, he waited until the two sides of the argument were firmly established, waited until the First Tiers were anxious to vote, waited until patience had eroded and tempers were rising.

By the time Cojax stood to speak, he was not just adding to the debate, he was acting as the tiebreaker. Remaining silent and apart from the conflict had made his vote much more potent. So when he did speak, everyone in the assembly listened.

Cojax cleared his throat, casting his gaze at all those around. He then stared directly at the Populi Party, and then the Restorationists, weighing their arguments in turn. "I've heard both sides and there are valid points. The Rifters did fall, but then they rose again. They had failed as warriors, but later proved their steel when they seized control of the Trinity. The most important thing that we must decide today is not whether the Rifters should be given a vote, but what sort of precedent we want to establish. They are Rifted and we are not because we were playing by the rules of the Numberless. Are we to let the Numberless still govern our city? Are we still subject to their will? If we are truly free, then let us make this decision as one that is not influenced by them. The Rifters were exiled because the Numberless ruled, but the Numberless fell because the Rifters rebelled.

"These are times that try a Validated's soul. We could very well be exterminated by the Decamont; we could very well be wiped off the face of the land, leaving nothing but scorched earth and ruins. And if that's the case, should our legacy be that we, once we gained freedom, denied it to the very people who fought for it. Or rather, should our last hour be our finest hour. Should we not only seek freedom from the Decamont but for all people as well? I vote for freedom. I vote that we give an equal voice to the Rifters."

These words were met with thunderous applause. Cojax initially thought that most of the noise was coming from the Populi Party, but he was wrong. Throughout the entire assembly, pockets of Validated were applauding.

The Statesmen submitted a formal proposal to give all those previously in the Rift a full vote. The motion was sustained by the Populi Party. The final vote was narrow, but Rifters were granted an equal vote. The Restorationists were livid; the Populi Party was elated.

Once the tumult died, Marcus took the stage, locking eyes with only Cojax in the room. "Then, in order to accomplish this task, may I propose that we form a group of individuals to meet with the Rifters, explain the situation, and assign them ArmGuards."

Cojax's heart thundered in his chest. Before he could even celebrate his victory, Marcus was already undermining it. Cojax was going to propose that the BloodBorne be in charge of disseminating the ArmGuards and information to the Rifters, not a collective group from all political parties. Most of the Rifters, after all, did not even know that they had won their freedom. They were still under the control of Brutus and were working in food production and allocation.

Orch leaned forward. "That's not good."

Cojax stood again, his rushed movement giving away his anxiety. "If I may, Arbiters, address the First Assembly."

"The Assembly recognizes Cojax of the BloodBorne Party and grants him the floor," one of the Arbiters stated.

"The BloodBorne Faction has already seen to the assimilation of the Rifters into society," Cojax said. "We have put them on our payroll and made sure that production and food allocation have been maintained."

"You've been paying them this whole time?" Marcus asked skeptically.

"The BloodBorne Party has made sure that they are cared for and informed," Cojax continued. "I think that if we involve other Factions in the process, it will complicate things."

"How?" Marcus asked.

"We've been paying them out of our funds. A simple and direct payment. If we involve other political parties, then it will complicate the dissemination of money. For example, would they each be paid by every political party? And how often? What if one political party wants to pay more than another? For the sake of simplicity, I suggest the BloodBorne be allowed to maintain payments to the Rifters."

"Why are you trying to hide them from us?" Marcus asked.

Cojax shook his head, his face flushing. "I'm not hiding them from anyone, but I do think that it's about time that the rest of the parties contribute money in exchange for the food and services received. They are on our payroll, but they serve all of you equally."

This had just the desired effect Cojax was looking for. The debate shifted from meeting with and speaking to the Rifters to figuring out how and who should compensate them. By the end of it, the general consensus was that if the BloodBorne could continue to pay and operate the food production without problems that they should be allowed to oversee the ArmGuard dissemination and Rifter assimilation into society. The Populi Party was not happy with the result, but none of the other parties wanted to be responsible for paying the Rifters, so they were outvoted.

"Quick thinking," Byron said.

Cojax shook his head. "Not quick enough. The Populi Party suspected something was not right. This won't be the last time they try to paint us into a corner on this issue."

SEVENTEEN

Abria was fuming by the time the First Assembly adjourned. She had smiled, she had waved, she had spoken to the other members of the political parties as if they were equals, and yet, the First Tiers had the slowest growth of all the rest. They were winning over dozens of talented First Tiers with their elaborate and showy banquets, but they were far surpassed by the thousands of Bottom Tiers that were joining everyone except their party. She stuck her sword into a table, stabbing it clear through.

"Don't destroy another table," Cineas said, his voice sharp and pitched. "I don't know if we can afford to buy one as nice as this." He stood rigid, his right hand on his hilt.

"We can just take one from the Numberless' private rooms—they've got loads of furniture that no one's using," said Bacis from the other side of the room. He was a giant warrior with broad shoulders. As of now, his foot was lazily slung over the edge of one of the armrests. His body posture reflected none of the tension that was so apparent in the other two. He picked up a pitcher of stock, which was within his grasp, and poured the liquid into his mouth, savoring every drop of it. A little dripped out the side, and he wiped it away with his forearm.

"And if someone sees us carting the furniture around the Trinity like thieving ants," Cineas said. "What then? The last thing we need now is to be accused of being common criminals."

"I don't understand," Abria said, her voice falling to a growl. "I'm an Omega, one of the few who was appointed to that position and yet wasn't a Numberless. I led thousands of Validated to victory time and time again against the Roaches. My name has been at the top of the Leader Board for the better part of a year. My blade has more Roach wax on it than any other in the city."

"Besides Onar," Bacis said.

Abria's chest tightened. "He seems more theatrical than

dangerous. Honestly, who's impressed by him taking his shirt off and bending a bar of metal? Does he really think that he'll win more followers with that display?"

"He has," Cineas pronounced. "His growth is not the strongest, but it certainly has outpaced us."

"We need to change our tactics," Abria said. "We've got all the talent in our ranks, but none of the votes. Blazing fools. They can't see that their best option is to follow the most talented."

"That would be Onar," Bacis added.

"He's only one man," Abria said, "we represent a whole host of First Tiers that are the best and the brightest. If there's a solution to the mess we're in, our political party will be the one that comes up with it."

"We need more money," Cineas proclaimed. "We have a logical argument: if you want to have the greatest chance of success, elect those leaders who have proven themselves the most. The problem is, between the ads about the downtrodden put out by the Populi, and the scare tactics that the BloodBorne employs, the price for airtime has gone up. We still have cash flow, despite how quickly you two like to spend it. If we want to beat them, we need to do it on their playing field."

Bacis sat up, his face suddenly serious. "Are you suggesting that we don't try to win over the First Tiers by playing to their palates?"

"That strategy was temporary at best," Cineas said. "But to increase our taxable base, we need more support. I suggest we funnel our money into advertisement. We'll come up with a comprehensive argument, and lay it all out there, point by point."

"That sounds horribly boring," Bacis said. "And, if we stop the fancy banquets, you cut off the teat that the First Tiers suck on. They won't be nearly as inclined to support us."

"Why don't we do both?" Abria asked. "We increase our tax rate until we can satiate the First Tiers while simultaneously getting our message out to the Bottom Tiers."

"We'd have to raise the tax from ten percent to somewhere near sixty-five," Cineas replied. "I've already worked all of this out. We're already spending more than we're taking in, and if we aren't careful, we'll be insolvent within a month."

"Sixty-five percent!" Bacis said, taking another long pull on the pitcher of stock. "Now, that's a great idea if we want to lose what little following we have."

"Well," Abria said, her temper flushing her face red, "if you didn't spend half of our money buying overpriced pitchers of stock, I don't think we'd be in this mess."

Bacis stood up, wielding the pitcher of stock as if it were an Arc Blade. "I'll have you know that because of my foresight, we still have stock left. As soon as prices started to climb, I bought all of the suppliers out."

"And you did it without consulting the two of us," Abria hissed.

Bacis took two large steps forward, his free hand going for the hilt of his blade. "What do you think draws First Tiers to our gatherings? Do you think it's your long-winded speeches about nobility and honor? Do you really think people want to hear you wail on about our new, perfect society?"

"What more can we offer!" Abria countered.

Cineas raised his hand between the two, apparent exhaustion and annoyance in his tone. This had not been the first time he had to act as the intercessory between Bacis and Abria. "I propose an alliance."

"We're already in an alliance," Bacis said, his eyes still locked on Abria.

"Not amongst ourselves," Cineas replied, "but with one of the other political parties. I've already made arrangements for them to be here. They should be arriving any minute."

"Arrangements?" Bacis asked.

"Who?" Abria asked.

"Onar," Cineas replied.

"That arrogant, Rifter," Abria said, throwing her hands in the air to accent her disgust.

"He doesn't want anything to do with us," Bacis replied just before he took another swig of stock.

"The beliefs of our political party most closely align with his," Cineas said. "Instead of having a collection of leaders—like we propose—he has deemed that he has all the power as a king…." Cineas stopped speaking and looked at his ArmGuard. He pushed it a few times until a Comm-Link was raised between him and a guard who was standing outside the room. "Show him in."

Cineas turned to the other two. "Let me do the talking."

"Oh," Abria said, folding her arms. "I didn't realize that you're now telling everyone else what to do."

"It's my idea," Cineas replied. "So, let me be the one to see it through."

Bacis rolled his eyes and returned to his supine position on the couch. "You're wasting your time with Onar. That fool has an even bigger ego than Abria, and that's saying something. The only way he'll even consider joining forces is if we swear allegiance to him."

Abria nodded. "I agree with Bacis."

"Hah," Bacis said quickly, "so you admit that you have a big ego? Well, recognizing the problem is half the battle."

Abria waved the comment off with her hand. "Onar won't want to join us; he'll want to rule over us."

Just then, a Validated entered. Despite his rigid appearance, he wore no shirt or helm. On his back, formed into an 'X,' hung two short swords. At his waist, he had another two. It seemed excessive, even to Cineas, who believed whole-heartedly in redundancy. The shirtless man cleared his throat as he stared down the occupants of the room. "I present the King of Acadia, the Lord of Blades, the Slayer of the Cracken, his mighty Lord, Onar the Grand."

Abria rolled her eyes with each word in the lengthy title.

"How can he be a Lord and a King?" Bacis asked. "Why doesn't he just pick one and call it good."

Onar entered, his frame so large he had to duck under the entrance door. He was a mammoth of a man, his arms as thick as tree trunks, his face appeared as if chiseled from stone. This time, instead of being bare-chested, he wore an elaborate set of armor only granted to those in the rank of the Numberless. Its polished sides gleamed in the light, making Bacis squint because of the reflection. On the back of the warrior was a single massive Arc Blade, garbed in ornately designed leather. The blade was so long that it would have hung past a normal Validated's knees, but on Onar, it barely passed his hip.

Cineas bowed respectfully, not quite as low as he would to a Numberless, but a little lower than he would for a peer. Onar did not respond, his eyes not giving away any emotion.

Cineas gestured to a chair. "Join us, my friend, in raising a pitcher of stock to both our noble political parties. For it is a great occasion to have all four of the top Validated from the Leader Board in one room, wouldn't you say?"

Onar still did not move.

Cineas swallowed nervously, grabbed a wooden cup, and poured some stock. He was about to take a drink but instead nervously offered it to Onar. Onar took the mug, his large hands making it look more like an upside-down thimble. Then he slowly poured the stock to the floor.

Abria and Bacis exploded into action, drawing their Arc Blades and donning their helmets as they rushed forward. Onar did not react, he still barely breathed. Abria and Bacis stopped short of attacking as Cineas stepped in between them.

Cineas turned, his chest swelling, his voice demanding. He was no Disciple in the Mahghetto. He was no struggling Dependent, weighted by vices. Cineas was a Tier Setter, a man who dedicated his life to the pursuit of perfection. A man who had achieved that perfection by denying himself of everything that gave anyone pleasure. He trained harder than all those around him; he fought with a skill that rivaled the Numberless. He had been an early riser, taking to the Tiers as a bird takes to flight. He achieved his First Tier status faster than almost all before him. He slept little, drilled constantly, and deprived himself of every luxury ever afforded. This man held the third position on the Leader Boards for the better part of two years—a feat that not only was unheard of, it was likely never to be repeated.

Cineas narrowed his eyes, his voice cold and condescending. "Be careful, Onar. Although you may be large, even a small dagger in the right hands can fell the biggest of beasts. Take care to have a little respect."

"I only respect those with greater power than my own," Onar said. "And you, like children, have beckoned me before you, as if you could hold my attention, as if you have something you can offer. You are little fledglings who succumb to their basest desires at the earliest point possible. I hear this house has become a place of drink, foolishness, and debauchery."

Abria shook her head, amazed at Onar's boldness. "Do you realize who we are? We are not some fools who started a club just for the fun of it. Our party holds the greatest talent since our city was first established."

"Mothers have value, fathers have value, warriors who keep to their oaths and serve with loyalty, have value," Onar said. "But, you three are the dross of our society, calling attention to yourselves because of your position, but never truly adding value. You are the cancer that must be cut out—"

Abria screamed, rushing forward, her sword raised. She swung quick and wide, hitting Onar across the chest. Light exploded, blinding all those in the room. The attack had been perfectly executed, a flawless demonstration of Abria's skill. Most Validated would have been thrown against the wall, their shields drained, their will to fight gone. When the light dissipated, Onar stood where he was before, his expression unchanged.

The giant slowly reached for his sword, his hands steady and calm. The blade made no sound as it was pulled free from the scabbard. As he placed a helmet on his head, Onar took a defensive posture. His movement was so smooth it seemed disconnected from the current situation.

"We invited you as a friend—in good faith—and you treat us as enemies," Cineas said as he pulled out an Arc Blade and donned his helmet. "We are the three greatest warriors in Titan, and you would treat us like dogs. Pride, my friend, is your weakness…that and thinking that you could come here, insult us, and leave with your head still attached to your body."

Bacis smiled. "I call dibs on his Arc Blade."

Abria stepped lightly, slowly surrounding Onar. Cineas approached from the other side. He leaned forward, taking an aggressive attack stance.

"Even now," Onar said, "when I'm outnumbered, you hesitate."

Bacis lunged forward, his blade becoming a flurry of attacks. Onar responded in kind, moving quickly out of the way, and then delivering a quick counter strike. Onar's massive blade hummed as it struck true, sending Bacis back into a couch that toppled over. Next, Abria came in, at first feinting a quick strike but then pulling back. Onar misjudged the attack and was hit twice before he could respond. When he did, Abria was sent sprawling across the floor. Cineas' attack followed, striking Onar in the legs. Onar exploded into a rage, swinging his blade so quickly he almost caught Cineas in the head. Cineas ducked in time, but a follow-up swing caught him in the legs, and then the shoulder. He fought back, attempting to regain the initiative in the fight. He was struck again and again, his body pushed from one side to the other. Energy leached from his frame with each tremendous swing. Abria attacked from behind, but by some incredible sense, Onar felt it coming. The giant dodged and hit Abria across the shoulder, sending the woman twisting to the side. Bacis rushed in next but received the same treatment.

All three First Tiers withdrew a step, their swords now being held in defense.

"We take him down together," Abria ordered. All levity from before was gone, all hurt egos were pushed aside. They now moved with greater respect for their opponent.

Onar did not move, his body was almost in the same position as when he started. As the attacks came in, he struck back, hitting Cineas down, and then Bacis. He took two swings to the side and then floored Abria. Onar then charged forward into Cineas, releasing such an animalistic cry that it disturbed the souls of all those who heard it. Cineas defended but was no match for the momentous force in front of him. In two heartbeats, Cineas' shields lost their charge. In three, Cineas was missing an arm, in four, his head was separated from his body, in five, his body hit the ground, in six, Onar's blade was put through his heart and stuck into the floor.

As Onar's blade wobbled back and forth in the center of Cineas' chest, Abria and Bacis shared a look. This had been a contest of strength, not one of butchery. They were used to spilling the blood of Roaches, but it was so rare to see one Validated cut down by another that it stole the breath from their chests.

Onar looked to Cineas, his expression solemn and reverent. "Find your way, brother."

"He's not your brother!" Abria hissed. "You have taken this too far."

Onar turned, pulling the Arc Blade from the body. "Do you think our enemy will give us quarter? Do you think they will not put a blade in your heart because you once achieved the First Tier?"

Bacis rushed in, scoring two hits. But he was then pushed back by an impressive attack by Onar. Abria took a turn, faring little better than Bacis. They circled Onar, trying to come from two different angles. When they attacked, it was with pure bestial instinct. The three exchanged a flurry of swings, Onar's body moving with surprising agility and speed. Their blades hummed with power, cracking like thunder with each impact. Onar ducked under one of Abria's attacks, and swung, his sword connecting with Bacis' body with such tremendous force that not only did his shields fail, but his body was cleaved in two.

Again, Onar's movement slowed, his expression solemn. He bent down, gently patting Bacis' shoulder with his free hand. The scene was so surreal that Abria could not help but watch. As gently as a mother is with a new child, Onar removed Bacis' helmet, pushed back his hair, and closed his eyes.

"It pains me greatly to see one of you fall," Onar said, his voice sounding vulnerable but strong. "But if it needs be, the few must perish to protect the many."

Abria tightened the grip on her blade. "What do you want from us?"

"Us?"

"What do you want from me?" Abria corrected.

"I sue only for your humility," Onar replied. "You must choose to serve someone greater than yourself, or you will die—either by my hand or by the Decamont, it doesn't matter. Yield to me now, and live."

Abria laughed, an arrogant noise that echoed in the almost deserted room. "You are strong, but your shields can't last much longer. And when you fall, I'm going to mount your head on a pole for the city to see." With this, she rushed in, her stance changing from low to high as she moved. Onar fell back, using distance as his defense. Abria pushed harder, her movement becoming a blur. She was the perfect warrior, her strikes flawless. But it was not enough. She was not enough. Her body eventually fell like the other two, in a flash of light and a splash of red.

Onar paid this third body even more respect than he did the other two. Then he stood, returning the way he had come. He turned to the shirtless man, who had surreptitiously entered just before the fight began. "Did you record it?"

"Yes, my King," said the shirtless servant.

"Good," Onar responded. "I want our first proclamation to be our most powerful."

EIGHTEEN

Adriana did not venture to the Rift often, and each time she did, she felt more and more disdain for this dark and dingy world below the city. Like her surroundings, the people she encountered in the Rift were empty and filthy. Brutus had cut this path for her, branching it off from a lower BloodBorne apartment building. And although she was the only one that knew it existed, she could not help but glance back to ensure that she was not being followed.

The news of the three leaders of the First Tiers being slaughtered had been unnerving. Even more disturbing than that was the video that was broadcast shortly thereafter. It was only shown once on the CityScreens, but it had been copied and replayed thousands of times by other Validated.

She found her way quickly into Brutus' office. It was disheveled and disorderly, having pitchers of stock and half-eaten plates of food. No one was there, so she made herself comfortable, plopping down on a chair behind a desk. She considered the situation, surveying her surroundings. *He was never sloppy in the Mahghetto. Has he become so because he has lived in the Rift? Or did the Rift merely reveal who he truly is? And now he's late.*

She waited another fifteen minutes before Brutus stepped through the door. Adriana opened her mouth to speak, a sharp quip on her tongue. But Brutus did not see her; he was too focused locking lips with the scantily clad female in front of him. The woman pushed against him, driving him deeper into the office and back onto the desk. Adriana pulled back in disgust. Brutus and the woman became a mess of hands and lips. Adriana was sure that she would have gone entirely unseen had not another, barely clothed female appeared, a large pitcher of stock in her hands.

The second woman first greeted Adriana with a smile, but it soon shifted into a grimace. Adriana was devoid of the crisscross scars all the Rifters bore. Her back was straight, her posture steady. She wore the armor of a true Validated. So, when Adriana stood up, her hand resting gently on the hilt of her blade, the woman shrieked, dropping the pitcher of stock to the floor.

Brutus looked up, first meeting eyes with the woman that dropped the pitcher of stock, and then with Adriana. At seeing Adriana, Brutus sighed, his voice falling to a growl. "You again?"

The woman who was wrapped around Brutus looked up with first anger in her eyes and then annoyance. She had once been stunning, but when the sensory implants were ripped from her body, the process seemed to have been particularly cruel to one side of her face. Her body was still something to behold, however, as Brutus' hands were finding out.

Adriana sat back down again and kicked her feet up onto the desk. "Can't we have a little privacy?"

"Depends on what you want to do with it?" Brutus asked as he gave a roguish wink.

"Ehh," Adriana said, covering her mouth as if she was going to vomit. "Even when your face didn't look like it had gone through a cheese grater, you were never that good looking."

Brutus became serious, all levity gone. "Leave us." One of the women looked as if she was going to protest, but a stern look from Brutus killed all arguments. Once they were gone, Brutus picked up Adriana's feet from the desk and dropped them to the floor, making room for him to sit. He reached across the desk, finding a dirty mug and a pitcher of stock. He tentatively smelled the cup, pulled back in disgust, and instead drank right from the pitcher.

"I see you've gotten rather comfortable down here," Adriana said, her voice cold and distant.

Brutus picked up some grapes, threw one in the air, and caught it in his mouth. "I was born to rule."

"Well, you certainly weren't born to clean."

Brutus narrowed his eyes. "To what do I owe the pleasure of your visit?"

"This is our weekly meeting."

"Has another week gone by already?"

Adriana shook her head. "You're slipping, Brutus. What did you have to promise those women to get them to be with you—an extra meal? A room to themselves? You're giving in to the temptations of the flesh."

Brutus leaned forward and lowered his voice to a whisper. "I could show you just how enjoyable that can be."

Adriana stood up, beginning to pace the room. "I have no problem with you rolling with whoever you want on your time. I don't care if you drink stock until it pours out of your ears, on your time. But, when it comes to my time, when it comes to my future, I will not stand for it. We are playing a dangerous game—"

"—And what makes you think you can make demands of me!" Brutus yelled.

"I made you," Adriana said with just as much fury. "And I can just as easily unmake you. You know nothing of the world above, of the moving tides of power. How quickly I could convince Cojax to rally his forces and wipe you out."

"Do not speak his name," Brutus hissed.

"You are such a child," Adriana replied. "Still holding onto your grudge, are we?"

"I will end him."

"Then, I will end you."

Brutus shook his head. "Why are you so loyal to him of all people? Don't you remember how he destroyed your position of power in the Mahghetto? Do you not remember what he did to me—how he claimed my eye because of his vanity? He would sacrifice your life in exchange for the Aberration without a moment of hesitation."

"He's one of the most powerful Validated in the entire city," Adriana replied. "And know this: if you ever make me choose between him and you, I've already chosen him. He is a Nova. He is a leader."

Brutus took another pull on the pitcher of stock. "Why are you here? What do you need from me?"

"That's better," Adriana cooed. "We need to expand our clandestine operations. The spies you have provided me have proven effective, but I need a group with a slightly different skill set."

Brutus crashed into the seat that Adriana had left. "I'm not a wizard. I can't make more available workers appear. Since the AC fell, I've had to divert personnel into cultivating new crops, I've had to bolster security forces to ensure the Rifters don't revolt, and I've had to provide you a host of spies, looters, and street thugs. All of that, I did because of your orders. And, keep in mind, no one else is being

Rifted right now, so we are short on new recruits."

"And you did well, but I need more."

"There's no one left," Brutus replied. "I've increased the Rifters' workday by two hours just so we can make up for the loss of personnel."

"What about the Hoarders? I thought they were the largest and least taken care of group down here. Make a promise of food to anyone of them, and I'm sure they'll do anything for you."

"They're gone."

Adriana leaned forward on the desk, the angle accenting her ample breasts. "What do you mean, gone? There were thousands of Hoarders roaming the Rift just weeks ago. They couldn't have disappeared."

"Well," Brutus said, "they did. And I'm glad. Without any more conflict between the Roaches and the Validated, they didn't have any more armor to trade for food. I thought for sure they'd try and raid our warehouses. That's why I had to beef up my security forces in the first place."

Adriana was not listening. Instead, she was considering the implications of the Hoarders' disappearance. She first thought that it could be a move by another political party—a way of leveraging the Rifters' vote. Now that the Rifters had been given a full vote, there was a real motivation to control them. A party offering food or shelter to the Rifters would undoubtedly receive a boost of support. *But, until now, no one has thought of them, let alone plotted to use their votes. Who would be motivated to protect them?* Then in a horrible instant, she knew exactly who was behind the surprising exodus. *Jessica.* Adriana pushed the disgust out of her mind and focused on the moment at hand.

"Regardless, we need a group of individuals to specialize in a particular task."

"What's that?"

"Assassination."

"Oooh," Brutus said, his voice taking on a chiding tone. "You are a bad girl, aren't you? What? Can't you manipulate everyone into doing your bidding? I thought all you needed was Cojax's winning personality?"

"Just a precaution."

"How many do you need?"

"Twenty that are trained and loyal. They need to be able to kill a First Tier and get out quickly."

"I'll make it work, but I have a few demands of my own."

Adriana frowned. "What?"

"We need equipment to train this special team."

"No problem."

"And…I need a CityScreen that's connected."

Adriana shook her head. "No, I don't think so. Something like that could be traced to its source and draw attention down to the Rift. If you like to continue to be the king of the land that no one cares about, you must make sure no one cares about it. I will get you an ArmGuard, however. As per law, all Rifters are to receive them."

"If we give the Rifters ArmGuards, they'll soon find out that they're no longer slaves. And just so you know, that's not good for this arrangement. They'll start making demands."

"Don't worry," Adriana said. "Cojax isn't planning on giving them ArmGuards any time soon. But, I will give one to you."

"Well, I'm glad that Cojax is there to make the tough choices," Brutus growled.

"Just worry about getting your team ready to take a First Tier down. I'll handle the rest."

NINETEEN

It had been weeks since Cojax first began training with Horace, and yet, his chest still constricted every time he received a summons. The pages always came at odd hours, either early in the morning or late at night. Cojax began to wonder if the old Numberless even slept. Dutifully, he always went, armor on, sword in hand. In truth, he often enjoyed the training more than he liked to admit. Despite being insulted and berated the entire time, and the fact that Horace would slap him on occasion for no apparent reason—Cojax preferred the overt abuse compared to the subtle attacks he received from his political opponents in the First Assembly.

This time would be different. And for this reason, Cojax felt even more nervous than he had ever before. This time, Finn was with him.

Finn did not ask any questions as Cojax led him through the Trinity. Instead, he approached the situation as he did with everything, with a silly grin on his face and a few jokes. As they drew closer to the area that was once only used by the Numberless, however, Finn's smile slipped ever so slightly. After seeing how Cojax's hands began to shake, his smile disappeared completely.

"You're not taking me to a deserted part of the Trinity so you can kill me, are you?" Finn asked.

"I'm not going to kill you, but it doesn't mean that we both won't end up dead."

"I don't know if anyone has ever told you this, but putting someone at ease is not your strong suit."

Cojax stopped before a large door, his hand hovering over the sensor. "Let me do the talking."

Finn nodded and the door slid open. Cojax entered, followed by Finn. Horace was there, his back to the entrance. "I said you were to come alone." The voice was barely audible, but the tone suggested a lethality that surprised the other two.

"Horace, give me a minute to explain."

Horace turned, one hand holding his massive battle-ax.

"You've got thirty seconds."

"Well then," Finn said quickly, slapping his hands together. "I'll give you two some space." He retreated backwards towards the exit but found that the door would not open.

"No, you don't, string bean. You're staying right here."

"String bean?" Finn asked.

Cojax took two steps forward, his hands out to his side. "Horace, we're not doing enough by just training me. We've got to do more if we are to have a chance at winning."

"This is not my war!" Horace yelled. "I'm only doing your father a favor to make sure you don't lose your head in the first battle of your revolution."

"It's not my revolution—if it was, my life would be the only one at stake. It's *our* revolution—it belongs to all of us in this city."

Horace shook his head, throwing his ax against the table. He looked up, his eyes burning with emotion. "So you made the decision to start a fire, and now that you can't control it, it's all of our responsibility to help you put it out? At what point can I just say that this is your mess, so you deal with it?"

Cojax took several steps forward before placing a heavy hand on Horace's shoulder. "You're right. A decision was made by a few that affected us all. I don't know if we were right in tearing down the AC, I don't even know if it's moral or justified to do any of the stuff we do now, but I do know that unless we do something different, all of us will end up dead. That's not a guess—that's a fact. Whether we're fighting for something moral or out of pure survival instinct, the results are the same. At the very least, if I do die, it will be with a sword in my hands."

Horace nodded. "A bit dramatic, but at least you're finally talking sense. What are you proposing—that I train this little lost boy on how to avoid stabbing himself?"

Finn shifted uncomfortably. "Validated."

Horace leaned forward, straining his ears. "What did you say, string bean?"

"I'm a Validated."

"Oh, you are, are you?" Horace said. "Well, do you know how

I already knew you were a Validated?"

Finn stepped forward, surprised that the Numberless even heard him. "No…I don't…sir."

"Do you see what I have written on my boot," Horace said.

Finn stepped closer, his eyebrows arching in curiosity. He approached slowly at first but then picked up his pace as Horace gestured him on. Finn kneeled, carefully studying the intricate lines on Horace's boot, looking for some legible text or visible number. Then Horace grabbed his head and farted on him.

Finn shot upright, his expression stiff. He stepped back, fixing his hair.

Cojax leaned in, whispering in Finn's ear. "He does that sometimes. I think it means he likes you."

"So, Lord Cojax, what's the plan?"

"It's Lord Cojax Artino now," Finn corrected.

Horace chuckled, an amused look on his face. "Are you guys picking last names now?"

"I didn't pick it; my brother Marcus did. All the First Tiers get to pick their last names—everyone else gets their name assigned to them."

"Yeah," Finn replied ruthfully, "I'm Finn Dom, now. I guess the First Tiers could only spare one syllable for me."

"Dumb?" Horace asked.

"Dom," Finn asserted.

Horace frowned. "Somebody must not have liked you very much in the naming department."

"That's beside the point," Cojax said, pulling the conversation back on topic. "The Decamont are coming. They already know the weapons we carry, they know about our shields, our armor, our flying craft, our battle formations. With all this knowledge, our survival is not so much a matter of tactics as it is a mathematical equation. Whatever they need to defeat us, they will bring. We have to change how we come at the problem if we want to achieve a different outcome."

"Said like a true politician," Horace said.

"We need to win over other cities to our cause," Cojax said. "The Decamont might know how to extinguish the fire of our rebellion, but what if that fire spreads?"

"So how does string bean fit into this?"

"Finn? Oh, well, I want him to go with you."

"You want the two of us to start spreading the rebellion to other cities?"

"There has to be a way we can sow rebellion among the other cities."

Horace rubbed his beard with one hand and folded the other arm across his chest. "There's no way to communicate with the other cities—at least, not directly." Cojax and Finn leaned forward as Horace continued. "But that never stopped a few of us from dropping in and partaking in their hospitality."

"You've talked to the Numberless in other cities before?" Finn asked. "How's that possible? The Validated of that city would detect you as you approached and shoot you down."

"Tell me," Horace said, "have you ever seen any other city pop up on our sensors? Some of these cities are easily within the range of our strongest detectors, and yet, they never have."

"The Decamont made them so that they won't detect the other Validated in other cities," Finn said.

"Are you always going to state the obvious every time you speak, string bean?"

Finn swallowed. "I just thought you wanted an answer."

"We can't detect them, and they can't detect us," Cojax said. "But then how did you know they were out there? How did you manage to first make contact with them?"

"The Decamont told us they were out there, but we never could know for sure until we looked," Horace answered. "So, when we were bored, we went and found a few cities. Soon, it became almost a rite of passage for the Numberless of one city to visit that of another city."

"How many cities have you visited?" Cojax asked.

"Two," Horace said, "well three if you count the one that outlawed our visitations. Four, if you include the one that ended in Titan starting an all-out brawl. Five, now that I'm counting, but we were technically flying by when they opened fire on us."

"I thought they couldn't detect you," Cojax said.

"The conventional detectors used by the Validated couldn't, but after discovering the other cities, a few of the Numberless adjusted some of the sensors so that we now can. Our sensors have picked up the location of every city within a thousand miles—probably more."

"Excellent," Cojax said.

"You were banned from one city, engaged in an all-out brawl in another, a third city fired upon you," Finn said. "That doesn't sound like you've planted the best seeds of friendship."

"Sometimes getting into an all-out brawl with someone is the best way to get to know them," Horace said, winking at Cojax.

"Or, you could just talk," Finn suggested.

"This new generation is so weak," Horace said.

"Or, we're just smart," Finn answered.

"I like the string bean," Horace said. "He can come with me to the city of Ephesus."

"Will they be receptive to your visit?" Cojax asked.

"No, but they have much better food than we do," Horace replied with a grin. "Now, are we done chatting like a bunch of squirrels? We need to get to training."

Cojax nodded. "Alright, you want to start where we left off?"

"Can't remember what that was," Horace said as he turned his attention to Finn. "Why you just standing there, string bean. Grab an Arc Lance from the wall."

"I prefer the Arc Blade," Finn said.

"Then you won't live long against a Nova," Horace replied. "The only chance you'll have against a trained Nova is to keep them back with the Arc Lance. If they close the distance, you might as well lop off your own head. If you're to train along with Lord Cojax here, I'll need you to trust me that I know what I'm doing."

"You're going to train me?" Finn asked.

Horace shrugged. "Let's find out what you can do, string bean."

TWENTY

Jessica carried a stack of food so high that she could barely see over it. She was trailed by twenty Rifters, each with arms as full as her own, but because she was so much shorter than the rest, her stack of food always looked bigger. This had become a daily routine: ordering the food, paging Rifters to meet her, and carting it through the city.

When she arrived in the Mahghetto, her provisions were quickly taken from her by other Rifters eager to prove themselves. Jessica wanted to object, but she thought it would be rude if she did. This part of the Mahghetto was buzzing with activity. It was no longer the austere, bleak part of the city where Disciples were trained. It was now where the Hoarders converged, forming into a well-organized and disciplined army. The Hoarders had been told the truth from the beginning. Jessica had insisted on it. That, coupled with the increased food Jessica provided, proved to be all the incentive they needed to recruit the rest of the Hoarders.

Aias met her in one of the tunnels to the cafeteria. Despite looking healthier and better fed than he had in weeks, he also looked more exhausted. Dark lines lingered around his eyes that never seemed to fade. When he spotted Jessica, however, a smile spread across his face.

Jessica nodded, now feeling more self-conscious than ever that she was not carrying any of the supplies.

"As timely as ever, Lady Jessica," Aias said with a bow. He gestured Jessica to the side, allowing the others to pass and head to the central kitchen.

Jessica obediently followed. "You've made some great progress down here."

"Much of it because of you."

"Everyone here seems to be of one mind."

"That's the benefit of having everything stripped from you," Aias replied. "You're just grateful for anything you can get back."

"Have you found all the Hoarders from the Rift?"

"I do believe we have," he replied, "but we still have a few teams searching, just in case. The Rift is much larger than you'd think."

"How many do you have here?"

"Around one hundred thousand," Aias replied.

Jessica shook her head. "That many? I just hope our food is enough."

"We've started preparing some of the ground to grow crops, but in the meantime, we'll make do with the food you bring us, what we can scrap from the kitchens, and what we can hunt in the Rift. But we'll have to get some seeds and UV bulbs somehow for that to work. I just feel bad that you have to deliver this food every day personally."

"I have to be the one that drops it off because we can't afford someone finding out."

"Where are you getting your supplies?" Aias asked. "I doubt Brutus is willing to share any of it unless he's forced."

"The Numberless were allotted more food than anyone else in the city. But the Numberless that were awake are now dead, and so, their food orders were not being used. It was a simple solution: I took all the ArmGuards of the fallen Numberless and have been using them to order their individual meals every day. The Numberless were able to order just about anything and everything they wanted, so for each fallen Numberless, I'm able to order a lot of food. I think I could order more each day, but I don't want to push my luck. I'm not sure how the First Assembly members would act if they knew what I was doing, not to mention Brutus. The rest of the food comes from the Validated in the BloodBorne. Every other day, they are required to skip a meal, by order of Lord Cojax Artino."

"That's brilliant," Aias said, "and much appreciated. For all of the high-minded ideals that they speak about in the First Assembly, I'm pretty sure they would let us starve." Aias led them to a ledge that overlooked a large training field. The field was impressive and expansive, stretching on for at least four hundred yards. Jessica had never seen a field so big in the Mahghetto during her time as a Disciple, but then again, she only saw the area that was utilized by the BloodBorne. On the field, thousands of Hoarders were drilling various battle formations.

"How's the training going?"

"Good," Aias said. "I don't know if the Hoarders are just excited for a second chance or something, but they have all taken to it like nothing I've seen before. No complaints. No insubordination."

"Have any of them expressed ideas of going to the surface?"

"A few," Aias said. "But we're different than the other Validated, as evidenced by our scarred faces and bodies. We will never be viewed as equals by them, even by the most open-minded. No, we failed in the past, and so they will always see us as something broken. My people won't journey to the surface willingly, at least, not without wearing a helmet and a full suit of armor to cover their scars."

Jessica studied the warriors below. Their training regimen seemed just as harsh as it was in the Mahghetto, but with one significant difference. By the end of the day, none of these people would be Rifted. And so, instead of competing with each other, the Hoarders encouraged each other. There was no Score being taken here. There was no ranking system that would allow some to live and leave others to die.

"I wish we could take the unity you see down here and implant it into the minds of all those in the First Assembly," Jessica said.

"Ironic isn't it," Aias said. "Those in the First Assembly would be much better off if they had the perspective of a Hoarder, but if they did, that would mean there would be no chance of them being on the First Assembly."

"Things are changing," Jessica said. "Onar, the self-proclaimed King of Acadia, just killed the leaders of the First Tiers."

"What? How?"

"Technically, they attacked him, and so he was defending himself," Jessica said. "But he knew what he was doing. He insulted them, and their egos demanded retribution. But he cut through them as if they were nothing. And then he broadcast the carnage to the rest of the city. It was one thing to shed the blood of our fellow Validated when we rebelled, but this is something different entirely. I'm worried that it might give license for others to kill as a way of solving their disputes. We never had to worry about this sort of violence during the AC, because everyone was constantly being monitored. Any insubordination to someone of a higher Score would cost someone dearly. Now, there's nothing to stop one person from killing another. There also have been reports of regular citizens being attacked and robbed in the streets. Sometimes the attackers don't take anything from the victim and just beat them for no apparent reason. The whole city is on edge, and incidents of violence are starting to break out all over. What's more, after Onar killed the leaders of the First Tiers, their political party fractured and a good portion of them joined Onar, which validated the use of violence."

"Did the First Tier Party dissolve completely?"

"No, but they are weakened. They barely have enough support to remain a political party."

"What do you need from us?"

"We need to make sure the Hoarders are loyal to Cojax," Jessica said. "If conflict arises to the point of civil war, we have to be sure that they choose to follow the BloodBorne."

"They are loyal," Aias said, turning to Jessica, "but not to Cojax."

"What?"

"They're loyal to you," Aias said.

"What are you saying?" Jessica asked.

"You led them to freedom, you gave them a second chance, you are the only one that comes down here regularly, and you bring food. Look at the Hoarders down there. Did you not see it before? Even though we succeeded in taking over the Trinity, they still bear the mark of the Aberration."

Jessica studied the warriors in earnest, spotting it almost immediately. She had known that they had persisted in marking their helmets with an "X," but she did not know why. She ran a finger on her scarred face; the place Atlas had dragged a blade across it in the shape of an X. It had been Atlas' way of singling her out, a way of indicating to the rest that she did not belong among them. But now, that symbol had become something different entirely.

"You've become a legend among them," Aias said. "You started as the Aberration, almost as a Rifter, and rose to the rank of a Validated. You usurped the Numberless, granted the Hoarders freedom, and you continue to provide for and protect them. Each one of them would die if it meant they could protect you."

"You organized them, trained them, protected them," Jessica replied, "I can't believe they would choose to follow me over you."

"Perhaps," Aias said, "I did train them, but I also punish them.

With me, they have to take the good with the bad, but in their eyes, you're above all of that."

Jessica hoped that the dark room would prevent Aias from seeing her red cheeks. She wanted desperately to change the subject. "We'll be receiving the first shipment of ArmGuards soon. Most used, but some are new. We'll have to figure out the best way to distribute them among your ranks."

"That won't be a problem."

"And," Jessica began slowly, "I've got a concern with Adriana."

"Is she making a move against Cojax?" Aias asked.

"No, just the opposite," Jessica said. "She defends him as if he is infallible. After Cojax put her on the BloodBorne High Council, she's been nothing but loyal."

"I don't see what the issue is then."

"She's never been loyal, not to her friends, not to her commanding officers, not even to the Numberless that ruled the city. Her pursuit is that of power."

"So then, how can I help?"

"I think we need to start stockpiling vehicles in the Rift, if that's at all possible," Jessica said. "If we take a few every once in a while and power them down, I don't think they'll be missed."

"We've already secured a few HoverBuckets," Aias said, "but I can increase the effort. The Rifters are also building a secret tunnel that leads out of the city—one big enough that we can drive our vehicles through. As long as it's constructed slowly, I don't think it will attract too much attention. But what else do we need to do?"

"Apart from vehicles, we need spies," Jessica said. "Put together a team and see if someone can infiltrate Adriana's ranks. We have to find out what she's up to. Maybe she's changed. Maybe Cojax has won her loyalty, and all this is for naught. But, if that's not true, I want to be the first one to know about it."

"But the Rifted stick out because of their scars."

Jessica nodded. "With armor on, no one can tell the difference. Besides, I bet most of Adriana's spies are Rifters too. So if anything, they'll blend right in."

Aias saluted and bowed. "It will be done."

TWENTY-ONE

Sejanus could not help but smile—this was one of the rare times it was genuine. He had just finished the last political rally of the day, and by the end of it, the crowd chanted Sejanus' name until he sat down. He and Marcus were now among them, shaking hands and clapping friends on shoulders. This rally had gone flawlessly—no critiques from the crowd, no claims of hypocrisy, no accusations of being disingenuous. Even though they did not initially receive any support from voting to reinstate the Rifters, it seemed that the proposition at least validated their political argument.

The other event that seemed to solidify their support was when Onar had slaughtered the First Tier's leadership. The Populi Party received a healthy boost in support, not only from a portion of the First Tiers, but also from the Statesmen and the Restorationists. The conflict had forced everyone to reevaluate their position, and the Populi Party benefited the most because of it. The BloodBorne had also received some support, especially since the Rifters had been given ArmGuards, but it would be too little, too late. Despite the BloodBorne's overt scare tactics utilized in their advertisements, their campaign was not nearly as successful as they had hoped.

Even though the Statesmen were still technically bigger, the Populi Party was now the party to beat. They had momentum and it showed in all of their recent rallies. More and more, people were bowing to Sejanus as if he were a Numberless. He enjoyed this universal respect, enjoyed the fact that they cheered his name as he walked through the city. A few times, he had even been referred to as the city's Savior.

Sejanus was fueled by the political rallies while Marcus seemed drained by them. By the end, Marcus was leaning against a building, his eyes sagging with the want of sleep. Sejanus, on the other hand, felt like he could storm a Roach stronghold by himself.

Marcus smiled, arching his eyebrows. "You really get into these things, don't you?"

"It's the people," Sejanus replied. "The more worked up they get, the more their energy seems to translate to me. It's an intoxicating feeling. And we're right in the middle of it. We are the architects of this whole government. And we're going to win this fight—and for a good reason too. What other government offers as much freedom as we do?"

Marcus looked around, making sure no one was close enough to hear him. "What of the Decamont?"

Sejanus scoffed. "Don't tell me that your brother's ads are starting to get to you."

"I'm serious," Marcus said. "If we win, what does that mean?"

"If the Decamont was so hell-bent on destroying us, then where are they? If they could wipe us out so easily, why haven't they?"

"But what if they do eventually show up?"

"Then we face the Decamont as a united people."

"What does that mean?"

"Where is this coming from, Marcus?" Sejanus asked.

"If we're going to institute our form of government, we need to start making preparations for defeating the Decamont," Marcus replied.

"Well," Sejanus said, "we'll have someone in the Senate draft a proposal for war, we'll ratify it in the house of Prolits, and then present it to one of the two Consuls. If they pass a clean bill, the Consuls should have no problem signing it. Then we'll take the appropriate measures to elect a military leader, allocate funds for operations and supplies—as is the job of the Senate—and prepare our defenses. Once our political party wins, we'll have a government worth saving."

Marcus slowly nodded. "Perhaps."

"Listen," Sejanus said, "why don't you come back to my apartment and we'll crack open a new keg. You get so focused on what we need to do, you frequently forget to celebrate exactly what we have done."

Marcus shook his head. "I'm too exhausted."

The Populi Party had acquired a new shipment of stock by leveraging their control over the power grid with the individuals involved in stock production. Marcus did not think the Populi Party would actually follow through with the subtle threat, but regardless, either through fear or hope of future favor, the stock producers began selling to the Populi Party at a steep discount. Marcus refused to buy directly from the stock producers, but, much to his dismay, Sejanus had publicly presented Marcus a few barrels of stock purchased with the Populi Party funds. Marcus accepted the gift, much to his shame, mostly out of a show of solidarity, but he hated that Sejanus had cornered him into it. This had been a point of contention between the two friends.

Sejanus nodded. "Alright, but get some rest tonight. We have three rallies in the morning. Plus, we need to review some of the new political ads."

Marcus nodded and saluted. "I'll get Karpas and Lentios to escort you home." He turned to his ArmGuard, about to hail the two Validated, but Sejanus put his hand on Marcus' shoulder.

"You need to have more faith in the people," Sejanus said. "We're not barbarians, born to caves and destined to fight with clubs. We are the most advanced and sophisticated humans ever to walk this earth. I live just a few blocks from here. If we want people to believe in us, we have to believe in them."

"Whether someone bashes your skull in with a club or cuts your head off with an Arc Blade, the result is the same. You're dead. And after what Onar did—"

"—As your Consul, I order you to relax tonight," Sejanus said, his good-natured face cracking into a smile.

Marcus mirrored his friend's expression. "Can you order someone to do something in a Republic, or is that something we have to vote on?"

The two laughed.

Sejanus slapped Marcus one last time on the shoulder. "I'll see you tomorrow." With that, he turned around, his feet light. He felt another rush of pure euphoria as he thought about the political rallies that were scheduled for the next day. Eventually, however, his thoughts drifted back to Marcus, a good man who worried far more than Sejanus thought was healthy. To Marcus, equality and liberty were not just ideals to strive for, they were things that could actually be obtained. *I won't be able to keep him as one of the party leaders after we win. He'll eventually undermine and fracture the Populi, complicating even the most basic of issues. His passion will gain us control, but his morality will make it hard to keep it.*

The streets were barren, a marked difference from when the AC existed. In the time before, there were always Validated in the street, no matter the hour, either on their way to guard duty or some other task. Now, Validated returned home when they wanted and stayed there as long as they desired, leaving the city absolutely desolate during the later hours of the night.

Sejanus began structuring his speech for the next day. Honestly, it really did not matter much what he said anymore. They had the momentum. But, creating a well-thought-out speech still thrilled him. He liked to see the effect of his words; he liked to see the emotions of the crowd, their expressions as he promised them equality.

Then Sejanus was pitched forward, his body rolling once before it stopped. He reacted quickly, off lining to the right, and drawing his Arc Blade. He had, after all, risen to the First Tier and was a master with the blade. They came from the shadows, their weapons drawn, their faces unseen behind dark helmets. Before Sejanus even saw them all, he knew he was surrounded. By the spacing of those in the front, Sejanus guessed that there were nine, plus one sniper, bringing the number of attackers to at least ten.

Sejanus laughed, his confidence still sailing high from the political rally. Then he attacked in earnest, slicing one attacker in the leg, another in the back. The movement was so fast that the hits seemed more like one flash of light than two. The rest of the attackers rushed in, drowning Sejanus in rays of light. Sejanus was so fierce in his attacks that it was not long before he broke through the attacker's ranks, giving him a clear path of retreat.

But pride did not allow him to take it. *If these fools are crazy enough to start a fight, I will be the one that finishes it.* The next second, Sejanus sliced an attacker in two. He removed the helmet off the fallen warrior's head and placed it on his own. Fortunately, the helmet synced with his armor, protecting him from someone scoring a lucky headshot.

Sejanus laughed, walking around the circle as if this was nothing more than a social call. "Is this your ploy Onar? If you want to take down a lion, you better send more than sheep."

The attackers regrouped, this time using more caution as they approached. Instead of an all-out charge, they began to toy with Sejanus, charging in and then retreating quickly. Each time they did, it opened up a perfect shot for the sniper, who took it with the greatest of zeal. Sejanus curled his hands at the cowardice, lashing out at his attackers in frustration. They only engaged briefly, just enough to push Sejanus back into the center of the attackers. Then the sniper whittled him down, as a master carver does to a piece of wood. Shot after shot hammered the First Tier in the upper torso, leaching more and more power with each hit. He could feel his shields disappearing, feel his control of the situation slipping.

As Sejanus' desperation grew, so did the attackers' boldness. This time, when they came at him, they did not fall back as quickly as before. Sejanus was able to cut down two more attackers, but then his shields broke, and his body lost all of its strength. Despite it all, he still refused to surrender. His attackers took him piece by piece, slashing first his arms, followed by his legs. He fell heavily to his knees, his breath coming in sharp gasps.

"At least," Sejanus said. "Tell me who you are?"

The only answer came in the form of an Arc Blade. Sejanus' headless body fell hard to the ground, his once beautiful armor now discarded in the gutter. They left the Arc Blade that finished the task, but they took Sejanus' head, as per their instructions. It was found the next day at the end of an Arc Lance in the middle of the main forum, right where the Populi Party had scheduled their first rally of the day.

TWENTY-TWO

Cojax slammed his fist against the door. He waited precisely half a second before he knocked again, this time with much greater force. "Adriana, open this door. I know you're here. I know—"

The door opened, but it was not Adriana.

"Ion?" Cojax asked.

"Oh, Cojax, hello," Ion replied, his hands shaking at his sides. "I didn't expect a visit from you."

"I'm not visiting you," Cojax said. "I was looking for Adriana. This is where she lives, is it not?"

Suddenly, Cojax saw her walking past. He pushed past Ion, catching Adriana in the kitchen. She was wearing nothing but a bathrobe, as was evident when she turned around.

Cojax looked the other way, directing his voice to the wall instead of her. Despite his tone, it was difficult to maintain his venom when he was now talking to the wall. "Did you do it?"

Adriana laughed. "Hmmm...please be more specific."

"Did you kill him?"

"What a wild accusation," she replied. "Ion, be a dear and leave us."

Ion nodded once, stumbling on an awkward farewell as he did. He left as quickly as Cojax had arrived.

Adriana let out a long sigh. "Is that why you rushed over here in such a rage? A man that's not even part of our party disappears and you get all worked up over it."

"His head was stuck on a pole and placed in the main forum. There's no excuse for that kind of butchery. Now, I will only ask one final time: did you kill Sejanus?"

"Not directly," Adriana replied.

Cojax turned towards her, ignoring all sense of propriety. "What do you mean? Did you send people to kill him?"

"Yes."

Cojax punched the wall, putting a gloved fist clear through it. Concrete exploded, a trail of dust followed.

"You know," Adriana said, her voice taking on a sexy tone, "Since the AC doesn't exist anymore, I don't know how I will get someone to fix that."

"You have blood on your hands," Cojax said.

"And you don't?" Adriana asked. "Don't you remember, it was your plan to raid the Trinity? And you led one of the main bodies in the attack, spilling the blood of thousands. So, don't play the part of a saint when you're much more suited to be a soldier."

"That's different," Cojax yelled, "and get some clothes on."

Adriana frowned, folding her arms. "You're just no fun. Alright, but do me one favor."

Cojax frowned.

Adriana took off her robe and handed it to Cojax. He blushed bright red as she took her time to disappear into a back room. Minutes later, she reappeared, wearing formal BloodBorne attire. Cojax had sat down while he waited, his temper rising in degrees.

She raised a hand before he could speak, "Let me explain before you throw out your accusations."

"I'm waiting."

"You and I agree on one thing—that if our people squabble and whine about who controls what, the Decamont will come down here, use our own divisions and differences, and wipe us out. For some reason, everyone else in this blazing city can't seem to grasp that concept. Instead, they whine about some pretended authority that they want but don't have. Cojax, if they show up tomorrow or the next day, we're all dead. How vain are we to believe that the very creatures who created this city would be fought off so easily."

"What does that have to do with Sejanus?"

"Shut up," Adriana said. "Let me finish. But, you and I disagree on something fundamental: how far you are willing to go to protect our people. You were willing to defy the Numberless, you were willing to kill, to raid, and to take over the Trinity, and you were even willing to lie and subvert the authority of other political parties. But you stop short of killing one man. For some reason, you still don't believe your political party will win control. The only reason you're willing to continue on is the hope that your political party will influence whatever government is eventually put into place into believing that the Decamont are a real threat.

"Well, Cojax, wakeup. Titan put you in charge of the BloodBorne for a reason, and not because you're an awesome warrior, not because you're a phenomenal speaker. He put you in charge because you see the threat that is before you. You see the Decamont for what they are: exterminators. And no one besides you and me, and maybe a hand full of others see it the same way. Yeah, everyone knows they're out there, and they'll be coming, but either because they can't see the threat, or they are so arrogant they believe that we can soundly defeat them, they aren't afraid of them."

"I want our party to win," Cojax defended.

"Do you?" Adriana asked.

"It doesn't matter," Cojax replied.

"I truly believe that if you don't win, if you don't become our Lord, that we will be as wheat before the harvest. The Decamont will mow our city down and salt the ground with our bodies. We can't just let the Populi Party win and then try to influence them to take the Decamont seriously; we can't let the Statesmen rule and expect that they will suddenly deal with the external threat. So, Cojax, I am not fighting for a new government; I am fighting for our very survival. And if one man has to die—just one—for us to preserve ten million, then I will rip that man apart with my nails if I have to."

Cojax looked to speak, but Adriana cut him off.

"How many weeks have we spent in the First Assembly—four, five? What good has that done? Have we sent out scouting parties to get a lay of the land? Have we tried to contact other cities to see if they will join us? Have we tried to increase the production of weapons? Or doubled our defenses? Or organized our armies into one cohesive unit? Why not? Because, in a city of ten million, there will be ten million ways to approach this problem. We need one voice—one direction. You must be that voice. You must be our Lord."

Cojax swallowed. He opened his mouth to speak but did not know what to say. Finally, he decided to steer the conversation back towards the morality of the situation. "Why did you kill Sejanus?"

"Well," Adriana said, "because he was gaining momentum. If his popularity continues at this rate, his party will control the government in a matter of weeks. No one has appeared on the ads as much as him; no one had as much influence over the party as he did. This will, at the very least, slow their growth."

"You could have just as easily made him a martyr, a symbol the Populi Party can rally around."

"There will be some of that, sure, but I think it was worth the risk."

Cojax shook his head. "Adriana, you can't just kill people like that. We cannot let ourselves become as bad as the Decamont. Do you understand?"

"Yes, but do you understand?"

"I can see why you feel that way."

"No, you still don't get it. Cojax, you have to believe that you're going to win. You need to make decisions as if you will win. You must be our Lord. You must rule Titan—no matter the cost. They may judge us in the future, they may condemn our actions, but without us, there will be no future."

"Do you really believe that?"

"Yes, I do," Adriana said. "If the Statesmen win, what will happen? We'll fracture into our original Factions. Instead of having one government, we will have many. If the Populi Party wins, then we will function just like the First Assembly—with much discussion, but little progress. If Onar wins, we'll likely suffer more under his rule than we did under the AC. The Restorationists will attempt to put us back under the yoke of the Decamont. Hah, I don't even want to think about what will happen if the First Tiers gain control."

"Their party can't last much longer now that they've lost their leadership."

"True, but that's not my point. My point is this: it has to be you. For whatever reason, fate has decided that you must be our ruler. Now is the time where you must begin acting the part."

Cojax stood, turning away from Adriana. He walked to the window studying the city as it was just starting to come alive with the morning light. It was a while longer before he finally spoke. "I think you might be right."

"You think?"

Cojax shook his head. "But I'm not my father. He was a leader. He was a warrior. A man that not only commanded respect but inspired those around him. I think that many in the BloodBorne follow me solely out of respect for my father."

"That may have been true at first, but I don't think it is now."

"I'm in the Tenth Tier. I've never been an Omega or led armies. I've never even been an Arch Hoplite or an Alpha."

Adriana stepped closer, "Didn't some ancient philosopher once say that 'he that should rule is the one that thinks he should not.' It's your humility that makes you the only person that can rule our city with equity and strength."

"I don't know how to command armies," Cojax replied.

"That's why a Lord appoints Omegas to lead," Adriana replied.

"I'm still debating with myself if we did the right thing by ending the AC."

"Let go of your morality," Adriana said. "As a Lord, you cannot afford to make decisions based on right or wrong. Sure, you want to be in the right most of the time; otherwise, your people will rise against you. But the most difficult decisions you have to make must be made with your head, not with your heart. You may hate yourself for it, but you will save your people because of it."

"So, you see me as your Lord?"

Adriana bowed low.

"Then I order you never to kill someone like that again without first consulting me. I also want to be fully informed on your spy network. Don't mistake my intentions, Adriana, you've already proven your value, but we must make these types of decisions together. I want to know who your informants are, where they're positioned, and what sort of compensation or promises you have made to them."

Adrian bowed again, this time saluting. "I will prepare a detailed brief. But I warn you Cojax; it might not be wise to know everything I'm involved in. That way, you can always claim ignorance if something goes sideways."

"I need to know everything," Cojax replied. "Tell me about Ion? Why was he here at your apartment? He's clearly aligned with my brother in the Populi Party."

"He's a source of information," Adriana replied. "That's how I knew that the Populi Party was going to propose that the Rifters get a vote."

"He might be getting information from you just as easily."

Adriana smiled. "No, I'm better than that. I keep him...

distracted."

Cojax blushed red.

Adriana continued, pretending not to notice. "Ion is incredibly intelligent in some aspects, but he completely lacks the most basic social awareness. He's also well positioned in the Populi Party and just as naïve as someone can be—a perfect mark."

Cojax nodded. "Alright, when can you get me that brief?"

"Promise me first that you'll be our Lord."

"I will…try."

Adriana shook her head. "I need you to have more conviction. Answer me this, if the city hands you a crown, will you accept it?"

Cojax nodded. "I guess I'll have to at that point."

"Then," Adriana replied, "I'll send it to you by tonight, my Lord. Although, I will say, my spies are completely useless as soon as their identities become public knowledge. I must impress upon you the importance of keeping their identity secret."

Cojax nodded, "Only myself and my two Counselors will know about them."

Adriana rolled her eyes. "Oh, so you're planning on telling Jessica. I might as well blast their identities on the CityScreens."

"Why do you hate her so much?"

"You're handsome, smart, and talented, and yet, you can be so incredibly naïve sometimes. Tell me, does she make you happy?"

"Please don't attack her. Out of everything that has happened, she is the only thing that makes sense to me. I love her, love her determination to tackle the most daunting of tasks, love her compassion for others, love the way she somehow makes a room have more light as she walks into it."

"Blood and bile," Adriana said, her hand covering her mouth. "Please never talk like that again."

Cojax laughed. "I'm not naïve. I know, for some odd reason, either to get something from me or for some political advantage, you think you'd be a better fit for me than Jessica. But my heart already belongs to her. You are one of the most stunningly beautiful and talented women I have ever met. In another life, perhaps, I would be lucky to have someone like you at my side."

Adriana laughed, but it seemed somewhat forced. For the briefest of moments, Adriana appeared vulnerable and weak, like a baby bird that had fallen from its nest. The moment passed quickly, and the mood changed. They spoke for only a few minutes longer before Cojax exhaled and left. As soon as he was gone, Adriana put one of her fists through her bedroom wall.

TWENTY-THREE

Marcus took the stage, addressing the crowd with a solemn air. "Sejanus organized these debates, and so, in his honor, the Populi Party has decided to continue them. Now, more than ever, I think we need to push ahead, remembering Sejanus for not only who he was, but what he wanted to achieve—an equitable government, based on principles of morality. Before we begin, let us have a moment of silence for our fallen friend and hero—Sejanus."

Marcus was at a podium on the far side of a stage. To his right, at another podium, was a Validated named Nicodema, who was one of the leaders of the Statesmen. To her right was another podium with a Validated named Tidas, who was the principle and newly elected leader of the First Tiers. Finally, the last podium on the opposite side was Deo, leader of the Restorationists. There were also two empty podiums, one for Cojax of the BloodBorne and another for the self-proclaimed King of Acadia, Onar the Slayer. Neither one had accepted the invitation, much to Marcus' dismay. Of all the people to have not accepted the invitation, Marcus was hoping it would be the Statesmen. Their crass language and words would do little to elevate and validate the debate.

This was to be the first of six debates, each one monitored and sponsored by a different Faction. In order to set the tone right, Marcus made sure that the first few debates were hosted by a Faction that was sympathetic to the Populi Political Party.

After a brief moment of silence, a moderator, dressed in formal attire and wrapped in a blue cape, organized and structured the debate. She was an imposing figure, her face marked by age that seemed to validate her wisdom and her position. She took this assignment very seriously. Her words were exact and sharp.

The debate opened with a brief statement from each of the delegates and then the war of words began. The moderator asked a question concerning the recent increase in violence. Marcus was first given the floor. He came in strong, denouncing the violence committed by Onar and the assassins of Sejanus. His words were more potent than they had ever been, and all those who listened could not help but be entranced by them. The other debaters continued the trend, denouncing the violence. It was not until Deo of the Restorationists spoke that the real debate began. Deo assigned culpability to every party present, especially the Populi, who encouraged this type of violence with their inequality. He argued that they should, if only temporarily, revert to the Acadian Code.

Nicodema of the Statesmen Party quickly reacted to these accusations, charging at the Restorationists as a wolf pursues prey. After only minutes, any pretended civility disappeared, and the arguments descended into insults—the most crass of which were produced by Nicodema. The Restorationists countered, accusing the Statesmen of working for the enemy. They even claimed they had proof. The audience that supported the Restorationist Party erupted into cheers, while those that supported the Statesmen turned absolutely manic.

The moderator had a tough time restoring the peace, but the debate finally continued. On and on the questions came, each one dividing the leaders behind the podiums as well as the audience. Every chance Marcus got, he tried to elevate the discussion, presenting facts and logical points. For two hours, this continued, all sides being bruised and dirtied by the conflict.

After the debate concluded, Marcus was surrounded by members of his own party. They hailed him as a hero, declaring him a decisive victor. The polls from the audience were not nearly as convincing, giving him only a slight edge over his competitors.

Marcus returned to the Populi headquarters, his head pounding with pain. He could not help but feel frustrated over the entire debating experience. It had not been so much a matter of presenting logic as it was a series of quick quips and rebuttals. These sorts of events drained Marcus as a battery connected by frayed wires. After Sejanus was assassinated, Marcus had been elected as the Consul. He did not want it, but since it was unanimous, he felt obligated to take it.

It was not long before Validated were approaching him, presenting various details of upcoming events. Finally, he took his leave, a little more abruptly than seemed socially acceptable, and returned to his apartment. Since he was now one of the two Consuls, four Validated escorted him everywhere, a rule he instituted himself. Despite the company, he felt alone, his one true friend had been cremated two days before.

Once arriving at his apartment, he allowed the Validated inside so they could check for intruders. Once clear, he entered his room, his eyes drifting longingly to the bed. Instead, he headed for a small desk where he found a mess of paper and writing utensils. He preferred real paper and pens to the electronic notepad and stylus, despite the cost. Even before the AC had fallen, he had acquired these items as soon as he had enough points to do so. He sat down, his hands putting ink to paper, ideas flowing through him. This is what he was good at, what he always preferred. The quiet pen to paper and the flow of ideas. He was never meant for the stage, that was always Sejanus' arena.

Marcus pulled up an interface on his ArmGuard, searching it for a specific picture. He found it not long after, a picture of when the Populi Party was first organized. Sejanus was in the front, his back straight, his eyes commanding but warm. *Your sacrifice will not be in vain. I swear by everything I hold sacred, that those who sought your death will be revisited in kind.* Sejanus had been flawed, but he had been earnest. He did not seek power for his own gain but to help those around him. For the first time, Marcus now felt that he was fighting against something purely evil. Something that would not just be defeated through words and logic, but something that had to be cut out and burned, like some diseased tree amidst an orchard. *I will find out who committed this sin—who thought his life was naught—and I will crucify them before the city.*

The debates continued every night for the next week. They demanded everything from Marcus, seemingly draining his soul. He became a recluse, retreating to his apartment as soon as he was able. The war of words degraded into a cesspit of lies, accusations, and the occasional challenge to mortal combat. Marcus hated all of it. At some point during the debates, he began to see his opponents as the would-be assassins of Sejanus. Every jab they took at the Populi Party, Marcus took as a personal affront on Sejanus' life.

The Great Debates, as some Validated had taken to calling them, did prove worthwhile, and by weeks end, the Statesmen began to show interest in joining the Populi Party. But this came at a cost, however, that Marcus was not willing to pay. The Statesmen demanded substantial concessions to how the Populi Party was structured. Marcus absolutely refused. He would not trade moral principles for votes. But then, it was put to a vote, and he lost by a small margin. With the concessions, however, the Statesmen Party joined the Populi. Soon, Marcus' party was the dominant political force in the city.

TWENTY-FOUR

Horace walked Finn to the inside of the CargoLifter, pointing to a metallic plate. "Hold that down tight, or the whole ship might come apart."

Finn looked to Horace, his eyes going wide. "What? The whole ship? How's that possible?"

"Oh, and I've got a friend coming along, so mind your manners."

Finn nodded. "You've got friends?"

Horace straightened his back. "Of course I do."

"Is he a Numberless?"

"Who else am I supposed to bring?"

"You woke up another Numberless?" Finn asked, his eyes again going wide.

Horace gestured to the metallic panel. "You need to hold that tighter."

Finn nodded again, pushing harder against the interior wall.

Horace went to the captain's cabin at the front of the craft, flipping switches as he went. The vehicle's engines fired, the lights popped on. Finn took a chance and glanced around. He had ridden in a CargoLifter at least a thousand times in his life, and yet, this craft was like nothing he had ever seen. It was a smooth, sleek vehicle, built with every luxury in mind. Plush couches circled the cargo bay. In one of the corners, there was a small kitchen; in another, a door led to a bathroom. Even the air smelled fancy, and Finn could not help but inhale it deeply as if it was in short supply.

Another man entered the craft. He was tall and thin, garbed in the armor of a Numberless. His eyebrows were thick and unkempt, much like the beard that clung to his chin. A thick Arc Blade hung from his back, another smaller one from his waist. He held a helmet in one hand, a pitcher of stock in the other.

Finn redoubled his efforts in holding the metallic panel in

place. He was not going to make a bad impression with this new Numberless. There was an awkward moment while Finn and the Numberless locked eyes.

Finn gestured to the metallic panel. "Don't worry about a thing. I've got this locked down tight."

The man nodded and continued on, entering into the captain's cabin a moment later.

After shutting the door so Finn could not hear, the Numberless turned to Horace. "What's wrong with the kid? He was leaning against the wall of the Lifter with so much force I thought he was trying to walk through it."

Horace laughed. "I told him if he didn't, the ship would fall apart."

The Numberless returned the laughter, slapping Horace on the back. "That's a good one. I didn't think it would be a good idea to bring him along, but now, I'm starting to warm up to it."

"You ready to get out of here, Seleukus?" Horace asked.

Seleukus plopped down into the copilot chair, waving a hefty pitcher of stock in the air as he did. "I've got all I need right here."

"You're only bringing one pitcher?" Horace asked. "We're going to need more than that."

"This is just for the trip," Seleukus said, "the rest is already packed in the cargo hold."

Horace leaned forward, reaching for the pitcher. "Good man! Let me have some."

"Oh," Seleukus replied. "Were you under the impression that I was sharing?"

"Come on," Horace said. "You've got an unlimited supply. Blood and bile, you make the stuff in your quarters. You can at least share a taste with your friend."

"My friend? My friend? I half think the only reason you woke me up is so I can start making more stock for you."

"You say that as if it's a bad thing."

Seleukus rolled his eyes and poured a cup from the pitcher, handing it to Horace. "I've been experimenting with new recipes. Actually, they're new to me but old to our race. Our ancestors were weak, whiny, and worthless, but in this art, they far surpassed us. Go ahead. Give it a try."

Horace sniffed the cup.

"Come on, you greedy Rifter," Seleukus said.

Horace took a sip, followed by a large drag. "That's fantastic. How did you manage it?"

"Well, I've been using Hallertau hops, and I haven't regretted it yet."

"Now that we've got the beverage situation under control," Horace said, "we better be off." With one hand on his mug and the other on the ship's controls, he revved the engines, and the shuttle shot directly up into the air. Even if one was looking for it, a Validated would be hard-pressed to see it. It was not long before they were in the clouds.

"Watch this," Seleukus said. He flipped on a camera that showed the back of the CargoLifter. Finn was still there, holding the metallic panel as if all of their lives depended on it. Then Seleukus began rocking the ship, first one way and then the other. Finn, despite himself, was thrown around the cargo bay, like lint in a dryer. Each time he was displaced, the boy would run back to the panel in a panic. And each time he did, Seleukus would tip the ship the other way, making Finn collide into the wall.

Once the two Numberless got their laughter under control, Horace activated the loudspeaker, "Finn, what's going on? We're losing power. Are you still holding onto the panel?"

Finn did his best to fight the turbulence. "I'm on it. I keep getting bounced around, but I'm on it."

The trip only took thirty minutes. Before long, they were dropping out of the sky almost as quickly as they had shot up. They landed hard, forcing Finn onto the floor. While on the ground, the boy reached up, trying with all his might to maintain his grip on the panel.

The door of the CargoLifter hissed open, revealing a landing pad at a structure that was identical to the Trinity in Titan. Finn pulled himself off the floor before the other two men could see him. Horace exited the CargoLifter first, followed by Finn and Seleukus.

"Good job, boy," Seleukus said. "I don't know what we would've done without you keeping the ship together. I almost thought we were going to lose it back there."

Finn nodded, a smile spread across his face. "Not a problem. Glad I was of use."

Then Finn was shot in the chest. His armor exploded with light as he was knocked over by the sudden blast. It had been a large projectile and a clean shot. Instead of going on the offensive, Horace and Seleukus raised their hands, seemingly surrendering to the enemy.

"Easy now, Tiberius," Horace said. "We come bearing gifts of a fragile nature."

Tiberius was a thick man with a white beard and bushy eyebrows. Besides the color of hair, Tiberius and Horace looked as if they could be brothers.

"I thought I told you that you weren't welcome here anymore."

Horace pointed to himself, a look of surprise on his face. "You said that to Titan; I didn't think you meant me too."

"I couldn't have been more clear, and nothing you say will change my mind."

Seleukus began inching towards the CargoLifter, his hands still raised. He then popped the cargo hold open, revealing at least a dozen kegs of stock. Seleukus nodded towards his cargo, a mischievous smile on his face. Then he winked.

In reply, Tiberius pointed the Blazer at Seleukus. Slowly, the man's finger began pulling back on the trigger. Finn rolled to his feet, his right hand pulling free his Arc Blade. If it was going to be a fight, at least they outnumbered Tiberius three to one.

Then Tiberius threw his gun on his shoulder, a grin replacing his former grimace. "You Acadians always knew how to make a persuasive argument. Come on then, bring it inside." The thick man turned his back to the CargoLifter and headed to the Trinity.

Finn looked to Horace and Seleukus in turn, an expression of pure terror spread across his face. He did not want to come near these people if that is how they said, "Hello."

"Grab the stock, string bean," Horace said to Finn.

"You can't seriously think about sharing a drink with that man," Finn protested. "He just shot me."

"I really can't blame him after what happened last time," Horace said. "After Titan ripped apart their banquet hall with a Blazer in each hand."

"This is the city where you had the Blazer fight?" Finn asked, his voice becoming increasingly higher pitched. "And you decided to come here first?"

"It's the closest," Horace replied.

"Plus, old Tiberius would never refuse good stock," Seleukus replied.

The two Numberless followed Tiberius, disappearing behind double doors that opened and then closed again. Finn hefted two kegs under one arm, a third on his shoulder. He followed the three men but was stopped short at the door. It did not open as it did for Horace and Seleukus. Finn decidedly stepped back, approaching the door again, hoping that the sensors would pick him up. No success. He tried a third time, moving as slowly as he could.

He decided to put the kegs back in the ship and hail Horace on his ArmGuard. As soon as he was halfway back, however, the doors hissed open. Finn twisted around, almost dropping one of the kegs to the ground. He came at the door at a quick jog, but just before he could walk through, it slammed closed and he collided into it. Again, the door would not open for him.

Horace and Seleukus, who were already inside and standing next to the door's terminal, could not keep back their fit of laughter. Every time Finn was about to walk through, Horace used the manual override to force it closed.

"I could do this all day," Horace said.

"Oh, I don't think so," Tiberius responded, using his ArmGuard to force the door open. "I've got a thirst, and that boy is carrying the stock that's going to quench it."

Finn came in looking flushed. "Something's wrong with the door."

"Must be…uhh…sticking," Seleukus said, repressing a grin.

Tiberius led them to a large banquet hall not far from the hanger doors. He gestured to some seats, easing Finn's burden as he grabbed one of the kegs. Instead of using a glass, he used an Arc Blade to slice open the top, making a massive mug out of it. The Numberless' eyes widened as the brew hit his taste buds. "That's the best stock I've ever had. What'd you put in it?"

"Family recipe," Seleukus replied.

Tiberius took another swig of the keg, this time accidentally spilling some down his beard. "Well, invite me over next time you have a family reunion."

Horace and Tiberius took their own kegs of stock, tapping it as Tiberius did before them and taking a long swig each.

Horace looked at the brew anew, his face beset with wonder. "Seleukus, you old dog of war, you're an artist. A man ahead of his time."

Finn was feeling like a fly in soup, his stance rigid, his expression stoic. He felt so out of place being amongst three Numberless. His hands alternated between resting on his hips, then on the grip of his Arc Blade, then folding across his chest. Each hand position felt awkward as he worried that he would be conveying the wrong sort of demeanor. His worry was in vain, however, as the three Numberless seemed more intent on discovering the bottoms of their kegs than anything else. The first round was quickly finished, and Finn was sent for another round of ale.

He brought more barrels, this time the door did not stick. By the time he returned, the three men were eating the thickest and juiciest steaks Finn had ever seen. Somehow, the empty table was now teaming with food, buffet style. Horace was garnishing his steak with shrimp while Seleukus was helping himself to a spoon full of garlic potatoes.

Finn brought four kegs this time, one specifically for him, but as he was about to slice it open with his Arc Blade, Horace slapped him in the shoulder, pitching him to the side. The blade went in at an angle, leaving his keg looking more like a triangle then a cup. Brew dripped to the floor, but none of the other three seemed to mind. Finn tipped the keg back, expecting a wonder of sensations. He was quickly disappointed, as evidenced by his coughing fit moments later.

"That's it," Horace said, again slapping Finn on the shoulder. "The boy has just had his first drag on a true drink. What do you think?"

Finn felt he should lie, but before he could, the truth slipped out. "It's disgusting."

For some odd and horrible reason, the other three men laughed, kicking back in their seats with the greatest sense of levity they could muster. Finn tried the drink again, just to be sure he had not somehow mistaken the taste. *No,* Finn thought, *it's still disgusting.*

Tiberius pulled Finn into a side hug, all animosity that was in his face before now completely gone. "It's an acquired taste."

"Ain't nothing better when you do!" Seleukus said, his face a bright red.

Finn was so confused right now, he did not know how to respond. Even worse, it seemed that no amount of questions answered would make his confusion disappear. This had been a political envoy sent from one city to another. They were representatives of their city; they were here looking for allies in a coming war. Or, at the very least, information on the enemy's movements. Neither Horace nor Seleukus seemed even the least bit inclined to talk about the task at hand.

Tiberius then started paging some of the other Numberless, explaining in terse but convincing detail that they needed to try some of this "stock." Despite only calling three or four of the Numberless, the word spread quickly, and soon Finn was in a room filled with some of the most powerful men and women he had ever been around. The unfortunate boy found himself the unofficial waiter of all the Numberless and kept himself busy taking orders of stock and picking up and dropping off food from a nearby chute. This allowed him to drift from person to person, hearing bits of their conversation. The Numberless looked and acted very much like the Numberless in the city of Titan. The most significant difference was in their armor. Instead of using armor that was derived from the Greeks, they seemed more influenced by the Romans. Their breastplates were segmented and their helmets were more open. They also carried a different kind of Arc Lance. Instead of having a large blade on the end, the tips were much smaller, being only the size of a finger. Their Arc Blades and Blazers seemed similar with only cosmetic differences.

An hour past, and then two. And yet, Horace said nothing about the city of Titan. He said nothing about alliances or treaties or mutual aid. It seemed every topic was fair game except for the one they were assigned to bring up. Finn's frustration began to peak. While the Decamont were planning their city's demise, these Numberless drank to excess and ate until their armor barely fit.

Finn walked past Horace, trying to signal with raised eyebrows. Horace only smiled back and winked. "Yes, I'd love another pitcher! Will you look at this boy, always anticipating my thoughts."

Finn went and retrieved another sixteen kegs from the CargoLifter, taking multiple trips. This represented the last of it, much to Finn's relief. The kegs disappeared almost as soon as he returned. Horace was circled by a lively group of Numberless, all of which were competing with tales of their heroic deeds. Finn moved in closer, trying to whisper in Horace's ear. But just then, Tiberius was finishing a harrowing tale of how he once fell thirty stories down into a Roach's nest.

Horace put his arms around the two individuals who were at his side, shaking them vigorously. "What's the harm in this? Why don't we do this more often?"

Tiberius grinned. "Yes, why not? Although I'll be honest, I like your stock much better than I like you." The room filled with scattered laughter.

Seleukus straightened up, his arms folded across his chest. "Why does Horace get all the credit? I'm the one that brews it."

"Then why did you even invite him in the first place," Tiberius said. The group of Numberless again broke up in laughter.

"If I weren't here, who else would 'one-up' each one of your lame stories," Horace retorted. Then he stood, raising a keg to the other Numberless. "I would like to propose a toast to the inhabitants of the city of Ephesus—a beautiful city, almost as nice as our Titan."

Kegs were raised in a show of appreciation.

After the noise died down again, Tiberius continued his jibes. "Horace, you've drunk too much. The name of your city is Acadia, not Titan. Where is Titan by the way, that old bloodhound?"

Horace stood up again, his voice taking on a rare somber tone. "Titan was a great man, one of the best. But he has passed from this life to the next."

The Numberless stopped talking, all turning Horace's direction. Tiberius straightened up. "What?"

Horace studied his cup for a moment before he continued, acting as if this was a topic he was trying to avoid. "He died overthrowing the Decamont's control of our city."

Again, the room filled with stunned silence.

"What?" said a large, thick Numberless. "What are you saying? Your city has rebelled?"

Horace shrugged his shoulders. "Yes, and we won our freedom. The name of the city was changed to Titan after his heroic actions and selfless sacrifice. Because of what he did, our city is no longer under the tyranny of the Decamont."

"But what happened to your power grid?" a large woman asked.

"We still have power," Horace replied. "Titan figured out a way to sever the Decamont's control before they could shut the power down. And now we live free."

A tall but thin Numberless stood up. "Wait a minute, wait a minute. Are you saying that you've rebelled against the Decamont?"

"Yes," Horace replied.

"So, they don't control you anymore?" said a thin Numberless,

"Yes," Horace replied. "Am I not explaining this well? We've won our freedom. We are no longer subject to the Acadian Code. There are no more Riftings, Releases, or senseless deaths in our city."

"How did Titan sever the connection with the Decamont without sacrificing your power grid?" said the thin Numberless. "That should've been impossible."

"I can show ya," Horace said.

"Whoa, whoa, whoa," Tiberius said, raising his hands in the air. "Are you suggesting we should rebel as well?"

"No," Horace shook his head. "You were just asking me, and I was just tellin' you."

A Numberless on the other side of the room stood up. "You do know that they'll be coming for you. They'll gather a Roach army so large that it will shake the very ground as they approach. Then they will send a tide of carapace against your walls until every last man, woman, and child is drowned by it."

"It will be a war for the ages," Horace said. "Akin to the three hundred Spartans at Phybolis. But I don't want you thinking we rebelled just so we could be slaughtered. The son of Titan, Cojax Artino of the BloodBorne, a brilliant warrior and a Nova, has been named our Lord. And he is no ordinary man. He has vision and strength, a genius tactician."

"Let us know how that works out for you," said a Numberless who had her legs kicked up on the table.

"Wait a minute," said the thin Numberless, "we're not even going to entertain this? I at least think we should put this to a vote."

"Tigris, why would we want to risk losing everything? Titan didn't talk to us before he incited his little rebellion, and now that he realizes what he's done, he wants to drag us into it."

"Kyscene, how could he have let us know?" Tigris asked. "He was about to do something that has never been done before. He couldn't tell us, someone might have prevented it."

Tiberius turned to Horace. "What's your objective?"

Horace scratched his chin. "For the first time since our planet was dominated by the Decamont, we have a chance to stand up against them. I, like you, did not plan this with Titan; I was forced into it. But I'm a free man now, able to lead the life I choose. Able to come here and break open a keg with you worthless lot."

"Free now, dead in a few months," Kyscene replied. "I've already transmitted my vote on my ArmGuard. Don't want to ruin the surprise, but I chose the option where we don't end up dead."

"Don't you want to discuss this a little first?" Tigris asked.

"Let's just vote," Tiberius said. "We all know what's at stake."

"We don't even have everyone here," Tigris answered.

Finn felt slightly disturbed at how lightly each Numberless took the idea of rebellion. Many were not paying attention to the conversation. He felt he should do something. Say something. He was not as passionate as Cojax. In fact, he was usually the guy trying to make light of serious things. But who else was there? Horace seemed just as carefree as the Numberless, and Seleukus even more so. The tone of the conversation suggested they were speaking about something trivial—like which Blazer functioned the best—not the future of their people. Finn ran a few sentences through his head, trying to think how Cojax might phrase them. They sounded powerful the first time he thought of them, but less so each subsequent time he repeated them in his mind. He finally rested on a short, positive speech, one that would not embarrass him too much if it fell flat. He stepped forward, opening his mouth to cut in, but before he could, a cup of stock was thrust in his face.

"Hold your tongue, boy," Seleukus said as he forced Finn to take a drink of stock. "Horace is no fool, nor am I."

"But…," Finn began, but the stock was forced down his throat. It was not as disagreeable as the first time he tried it, but it certainly was not much better. He forced the liquid down, seemingly placated for now.

But Horace did not win the crowd over, nor did he seem to particularly care how any of this was going. When a vote was finally called and counted, not a single Numberless voted in favor of revolution. Horace took the news so well that Finn thought that he must have been drunk. Instead of pushing for another vote, or even trying to persuade the Validated to reconsider, Horace spent his time telling the story about how Titan woke him up in the middle of the rebellion and led them to fight against the other Numberless.

Horace told the story with a practiced art, describing in detail the great clash of the two sides—Titan leading one side, Atlas on the other. Horace listed name after name of the fallen from both sides, sharing with the audience some epic deed that they had done in the past.

"Only I survived, and even then, it wasn't all of me," Horace said, gesturing to his mechanical leg.

It was the exact sort of story that Finn thought should not be told—especially from someone who is trying to convince others of their chances of success. But this story, despite its gruesome end, was well-liked among the Numberless, who for the first time during the conversation were not trying to one-up Horace. These Numberless had known Titan, known his skill with a blade, and they showed great reverence for his death. A few of the Numberless in particular seemed to revel in the idea that a smaller force could and did defeat a more substantial force by sheer skill and determination alone.

Finn became more depressed as the conversation progressed. He finished his glass of stock but did not care to retrieve another. Instead, he found a plate a food, helping himself. He was not sure if this would be allowed, but no one stopped him, and frankly, he was beyond caring at that point. The food was abundant and filling, but Finn found no pleasure in it. They had failed. He had failed. And worst of all, he had no idea how he could have done any better, no matter what avenue of approach they would have taken. For the first time, he began to realize how hopeless this task really was. They were trying to convince these Numberless to give up all the comforts, freedoms, and security that they had obtained through a life of struggle, for what…the chance of getting a little more freedom. These Numberless already ruled and acted like gods—what motivation could they possibly have to risk all of that.

The meeting eventually came to an abrupt end when the stock ran dry. The room was a mess. Empty kegs and tipped chairs littered the floor. Most of the Numberless had disappeared by now, leaving none behind but the verbose and opinionated. Half-eaten food was scattered across plates and tables alike, creating a minefield of gluttony. At a gesture from Horace, Finn finished his meal and began heading for the door. Seleukus followed, saying his goodbyes as he went.

Finn led the way towards the exit, not bothering to wait for the other two. His frustration was peaking just as the door to the landing platform opened. A second later, he stopped short, his hands mechanically reaching for the sword at his side. At least a dozen Numberless stood before them, their weapons out, their faces hidden by helmets.

Finn took half a step back, bumping into Horace. Horace tucked Finn to the side and stepped forward, his grin gone. "I appreciate you walking us to our ship, but I think we can take it from here."

One of the Numberless pulled off his helmet as he lowered his sword. It was Tiberius. He locked eyes with Horace, his expression stern and unreadable. "That's far enough. You think you could go start a war without asking us first? You think you could try to take on the Decamont in all of their power alone?"

Horace did not respond.

"You think you can have all the fun and not invite us," Tiberius continued.

Horace grinned. "I'd invite you, but I didn't want you to wet your armor in front of your friends."

"The only thing that would scare me," Tiberius replied, "is if you're the one leading this endeavor."

Horace nodded. "I can't argue with that. There's not much room inside for all of your gear, but we should manage." Horace pushed past the Numberless, opening the side door of the CargoLifter by fiddling with his ArmGuard. He stood by the entrance, allowing the other Numberless to enter first.

Finn was so confused he did not know what to do. He stood there, his mouth slightly ajar. Finally, as the last Numberless boarded, Horace called to him. "You coming, string bean?"

TWENTY-FIVE

Finn felt awkward as he traveled, sandwiched between two large Numberless. His own ornate armor seemed dull and plain compared to this new company. He did not hold the metal panel on the wall of the CargoLifter, as he did on the way over. He had attempted to, but as Horace passed him, he pushed Finn into a seat, mumbling something about the panel being fixed. Finn began to think that there was nothing wrong with the metal paneling in the first place.

The CargoLifter did not take long to make the trek back to Titan. They landed with a hiss and filed out. Seleukus followed behind, instructing the Numberless where to go to find their new quarters. They obeyed without complaint, disappearing into the Trinity.

Finn stared at their backs as they walked away, disbelief still evident on his face. Horace slapped him on the back, directing him towards the entrance.

"I'm confused," Finn said. "I thought they voted not to join us in our conflict."

"They voted not to involve their city," Horace said. "But that didn't mean they wanted to avoid the conflict."

"What?"

Horace walked him through the Trinity entrance and directed him to a training room on the Northside. "You've got to understand the mentality of a Numberless. These are they who have never been beaten, not while they went through the Mahghetto and not on the battlefield. They have risen steadily through the ranks, far surpassing each and every one of their peers. They have dominated every challenge and laid low every enemy. And then, they reached the level of the Numberless—and there was no one left to fight. Of course, we do spar each other, honing our skills, but that's a far cry from the melee of battle."

"But why don't they want the support of their city? They all voted against rebellion. I counted twenty of them on the CargoLifter.

Why would they all of a sudden want to join us?"

"They don't want the responsibility of their city being destroyed, but that doesn't mean they shy from the fight."

The doors to a large training room hissed open, revealing even more Numberless inside. Some were training with Arc Blades, others were lounging at a table, and a few others were lifting weights in the far corner of the room.

"Who are all these Numberless?" Finn asked.

"Old drinking buddies," Horace replied. "I've awoken them, explained our situation, and most of them have joined our cause."

"How many have you awoken?"

"Forty or so," Horace replied.

"And those that aren't with us?" Finn asked. "What happens to them?"

"Same as those who are with us," Horace replied. "They go about doing what they would normally do as a Numberless."

"But they could betray us," Finn replied.

"Nah," Horace replied. "There are some who might, but none of these who I've awoken will."

Finn was in an all-out panic. "You can't just let them wander around the city. The Validated will think we are under attack or something. The Numberless were the enemy during the rebellion."

"Relax," Horace replied. "They'll only go in areas where I've restricted access to everyone else. And if they ever do take a stroll through the city, it will be in First or Second Tier Static Armor. So, no one will know."

"Does Cojax know about any of this?"

"Not yet," Horace said. "But, now that you've seen it, you can tell him."

Finn shook his head, trying with his might to wrap his head around their current situation. "Sixty extra warriors—what good will that do? We need the support of a city, not just a few Numberless."

"Ahh," Horace replied. "You haven't seen a Numberless in battle before, have you? Otherwise, you wouldn't be asking such a stupid question."

Finn shrugged.

"Give me a hundred Numberless at my back," Horace said, "and I will destroy cities."

"Well," Finn said. "I don't think we need to destroy them as much as we need to win them over to our side. So was this your plan from the beginning?"

"A city will never come to our side on its own," Horace said. "If that wasn't obvious before, it should be now. But, that doesn't mean we can't take some of the best of their Numberless. You did well back there."

"But I didn't say anything."

"Exactly," Horace replied.

"How many of them could you pull to our side before the Decamont arrive, a hundred? Perhaps two hundred? You think that'll make that much of a difference? Even with a thousand Numberless at your back, how would that change our fate if they sent an endless horde of Roaches against us?"

"Two hundred?" Horace said with surprise. "That sounds a little ambitious. I was only shooting for one hundred, and even that seemed a little steep. Find Seleukus and help him load up some more stock in the CargoLifter."

"Stock?"

"That's only the first city of many. We ain't done yet, string bean."

TWENTY-SIX

Jessica looked down, her mind spinning with the new information. "Can we trust these new Numberless?" It had been a long day of meetings that had turned into debates. These sorts of social encounters drained her energy as much as they seemed to energize Cojax. They walked under an archway, a structure built as a memorial to Achillian, a Numberless who was known as the best tactician to have ever lived. She wanted to hold his hand, but she held back, afraid of how their two BloodBorne bodyguards might react. Ever since Sejanus was killed, the bodyguards were something that Byron insisted upon. Initially, it was to be a group of ten Validated, but Cojax had convinced him only two were needed for the task. It was late. The streets were almost deserted. Even though there was no curfew, most of the Validated preferred to return home early.

Cojax shrugged. "I trust Horace, and he seems to trust them."

"Finn said that some of them aren't even supporting the rebellion. How can we possibly let those individuals run around in the Trinity knowing that at any moment, they could sabotage our power grid, or pass information off to the Decamont? We don't even know what they're capable of."

"We discussed this issue weeks ago in the First Assembly," Cojax replied. "They've taken measures to make sure a Numberless can't access the power mainframe—or have the same privileges they once had."

"Horace still has access to the entire Trinity—as if he owns it. You told me that he once locked you in the training room, and you weren't able to leave. Whatever the First Assembly thought it was doing as a precaution obviously didn't work."

"What are you suggesting?"

Jessica shook her head. "There's sixty of them already—that's even more than they had when we raided the Trinity. Really, we have just two options: we could try to storm the Trinity again, rooting out the Numberless. At least this time, we'd have the backing of the entire city."

Cojax nodded.

"Or we could just trust Horace," Jessica said, her voice taking on a defeated tone. "If we started a war with the Numberless now, I don't think we could win. We have the numbers, and we could eventually wear them down, but at what cost? How many of us would die before we could even fell just one of them? They could just as easily destroy the power grid or sabotage our shields as soon as the conflict started."

Cojax rubbed his hands together, a nervous habit that he had picked up lately. "So once again, our fates are controlled by the Numberless. At least we can trust these ones a little more."

"It only takes one traitor among them to destroy everything."

"But you're right," Cojax said. "If we attacked them now, it would be like trying to take down a wolf with a flock of sheep. And if we did, we'd never have another Numberless fight by our side. And we need them. We need all of them."

"The biggest problem with this situation," Jessica said, "is that we don't know if they serve you or if they serve Horace. Until today, Horace kept this all from you. Until today, Horace is the only one that has communicated with the Numberless he has freed. He could've told them any number of things."

"That's a good point—"

Just then, Cojax was sent pitching forward, a flash of light blazing behind him. Cojax rolled, his Arc Blade in hand. He mechanically attempted to put his helmet on but discovered it had rolled free from his grip in the attack. Jessica donned her own helmet and drew her blade a second later. Several attackers were perched high, their Blazers ripping with light as they shot at the two bodyguards. The two BloodBorne Validated held their ground and faced the threat with Repulse Shields raised and Arc Lances out. They were both First Tiers, elite warriors with tremendous talent.

Jessica linked Comms with Cojax and the bodyguards, "We need to run." She grabbed Cojax by the arm, who seemed stuck between a decision of looking for his helmet and lining up with the other two warriors.

"Come on," Jessica said, her voice becoming more urgent.

"We'll hold them off," replied one of the bodyguards. "You get to safety."

These words seemed to inspire Cojax to action. He took a position behind one of the BloodBorne, his sword at the ready. He linked his shields to the other two, providing additional power to their defenses.

Jessica could not believe what she was seeing. Three men standing their ground against at least a dozen others. The Blazer shots continued to ring out, striking mostly the locked shields of the BloodBorne. They would be able to hold this position almost indefinitely, entrenched behind their shields.

Cojax linked his Comm with the BloodBorne Leadership, conveying the situation and their position. Byron dispatched an entire Phalanx a second later. The estimated time of arrival was two minutes.

Jessica hailed Cojax on the Comm. "If you think their plan is to try and shoot us down with Blazers, you're mistaken. We've got to run. Unlock your shields and—."

She was interrupted by the real attack, which came from behind. Two dozen armed and battle-ready Validated charged, effectively making a horseshoe around them. The bodyguards proved their Tier, reacting quickly, unlinking their shields and facing this new threat. They charged forward with the air of certain victory. But the Blazers still burned from behind, slowing their movements and catching them at odd angles. Then blood began to spill.

The attackers focused their attention on Cojax, giving the other two BloodBorne Validated an opportunity for a vicious counter-attack. Two bodies fell, followed by a third. The attackers were not prepared for such a forceful counterattack. By the time a fourth body fell at the hands of the bodyguards, the attackers were forced to adjust their strategy.

Jessica linked Comms with Cojax, "We've got to leave now!"

Cojax spared Jessica a glance and received a blow to his shoulder for his effort. He refocused on his opponent. Jessica shook her head, scooping Cojax's helmet off the ground, and charged into the mess of Arc Blades and armor. She cut in front of Cojax, throwing his helmet to him while engaging two opponents at once. She was not the better warrior, but her sudden appearance gave her just the right edge to deliver two powerful strikes. But it took a turn for the worse quickly as two Blazers hit her in the leg and shoulder, spinning her to one side. She was hit again by the attackers in front of her and another time from behind. During the brief moment when Cojax was separated from the conflict, Jessica was quickly overwhelmed. The next instant, one of the bodyguard's shields gave way, allowing an Arc Blade to slash him from shoulder to hip. He mechanically continued his fight for seconds longer, not even realizing he was already dead.

Cojax rejoined the fight just long enough to pull Jessica back. The second bodyguard died, putting his body between Cojax and an oncoming attacker. Cojax pushed Jessica into a building, his Arc Blade paring two attacks destined for her back.

The attackers charged forward, encouraged by their retreating quarry. Jessica led the way with Cojax not far behind. They passed into an apartment complex and continued down a hallway. Cojax took two Blazer hits in the back just before they turned a corner. They ran to the end of the hall, where Jessica used her blade to open a door. They found themselves in a small, clean apartment. Jessica pushed on, not waiting to see if the occupants were present or not. At the rear of the apartment, she made quick work of the wall, opening up a small passage into an adjoining room. Cojax slid through, taking a defensive stance just inside. The first unfortunate attacker that followed found Cojax waiting with a blazing Arc Blade. With one terrific swing, head was separated from body. This slowed the subsequent attackers, who hesitated at the entrance. After several long moments, the attackers opted to make their own entrances rather than use the one Jessica had carved.

Jessica used the time to cut another hole in a far wall and a much smaller one in the floor. "Come on, Cojax."

Cojax nodded, following Jessica as she jumped down the hole and disappeared into the darkness. She landed hard on a bed. Cojax landed on the person that was sleeping in that bed. Before the unfortunate woman could activate the lights, Cojax and Jessica were gone, cutting themselves out of the apartment and into a long hallway.

"Where're you going?" Cojax asked through the Comm.

"We've got to backtrack to where we started," Jessica replied.

"Backtrack?" Cojax retorted. "Most of them are probably still back there."

Jessica did not stop, forcing Cojax to follow. When they

reached the end of a hallway, Jessica, using a series of discreet incisions, cut the lock off a storage closet. They stepped inside and shut the door. The locking mechanism no longer worked, but the door closed just as tightly as it had before. Cojax was about to cut another hole down, but Jessica rested a hand on his arm, stopping him just as he pulsed into his Arc Blade.

"We've got to keep moving," Cojax whispered.

Jessica removed her helmet and shook her head, pulling herself closer to Cojax. Cojax did the same and found the closet was barely lit by a small red light high above. Jessica's features almost completely disappeared except for her nose and lips.

"Why'd you stop?" Cojax asked.

"You called the Phalanx to this location," Jessica replied. "Which means it's the last place those attackers will want to be when they arrive."

"*When* they arrive," Cojax reiterated.

"If they haven't started to arrive already, then it won't be long before they do," Jessica replied. She was about to continue speaking, but before she could, Cojax put his finger to his lips. He pulled her close, his hands finding the small of her back. She looked at him, reading his expression. Someone in the hallway was approaching, their steps heavy and careless. The steps became louder until they were just outside the closet door, where they stopped and waited.

Cojax's grip tightened on his Arc Blade, while his other hand readied to don his helmet. Someone was just on the other side of the door. Moments passed. Cojax was torn between charging out and staying where he was.

Then there was shouting further down the hall. Whoever was just outside the door reacted quickly to the coming voices, running in the opposite direction. A pursuit down the hallway ensued.

Cojax and Jessica's ArmGuards began to flash in earnest, signaling an incoming message. They placed their helmets on and were patched through to Byron.

"Cojax…Jessica, where are you?" Byron asked. "Are you alright?"

Cojax sighed. "We're fine. Are you here?"

"Yes," Byron replied, "in force. Send me your coords, and I'll dispatch an escort. We need to extract you as soon as possible."

Cojax was about to, but Jessica stopped him short. "How do we know if we can trust him?"

"Because it's Byron," Cojax answered. "He might lecture us until our ears bleed, but he would never betray us."

Jessica stopped to consider, running the variables through her mind. She finally nodded, and Cojax dispatched the coords.

"We're right next to you—where are you?" Byron said.

"We're one level down," Cojax replied.

"Standby."

Within a few moments, they could hear more Validated running in the hallway, collecting just outside the closet. The door opened, revealing a dozen BloodBorne Validated—Byron was chief among them. He removed his helmet, his expression turning from panic to relief in a matter of seconds.

Cojax stepped out into the hallway, clasping Byron's forearm. "Glad to see you."

Byron's expression shifted again, this time to annoyance. "Well don't just stand there like a fool. We've got to get you out of here." He then turned his attention to Jessica. "We've got to get both of you out of here. Several of the other BloodBorne High Councilors were attacked as well."

"Everyone alright?" Cojax asked.

"Amphis was killed, and Parmenion was wounded. Everyone else is safe and accounted for. Let's get you two to a safe location. Follow me."

TWENTY-SEVEN

"And I say that's not enough," Bryon said, his voice soft but firm.

"So what would you have? An entire Phalanx follow the boy?" Cato replied, his voice full of judgment and condescension. "The only thing he will be in danger of at that point is causing a public nuisance everywhere he goes. If we overreact, it shows fear. It shows weakness."

"If we don't react enough," Byron said, "the Lord High Councilor could end up dead. Then we truly will be weak—we'd have a kingdom without a king."

Orch slouched deeper in his chair as he rotated his head from side to side. "Please don't tell me we're debating this again. I still have a headache from the last four times we discussed it."

It had been three days since the assassination attempt, and in that time, Byron had managed to call five meetings to discuss changes to the security protocol. As of now, Cojax and Jessica's freedom had disappeared entirely. Their personal escort went from two to twenty, with a Phalanx always standing by in a CargoLifter just seconds away at any moment. They were forced to abide by a curfew; they had to change apartments almost every night; they were not allowed to eat their food without it first being tested; and no one was allowed within twenty feet of Cojax unless their loyalty had been vouched for. Jessica took the changes in stride, adjusting to them as quickly as one changes their clothes, but for Cojax, it was altogether more difficult. He felt trapped as if he were once again in the Mahghetto. More and more, Cojax envied Finn's assignment, who spent most of his time going with Horace to various cities.

There had been a gradual change in the way people treated Cojax, which was only made worse by the assassination attempt. It seemed that now that someone thought he was worth killing, it somehow made him much more worth protecting. He became separated from the public, isolated and insular, the exact opposite of his brother Marcus, who encouraged interaction with the crowd. Not a day went by where Cojax did not see some ad with Marcus in it that had him kissing babies or shaking hands with important Validated.

Cojax raised his hand, silencing those around him. That, too, was another thing that seemed to be changing. His voice was metaphorically louder, and although the Council rarely agreed with him, they did listen to what he said. "I thank you, Byron, for your concern. The safety measures have been…comprehensive, to say the least. I agree with Cato. If I'm not safe now, I never will be. If we do more than we've done, we risk broadcasting a message of weakness at best, paranoia at worst. We can't become the political party that's so scared of assassins that we can't function."

Byron nodded respectfully.

Cato rolled his eyes and sat back down.

They were in their assigned conference room at the Trinity. The room was large, domed, and functional, having more than adequate seating for the BloodBorne High Council, attendants, scribes, counselors, and Cojax's new retinue of bodyguards. More and more, it was becoming a political hub, receiving emissaries and visitors from various parties. Their party was not the biggest, by a large margin, but its support was consistent. The Council first met these new situations with chaos and disorder, but now, as the weeks passed, they addressed everything with protocol and procedure. Each meeting was not a shouting match, as Cojax heard it often was in the Populi Party. It was usually governed and controlled, not giving way to vain passions.

In the center of the room was a long, oval table, which mimicked the roof above. High backed, wooden chairs with small cushions circled the room, all of them equal in height and elegance. The only exception was Cojax's chair, which was larger than all the rest and more elaborately carved. It had been made for a mountain of a Numberless, but Cojax seemed to fill it well. It sat apart from the table, dominating it, as a hill before a valley. That, coupled with the four elite bodyguards that surrounded Cojax, made it apparent to anyone who entered who was in charge. Cojax felt self-conscious every time he sat in the carved monstrosity—every time everyone rose when he entered, and when they waited to sit until he had. Byron had insisted on these procedures, and Cojax felt obligated to follow them.

"When will the First Tiers arrive?" Cojax asked one of his

attendants.

"They are scheduled to arrive any time now," the attendant replied.

After a brief investigation, Byron began to suspect that the First Tiers had attempted the assassination. Cojax, however, was not so sure. After the deaths of their top three leaders at the hand of Onar, they were hemorrhaging followers. But Cojax could not see how his death would aid their climb to power or avenge the deaths of their fallen leaders. If anything, the First Tiers would have gone after Onar. He was, after all, the one that started the carnage in the first place. Besides, Cojax had reasoned, the attackers were skilled with the sword, but were certainly not First Tiers. They had been vastly outnumbered and outflanked, and still, were able to hold their own, at least for a time.

Cojax felt nausea return as he thought of the two Validated that gave their lives to protect him and Jessica. He did not even know their names until after they were killed—Simon and Quintus. Jessica had seen how foolish taking a defensive position was. She had known that to stand and fight would be death. Had Cojax ordered the bodyguards to retreat, they would have followed, and they could very well have stayed alive. Retreating, however, did not come naturally to a Validated, and Cojax could not stand to give the order. And now, two Validated were dead because of it.

The conversation continued for another fifteen minutes, Cojax's attention fading in and out the entire time. Finally, an attendant appeared, his face stoic as he bowed before the assembly. "The First Tiers have arrived."

This brought silence to the room, one that was only interrupted by Orch commenting on how late they were.

Cojax nodded to Byron, who, in turn, spoke to the attendant. "Show them in."

"They refuse to give up their weapons," the attendant replied.

"How many are there?" Byron asked.

"Ten."

Cojax again nodded to Byron, who, in turn, spoke to the attendant. "Show them in. They are allowed to retain their weapons."

This, in itself, Cojax meant as an insult. By allowing them to keep their weapons, it signified that even with them, they would be powerless to do much. And indeed, they would be. The twelve BloodBorne High Councilors were almost all First Tiers, each one as talented and as deadly with a sword as the very best in the city. Besides that, the room was circled by guards, attendants, and counselors, who were all armed and armored, as if on the precipice of war.

The First Tiers entered slowly, matching the gaze of everyone that would meet their eyes. They were arrogant and self-assured, acting as conquering heroes returned from war. Their armor glistened with polish; the hilts of their Arc Blades were shiny from regular and repeated use. He had seen many of them on the CityScreens in their glory as they climbed up the Leader Boards. Now they stood as ten suns, their splendor illuminating the room.

Cojax let Byron talk while he simply observed. Byron laid out the facts, gathered either from Adriana's spies or through video evidence obtained of the assassination attempt. The argument was compelling, even to Cojax, who believed it to be false.

The First Tiers endured it well, showing no emotion as Byron levied one accusation after another.

Byron was firm and bold in his word choice. "And so, I lay the evidence bare before you. We have called you in an attempt to resolve this quickly and quietly. It is my opinion, and the opinion of the BloodBorne High Council, that this attempt on Cojax's life was arranged and conducted by the First Tiers. How do you answer these charges?"

"I had knowledge of the assassination attempt," Tidas said, his face curling into a smile, "but I do not know who orchestrated it."

"Was it someone in your political party?" Byron asked.

"Yes, of course."

The room filled with gasps and cries of contempt.

Byron's expression turned rigid and bestial, like that of a bear protecting its cub. "Who was behind the attempt?"

"I already told you," Tidas said, "I don't know, nor do I care. For they failed in their attempt, and so they failed to get my attention."

"Aren't you the leader of your party!" Byron railed. "How are you unaware of what goes on with your own people? Do you have so little control that you can't stop them from attempting to assassinate another party leader?"

"I know my people better than you," Tidas replied. "The

would-be assassins attempted to gain my favor through Cojax's death. We don't have Reevers to slay anymore. We don't have SataniKahns to lay low. So how does one climb the ranks among the First Tiers if they can't prove themselves with acts of bravery?"

"Is this a game to you!" Byron shouted, his face turning as red as blood.

"It is how we govern," Tidas replied. "Those who want title and prestige must prove themselves. It was true before the AC fell, and it's true for the First Tiers now. I did not arrange the assassination of the boy, but I did not stop it either. Had they succeeded, those who planned it would have risen in rank and prestige. But they failed, so they are not here among you."

"This is an act of war," Byron proclaimed. "An attack on our sovereign is an attack on the whole of the BloodBorne. The support for your political party is weak and weakening every day. Ever since you let Onar slay your leaders, your party has been crumbling. And you would challenge us? We have ten men for every one of yours? Is that your aim? To bring us into civil war?"

"It would provide an opportunity for the strongest among us to rise," Tidas said.

"Onar is the strongest one among us," Byron shouted. "He proved that by killing your leaders. And he did so with his shields intact."

Tidas narrowed his eyes, his hand drifting to his sword. "Mention their deaths again, and I will use my Arc Blade to split your body in two."

Byron grabbed his own Arc Blade, sliding it out of the sheath with practiced skill. Before it was free of the scabbard, Cojax stood, raising his hands to silence the hall.

This worked on the BloodBorne, but only encouraged those of the First Tier to laughter.

"So the boy king thinks he commands us as well," Tidas said.

"I don't command you," Cojax said. "But do not mistake me. I don't stop this conflict out of fear, but out of respect."

"Perhaps," Tidas said, "I should be teaching you respect, instead of dealing with one of your minions."

Cojax ignored the insult and continued, stepping down from his seat and circling the room. "I see Ajax here among the First Tiers.

I remember you well. I was in my fourteenth year when you carved into a SataniKahn with nothing more than the end of an Arc Spear. They played that infamous clip for weeks after. And you, Aria, I remember when you led six Validated—what remained of your Phalanx—into the flank of a horde of Roaches. It was insane, and yet you turned the tide of the battle. Tristan, when the Wall was cracked and broken from the enemy, leaving behind a hole only wide enough to fit one Validated, you stood alone and held your ground against countless Roaches. They could not enter because you were a gate that refused to open."

"Are you looking to get our autographs?" Tidas asked.

The other First Tiers shook with laughter.

Instead of being offended, Cojax laughed with them as if he was part of the joke and not the butt of it. When it fell silent again, he continued his walk around the room, meeting each of their eyes in turn—not with intimidation, but out of admiration. He spoke of Critius, who, when trapped in a Roach hole, defended ten other wounded Validated for the better part of a day before they could be rescued.

"And then there's Clandis, someone I have long admired and studied. Clandis is different from so many other Validated I've seen on the CityScreens. He has skill with the blade and is a god on the battlefield, but his real genius is that of a tactician. I've seen Clandis perform the same perfunctory battle formations as so many commanders before him, but then employ subtle, unique orders to his unit. These small differences added up to dramatic results. What so many before took as gospel, Clandis questioned, changed, and improved upon."

Cojax went through each of the First Tiers, citing their glorious deeds. The only person he failed to mention was Tidas. When Cojax finished his natural pace around the room, he arrived at his seat almost at the same time he stopped speaking.

"I'm glad to see we've got a fan among us," Tidas said.

"You have more than that," Cojax said. "Your deeds are those that protect the weak from the strong, and for that, you have my respect. You and I are not so different—just different sides of the same coin. I'm blessed with a myriad of followers, but I lack leaders, and you have the leaders, but are losing followers."

"Do not think you can flatter us into joining you," Tidas replied, his voice taking on a hint of annoyance.

"No flattery," Cojax answered. "Words are worth little once spoken. Even if I could convince you to join our ranks, what's to say someone else can't convince you to leave just as easily? Loyalty begets loyalty—so let me be the first to be loyal to you."

"I'm confused," Tidas said. "Did you not hear? One of our rank tried to kill you not three days prior."

"I'm reorganizing my armies," Cojax said, ignoring the previous comment.

Cato raised his hand to interrupt, "Cojax, if I may interject…."

"No, you may not," Cojax replied. He turned his attention back to Tidas, who arched his eyebrows with curiosity.

"I have found that they are strong, but, as with all blades, they'll become dull unless they're sharpened. I'm in need of six Omegas to rule over my armies—to direct them as needed. To be the sword and shield of our great city."

"Now you mock us," Tidas said. "What you offer is title only, something to satiate pride."

"No," Cojax shook his head. "Did I not begin with your great deeds? Did I not explain to you how much capacity all of you have? You are truly some of our greatest Validated—why would I not invite you to our table?"

"You would not offer command of your armies to us," Tidas said.

"I need six Omegas to command our armies," Cojax said. "And I offer these positions to you—without reservation or hesitation."

"Sir," Cato said, "this is something we need to discuss before the Council."

Cojax shook his head. "Not this time. These men and women here have proven to be the most capable—which is exactly what we need. If I were a butcher, wouldn't I use the sharpest knives to cut the meat?"

"What sort of fools do you take us for," Tidas said, his voice taking on a mocking tone. "We won't serve you!"

"I cannot use all of you," Cojax said in a low, contrite tone. "Unfortunately, your numbers outpace my needs. I only need six Omegas to lead; I already have another six that have proven their command. I can't take all of you, despite your skill. So, who can I trust to lead my armies?"

Tidas looked at each of the First Tiers in turn. None of them seemed willing to meet his eyes.

"You might be asking yourself," Cojax said, "what kind of treatment can you expect in my army? You'll be granted title and privilege, respect, and notoriety. There is a great need for your skill and talent, and so you will be well received."

Tidas laughed. "You are absurd—no one here would—"

Clandis stepped forward, his hand collapsing into a salute. "I will serve you, Cojax Artino, Lord of the BloodBorne, Son of Titan. Give me command of some of your best soldiers, and I will ensure that when battle comes, the Decamont will fall."

"Get back in formation," Tidas yelled.

"That's one," Cojax said. "Since you were the first to speak, your force shall be the vanguard of my army. Only five more positions are still available. Who shall answer the call and lead our warriors against the Decamont?"

There was a pause before three of the First Tiers spoke at once, all of them stepping forward with a rush, all of them swearing their fealty to Cojax.

"Two positions left," Cojax said.

Tidas' face was burning with rage. "First Tiers, on me. Let's leave these Dependents and traitors." He turned and fled the room, his cape flapping wildly as he did. Of the five that were left, only two followed. The others competed with each other to swear to Cojax their allegiance.

"Because you three were so eager," Cojax replied. "I will accept you into our rank with honor and privilege as Omegas. But my army is in need of Invictors and Gammas to command my Decurias. I need Magisters to train my men; I need Kappas to command my Quorums. Now that you serve me, seek those of talent among the First Tiers and bring them to our side. If they want a position of privilege and power, they have only today to swear to me their loyalty. Now go."

TWENTY-EIGHT

When the seven First Tiers left, the room exploded with noise. Shouting, yelling, and even some applause echoed in Cojax's ears. He was still standing, his hand on his chest from the salute he returned to the First Tiers.

Cato took to the center of the room, "You go too far, Cojax. Even for you! You talk of loyalty, and yet, you just demoted half of the leadership in your army to accommodate those arrogant Dependents. We already have structure and rank. We've already assigned those positions to those who now faithfully serve you. Why would you even contemplate such an idea?"

Orch stood, his hands slamming on the table. "Because he just prevented civil war! Are you so blind that you can't see past your inflated pride? Ten of the most talented warriors entered this room, and when they left, seven of them had sworn allegiance to the BloodBorne."

"You offered them too much," Parmenion said. "We'll have to adjust the entire command structure."

"We won't offer them real positions," Byron said. "Cojax did what he did to prevent war, but we won't be offering them actual positions of power, right Cojax?"

Cojax lowered the hand from his chest, seeming to notice everyone for the first time. He sat down, his chest heavy from the weight of his office.

"Cojax," Byron said anew, "you can't seriously be contemplating giving the leadership of the army to those First Tiers. Give them titles and hollow positions but nothing more. We can't demote those in the BloodBorne who have served you faithfully."

Cojax looked at Byron for the first time. "It won't be easy, but it is necessary."

Again, the room exploded into vehement protests. "You would reward the very people that tried to have you killed!"

"Where is your honor!"

"This is an outrage!"

Cojax raised his hands. "We are not a disorganized rabble. If we can't have a civil conversation about this, then we will not have one at all!" Despite his best effort, Cojax could not regain order. He tried again. This time his words were drowned out even before they left his mouth. Private feuds broke out. Some shouted in favor of Cojax, the vast majority were against. They were only seconds away from weapons being drawn and blood being spilled.

Then three precise Blazer shots ripped through the air, slicing a chandelier free from the roof above. It came crashing down, sending crystals flipping in every direction. The noise was deafening and sudden, sending the BloodBorne High Councilors into a panic. Weapons were drawn as they sought to find the enemy in the room.

Orch leaped onto the table, landing heavily on the chandelier and crushing it underfoot. In his right hand, he held the Blazer that shot free the chandelier. Silence fell as all eyes turned to Orch. The slender man spoke, his voice dominating the room. "I guess it's true what they say that he who makes the most noise is the most correct." He stepped over the chandelier, sweeping the barrel of his weapon past each Councilor. No one had their helmets on and a precise shot from the Blazer could very well split a skull.

"I have known Cojax since the Mahghetto, where I trained him in the use of the Blazer," Orch proclaimed. "Of all the blazing foolish things I saw him do, this was by far the most brilliant. Can't you see what he just did? Can't you recognize what he just prevented? We were on the precipice of civil war, were we not?" With hardly even aiming, Orch fired his Blazer again, severing a thin cord of another chandelier on the opposite end of the room. The shot was impressive by anyone's standards, but especially since it took so little effort. The chandelier came crashing down, exploding into metal and crystal fragments.

"Let's look at this logically, shall we?" Orch said. "Byron is an honorable man and would have been honor-bound to demand justice on behalf of the Lord he serves. We would have presented the evidence to the First Assembly, and they would have condemned the First Tiers, but no action would have been taken. The other parties would like nothing better than to see our party fight it out with the First Tiers. Remember, the other political parties are our competitors, not our comrades. We would be disappointed with the inaction of the First Assembly, and so the conflict would escalate. And the First Tiers would have gotten what they wanted all along—civil war. We have the numbers; they have the skill. It's a last-ditch gambit to seize power, but it's all they have left.

"Whether by some luck or by the grace of providence, Cojax was able to see what most of these First Tiers really wanted—that is, to be seen as they once were. As men and women of respect and power. They will not be placated with soup when they know they deserve steak. We would be stripping several BloodBorne of rank, yes, but did they earn those positions? Did they climb up the ranks as did the First Tiers, sacrificing all to reach their post? No, they were given them because many of the First Tiers were no longer available to command. Remember, it was the First Tiers that commanded our armies and governed our people. They are by far the best suited for the position, so why should we not give it to them?"

"How can we trust them?" Cato asked, his tone even but unyielding.

"They're not traitors," Orch said. "They're just men and women who know they deserve more than what they're getting. As Cojax said, 'loyalty begets loyalty.' We can put in place measures that ensure our armies are loyal to Cojax and not to the Omegas—just in case they have nefarious goals. But how can we deny the best tools for the job? They are brilliant on the battlefield and skilled with the Arc Blade, and so, with their backing, we will have one thing that no other political party has—a real army."

Orch shot free the last chandelier at the furthest end of the room. It came smashing down like the two before.

"Why'd you shoot that one?" Byron demanded. "You've already made your point."

Orch shrugged. "The room was uneven with only one chandelier still in place."

The BloodBorne High Councilors continued to debate the topic, and eventually, a vote was called. Adriana and Orch voted to uphold Cojax's plan, several others voted against. The deciding vote came down to Byron, who stared directly at Cojax as he cast his vote. It was close, but Cojax's plan was upheld.

Once the final tally was completed, Cato stood, removed his

sword from his side, and dropped it on the table. "I can't in good conscious spit on the faces of our brothers and sisters, whose only crime is loyalty to a false king. I thought I could help lead the BloodBorne to become something better, but that's impossible—now that the BloodBorne is ruled by a self-absorbed Dependent. We will all end up dead if we remain on this path, mark my words. I will no longer follow a child, who, by the way, was in the Tenth Tier when the AC fell. Titan was blinded by his own affection for this boy, but I am not. I urge all of you to come to your senses." With this, he left the room never to return again.

Parmenion stood as well, removed his sword, and dropped it onto the table in dramatic fashion. "Ten years I have carried this blade given to me by the BloodBorne, and for ten years, I have not dishonored it. And now I see that, for me to retain my honor, I will have to leave my blade." Then Diagoras stood, a tall powerful woman with sharp eyes. Without a word, she saluted Byron and exited the room. Seven aids and assistants followed not too far behind.

"At least there will be more food to go around when lunch is served," Orch said.

"Oh, Shut up," Byron said.

TWENTY-NINE

"No peeking," Cojax said.

"Even if I could see through this blindfold, I think it would be too dark to see anything," Jessica replied.

Cojax shook his head. "You are peeking! I knew it."

"What?" Jessica said with feigned innocence.

"How did you know it was dark unless you were peeking?"

Jessica laughed with such warmth it made Cojax smile. "Well, maybe a little."

Cojax kissed Jessica gently on the lips. As he pulled away, he untied the blindfold, revealing their surroundings.

Jessica looked around, instantly recognizing their location. They were in the belly of the Mahghetto, in the training room where they first were introduced to the Blazer.

Jessica raised her eyebrows. "Isn't this the room where a group of ten Disciples tried to kill me with their Blazers?"

"Umm," Cojax said, his mind thinking of a reply. "I like to think of this as the room where you kicked all of their butts."

Jessica laughed. "I guess that's one way to look at it."

"Well," Cojax replied. "It's one of the few rooms I could convince our bodyguards to give us some more breathing room."

"There are no bodyguards nearby?"

"Byron insisted on there being a dozen or so in a room down the hall, but they won't interrupt us as long as we don't hail them on the Comms."

"So, they can't hear us?"

"No."

Jessica stepped forward, her head tipped up to Cojax. "Well, why didn't you say that earlier?" She kissed him softly, enjoying the taste of his lips. As the kiss persisted, it became more passionate. She raked her fingers through his hair and down his muscular arms. He kissed back, his hands pulling her closer.

As the kiss broke, Cojax's lips drifted to the side of her neck. She closed her eyes, letting a feeling of ecstasy twist through her body.

"And this was usually the time in the Mahghetto," Jessica whispered, "when your Static Armor would begin holding a charge."

Cojax laughed. "Yes, it was. But we don't have to worry about that stopping us now."

She pushed him against the wall, knocking the breath from his lungs, and resumed kissing. As their bodies pressed closer, they could feel each other's quickened heartbeat.

Cojax pulled back, his hand brushing Jessica's hair from her eyes. "I love you Jessica, and I always will. I love you for who you are—for who you have always been. I love your compassion for others, your humility, your endless determination."

She closed her eyes, a sudden pain in her chest.

Cojax noticed the change and looked down, a frown replacing his smile. "What's wrong?"

"I love you too, Cojax," Jessica said, her voice turning into a monotone. "But there's something I need to tell you."

"What? Tell me."

"Let's sit down."

Cojax gestured to an area across the dimly lit space. "Of course. I've got something to show you. I've got it all set up." He excitedly grabbed her hand and pulled her across the room to a blanket that had been set out on the floor. On the blanket was a large metal tin, two candles, and a small barrel of something she did not recognize.

Jessica covered her mouth, her body overcome with emotion. "You did all of this?"

Cojax busied himself lighting the candles. "You have no idea how rare candles are in this city. I had to turn the Trinity upside down before I found a Numberless who knew how to print a few." As the light increased in the room, he was able to notice that she was crying.

He stood up, his hands finding the sides of her arms. "What's wrong? Are you still thinking about the assassination attempt? It was certainly close, but—."

"—It's not that," Jessica replied.

Cojax pulled her into an embrace, her head fit perfectly below his powerful jaw. He squeezed her tightly. "You can tell me anything. What's wrong?"

Jessica wiped her tears away. "I can be so foolish sometimes. I should have told you earlier. It's just that everything has happened so fast since the Mahghetto."

"You're starting to worry me," Cojax said in a teasing voice. "Come on. It can't be that bad. Am I a bad kisser?" This seemed to ease the tension ever so slightly.

Jessica laughed. "You're perfect. You know that. I hope you always stay that way. I hope you always stay someone who is quick to smile and slow to judge."

"Well, I could just as easily say the same about you."

"That's just it, Cojax. You are not the same as me."

"What do you mean?"

"I won't blame you if you don't want to be with me once you know. I will still support you regardless. I always will. I truly believe you are the only one that can get us ready to face the Decamont." Cojax began to speak, but Jessica cut him off. "Please, let me finish. You have to know this. I am different than you. Humans are not Acadians. When I first arrived in this city, I had no chance to complete the Mahghetto. You know I had help, but I don't think you know how much. I could not physically handle the training, and so Elena began an experimental gene manipulation and hormonal therapy on my body. The process could have killed me, but by some miracle, it didn't. It initially turned my bones to iron and my muscles into cords of steel. It increased my reflex speed, my senses, and mental function until I could almost pass for an Acadian."

Jessica sat down, pulling Cojax to the floor with her. "But that all came at a price. A very high price."

"What price?"

"I will die in a few years."

Cojax felt a hammer hit his chest. He swallowed, straining his eyes in the low light. "We have the most advanced medicine in the world, Jessica. I'm sure the Numberless know about some treatment that can reverse those things. At the very least, I've heard that the Stasis Chambers are designed to not only keep someone in stasis, but heal them as well."

"It can only heal those who have external wounds, not the decay of internal organs. I've looked for answers through the Numberless Information Network, and so has Finn."

"Finn?"

"Well, Finn actually asked Horace about it."

"So Horace knew about this before I did?"

"I didn't want to burden you with it if there was an easy fix. But, Horace, after looking at recent scans of my body, didn't seem optimistic. He said he would get the smartest individuals he knew to start working on the problem, but that he didn't want to give me false hope."

"There has to be some way around this."

"I won't ever just give up, but I could not stand to deceive you anymore. There are things that might work to delay the inevitable, but the process wasn't just hard on one part of my body. It damaged all of it."

"How long do you have?"

"Well, Elena's calculations were much more optimistic: she calculated that my bones would become brittle by the time I'm twenty-two and that my nervous system will begin to lose connectivity and result in eventual paralysis. She said that I would begin to experience memory loss, decrease in motor control, hand-eye coordination, and vision by the time I am twenty-five. She said my liver would be eaten through by the time I'm twenty-six; that my heart will fail around the age of twenty-eight; and that my lungs will collapse by the time I'm thirty. But that was only her best guesses. Horace, however, thinks I have much less time."

"How long?"

"He thinks I'll be dead by twenty-two, maybe sooner. But even before that, my body will begin to fall apart."

"How are you feeling now?"

Jessica swallowed. "My hands are starting to go numb. Sometimes, I can't feel my fingers for a few minutes each day. That's what prompted me to talk to Finn about it in the first place."

"That's far sooner than Elena predicted."

"She was only guessing."

"Why didn't you tell me this?"

Jessica shook her head, unable to answer the question. Her chest tightened with emotion before she was able to push it down. "Please, don't waste your love on me, Cojax. You must be the Lord of our city, and I can't let my problems weigh you down."

Cojax felt tears welling in his eyes. "It's not your problem alone; it is *our* problem. And If I am ever elected to be the Lord of this city, you will be at my side, as my Queen. And together, we will come up with a solution."

"But, Cojax what if there is no solution—."

"—Then I would rather spend a few good years with you than live a thousand years with anyone else. Jessica, you mean more to me than life itself. I love you."

He kissed her, tasting her tears on his lips. Then he pulled her into a deep embrace.

Jessica clung to the embrace with desperation. "You're such a good man."

"I don't know how good I am," Cojax replied, forcing levity into his voice. "I let our food get cold while we talked."

She laughed.

Cojax wiped at his cheeks before speaking. "Horace put in this food order for me specifically, so we'd better not let it go to waste. Come on, let's eat. Have you ever had lobster before?"

"What is it?"

"Let's find out together."

THIRTY

The members of the First Assembly were much more subdued than normal, their burdens of state had now begun to show on their faces. Even the Populi Party was quieter. Roll was called and all political parties were found to be present.

"We must take into consideration," Melina said, her voice amplified by speakers. "The sudden shift of support away from the First Tiers. Upon complete investigation, it has been deemed that the total support for the First Tiers has fallen below a consequential level. The First Tier Political Party is hereby dissolved and will no longer be recognized by the First Assembly."

This brought the noise that was so absent before. The First Tiers, although only a few remained, were in an uproar, crying foul and asking for a recount. It was all in vain, however, as no political party would come to their aid. Tidas went on for a minute about how unfair voting practices led to this travesty and that all voting had to be suspended until a complete investigation could be conducted. This was put to a vote and, unanimously, denied by the other political parties. Tidas continued his grievance, appealing to the sympathies of the highest Tiers, but it all fell on deaf ears. Eventually, the Arbiters lost patience and had the remaining First Tiers escorted out.

"It has been found that among the remaining political parties," the Arbiter continued, "that the Populi Party has forty-five percent of the vote, and the BloodBorne Faction has thirty-five percent. The Restorationists have ten percent, while the Unbroken, who are led by Onar, have five percent of the voting bloc. As a reminder, whichever political party obtains sixty percent of the voting block will be declared the dominate party and will be instituted as the governing body."

As usual, the remaining four political parties were given some time to present the precepts of their party in an effort to convince those that were watching from their apartments to join. The Populi Party went first, as was their right as the prevailing party, followed by

Cojax, the Restorationists, and the Unbroken. The Populi Party leaders tried something new, involving multiple individuals from various Tiers. Each one briefly related their personal history as well as affirming their support of the Populi Party.

Cojax allowed Byron to speak when it was their turn. He stood and in a bold voice spoke of the coming invasion of the Decamont. When it was the Restorationists' turn, they spent their time railing on all the inefficiencies that had occurred since the fall of the AC and how all problems would be solved if they restored the meritocracy. Finally, when the time was turned to Onar, he said nothing.

The floor was then opened up to the various political parties. In a surprising move, the Restorationists requested the floor, which was granted. Deo, a lean, toned man in the twilight of his life, stood and approached the assembly. He had black hair that, in parts, was turning white, an uncommon feature in a Validated, but not unseemly. The man was tall and stately, his armor worn but well maintained. On his chest, in the middle of his Placard, he had written his Score, as was the custom of the Restorationists, but he had done so with a calligrapher's hand. His regal voice carried to the whole assembly without the use of a microphone.

"Once again, I address this assembly, and once again, I find it lacking," Deo said. "My people have been under attack since the AC first fell. We've been subjected to muggings, thefts, and murders. None of these crimes existed when the AC still stood. My people require order; we need protection. And despite all of the talking we do here, nothing changes."

"Do you wish to submit a proposal to the First Assembly?" an Arbiter asked.

"For the time being, until a dominant political party is established, I propose that the Acadian Code be reinstituted in its entirety—with the exception of Riftings and Releases. Must I remind you that at no other time have we been stronger as when we were under the AC."

Marcus raised his hand. When the Arbiter called on him, he stood, addressing the First Assembly. "Why don't you police your own people? As do the rest of us?"

"And let's just ask your friend Sejanus," Deo said, with a tight smile, "how effective that was." He paused for a moment to let his words sink in. "The Restorationist Party has made their stance clear on this matter: we will not form a policing force, nor a system of laws, judges, or incarceration because it is ineffectual at best, corrupt at worst. We will not sustain an unsustainable system. History has well proven this over and over again. If we form a policing force, we sow a bed of corruption, incompetence, and injustice. And once instituted, it will not be easily discarded. This has been true among all societies, without exception. All of us have been subjected to the increase in crime. And just last week, an attempt was made on the leader of the BloodBorne Party. Sejanus of the Populi Party was murdered in the middle of the street. Let's not forget the assassination of Abria, Bacis, and Cineas, former leaders of the First Tiers. From our own Restorationist Party, we have lost Demetrius and Tarsus, who were mugged and murdered while on assignment. If we do not act quickly, whatever action we eventually take, will not be enough."

Marcus continued, "I understand why you believe a policing force would hamper your political movement, but why doesn't your party institute a temporary policing force?"

"Why would we revert to something so archaic," Deo answered, "when we had a system that has proven so efficient? Can't any of you understand that? Crime, theft, beatings, and even murder were words we only read in books. Now we face these atrocities, and we pretend we don't have a solution. I demand that if you will not grant it to the entire city, that at least the Restorationist Party be restored to the Acadian Code."

The debate continued, each of the other three parties denouncing the plan in turn. A final vote was called, and the motion was not carried.

"I see, once again," Deo said, "that you have chosen the path of fools. The truth is, this First Assembly is no better than the Numberless. They used the threat of the Roaches to hold freedom over our heads. Now, members of the First Assembly use the idea of the Decamont invasion in much the same way. You're a bunch of fear mongers and hypocrites. If the Decamont was going to attack, where are they? Can you answer me that, Lord Cojax of the BloodBorne? If they are so powerful, why do they wait? The answer is simple: because there is no Decamont invasion coming. It is a lie. Lord Cojax Artino used this lie to abolish the Acadian Code. And we went along with it so willingly, as lambs before the slaughter. And once the AC was ripped down, it allowed all those in this room to live beyond their means. Have you noticed the smaller portions of food? Or the frigid showers? Or the delays in waiting for a HoverBucket to transport you throughout the city? There was always plenty under the AC, but there is not enough now. So what has changed?" Deo pointed a cruel finger towards Cojax. "Those in this room now take more than they've earned, leaving much less for the rest of us. Restore the AC, and you restore order. Restore the AC, and you take away the power of these new tyrants."

THIRTY-ONE

The HoverBucket landed heavily on the landing pad. Finn's heart felt just as heavy. He had been traveling with Horace and Seleukus for the better part of a month, gaining few followers, but never the support of an entire city. They were now landing in a city called Rome, which was located on a narrow piece of flat land on the crest of a hill. The city was built higher than any Finn had seen. The tallest building in Titan would not have even appeared in the skyline of Rome. The Romans preferred columns and terracotta tiles, as did the Titans, but they were much more liberal with their use of domes, triumphant arches, and ornate Corinthian columns.

Horace was the first to exit, followed by Seleukus. Finn was slower to step off the craft, especially since he was required to leave his Arc Blade, Repulse Shield, and Helmet behind.

There were three Numberless who greeted them, all with blades in their hands and helmets guarding their faces—a colder reception than usual. Their armor had a much different appearance, despite having the same function. Their helmets were flat on top with no frill, and more open around the face, granting the wearer increased vision. Their breastplates were segmented, like a lobster's tail, and they seemed to prefer a straight short sword called a gladius to the curved falcata.

Horace had never been to this city, nor had anyone else from Titan. They only knew about this location from Tiberius, one of the other Numberless they had recently recruited. Despite a few differences, Tiberius insisted that Rome's government functioned like every other city they had visited and that the Trinity had almost exactly the same layout.

Finn swallowed hard, trying to keep his fake smile fixed to his face. He had played this role so many times, he had begun to believe he was mastering it. But then Horace told him he was more likely to sprout a set of wings than to fool anyone with that smile.

Horace opened his arms wide, carefully showing that he had no weapons in his hands. Up to this point, they had been received in many of the cities they had visited in large part because the people there knew Horace personally. But the further they ventured from cities that knew Horace or Titan, the colder their receptions became. And consequently, fewer and fewer Numberless seemed willing to join their ranks.

Their strategy—as Finn pointed out to Horace one day—would not last forever. So, when it came to the unknown and unvisited city of Rome, they were going to try Finn's idea.

As with so many times before, Seleukus opened up the side panel of the CargoLifter, showing off his kegs of stock. The Romans did not appear interested. They stood as still as statues, not even lowering their weapons.

"Come now," Horace persisted. "Just because we've never met, doesn't mean we can't crack open a keg. This is an envoy of friendship, not war."

One of the Romans approached, pointing with his sword as he did. "Your presence is a violation of the RC. Leave now."

"Easy there, lad," Horace said. "I think you misunderstand our intentions. We've come bearing gifts. You've heard of stock before, right? You don't need a blade so much as you do a mug."

The Roman was obviously speaking over the Comm with some of his companions because he took a long time to respond. "Are you from the city that has rebelled?"

"Rebelled?" Horace said. "Is that how people have been phrasing it? We answer to no one but ourselves—if that's what you mean. But I'm not here on orders anyway. I just like visiting other cities."

"By order of our Infinite Council, we cannot abide you here," the Roman responded.

"Abide me?" Horace asked. "I haven't heard anyone say that before.'"

"The Council has spoken," the Roman replied. "If you fail to leave, we will use lethal force."

"If you're going to act like this, why didn't you just shoot us out of the sky as we approached?" Horace said gruffly.

"So that we could tell you directly," the Roman replied. "Leave now and never return. And if you ever do, you'll be treated as an enemy of Rome."

"Alright," Horace laughed. "As a parting gift, let me at least leave you a keg."

"No," the Roman replied. "We don't want anything from you. Return to your CargoLifter."

Horace stared blankly at the man, waiting for something to happen. It turned awkward as the seconds past, the two men staring at each other.

Then they both spoke at once.

While Horace spoke, he looked up into the clouds, as if he was trying to barter with the gods above. "As a parting gift...."

"This is your last warning—"

The Roman was cut short as a Numberless from above landed on top of him, an Arc Blade slamming into his shields. Six more Numberless fell from the sky, as fiery bombs, landing in a flurry of light and speed. The sight was so impressive, Finn nearly forgot to do the one critical task that he had been given. The platform turned into a battlefield, as swords met with shields. Outnumbered and overwhelmed, the Romans were soon subdued, their shields drained. Finn reached the platform door, just as it was closing. Using his shield, he sent a pulse into it, creating an energy bubble. This shield, despite its normal appearance, had been adjusted and its power amplified. It was no longer a defensive tool used on the battlefield, but it had been changed into a miniature shield generator. As the gate to the Trinity was closing, it was stopped short by Finn's shield.

"Come on," Finn shouted, "the gate is down!"

More Numberless fell from the sky, hitting with so much force the landing pad seemed to groan. Ten, fifteen, twenty. With each second, their numbers grew. They poured in past Finn, who shouted them on.

Inside the Trinity, Roman defensive measures activated, powering two Gouger cannons that opened fire. These would have stopped a Phalanx in its tracks, but they did little against a Numberless. The elite warriors spread through the room, wreaking havoc on every threat present. Within seconds, the Gougers had been grated to pieces. More Numberless flooded in, eager for battle. Forty, fifty, sixty. Finn looked at his shield generator; the power indicator was blinking red.

Seventy. Eighty. Ninety.

"Push through!" Finn said. "The gate is about to collapse."

From outside, a Roman CargoLifter appeared, armed with massive cannons that burned with light. The next moment, the CargoLifter they had arrived in exploded into white flames.

Horace was the last one to enter. In his hands, he had Finn's helmet, Arc Lance, and Arc Blade. "Here you are, string bean. Keep your head down and stay alive."

"But the CargoLifter," Finn said. "We've just lost our retreat."

"Nothing compels a group of warriors to fight as hard as when they realize that they have no other choice," Horace replied. He grabbed Finn, pulling him forward. The next second, the shield generator gave out, allowing the gate to slam shut, barely missing Finn. Finn looked between the now shut gate and Horace, his expression unreadable.

"That would've killed you, string bean," Horace growled. The broad warrior turned to go, but Finn called him back.

"Where do you need me?"

"I need you to survive," Horace replied.

Finn blinked twice, his mind not comprehending the old warrior's words. "I can handle my own. I was there when we stormed the Trinity the first time."

Horace winked just before he put on his own helmet. "Stay here—that's an order from Cojax. If we do need to withdraw, we will need this landing pad open so our ships can land." He then joined a group of Numberless that were advancing down a hall.

Finn shook his head, knowing that almost as quickly as the battle had begun, he had been cut out of it. What's worse, this had been his plan, and now he would not be able to see it through. He had no fantastical notions that he could take down a Numberless on his own, but he had, at least, hoped to fight alongside them.

The Romans were caught off guard, but reacted quickly, recalling all Numberless to the Trinity. For a time, everything went quiet. Horace divided his forces into three parts: one heading for the Stasis Chambers, another to the Main Control Room, and the third to blockade any entry point along the way. Horace took the command of the warriors heading down to the Main Control Room. They took their time through the hallway, hoping that their caution would be worth the delay.

Upon arriving at the stairs, they took them three at a time, their heavy armor announcing their presence as they went. When they finally arrived at the correct floor, they fanned out, weapons raised. This level opened up to a large, domed room—much larger than any room they had in the Trinity in Titan. There was a podium on one side, as well as several benches that were draped in red and white. It was some sort of city forum. But Horace did not focus on the benches so much as he did the amassing ranks of Romans who began forming into tight, unique formations. It took Horace a second to realize it, but these were not Numberless that they faced, but simple Validated.

Horace began the death rattle, beating his Arc Spear against his shield, and linking his shields to those around him. The other Numberless picked up the beat, and soon it grew to a deafening sound. "Spare them if you can!" The Titans picked up the pace, heading straight for the Romans' center. The Romans opened fire, not with Blazers, but with some sort of Arc Spear that was meant to be thrown. The weapon would have effectively slowed the charge of unarmored Roaches, but it did little to impede the Numberless.

The Numberless crashed into their opponents in a terrific, blinding light. The Romans stood their ground, using their small, straight blades to stab the Titans whenever possible. Romans began to fall, first a few, then several dozen. Blood mixed with bodies, as they fell as wheat before the harvester. Horace quickly realized that the Romans used a different system of armor linking than did the Titans. When shields were locked in a Phalanx formation it created an impenetrable wall that disappeared only when the majority of shields were weakened beyond a certain point; the Romans, on the other hand, were only protected for a few blows by their shared shields before it reverted to the exclusive use and charge of their personal armor, allowing them to be individually cut down. Instead of an entire unit's shields going down all at once, this allowed new warriors to file in from the back, taking the place of the fallen, which constantly rejuvenated the overall collective shield.

Horace pulled back from the conflict, his warriors giving him a wide berth. He fiddled with his ArmGuard until HoverCams were released from his armor. They rose into the air, giving Horace a tactical eye over the field of battle. They were winning, of that, there was no doubt, and this conflict would undoubtedly end in their victory. But it was taking too long, far too long. They were gaining ground, but only inches at a time. At this rate, it would be half an hour before they could reach the first door to the Main Control Room.

Horace shook his head. "Something's…not right. Why are they stalling? Where are their Numberless?" The old warrior linked his Comm to Finn. "Are you there, string bean? We've run into their forces, but there are no Numberless here. I don't like it. This could be a trap."

Finn was about to respond when the rear gate flew open. He now stood face to face with a dozen Roman Numberless, all armed and ready for war. They raised their weapons and were about to rush in when Finn used the manual controls to shut the door. A second later, the door opened again. A half-second after that, Finn shut it again. When it opened a third time, and Finn closed it for the third time, one of the Numberless stepped forward just in time to have the door crush him against the frame. The shields of the Numberless prevented him from being turned into a grease spot, but his helmet popped off from the impact.

Finn's face was only inches away from the man, whose blood-shot eyes stared intently at him. The man reached with a free hand, swiping at Finn's helmet. The gate opened again, and the man fell to the floor, allowing the other Numberless to pour in. Finn tried to shut the door again manually, but this time his controls had been overridden.

He raised his Arc Blade, his mind a blur. Horace had been trying to keep him from the conflict, but now, he was neck-deep in it. "Don't do me any favors in the future, Horace," Finn whispered.

"Surrender or we—"

Finn dropped his Arc Blade to the ground before the Roman could finish her sentence. The Romans looked at each other, unsure of how to proceed. They expected more resistance. They planned on cutting down their opponent as soon as he raised his blade. Now they were in unknown territory, never having to take another Validated as a prisoner of war before.

Finn raised his hands, placing them behind his head, which allowed his fingers to barely touch the Arc Spear that was fastened to his back. Finn had noticed early on, that these Romans did not carry

Arc Spears, and so there was a chance they were unfamiliar with the weapon and its placement on the back. He could grab it, he was sure. *"But then what?"* He asked himself. *"What does that do?"* He pushed the thought down, not wanting to consider his rash actions. His heart pounded against his chest, sharpening his senses. One of the rear Numberless seemed to become restless and was trying to circumvent his comrades. Another in the front teetered on her back foot as if she was preparing to charge.

Finn yelled, ripping the Arc Spear off his back in dramatic fashion. He sent a pulse through the weapon and it expanded to its full length. He whipped the spear through the air, twisting it around his body. Horace had neglected to teach Finn the Arc Blade but had been liberal with his instruction of the spear. He pushed Horace's recent training to the front of his mind, and he began to move around the room, putting one opponent in front of the rest.

Unimpressed by the display, his opponents attacked, all twelve of them rushing in with an appetite for blood. Holding one Numberless at bay with a spear was possible, as Horace had instructed him, but a group of Numberless was an entirely different matter. He struck a Numberless in the chest, swept the leg of another, hit the helmet of a third. Between his spear and his agility, he was just barely able to keep his distance from the tide of elite warriors. He passed into a narrow hallway, shutting a door as he went. When the Numberless opened it, he jammed his spear into an opponent's neck, which exploded with light.

Too late, Finn realized his mistake. He now was in a narrow hallway, making his spear much less effective. He managed two more strikes before a terrific blow sent him spinning to a knee. Two more followed, completely neutralizing his shields. He fell to both knees, his energy suddenly drained. He tried one more thrust of the spear, but it was taken from him as soon as he raised it.

"Take him," said one of the Romans, "and hurry. The ProConsul is making my ears bleed with how many times she's asked me to pick up our pace."

THIRTY-TWO

Finn's helmet was removed. He took some satisfaction when one of the Numberless commented on how young he looked for how well he fought. That satisfaction disappeared as another laughed and said, "It doesn't matter how young the rabbit is as it evades the fox. Eventually, the fox will rip apart the rabbit."

The hallway was darker than he had thought, being lit only by small service lights that ran in the corners. Without a weapon or charged armor, and with so many elite warriors surrounding him, the Numberless neglected to bind his hands. He was ordered to stand, and he did. Finn reasoned that there was no point in fighting his fate now, and he would only expedite his death if he did. He was flanked by two warriors, making the chance of escape an impossibility.

He felt tired and worn as they marched him off, his breath coming in short gasps. His armor would need a half-hour or so before it was charged. They moved at an even pace, which seemed entirely too slow to Finn. Their city, after all, was being invaded. Finn studied the Roman Trinity as they walked. It had large, metallic arches and expansive rooms. This was obviously a place frequented only by Numberless, having vaulted ceilings, carpeted floors, crown molding, and silver chandeliers.

Finn was taken to a large conference room and seated at the very end, almost as if he were to be the keynote speaker. The Romans removed their helmets, placing them carefully in front of themselves as they sat down. As they did, the table beneath stirred to life with light.

He looked around the room, carefully studying his captors. For a few moments, all fear of losing his life was replaced by curiosity. The Romans were much more ceremonial than Titans, who were ruled by their passions. These Romans were a pragmatic people, governed by logic and reason. After their helmets were removed, they freed their Arc Blades from their sides, raised them up, and placed them on the table while shouting in unison, "Non ducor duco."

A Roman on the opposite end of the table stood in her chair, placing a golden laurel in her hair and gestured wide to those in front of her. "I am Julia, one of two ProConsuls selected for these six months, in the year of 243, from the time of the winter winds to the beginning of the spring. I call to order this emergency meeting to discuss key elements of a pending issue."

Finn was shocked by what he was hearing. *Do these people not know their city is under attack?* He looked around the room, searching for some sanity in the Romans' eyes. They were having a meeting, and all their Numberless, which totaled thirty-nine, seemed to be just fine sitting around the table while a battle raged several stories below.

Another elected official stood, recounting the major topics of a previous meeting and holding individuals accountable for assignments made. Some discussion went back and forth about the East Wall, which was currently under siege by a Roach army.

Finn reflected on the planning meetings with Horace and Cojax. *Did Horace purposely attack while Roaches were attacking, or was that just a coincidence? Don't the Numberless control the Roaches here? If so, why don't they pull them back from the attack?* Finn's question was finally answered as one of the Roman Numberless suggested what Finn was thinking, "Why don't we pull back the Roach invasion until other domestic matters are seen to?"

This was briefly debated and voted upon. The Roach army would be ordered to continue its assault on the city as it had already been previously scheduled. Finn blinked his eyes in disbelief. These people had no sense of urgency. *Isn't that a good thing?* Finn thought. *The more time they waste here, the more time Horace has to take over the Main Control Room.*

"Now to the matter at hand," said the ProConsul. "Approximately ninety-five Numberless from the city of Acadia have raided the Trinity, seeking—no doubt—to severe our connection with the Decamont and broadcast something throughout the city that would push it into rebellion."

An abnormally large Numberless placed his right hand on his chest and the other on the table. The ProConsul turned to him, calling him by name. "Aeneas, you have the floor."

Aeneas looked to Finn and then to the ProConsul. "We should have shot them down as soon as we knew they were on the landing platform. I guess it's too late for that now. Can we stop the Numberless from reaching the Main Control Room?"

The ProConsul looked to Saturn, a smaller, thin Numberless with an airy voice. "No, at their current rate, and counting each stop they will have to make as they access each control door, they will arrive in approximately one hour. Even if we reinforced them with our ranks, we would not be able to stand for long."

Another Numberless placed one hand on his chest and the other on the table in front of him. The ProConsul addressed this new individual. "Remus, you have the floor."

"We need to wake some of our brothers and sisters," Remus proclaimed. "We can double our numbers within ten minutes, and then flank the Acadians. Within half an hour, we'll have put down every last one of those Dependents."

The ProConsul nodded thoughtfully.

Saturn requested to speak, and Julia nodded to him in turn. "Half of the invading forces went to the Stasis Chambers where they've jammed the communication to each Cell. The only way we will be able to wake them up is to do so manually, and to do that, we'll have to cut our way through the Acadians."

"What's wrong with that?" Aeneas asked.

The ProConsul stiffened.

Aeneas suddenly realized he had spoken without permission and lowered his head. "My apologies, ProConsul."

The ProConsul nodded. "Despite the breach in protocol, you do have an interesting proposal."

Remus raised his hand to his chest and extended his other hand. He spoke after being called upon. "They also have a superior position. They could very easily use the narrow hallways along the way to hold us at bay."

"Then we cut through the walls," Aeneas proclaimed.

The Proconsul's features tightened. "Speak again without warrant, and you will lose the Privilege of Speech for the remainder of this meeting." Finn was starting to like the hairy Numberless named Aeneas. He seemed to be a taller version of Horace.

Remus signaled that he had a comment, and the ProConsul called on him. "We have to do something. If we cannot go for the Stasis Chambers, why don't we charge straight into the backs of the

Acadians that are heading for the Main Control Room? If we stop them, the invasion ends."

The ProConsul steepled her fingers, her face the image of concentration. "They would call for reinforcements as soon as they knew what we planned. Our flanking maneuver would leave our flank vulnerable, and they would outnumber our Numberless three-to-one."

Another Numberless was called upon. "We only have one real option: we have to stop the Acadians from reaching the Main Control Room. If they severe our connection to the Decamont, then we will be seen as much as traitors as they are. The Decamont will not reconcile with us, even if we're not at fault. They'll come upon us with the weight of all their armies, and we'll be helpless against it. As soon as they destroy Acadia, they'll come for Rome. What's worse, the Decamont has already been preparing their armies to deal with the Acadian revolution, so we won't have much time before they are upon us."

Artemis was called upon and took the floor. "Can't we convince the Acadians to withdraw? Perhaps we can trade them weapons or information or something else they value? There must be something that they want."

The ProConsul turned her gaze to Finn. All eyes followed hers and rested on the far end of the table. Finn gulped.

"Trade?" Finn said, his face arching up into a perplexed expression.

The ProConsul leaned forward, seemingly applying her weight to the gravity of the situation. "What do you Acadian's value?"

Finn arched his eyebrows. "I can't speak for our city, but I know one thing that I value above all else. And that's the one thing you cannot offer. My freedom."

"That's a funny thing coming from a prisoner," Aeneas said.

The room filled with scattered laughter. The ProConsul did not bother to scold the Numberless for speaking out of turn this time. The laughter burrowed into Finn's skin, like meat flies into flesh. It festered, twisted, pushing up a burning rage.

Finn slowly stood, meeting the eyes of everyone at the table.

"Sit," the ProConsul ordered.

"Listen, Romans," Finn said, his voice taking on a sharp tone. "I'm not the best with words and such."

"Or with an Arc Blade," someone interrupted.

Finn continued undeterred. "But *your* people are dying down there. Each second we spend up here, one of your Validated colors the floor red with their blood. How many have fallen already—one hundred, two hundred. How many more must fall before you see this is pointless."

"Sit," the ProConsul said

Finn was forced into his chair by the two Numberless that stood behind him. Still, he continued to speak. "We did not come here for vain glory, or to make you slaves."

"Then why are you here?" the ProConsul demanded.

"Our people are here to liberate you."

"Liberate?" the ProConsul asked. "All you've done is put us on the execution block with you. We Romans know better than most; we know how the Decamont slaughters a city of rebels." She looked poignantly at a man who was not sitting too far from Finn. The man nodded solemnly, standing in turn. He was in his thirties, but his eyes looked much older. His body was thin but toned.

"I am Aldeen, a Numberless from the city of Iberia," the man began. "And I am the last living survivor from that place now called Desolation. Our city rebelled, as yours has now. The Numberless were united in this decision, and so were the people. The Decamont remotely shut down our power collection and distribution system; we did not even know they could do that. Our shields disappeared, our food production ceased, our vehicles could not be powered. The only thing we had was our armor, our blades, and our bodies." The man looked to Finn, his left eye twitching. "But one cannot eat their armor or their blade. We took to the Killing Fields, feasting on the flesh of Roaches that we killed, but they soon withdrew. We held out. We would not give in. But, hunger drives one to do things… unspeakable things. Hunger is a weight that will break the strongest man, push the most moral into the greatest sin. We turned on each other, the weak becoming our prey. And finally, when we were completely powerless, they attacked. They did not offer terms of surrender or reconciliation. They wiped out every man, woman, and child. I alone survived."

"How?" Finn asked.

"When the final attack came, I was here in this city, begging them for aid as you do now," Aldeen said. "The Decamont won't try to cut out the disease from your city; they will sacrifice all of it so it doesn't taint the cities around it."

Finn nodded. "I've heard about your city, and I'm sorry. But our city is different. A Numberless named Titan learned from what happened to your city and disabled the Decamont's ability to cut off our power. We have since changed the name of the city from Acadia to Titan, in his memory. Our shields still run, our farms still produce food, our vehicles still operate as they always did. The Numberless that now invade your city are planning on doing that same thing here—severing your connection with the Decamont, but not sacrificing your power."

"And who rules your city?" the ProConsul asked.

"The son of Titan, Cojax Artino, Lord of the City of Titan," Finn said.

"You are ruled by a King, then?" the ProConsul asked.

"Technically a Lord."

"Then you would have us be subject to this Lord?" the ProConsul asked.

"I don't know how it will all work out exactly," Finn said with a boyish smile. "But, if our two great cities come together, think of how powerful we will be?" He turned to Aldeen. "How long was it before the Decamont attacked your city?"

Aldeen thought for a moment before answering. "After the rebellion started, maybe one month."

"See," Finn said, his voice picking up with excitement. "The city of Titan has been free from the Decamont for over two months now. They hesitate to attack us. Think of how much more they will fear us if our two cities stand together."

"We need time to consider the situation," the ProConsul said. "And I need to meet with this Lord before any decision can be made. Call off the attack, and we will begin negotiating."

Finn shook his head.

The ProConsul frowned, unaccustomed to rejection. "Speak up, boy. I can't hear you."

"No," Finn said flatly.

The ProConsul suddenly leaped into the air, her Arc Blade burning with light as she went. She flew the entire distance of the room, nearly brushing the chandeliers above. She landed in front of

Finn.

"I could have spoken even louder if needed," Finn responded. "You didn't need to leap over to this side of the room."

Despite himself, Aeneas laughed, easing some of the tension.

The ProConsul raised her blade, placing it along Finn's throat. "Think carefully about what you say next. We need time to talk; we need time to negotiate. Call off the attack."

"Even if I could," Finn said. "Why would I? We lose all of our leverage as soon as we withdraw."

"I give you my word that your proposal will be considered," the ProConsul replied.

Finn frowned. "In a very short time, our Numberless will disconnect your link with the Decamont, forcing you into rebellion. All that's left to decide is whether you will fight with us, or against. That was my plan anyway."

The ProConsul frowned. "What?

"I mean, that's the plan someone else came up with," Finn replied. "I was just in the room when someone else proposed it. But I definitely did not try to gain the Numberless' respect by proposing such a brilliant plan."

The ProConsul lowered her blade and looked back to the room. The anger she felt only moments ago was fading. She jumped off the table and walked behind Finn.

"Tell me about Lord Cojax."

"Lord Cojax Artino," Finn began, "is a good man. He and a girl by the name of Jessica Halworth started the rebellion, forcing all in the city to take a side. There was a learning curve, several thousand died in the ensuing chaos, but they pulled the city together."

"If we join you," the ProConsul said.

"You can't seriously be considering—," Remus said.

"Silence!" the ProConsul yelled. She turned her attention back to Finn. "If we united with you, we would want autonomous control of our city."

"I'm sure that wouldn't be an issue. The Lord already has enough headaches to worry about."

"We would insist our leaders commanded our own armies, and we wouldn't want to be subject to your Lord's command."

"Who would command your armies and develop your military

strategy?" Finn asked.

"The Roman Numberless, of course."

"Well," Finn said, "that probably wouldn't work."

"What do you mean?"

"So," Finn replied, "the Numberless we sent into your city have two objectives: first, disable the Decamont's ability to destroy your power remotely; and secondly, to release a video to every CityScreen in Rome that explains how things have really worked for the last two hundred years. The video that our Numberless are going to release to your city doesn't exactly put you in the best light. In fact, this video is more damning than the one we aired in our own city, and our people were ready to rip the Numberless to pieces by the end of it. If they see all of your crimes laid out before them all at once, they will come for you."

"So, you would have us kneel before your Lord, begging for our lives?" the ProConsul asked.

"No," Finn replied. "But, if you stand with us, you must serve our Lord, at least until the war with the Decamont is over. If we are not united, both our cities will fall. We can't have one city attacking, while the other goes on the defense. Swear an oath to serve Lord Cojax Artino during this time of war, and I will make sure your good names aren't tarnished by the release of that video. A second video that is more 'Numberless friendly' will be broadcast to your people instead. Their support for you will grow."

"We need more time to discuss this," the ProConsul said, a hint of pleading in her voice. "Call off your dogs of war."

Finn shook his head. "I'm not the Lord—I don't command them."

Across the room, Aeneas stood, Arc Blade in hand. "I will take your oath, boy. I will serve your king."

"That's enough, Aeneas," the ProConsul barked. "Your Privilege of Speech has been revoked."

"You're no longer my sovereign," Aeneas said with a laugh. "So, I don't think that's something you can do to me anymore. I serve Lord Cojax Artinian now."

"It's actually Cojax Artino," Finn corrected.

"Then, I'll swear to serve him too!"

"I will also swear to your Lord," said Aldeen. At this, the whole room gasped and pulled back, staring in earnest at the hardened, thin warrior.

"How can you swear to them after what happened to your city?" the ProConsul asked.

"I swear to serve him *because* of what happened to my city," Aldeen replied. "I didn't know there was another way, but now that the choice is placed before me, how can I not take it? The brave may fall, but they cannot yield. I believe we have a chance if we unite our two cities—I believe we must follow this Lord Cojax Artino."

More Numberless began to stand, each one pledging their support. The phenomenon spread slowly at first, but more rapidly as those standing became the majority. Finally, the whole room was standing, their hands raised in a Roman salute. Finn was dumbfounded, his mouth slightly open. Something had changed but he could not quite figure out what it was or when it happened.

The ProConsul returned to her seat, facing each of the Numberless in turn. "If this is our choice, then let it be a united one. I, Julia, ProConsul of Rome and daughter of Claudia, do swear, during this time of war, to serve Lord Cojax Artino, ruler of the city of Titan. In taking this oath, I will give life and liberty until we are either free from the Decamont or our people are no more."

The rest of the room echoed the ProConsul's oath.

Finn grabbed the nearest Numberless. "I need my helmet! I've got to stop Horace from playing that recording."

THIRTY-THREE

Cojax had just returned from Rome, where the entire city pledged their loyalty to him. They had bowed when he entered, called him Lord when they addressed him, offered him the best of what they had to eat and drink. He took it well, considering how little Horace and Finn had prepared him for it. He remained silent most of the time, relying on Horace to convey most of the BloodBorne's proposals and ideas. After some concessions and debate, Horace and the ProConsul decided to form a Senate that would act much like the BloodBorne Council. This Senate could veto Cojax's decisions if they reached a majority of votes. A little over half of the Senators would be provided by Rome, the rest by the city of Titan. It seemed like a fair proposal, and both sides agreed to it reasonably quickly. They instituted other governmental structures and positions, each of which was filled by one Roman and one Titan.

Even though he had hardly said anything, Cojax felt exhausted by the trip. Never had doing so little drained him so much. Cojax went to a small room, where he changed his polished ceremonial armor for a practice set. He met Horace in the training room not long after, a sword and shield in hand. Horace had been so busy visiting other cities that their practice sessions could only be held every other day.

Cojax now looked forward to the sessions. They pushed his mind far from the drama of the First Assembly and the bitter politics that ensued. It was also the only time he could get away from his host of bodyguards.

"There's a problem with this new alliance, Horace," Cojax said as he stretched out on the floor.

"I hand you a city with a pretty ribbon wrapped around it," Horace replied, "and the best you can do is point out the problems. Oh, boyou, did I ever tell you about the story of the ungrateful boy who got beaten by his father's friend for being so ungrateful."

"No."

"Well," Horace replied. "That's pretty much the story: moral of it is to be grateful."

"The problem is," Cojax said, undeterred, "that the Romans think we have complete control over our city. They think that I am Lord of Titan. But I'm not even the leader of the leading political party—that title belongs to my brother, Marcus."

"Details."

"Horace," Cojax replied, "that's more than a detail. What happens when we want to mobilize our armies and only our political party shows up? What happens when a Roman Centurion speaks to an Alpha from Titan? And while talking to each other, they realize I'm not their official leader. At best, they'll end their alliance with us, at worst, they'll initiate a war."

"True…true," Horace said.

"But…," Cojax prompted.

"But nothing," Horace replied. "You made a good point, and I was agreeing with you. Come on now. Get into your fighting stance. Nothing clears the mind like training."

Cojax obeyed, raising his round shield and steading his Arc Blade upon it. He no longer trained with the small Arc Blade he earned from the Mahghetto, but with the Archaic, the much larger and thicker one that Titan had kept on his apartment wall. It was unwieldy at first. It felt like trying to push a button with a large stick, but the more he used it, the more precise he became. Horace now used a large blade as well, at least in training, although he still preferred his ax.

They exchanged blows. Although Cojax took the brunt of most of them, he returned an impressive number of strikes.

"Come on, boyou," Horace chided. "You're better than me. Now prove it."

Cojax lunged forward, exchanging a series of rapid swings. Horace blocked them all and returned his own, barely missing Cojax's head.

"Is that all you got, lad?" Horace said. "Prove your title and put me on the floor!"

Cojax stopped moving and lowered his sword. An idea suddenly struck him, along with Horace's blade. The latter sent him pitching to the side and rolling like a ball. Cojax pulled himself to his feet. "I've got it, Horace. I know how we can win Onar to our side."

Horace scoffed. "That big brute, what do you need him for?"

"Because he has five percent of the voting bloc. If we could win him over, we'd almost catch up to the Populi Party. And then, we'd only need one more shove on our side to complete it all. We have to consolidate our power before the Romans realize our city is still in chaos."

"What's your plan to win over the great King Onar?"

"What does he value above all else?"

"A big guy like that," Horace said. "I imagine he values shoes that actually fit him."

"Skill with the Arc Blade. Think about it. Everything he has ever presented to the First Assembly or anyone else has been to boast of his power and strength. He believes that in order to rule, you must be the most powerful. What do you think my chance of winning is if I challenged him to a bout?"

"About as much chance as me pooping a chocolate bar next time I relieve myself."

"I'm serious."

"None."

"Come on," Cojax said. "I've been training with you for the last few months. That has to count for something. You can't tell me that he's received one-on-one training from a Numberless."

"No, he hasn't. But he was selected to be a Numberless, which means he's a Nova. He's got the skill to cut down three of the First Tiers at the same time, without losing the charge of his shields. Boyou, I'm one of those 'glass is half full' kind of guys, and I don't think you stand a chance. Now, I've never seen him fight, but that guy is more beast than man. I wouldn't be surprised if he's fifty percent SrataniKahn or something. In all my years, in all the cities I've visited, I've never seen a human so large."

"Size doesn't matter when it comes to one-on-one combat."

"Not usually, but that man is like a boulder. Have you ever tried to stop a boulder with a sword?"

"I've seen him fight. I can beat him."

Horace shook his head. "It takes years of training with a Numberless to even begin to appreciate some of the minute nuances of one-on-one combat. You've got skill—both your dad and I recognized that right away—but you still need time. You've still got so much to learn, boyou."

"But time is the one thing we don't have," Cojax replied. "Horace, they are coming for us. And if I can't bring our people together, it's over. Who knows how much time we have. Tomorrow? Next week? Who knows what they are planning. If beating that creature is our only chance of victory, I've got to take that chance."

Horace lowered his shoulders in a consolatory gesture. "Alright, but may I make a suggestion?"

"Sure."

"Wear a set of my armor. It's bigger and bulkier, so we'll have to make a few adjustments, but it has a few enhancements that Onar's won't."

"But what if I damage it?" Cojax asked.

"Don't worry," Horace replied with a grin. "Even if you end up getting sliced in half, I've got three more sets that are identical to the first."

THIRTY-FOUR

Deo walked quickly through the streets. Delayed by a late summons from the Populi Party, he was eager to make up time. He had almost ignored the call completely. After all, that is precisely what they did when *he* summoned *them*.

The meeting with the Populi Party was filled with words, such as 'compromise' and 'uniting together,' but he sincerely doubted that even the supposed Consul believed them. The Restorationists had been abused, beaten, robbed, and murdered. And all the Populi Party could think to do was suggest potential solutions, debate over proposals, and eventually vote not to do any of them. By the end of it, Deo was so disgusted he abruptly departed.

The more he thought of it, the more the anger rippled through his muscles, forcing his hands into fists. His anger did not abate as he walked down the street, his eyes narrow slits of disgust. He was not asking for much, only the restoration of a system that would solve all their problems.

When he stepped into the Restorationist sector, he gave a sigh of relief. It was cleaner and more organized, not a piece of trash in the street. He demanded the same discipline of every Validated now as was required under the Acadian Code. And the data proved what all the other political parties could not see: that the Restorationists worked harder, consumed fewer resources, and maintained their absolute discipline. While the Populi Party trashed the streets with their political brochures, and the BloodBorne crowded the CityScreens with various threats of the Decamont invasion, his people resisted the urge to debase themselves. The Acadian Code was wrong, but not by much. End the Riftings. End the Honorable Releases. But keep the AC intact.

It was a mark of how frustrated Deo was that he carried his helmet in his arm instead of on his head, as would have been required under the AC. Every once in a while, Deo would pass a patch of road that had been stained in blood. The blood had long since been cleaned up, but it could still be seen in some of the cracks that scattered the street. He had seen many dead bodies recently, all of them from his own party, all of them killed for the few possessions they carried. Every other party had implemented some sort of policing force—but not his. And so his people became the target of the riffraff of every other political party. There had been a few times he had been tempted to organize a law enforcement unit, a few days he had even contemplated organizing an army, but he resisted the urge. If he gave in on that issue, how would anyone trust him with anything else? If they forged a policing force, it would be a clear sign that the people of Acadia would never be reverting back to the AC. He would lose face and popularity, perhaps even his position. Then there would be no resisting the other parties as they grew in power and prominence.

With him were his two counselors, Diocles and Diotimus, brothers who not only looked a lot alike but acted as if they were the same person. They were a somber group—their hands resting on the hilts of their blades. The Restorationists could never be at ease in their own section of the city, not with all the recent violence.

"Help!" cried a voice between two apartment buildings.

Deo drew his sword and donned his helmet. The two brothers did the same, tentatively spreading out to either side of their leader. They saw the assailant almost immediately as they approached the entrance of an alley. The attacker stood over the victim, alternating between fists as she delivered powerful attacks to the individual on the ground.

Anger as scalding as liquid metal twisted through Deo's veins, forcing him into action. He charged in, his blade raised. The closer he drew, the bloodier the ground became. A woman lay at the feet of the assailant, whose knuckles were now as crimson as her crime. The attacker turned, not even bothering to reach for her sword. A second later, Deo stopped dead in his tracks as the attacker's helmet was removed.

"You?" Deo asked.

"You do recognize me."

"Adriana, what are you doing here?"

"Very good," she replied. "You could even tell me apart from my sister. And here I thought that there wouldn't be much of a mind buried under all of those wrinkles. But I'm glad to see you at least remember one of your own daughters."

"Of course I remember," Deo replied with a bitter tone. "The biggest mistake I've ever made was choosing you over her. What are you doing in this sector? You belong to the BloodBorne."

Adriana walked forward, wiping her bloodied hands on the greaves of her armor. "You were once part of the BloodBorne, and now you're here. Why can't I be here too? And besides, I had business to take care of."

"Killing an innocent woman?"

"First of all, she's not dead. And second, she attacked me."

Deo scoffed.

Adriana stepped into a beam of light, which accented her sleek curves. "I have a proposal for you."

Deo turned, heading back for the main road. "I've heard enough proposals for today." He took four steps before he stopped. His exit to the main road was no longer clear, as a group of warriors now blocked it.

Deo's eyes narrowed into fine slits. "Is this how the BloodBorne gained so much support? Through intimidation and coercion? Are you the one who's behind these attacks on my people?"

"Mostly."

"What?" Deo said, his voice a mix of shock and anger. "You admit it so easily?"

"Yes," Adriana said, her face turning into a frown. "Messy work, yes, but necessary."

"Necessary? You would cut down your own people for what—their possessions?"

"It was never about what they carried, but about sending a message. You are weak. Your political party will fail. But most importantly, you cannot protect them."

Deo stepped forward, his sword raised. "You wretched beast." Before he could draw too close, a dozen warriors stepped out of the shadows and stood behind Adriana."

"Are we going to be able to have a civil conversation?" Adriana asked in a playful tone. "Or does everything you do devolve into bloodshed."

"You speak of civility?" Deo mocked. "How dare you accuse me of spilling blood? Look at your hands. Look at the blood that coats them. Add that blood to the hundreds of people slain because of your orders in the last few months. Who is really behind this? Did your Lord put you up to this? Is this how the BloodBorne recruits followers? With a smile on their faces and a blade in their hands."

"You have your blade drawn, not I," Adriana replied. "Come on, let's talk."

Deo looked around, scanning his surroundings. He finally nodded, sheathing his sword. "Alright, let's talk." As per custom, Deo and his two companions removed their helmets. Adriana gestured them to a place further down the alley where several chairs and a table were set up.

Adriana nodded to the chairs. "I'm glad we can settle this rationally."

As soon as Deo and his companions sat, he began to speak. "I want you to cease all of your attacks on my people—in this sector and throughout the city. Otherwise, I will tell everyone that you're behind the attacks on the Restorationists."

Adriana clucked her tongue. "Without any long-winded speeches, you dive straight into it. You've changed. Ok, let's break this down logically. If you were to accuse me, you would be accusing the BloodBorne. You've already blamed your problems on every other party. How do you think they'll react when they hear you have no proof? Your armor doesn't record anymore, remember? And I've already destroyed all the cameras that have any visual of this area. Even if I didn't, Validated now spend their time defiling each other and filling their bellies with stock. They'd stop you from pulling any footage so it doesn't interfere with their fun."

Deo bit down on his lower lip. "How long have you lived without honor?"

"Of all people, how can you speak of honor?" Adriana replied. "After what you did to me?"

"I didn't come here to talk about your childhood," Deo replied, "so spare me the speech and tell me what you propose?"

"I can end the attacks, the beatings, the murders."

"And what do you want in return?"

"Your life."

"What?"

Adriana leaned forward, her face curving into a wicked grin.

"You are stubborn. I cannot change you. You're beyond persuasion. You believe that a sense of duty motivates you—an urge that drives you to stick to the old ways. But those ways are weighted. They will drag us down as quickly as if our feet were lead. Our salvation relies upon one man and one man only—Cojax Artino, Lord of the BloodBorne."

"Do you actually believe a word coming out of your mouth? He barely has any combat experience, let alone skill in governing. If he's your answer to the future, don't count on my help."

Adriana sighed. "My point exactly. We could spend all day talking to you, and you'd come to the same conclusion. There's no reasoning with you, and so, you must disappear."

"I will never abandon my people."

Adriana nodded eagerly. "Yes, I know, and that's why you must die."

"Never."

"Then you must suffer," Adriana said with a whisper. "Your two companions must die. You must learn what your stubborn attitude is forcing others to face—the loss of friends and family. You must learn that as you resist our society, the people closest to you will be destroyed."

Deo stood. "You're insane—"

Before he could continue, his helmet was taken from his left hand, as were the helmets of his two companions.

Adriana folded her arms in pleasure. "Once again, you have followed the ancient customs of the city. When I asked you to sit down, you all removed your helmets. As I knew you would, as your honor dictated that you should. The Decamont have given you this system so they could control you; so that they could predict your every action. By embracing it, you're in effect, handing them a key to the city."

"I will sooner fall on my sword than make the choice between my life and theirs."

"You have ten seconds," Adriana chimed. "Choose between them or you. If you make no choice, then we will kill all three."

THIRTY-FIVE

Jessica felt uneasy every time she entered the Rift. It was not so much her surroundings as it was the unnerving news she received from her spies that made her body tense. The spies had been ineffective at first, many of them being caught before they could discover anything of value. Two of them that had attempted to infiltrate Adriana's inner circle were actually murdered in the process. After that, Jessica almost canceled the entire project, especially upon seeing how incomplete the last Rifter's body ended up. But then a select few proved effective.

Jessica arrived at the meeting point, located just on the edge of the area formerly used by the BloodBorne disciples during the Mahghetto. It was now becoming routine for them to meet every three days. She placed a helmet on her head before entering, as was the custom. Aias had insisted on hiding her identity, even though she was pretty sure everyone knew who she was after seeing how much smaller she was compared to everyone else.

The room was narrow and dark. Her helmet switched to night vision, highlighting all the individuals already in the room. There were seven, a group much smaller than their original number, but much more talented. They were all shrouded in dark cloaks so that their armor could not be used to identify who they were. Only Aias knew each of their names, and even then, he had only heard most of them once. Recruiting these seven spies was a result of attrition and sacrifice. What once was five hundred Rifters strong had now dwindled down to these few.

Aias arrived not long after, draped in a long cloak. The Seven gathered around at his arrival, each one taking a place so they were equally spaced apart in a circle. Jessica stood on one end, Aias on the other. She hardly ever spoke, but all of the Seven treated her with the same deference they did Aias.

"I apologize for being late," Aias said in his old, but firm voice.

"But, let's not delay any more." He then nodded to the person on his right, known as "One" by all the others.

As always, One began to divulge what she had recently learned. Sometimes her information was hardly better than rumors spread on the streets; other times, it included details of intimate conversations. The way the information was so helpful one moment, and so useless the next, made Jessica think that she worked for the Populi Party in some sort of servant capacity.

Jessica realized that despite coming from different backgrounds, the Seven had a few things in common: They all had smaller, unassuming builds; they preferred to speak quickly and quietly, avoiding taking too much time or drawing too much attention; and they all wore their Arc Blades on their backs, not on their waists.

After One finished, Two took over, sharing his information. This was a gruff sounding man that moved with a slight limp—although, that might have all been for show. He seemed to be positioned somewhere in the armed guard for the Populi Party, as most of what he shared came from the endless debates between Senate members. His information was insightful but rarely actionable.

Next was Three, a woman affiliated with the Statesmen. Her information was always accurate, timely, and direct. If the Statesmen had ever become a dominant party, Three's connection would have been invaluable. The Statesmen had already been absorbed by the Populi Party, however, and much of Three's information was not relevant.

Four, a thicker woman with a soft voice, went next. "The Damnattii are pulling out—and not in small numbers either. At this rate, there won't be too many left in the next few days."

"Where are they going?" Aias asked.

"To the East," Four replied, "as far as anyone can tell. They must know something we don't."

On and on, they spoke until finally, they arrived at Seven. Seven's information was always worth more than the other six spies combined. She had an airy tone to her voice as if she was prophesying more than she was relating the details of her acquired intelligence.

Seven paused for a moment before speaking. "Two of the leading Restorationists were murdered by members of the BloodBorne Faction. It was a well-executed assassination made to look as if it were a simple mugging. Diocles and Diotimus have been killed."

"When?" Aias asked. It was uncommon for Aias to interrupt, but it seemed to happen more frequently with Seven.

"It happened only an hour ago as Deo, Diocles, and Diotimus were making their way through the city."

Jessica did not need to know more. She could already guess who was behind the assassination, as well as her motivations. Despite this, Aias asked the obvious question.

"Who ordered the assassination?"

"Adriana," Jessica answered.

Seven continued, unfazed by the interruption. "She gave Deo the choice to either kill himself or let his two companions be butchered."

"That sick woman," Jessica said before she could stop herself.

"Naturally," Seven said, "he chose to live."

"She has gone too far this time," Jessica said.

Aias raised his hand. "Now is not the time."

She knew he was right. This was not the place nor the time to vent about Adriana's abuses of power. The information shared in the room flowed only one direction, and it was never discussed.

"There's more," Seven continued. "Adriana has secretly begun production on something in the Rift—something that will supposedly change all of our fates. To that end, I heard she is removing machinery from the Mahghetto and placing it somewhere in the Rift where it's being reassembled."

Jessica clenched her jaw, biting down hard on her teeth. "Is it something that could threaten Cojax?"

Seven looked to Jessica. Despite both being shrouded in helmets, Jessica could swear she felt the penetrating glare of the woman across the room. "From everything I've seen, she's more loyal to him than many on the BloodBorne High Council. I doubt it's anything that could threaten Cojax. If anything, I'm sure it's something to turn the tide in his favor."

Jessica took in a deep breath, holding back her anger.

"I believe she loves him," Seven said in almost a whisper.

Jessica's body tensed. "She loves no one but herself."

Aias stepped forward, cutting the rising tension in the room. "Your city appreciates your service. Stay safe until we meet again. You are dismissed."

The Seven bowed low to Aias first and Jessica second. They left almost as quickly as they came.

Aias stepped forward. "You seem to have a consistent theme in your questioning."

"This is it," Jessica replied. "Now, Cojax will be forced to see her for what she really is."

"I think he already does," Aias replied simply, "and what he sees is someone who is extremely effective."

Jessica's face flushed with anger. "But this time she has gone too far. Do you know what the other parties would do if they found out that she was behind those murders? Do you know how quickly the Validated would leave the BloodBorne if they even thought for a second Cojax might be linked to them? She's not effective; she's reckless. When she can't achieve something by legitimate means, she resorts to assassination. She's a liability."

"Yes," Aias replied, "but she is our liability."

"What do you mean by that?" Jessica asked.

"Well, we can take steps to ensure that her actions cannot be linked to Cojax or the BloodBorne. If we let her continue to operate how she chooses—allowing her to do our dirty work—we can also expose her treachery if she ever even thinks about betraying the BloodBorne."

"You make it sound so simple."

Aias nodded. "Just convince Cojax to remove her from her position in the BloodBorne—that should give her more freedom to operate how she wants. I'll make sure that we have evidence that links her to every sin she has ever committed."

"She needs to be tried and executed," Jessica replied. "I'm convinced that's the only way to deal with her."

THIRTY-SIX

Cojax surveyed the room, most were not meeting his eyes. The chandeliers had been cleared, the damage repaired, and the members that had left had been replaced. He was now surrounded by some of the strongest Validated in the whole of Titan, and yet he had never felt more vulnerable. His plan had worked perfectly, drawing over the vast majority of First Tiers to his ranks. They were funneled to the same positions of power that they held before the AC fell. And now, his political party had something no other party did, a complete and comprehensive command structure from the Tenth to the First Tier.

Clandis and Ajax had replaced Cato and Parmenion on the BloodBorne High Council. Again, Byron objected, and again, Cojax pushed the nominations through. Now that Cato was gone, Cojax's will, for the most part, went unchallenged. This sudden shift was amplified by Clandis and Ajax, who truly treated Cojax as if he was already the Lord of Titan.

Cojax started the meeting by nodding to Ajax, who reviewed the minutes from the previous session. They went over assignments and held all those accountable for things they did or did not do. Orch provided a report on the assimilation of the First Tiers into the command structure, stating that it "went better than expected." He then spoke at length on the new chain of command.

This sparked some debate from the other members of the Council, who insisted on a few changes. The positions were debated and reviewed until finally, all eyes turned to Cojax, who nodded his approval on the proposed changes. Then Orch opened up a discussion about appointing a committee to begin studying the Decamont technology so it could be better understood. Decima stated that she had already started exploring the personal notes of several Numberless, most notably Titan, which contained several observations with regards to Decamont technology. The committee was established and granted leave to begin a more comprehensive investigation into

Decamont technology.

After several other topics were discussed, Cojax took the floor, addressing the Council as a whole. "The BloodBorne has seen a surge in membership recently. Our new leadership, as well as our increased support, have now made it possible to begin a comprehensive training program."

Several of the BloodBorne High Councilors nodded in approval. Cojax continued, "This will be the largest and most comprehensive training regimen that any in our city has ever undertaken. We've trained in groups of fifty in the Mahghetto, we've fought together in Phalanxes of one hundred on the field, but now we must train all together."

"Where would you propose this training take place?" Byron asked.

Cojax turned the attention to his counselors. "Are there any suggestions?"

"In the Mahghetto," Ajax said, "where we already have all the equipment needed to conduct training."

Cojax's chest tightened. He was one of the few who knew that the Hoarders not only trained in the Mahghetto, but lived there too.

Adriana must have sensed the potential conflict as well. "If we want people to believe we are preparing to fight the Decamont, why don't we show them?"

"What do you mean?" Byron asked.

"Why don't we train in the streets during the middle of the day," Adriana suggested. "Let's show the other political parties that we not only have a large base of supporters but that we are taking the threat of the Decamont seriously."

Cojax nodded to Byron. "What're your thoughts?"

Byron shrugged. "It will be noticed, and I'm sure it will be opposed at the next First Assembly meeting. Some parties will accuse us of trying to intimidate Validated to join our ranks, others will see it as progress towards something we should have already been doing. So, I think it will neither hurt nor help us."

Cojax turned to Orch. "What do you think?"

Orch nodded. "I've gotten a little fatter, so hopefully I'll fit into my battle armor, but I like it. We should start drilling urban fighting in any regard."

Cojax went to his counselors in turn, drawing opinions from all of them. He finally approved the plan, as well as appointing Clandis as the Alpha Magister over all training.

After this discussion concluded, Adriana requested and was granted the floor. "I'm afraid I have bad news, Lord Cojax. I've been informed that Onar, son of Cleinias, is toying with the idea of an alliance with the Populi Party. He doesn't want to join their ranks directly, but he is contemplating supporting them in their push for control of the government. In return, the Populi Party will grant Onar and his followers absolute autonomy once the new government is established."

"What?" Orch said. "That goes against everything Onar stands for."

"He," Adriana replied, "now fears us more than the Populi Party."

"Why?" Cojax asked. "The Populi Party still holds more support than us by a good margin."

"I think it's a compliment," Adriana said. "Onar knows that if the Populi Party wins, he could manipulate and intimidate the government to his will. Whereas if we won, he would lose all of his influence."

Cojax looked to Byron. "If Onar sides with the Populi Party, will they surpass sixty percent?"

Byron fiddled with his ArmGuard for a few moments. "Not by my calculations, but it will be close. They wouldn't need much more support than that. I propose we entreat Onar with our own proposed alliance."

Adriana shook her head. "He will only ally with the Populi Party because of the lack of central leadership. I highly doubt he would even consider sitting down to the negotiation table with us, much less make an alliance."

"It's worth a try," Byron replied.

"It looks desperate," Adriana said. "At best Onar will think we are incompetent, at worst weak. Look at what happened when the First Tiers attempted to meet with the brute."

"What do you propose?" Byron asked. "We can't afford to lose Onar's political party to the Populi."

"Perhaps we could manipulate him into supporting the

Restorationists, at least for the time being," Adriana replied.

"How the hell do we do that?" Orch asked, his voice full of skepticism.

"The Restorationists have had one complaint since the AC fell," Adriana said. "That their streets are not safe, that criminals have taken advantage of their lack of security, that they are being murdered, robbed, and beaten. The Restorationists have repeatedly stated that they will not allow a policing force because of the precedent it would set. Onar, on the other hand, is the exact opposite, having followers that are more than willing to prove themselves in conflict. All we have to do is convince Onar to patrol the streets of the Restorationists' sector, which would, in turn, win favor from the Restorationists."

"It sounds overly complicated," Orch said. "Not only do we have to convince Onar to go out of his way to help a political party that has no interest in helping themselves; we also have to convince the Restorationists to allow Onar to roam the streets in their sector."

"I agree," Byron said. "Given Onar's reputation, I think the Restorationists will believe they are under attack and will reply in kind. They are morally opposed to organizing a policing force, but I don't think they would have any problem going head-to-head with Onar and his forces in full out battle."

"And besides," Ajax added. "Even if the plan worked as designed, it would just give the Restorationists more support. We'd be creating just another larger party we would have to deal with later on."

Adriana leaned back in her chair. "It's a working plan, I'll admit. Let me have some time to think it through, and I can fine-tune it."

The debate went on and on, each counselor throwing out their best ideas to either win Onar over or buy time by distracting the giant warrior with various tasks. To Cojax, the debate had ended long before it even began. He knew what he had to do. Now, he was just trying to work up the courage to do it. He had thought about it for weeks, and it seemed simple enough all during that time. But now, as his next words would set into motion a dangerous plan, he hesitated to speak them. He tightened and released his sword hand, studying his palm with earnest. His hesitation gave way to doubt, which then turned to fear. As he realized it was fear that held his tongue, he reconsidered the plan in its entirety. At the end of this long procession of thought, he came to the same conclusion he always did. *There is no other way. There is no other person.* For the first time since the AC fell, Cojax began to realize how his father must have felt when he was forced to choose between his own son, who was leading the rebellion, and his honor as a Numberless. *When did Titan decide to help me? Did he know about the uprising long before? Or is it something he decided upon the moment we charged into the Trinity?* It had never seemed important before, but now it did. Cojax did not know the gravity of the choice he was making at the time he had raided the Trinity; Titan, however, did know. *And now it's my turn to make the hard decision. Now it's my turn to take the risk.*

Cojax stood, and the room fell silent. "The anniversary of when my father became a Numberless will be in five days. On that day, we will hold a celebration of my father that will far surpass any gathering seen in this city. We will put out ads informing the entire city of the event, and we will provide food, music, entertainment, and the best stock. I know someone that should be able to get us stock at a steep discount. We will host a series of gladiatorial games, as did the ancient Romans. We will pair the best against the brightest. The strong against the many. The apt with the Arc Lance against the masters of the Arc Blade. We will present to them a spectacle never before seen on the CityScreens. And then, when the whole city is watching, I will challenge Onar, son of Cleinias, to single combat."

All eyes remained on Cojax. Silence pursued for several seconds longer before it became awkward.

Adriana looked down at the table in front of her. "If you do, you will die."

Cojax shook his head. "There are only three Novas in the city right now that I know of: Marcus, Onar, and myself. Marcus is not going to challenge him anytime soon, and so that leaves the opportunity open for me. I'm the only one that has a chance of beating him."

"Even if you challenge him to friendly combat," Byron said, "he won't stop once your shields are down. This will be too much of an opportunity for him. He won't stop until you're dead."

"That's a chance I will have to take," Cojax replied.

"No," Byron replied. "That's a chance you can't possibly afford to take. If you fall, so does this political party and everything else we've worked so hard to achieve. Onar is not a man as you know it. He is a creature beyond strength, beyond skill. If you step into the arena with him, he will grant you no quarter."

"He's right," Orch said, his usual playful tone gone. "You'd be committing suicide. Abria, Bacis, and Cineas did not stand a chance against him, and those were the three highest Validated in the city."

Cojax turned to Clandis and Ajax.

"I think the Lord knows his limits," Clandis said. "If you feel you can best him, I do not doubt you can. I've already underestimated you once; I swear I will not do it again."

Ajax nodded in agreement. "Take the fool down, and let the people of Titan see you do it. Then, there would not be a political party that could oppose us."

Byron shook his head. "No, no, you can't listen to these two. They hardly know you, let alone know anything about how you can handle a blade. Cojax, I beg you to reconsider."

"Make preparations for the festival," Cojax said. "Pass the word among the BloodBorne that we will need every able hand and body to pull this thing off. And let it slip that I intend to challenge Onar. That alone should create enough hype to make this successful. Spare no expense on food, entertainment, or ads. This is to be a spectacle that will never be forgotten."

"No," Byron said. "I can't let you do this. I can't. I promised Titan that I would protect and serve you. And I very much doubt that he meant to serve you up to Onar as a sacrificial lamb. If you plan on proceeding with this plan, then I'm afraid I cannot be part of it. I can't let you die, Cojax. I'm sorry. I can't let you die."

Cojax felt his chest tighten. He took a while to respond, not meeting Byron's eyes when he did. "We can't miss this opportunity."

Byron stood, his frown deepening. "Please, I can't let you do this."

"It's already done," Cojax proclaimed.

Byron shook his head. "Then undo it. I can't be part of this."

"It's already done," Cojax roared, his hands clenching into fists.

Byron slowly saluted, bowing low. "I took an oath to serve you until the day I die. But in this case, I think I serve you best if I don't serve you at all. With your leave, my Lord."

Cojax nodded.

Byron bowed to the BloodBorne around him as he slowly retreated out of the room. The mood was so heavy that not even Orch made a comment.

Finally, Cojax spoke, "We have a lot to do and not much time to do it. Orch, will you take over primary responsibilities of seeing to the organization of the festival?"

Orch nodded. "Of course."

"Then," Cojax said, "I think that will be enough for today. Everyone is dismissed except for Adriana. I need to have a word with you privately."

High Councilors, advisors, and bodyguards stood, saluted to Cojax, and retreated out the door. As the room cleared, Adriana looked uncharacteristically nervous. She took a few deep breaths, forcing calm into her body. The room looked massive now that only two people were in it.

Adriana pulled a box from under the table and placed it delicately before Cojax. "I have something that might help make amends with your brother. I was able to access a Numberless machine that allowed me to fabricate a metallic arm to replace the one he lost."

Cojax perched from the top of his chair, as a falcon studying its prey. He felt a tremendous amount of anger pumping through his veins, and he was not exactly sure where it was all coming from. He shifted in his chair, gripping the armrest with both hands until his knuckles turned white.

"Cojax?" Adriana ventured.

He did not respond. Instead, he waited until his anger reached a manageable level and then stood up, closing the distance between Adriana and himself. He spoke as he walked. "I've received a…disturbing report."

"Is that so?" Adriana replied with a wink. "Let me guess. Your girlfriend doesn't care for me much."

"This is serious," Cojax said, his voice rising with his temper.

"Then what is it?" Adriana asked.

"I received word that two of the leading Restorationists, Diocles and Diotimus, were killed while protecting Deo, their leader. They were drawn into an alley where they were promptly surrounded, outnumbered, and overwhelmed. Deo alone escaped the conflict."

"Their sector is certainly the most dangerous one."

"Don't be coy, Adriana," Cojax said. "Did you do this?"

Adriana remained silent for a time, considering her words.

"Cojax, I want you to rule this city, and I'm willing to do whatever is necessary."

"Is that what you have become? A person that will set aside all morals and ethics to achieve their aim at any cost?"

"That is not what I've become, that is who I've always been," Adriana replied simply. "I understand if you don't approve of my methods. As a Lord, it's probably best that you don't know about them. No one can link you to anything I've done."

"Why would you butcher the Restorationists?"

"Because they are proving the most stubborn of any political party," Adriana replied. "And, by the way, Deo didn't escape, as he may have suggested. I let him live. But Deo needed to know what his people were going through because of his hardheaded policies, so I killed his two best friends."

Cojax began pacing the room, his hands behind his back. "Deo is already saying far and wide that you were behind the attack. And that I have personally sanctioned the violence."

Adriana shook her head as a mother does to a mischievous child. "This won't affect us. The Restorationists have talked this way from the beginning, accusing all around them of similar plots and ploys. Deo has no evidence, and so this, like all of his other accusations, will fall flat. He will begin to lose control over his party, as well as his followers. It was messy but necessary. Necessity dictated my actions. The Restorationists could hold out for months on end, clinging to the AC as if it was their newfound religion. The end result would mean that neither the Populi Party nor our BloodBorne Party could win them over. We'd end up in a stalemate, one that would last until the Decamont arrived."

Cojax shook his head. "You don't even understand why I'm so angry. Those were people, Adriana. Our people. Validated of the highest rank and caliber. And just because it was inconvenient that they were alive, you eliminated them."

"Yes," Adriana answered, her temper also rising. "I do understand. When you put an ad on the CityScreen and talk about the coming invasion of the Decamont, I listen. When you say that if we don't pull together, we will all be ripped apart, I hear you. It is unfortunate that two of our noble and brave had to fall, but if it means we can save the lives of everyone else—"

"Enough!" Cojax roared. He turned his back to Adriana, his steps becoming heavy. He returned to his seat, the mantle of responsibility weighing heavy on his shoulders. Cojax shook his head one last time before he spoke. "These are crimes that I cannot ignore. I warned you once of acting to this degree without my prior approval. Your actions were unsanctioned and unwarranted. Effective immediately, you will be removed from the BloodBorne High Council. All title, power, and prestige will be taken from you."

"You're just going to get rid of me?" Adriana asked.

"No," Cojax answered. "Adriana, you have tremendous talent and ability, but I have to limit your influence, at least for now. I will retain you as an advisor, but you are to speak to me directly and no one else, do you understand?"

Adriana tried to speak, but her voice failed her. She nodded instead.

"This might even be a better way to manage your spy network," Cojax said. "Since it completely removes your connection to the BloodBorne."

Adriana's hands were shaking, and so she tucked them behind her back. "So, am I free to operate as I see fit now? Now that I won't tarnish the BloodBorne's reputation?"

"No," Cojax reaffirmed. "Gather your information as you have in the past, but you are expressly forbidden to conduct any overt actions that could endanger the lives of your spies or the lives of someone else. Gather your information and report it directly to me."

Adriana's hands clenched into fists behind her back. "Is there anything else?"

"Yes," Cojax said. "I hear you have removed some equipment from the Mahghetto and are setting up some sort of factory in the Rift. Tell me why."

Adriana pushed her emotions to the side, reaching for the placid demeanor that had become her hallmark. "Jessica's spies must truly be getting better if she found out about that."

"What are you doing in the Rift?"

"Ion discovered something while perusing the Numberless Information Network," Adriana said quickly. "It seems that in their spare time, one of the Numberless had been working on an advanced set of Static Armor. I haven't been able to recreate the armor just yet, but according to the Numberless' calculations, if we are successful in its fabrication, it will work four times more efficiently than our current Static Armor."

Out of all the things Adriana could say to him, Cojax did not expect that. He had assumed she had been constructing something more nefarious—perhaps a secret detention facility where she could keep political prisoners. But, now that she said it was to make armor, that completely coincided with Jessica's preliminary report.

"Why are you making armor?"

"For the Numberless," Adriana answered simply.

Cojax shifted in his seat. "How do you know about them?"

Adriana shrugged. "We both have our talents, Cojax. One of mine is finding out things that people try to keep hidden."

"Tell me."

"I wasn't spying on you—if that's what you were asking. I merely stumbled across the information. Ion was the first to notice it, actually. There was an abnormal drain of power coming from the Trinity in the areas utilized by the Numberless. At first, I thought it was another political party that was storing the energy so they could obtain some sort of political advantage. Turns out, you've been waking the Numberless without approval from the First Assembly." Adriana shook her head in mock disapproval.

It was not entirely true. Cojax had not been waking the Numberless, that was something that Horace was doing, but Cojax did not bother to correct her.

"So, what does that have to do with the armor?" Cojax asked.

"Well," Adriana replied as she sat down on the conference table in a way that accented her bust line. "We really don't have any idea what sort of force the Decamont will be sending against us. For all we know, they could be sending a host of Numberless to grind us into submission. So, when I stumbled across these plans and studied them, I realized exactly how much of an advantage we could gain if we fabricated this new armor. It would grant each Numberless four times more strength, protection, and power."

Cojax shifted again in his chair. "Why didn't you tell me this sooner?"

"We haven't even made our first set," Adriana replied, "and I'm never one to overpromise and under deliver. This idea is based on a

Numberless' design, so I didn't want to let you know until I knew the idea was viable."

"If it is viable," Cojax said, "you may have just stumbled onto our salvation. How soon do you think you could begin production?"

"I'll need time to conduct tests to make sure it's even worth our time."

"Adriana, this is huge," Cojax said. "This could change everything. Tell me what you need to make this happen."

"The most time-consuming element will be in recalibrating the existing machines that make the armor. I think if we get some of the best minds working on it, we can get it done within a week and a half. After that, it will be a simple process of getting each Numberless' measurements and fabricating the armor. Each set of armor will take two to three minutes to make, depending on the dimensions."

Cojax leaned forward. "How many machines do you have set up?"

"Well," Adriana said, "technically, not even one. We still are missing some parts, but I imagine it'll be completed by the end of the day."

"We need twenty more machines just like it. More if we can find them."

"The Machines are found in the belly of the Mahghetto. If we didn't bother to move them, we could begin production sooner."

"No," Cojax said. "I like your idea of moving them to the Rift. This is something we need to hide from the other Factions—otherwise, they'll each want to exploit it for their own goals. Move the machines to the Rift and set them up there. I'll get the Rifters to help you out. You can trust them to keep it secret. I want you to make this a major priority. I'll be diverting as many resources as I can to this endeavor."

Cojax's eyes snapped back to Adriana. She was smiling, but it was only a shadow of her usual smile. Cojax felt a wave of guilt wash over his body, seeping into his gut, forcing him to break eye contact with her. Out of all of the people that served him, she was by far the most earnest. By her advice alone, Cojax had avoided all sorts of pitfalls and mistakes. In no way would he have as much success now without her support. And just before she had brought him this news, he berated her like she was a little school girl that had forgotten her homework.

He began to regret his harsh rebuke of Adriana. He could not apologize for what he said before—he still stood by it. But he wished he could take back how he had said it. Cojax approached Adriana, placing his hands gently on her shoulders. "Adriana, I'm truly glad you're on our side. You understand that, right? I may not agree with the way you deal with things, but there's no denying how effective you are."

Adriana nodded. "Thank you, my Lord."

THIRTY-SEVEN

The people of Acadia never had a holiday, never celebrated a birthday, never even took the time to sit down and watch a movie. Those activities had long since been rooted out of the city. So, when the Day of Titan was announced by the BloodBorne Party, it was received with a variety of reactions: disgust, angst, excitement, disdain, trepidation. But by far, the most significant emotion was the people's sense of curiosity. Initial sentiment for the event was not good, as most seemed to think of it as a prodigal event. Surprisingly, however, when the BloodBorne invited each Faction to participate in the opening ceremonies, only two Factions refused—both of which were major supporters of the Populi Party. The other thirty-three Factions were quick to pledge their support, eager to represent their Faction as well as honor Titan.

Cojax was amazed at the decorations that were put together in such a short time. The main road that led to the Trinity was lined with banners, each sporting an image of Titan's blade on a red and white background. The closer one drew to the Trinity, the more elaborate and prolific the decorations became. Around the Trinity, several sets of Titan's armor and weapons were on display along with footage playing on a CityScreen of the heroic deeds accomplished while using them. Other Validated of note were also recognized, turning one of the main forums into a living museum. This, by far, was the most difficult thing to plan and prepare, because they had to use extreme caution in selecting the right Validated as not to offend any of the Factions. They were careful to include at least two Validated in the display from each Faction.

The BloodBorne had rented all of the major CityScreens for the entire day, an enormously expensive cost that would have had Byron stammering if he was still on the BloodBorne High Council. To offset the cost, a nominal fee was required to watch the events from any CityScreen at home. The large CityScreens that were situated at every major forum broadcast the games for free, which in itself, was an incentive for the Validated to leave their apartment for the day and join in the festivities.

The morning began with a march along the main thoroughfare that led to the Trinity. Each Faction sent through their most elite and seasoned warriors. Many Factions showed off their skill with the blade or lance as they walked, proving how unique each group was.

The Cretan Faction marched with the heads of several SataniKahns that they had taken down in battle. Those in the Saken Faction marched without their armor, showing off each tribal tattoo that they had earned in various conflicts. Onar was at the front of the Saken procession. The mountain of a man stared unblinking at Cojax, his gaze clearly conveying that he would relish in any challenge that was issued. Faction after Faction came forward: the Curetes, who were known for their emphasis and prowess with the Arc Lance; the Pelasgians who valued silence and order above all; the Prolits who preferred a Phalanx formation with three times the typical Validated; the Hellions, who prided themselves most on individual combat; the Dryopes; the Kranaoi; the BloodLetters, who had a habit of smearing waxy Roach blood on their armor before battle; the Temmian; the Aones; the Screamers, who reveled in their violent war cries; the BlackHearts; the BloodBorne; the Cynurians; the Lox; the Minyans; the Telchines; the Mycenaeans; the BlackStones, who marked themselves by wearing black stones in their pierced ears; the Cicones; the Aemones; the Calmeans; the Kylik; the RedEyes, who were known for tattooing the whites of their eyes red once they obtained the Fifth Tier; the Invictors; the Cutters; the GriefGivers; the Armstrongs; and the Braken.

Despite Cojax's vehement protest, he and his staff were strategically placed on a balcony where they could oversee the whole affair. They had rented all the other balconies in the area, but these they kept vacant so that only Cojax and the BloodBorne were seen above the crowd. It was a subtle difference, but one that sent a clear message. Cojax hated the message that it sent, but he found himself outvoted, even by Orch, who had never voted against him in the past.

After the march through the street, the opening ceremonies began as a flame was carried by all the Faction leaders to a wood pyre in the middle of the street. Wood was rare in Titan since it had to be cultivated in the city where land was scarce. It represented an enormous expense that again would have Byron swearing if he would have known about it. When the pyre caught fire, an almost reverent silence fell over the crowd. The fire went quickly as the wood had been mixed with an accelerant. Within twenty minutes, the HoverCams all panned to Cojax, broadcasting his image on the CityScreens throughout the city. He gave a brief speech about Titan and why they should never forget him. It was a somber lecture and, mostly because it was short, seemed like it was well-received.

Then Orch took over, telling a series of mostly inappropriate jokes as he announced the day's activities. Various competitions were organized and broadcast throughout the city to include javelin throwing, wrestling, sprinting, shotput, Vortex running, Blazer wielding, discus, high jump, and long jump. To ensure that not everyone in the city tried to compete, an entrance fee was required by all participants. The money was then used to reward those who placed in the competitions. At noon, the winners of these first competitions were announced, and a formal but quick reward ceremony followed.

Cojax was in awe as he watched some of the Validated compete. Every Innocent had participated in these sorts of athletic events before entering the Mahghetto, but no one had ever competed as a Validated before. The athletic skill brought out by the competition was enthralling to say the least.

Once these contests were completed, food and stock was provided in several of the main forums. To prepare for the massive distribution of food, Cojax had his entire Faction only eating one meal a day for several days leading up to the festival. Adriana also convinced Brutus to provide more of an exotic palate of meats and mushrooms, supplemented by grilled vegetables. The food given to the masses was only barely above what a Validated could expect on a daily basis. The food served to Cojax and his honored guests, however, was something else entirely. Instead of receiving their standard fare, they now ate foods that were previously only available to a Numberless. Jessica had arranged and preordered it utilizing the Numberless ArmGuards, and Adriana had made sure the food appeared without incident. All the leaders from every significant Faction and political party were in attendance, save a few in the Populi Party leadership and Onar. Cojax would have invited Onar, but he was afraid the large man would insult him or one of his guests until a conflict would break out, much like he had with the First Tiers.

They had rented the largest room in the Trinity and adorned it with flashy banners of red and white. The food was available buffet style while the stock was served by various waiters and waitresses. Cojax had arranged it this way so he could make sure the stock did not disappear before the food did. The stock had been taken from Seleukus' private stores, unbeknownst to Seleukus himself, and Cojax was not going to waste it if he did not have to.

Despite most of the Populi leadership not being present, the room immediately split into three groups, one supporting the BloodBorne, a smaller, formal group supporting the Restorationists, and a third, louder contingent supporting the Populi. This became readily apparent when sympathizers of the Populi Party won a particular event or competition and half the room filled with loud, obnoxious cheering. Cojax was confused at the behavior at first, having not even paid attention to which competitor was sympathetic to which cause. But then he noticed that a number of the competitors wore blue bands on their upper arms, a clear sign that they favored the Populi Party. What had initially been just friendly competition, now turned into a political tool.

Cojax purposely entered the buffet just behind Segundus, one of the foremost leaders of the Populi. Segundus pretended not to notice Cojax at first, focusing his attention on his ArmGuard instead. It seemed a weak ploy, especially since Cojax was flanked by two bodyguards dressed in BloodBorne attire.

Cojax nudged the large man in the shoulder, drawing his attention.

"Are you here to take my drink order?" Segundus growled.

Cojax frowned ever so slightly. "No, but I can arrange for something to be brought over." He gestured a hand towards a waiter, who immediately responded, bringing a rare variety of stocks.

"What would you care for?" Cojax asked with a gesture to the tray. "We have dark, light, and cinnamon here."

"I didn't know stock came in more than one flavor," Segundus replied. "I'm glad to see that you've spent your time so productively since the AC fell. Thank you, but no. When I can avoid it, I don't engage in any sort of Dependent activity that results in such a waste."

"I hear your party has stored up a great deal of stock," Cojax replied. "Doesn't your party use your leverage over the power distribution to get lower prices for it? I imagine in exchange for stock, they get indulgent five-minute showers whenever they want."

"Excuse me," Segundus said. "What's your name?"

"Cojax Artino, Lord of the BloodBorne, Son of Titan."

"Oh, yes. The boy who would be king. Yes, I've heard your name mentioned a few times…at least in jest."

"I imagine so," Cojax replied. "I seem to be the main star in all of your ad campaigns. Tell me, why do you fancy putting all your energy in attacking a boy?"

"If I'd known that I would have to endure a lecture to get some free food," Segundus replied, "then I would've gladly paid instead."

Cojax shook his head. "Today is not about our competing political parties; it's about honoring one of the fallen. Titan was a great man and an even better leader. My intent for this whole affair is to bring our people together and find common ground."

"And if it just so happens that you gain more support by using your dead father as part of your platform," Segundus shrugged, "so be it, right? That's why Marcus is not here. He would not disrespect your father's honor by capitalizing on his death."

Cojax clenched his jaw. For a few seconds, uncontrollable anger flared through his body, tightening his arms and muscles. He breathed deep, forcing it down. He would not play into this politician's hands. "Although, I see you showed up regardless. I guess for some people, free food is too good to pass up." Cojax let out a long breath, forcing down his anger. "Segundus, I know we are on opposite ends of the spectrum."

"Yes," Segundus replied quickly, "I offer the people freedom, and you bring them bondage."

Cojax continued, undeterred by the interruption. "But by the end of this process, whatever government is in control, we'll need the support of every able body in the city."

"If you're looking for able bodies," Segundus replied, "then why do you spend your time hanging around the Aberration?"

Cojax's hand drifted to the blade at his side. He almost drew it. The moment passed, and his focus returned. "Am I missing something? I came over here with an offer of friendship, or at least understanding, and you attack me as if I've always been your enemy. You don't know me or my Faction. You don't know what Jessica and I had to do to get where we are now."

Segundus turned, all pretense of civility gone. "I don't know you, true, but your actions speak volumes of who you are. And, you and I will be enemies now and long after our government controls the city. Your party has specifically won solidarity by placating to a Validated's basest of desires. You know, I think I've lost my appetite." With this, Segundus turned and headed back to the other side of the room, pushing through a small group of BloodBorne lost in conversation.

Cojax stared at Segundus, his expression betraying his confusion and surprise.

"Don't worry about him," said a voice from behind him.

Cojax turned, his face forming into a smile as he met eyes with Jessica. She smiled back in earnest, completely driving away the anger he was feeling just moments before.

"They hate me," Cojax said.

"As can be expected."

"But I'm such a great guy," he said in jest.

"And humble, too," Jessica replied. "You know Elena used to say something that has always stuck with me: 'Some people will hate you when you fail, but they will hate you much more if you succeed.' As long as you have success, you'll be at odds with many in the Populi Party."

"And my brother?"

Jessica nodded. "Hopefully, this won't come between the two of you. He's a good man, so I can't see him holding a grudge—at least not for long. But I wanted to talk to you about something else."

Cojax already knew exactly what she wanted to speak to him about, but he was not going to make it easy for her. He feigned ignorance. "And what's that?"

She pulled Cojax to the side of the room, out of earshot of those around her. "You can't fight Onar."

Cojax gave a cocky grin. "But I can."

"No," Jessica replied. "You can't. How many people have to tell you before you realize how foolish this idea is?"

"I've been training—"

"—For what, two months? That beast has been using his blade for years."

"My training is a specific kind. I have a Numberless teaching me how to use my blade. I don't think there's a person in the city that could say that. And I'll be using Horace's armor."

"It won't matter," Jessica insisted.

Cojax grabbed Jessica by the arms. "Please, Jessica, I need your support more than ever. I need you to trust me on this, without question. If I'm to succeed, I need you at my side. Can you do that?"

"Are you asking me to pretend to be alright with you going to your death?"

"Trust me," Cojax insisted.

Jessica shook her head, pulling Cojax into an embrace. He returned the embrace. They did not touch long, since physical contact was still seen as taboo by many Validated, at least in public.

"Alright, Cojax," Jessica replied. "But, if you die, I'm going to figure out a way to bring you back to life so I can kill you myself."

***

The evening was reserved for the greatest and most intense competition. Wrestling and lawn sports gave way to gladiatorial combat. When Cojax was first organizing this event, Clandis insisted that they establish firm and consistent rules of engagement for the gladiatorial matches. First and most important rule, fights were only to last until one fighter drained the shields of another. To ensure the first rule was not broken, Clandis used a device developed by the Mycenaeans Faction. During one-on-one bouts in training, the Mycenaeans used a smaller, secondary power source that attached to the armor. If a warrior's shields were drained completely, the secondary battery source would kick in, protecting them just in case they faced an overzealous opponent. Despite the simplicity of the device, the Mycenaeans were the only Faction that utilized it with any sort of consistency. Clandis insisted that they employ it during the festival, however, lest revelry turned to butchery. Cojax thought it showed weakness, or at the very least, a sense of paranoia, but Clandis' insistence won out.

And Clandis could not have been more right. As soon as the matches began, the opponents started battling as if they were mortal enemies. More than just a few of the bouts would have ended up in death had Cojax not followed Clandis' suggestion.

As in the Mahghetto, the matches were regulated by a Magister, who allocated points as well as issued punishments for broken rules. While under the AC, fighting in this style was common in the Mahghetto, but much rarer once one achieved the rank of a Validated—since as a Validated, no one had the time or energy to waste in personal matches. The only exception were the Numberless, who had turned dueling into an art form. Now, with the AC abolished, and with over two months of little to no combat, each Validated craved battle as they never had before. And it was not just the gladiators that reveled in it, but the audience as well. They had no shortage of contestants, and within minutes of opening the conflict to the public, each available slot was filled.

They held the highest-profile bouts in the same room that was utilized by the First Assembly. The BloodBorne had rented and reserved the room for the day. When the Populi Party heard what their intended use of the room was, they fiercely objected. They asserted that using it in that fashion would degrade and undermine the current political proceedings. But their arguments had little weight since the room had been specially manufactured, designed, and utilized exclusively for gladiatorial combat.

The BloodBorne had constructed a temporary box for Lord Cojax and his retinue. The addition included access to the sandpit as well as a changing room in the back. Despite the rush in construction, it had been well decorated and displayed a mess of red and white banners. After every bout, the BloodBorne panned the cameras to Cojax's box so they could record and broadcast his reaction live.

In the early afternoon, they started with high-profile matches followed by reenactments of famous battles. The battles were often staged in the large forums spread throughout the city. This allowed the greatest number of spectators to watch the conflict live, which proved a nice touch. The festival already had too many exclusive elements that separated the people by Tiers, something that both Cojax and Jessica hated but found unavoidable. There was just simply no way to include the entire city of ten million in every single event.

Then the main event began, pitting some of the best fighters against each other in single combat. Talent met strength in the arena, proving that the best had been saved for last.

Even though Cojax's conflict was to be the final match, he found himself in the changing room, donning the armor that Horace had lent him far before his time. It felt comfortable as it wrapped around his body, fitting far better than any of his previous sets. He hefted his sword, the very blade that Titan often carried into battle. It was large but elegant, a blade made for a true master of his craft. His nerves twisted and turned inside as he looked at the blade. "I will not dishonor you tonight."

Finn, Orch, and Jessica found Cojax alone, releasing and reattaching one of his ArmGuards in a rhythmic and consistent manner.

"So," Orch said, "I'm assuming that you'd prefer a closed casket?" The joke fell flat, earning Orch reproachful glares by both Jessica and Finn. "What?" Orch replied. "I know we were all thinking it."

"You'll be fine out there," Jessica said more to herself than anyone else.

Cojax applied his ArmGuard one final time. "Yes, I will be. Don't worry about me; I'll be just as safe as anyone of you."

Finn opened his mouth to speak but seemed to think better of it. He seemed torn between trying to convince Cojax to back down and showing his support. He finally settled on saying weakly, "You got this guy."

They passed the time trying to talk about anything but the impending conflict. They failed miserably. They seemed stuck between talking about the fight with Onar and dead silence. Finally, Cojax straightened his shoulders, eyeing the other three. "You guys sure know how to make someone feel nervous."

"You're right," Jessica said quickly. "We better get back to the stands. Come on, let's give him some time alone."

Orch followed, but Finn hesitated. It looked like Finn was going to pat Cojax's shoulder one last time, but he went in for an awkward hug instead.

"I'll be fine," Cojax said.

Finn nodded once, then twice, then a third time, each time with more conviction. He turned and followed Jessica and Orch out the room and into the stands. As with all things of this nature, the time went by too slowly and too fast all at once. Before long, Cojax received a notification on his ArmGuard that his bout with Onar would be next. Within minutes, he could hear his name being called out across the CityScreens. He grabbed his Arc Blade and Repulse Shield.

As soon as he appeared, the announcer began to speak. "May I present Cojax Artino, Lord of the BloodBorne." These words were met with tumultuous cheers. Cojax was surprised by the ear-splitting sound. The cheers were not divided by political party, as they had been for other bouts. Even many members of the Populi Party cheered openly. Apparently, most everyone wanted to see Onar be beaten, or at least humbled, regardless of their allegiance.

The CityScreens changed from Cojax to the tens of thousands who gathered all around the city, mostly in the public forums and before the massive CityScreens that were located there. The people were in a frenzy, screaming with all the fervor that they possessed. He tried to look confident and commanding, but the noise was so pervasive, it was unsettling.

"And the contender," the announcer said with a low voice. "This man is well known among the city, having been honored on the CityScreens many times before this night. He is known for killing the Byzine, a SataniKahn so large it could not fit through the city Gates. He solidified his reputation at the battle of the South Wall, where he earned the moniker 'Unbroken.' All those around him gave way to death, but he alone stood up against the onslaught of evil. May I present to you, Onar, King of the Unbroken."

The room filled with cheers, especially from the shirtless Sakens, who went absolutely manic. As Onar appeared, Cojax began to wonder why his name was not introduced with all of his heroic deeds.

Onar was so large, he had to duck to clear the archway that led into the arena. His armor was a brilliant sheen of black and silver. In one hand, he held his massive sword, in the other a circular shield decorated with black tribal symbols. Despite the mountain of a man wearing a helmet, Cojax could feel the intensity of Onar's stare.

Onar made a show of walking around Cojax with languid and

deliberate steps. Cojax did his best to look bored but had a hard time of it. Onar was huge, making Cojax look more infant than warrior. The audience went fanatical at the sight of the two opponents squaring off. A Magister appeared, gesturing both opponents to the middle.

Her voice was amplified and broadcast so the entire city could hear. "First to lose their shields will be declared the loser. Points shall be tracked in the unlikely event you both lose your shields at the same time and a decision must be made. Otherwise, may the best Validated—" The Magister looked distractedly at Cojax, her face pulled back into a question. "Where's your helmet?"

Cojax suddenly went crimson, his sword hand reaching up to his face, confirming he was indeed not wearing his helmet. In front of the entire city, Cojax had forgotten his helmet, like some fumbling Disciple in the Mahghetto. A mistake like that would have been death on the battlefield since it was through the helmet that one received and transmitted their orders.

The cheering gave way to laughter as Cojax turned and ran back to his changing room. He reappeared a moment later, his helmet on, his Arc Blade in hand. The cheering became so loud that Cojax's helmet began to reduce the sound to safer levels. As soon as Cojax returned, the Magister raised her hand, a sign for the combat to begin. And begin it did. Cojax charged in, swinging his blade with rapid succession, catching Onar by surprise. He was not used to being forced to fight defensively.

Cojax moved as if he were Horace, forcing his opponent into a quick series of exchanges. Onar tried to adjust, trying to find the pattern in the mad assault. But each time he did, he was disappointed as it suddenly changed. The large man was hit twice in the legs, glancing blows that only sparkled from the impact. Cojax pushed his opponent towards the arena wall. Just when Onar thought he saw an opening, Cojax rolled across the ground, and swung his blade back, catching Onar right in the head. Light and cheers filled the room. Onar jumped forward, catching Cojax just as he gained his feet. The large Validated returned his own terrific swing, hitting Cojax in the arm. Onar would have pushed on, but Cojax recovered quickly.

The two hesitated, eyeing the other's form. Cojax nodded, an acknowledgment of his opponent's skill. Onar did not respond in kind. They circled each other, waiting for the approach of their opponent.

Cojax feigned a retreat, one of Horace's favorite moves, drawing in his quarry. When Onar pursued, Cojax took two steps forward and one to the right in the shape of a large 'L.' Onar swung his blade, just barely missing Cojax, who rushed back in and placed a careful Arc Blade right into the behemoth's chest.

The audience roared.

Onar bellowed in rage. He went on the offensive, his calm demeanor giving way to an explosive anger. He hammered down on Cojax's Repulse Shield, but Cojax returned an attack to Onar's legs. The attack was so forceful, it almost knocked Onar to his knees. Cojax feigned an assault and then pulled back, his opponent swinging wildly but catching nothing but air.

The Lord of the BloodBorne moved back in, hitting Onar once in the head, twice in the chest, and another time in the legs. The attacks came so fast that if one had blinked, they would have missed them completely. Onar engaged again, responding to the blows with one horrific swing of his Arc Blade. By sheer random luck, he caught Cojax in the shield, ripping it free from his grip and sending it to the side. Onar now felt he had the advantage. In a unique move, Onar sprinted forward, using his shield as a ram. Cojax hit Onar once in the head as he came forward, but with the momentum Onar had gained, Cojax was unable to push back. Onar drove his quarry back across the arena until he slammed Cojax's body against the wall. At the same time, Onar used his Repulse Shield to send a pulse so strong that it cracked the concrete in the arena. Onar held Cojax against the wall with this Repulse Shield while using his blade to exploit any openings he could find. Cojax was hit twice in the helmet, a third time in the leg. Onar then shifted his shield to the side and went in with a terrific swing. Cojax ducked and rolled away, allowing the blade to slice clear through the concrete arena wall. A large slab teetered before falling backwards and kicking up dust on impact.

Onar thought victory was well within his reach—now that he had a shield and his opponent did not. He pushed the attack, alternating strikes between his shield and sword. But Cojax turned this advantage around, using Onar's limited visibility to attack from odd angles. Onar was hit again and again, each blow leaching energy from his shield. Finally, in frustration, Onar threw his shield at his opponent, which was quickly batted away.

Cojax moved in, attacking with a speed and skill unseen before by a mere Validated. Blow after blow struck Onar, and he was powerless to stop the onslaught. Light cascaded from Onar's shields in a waterfall of energy. He was pushed back again, and again, his counterattacks were anticipated and stopped short. The next second, Onar's sword was knocked free and sent skidding across the sand below. With a desperate roar, Onar lunged forward, trying to wrap his arms around his opponent and squeeze him into submission. This turned into his final mistake. With three horrific blows, Onar was brought to his knees, his energy depleted.

The audience was in so much shock that instead of responding with applause, they stood there in silence, their minds not quite comprehending what had just happened. Even the announcer and Magister failed to speak.

Then the applause began. It was slow at first but then quickly gained momentum. Soon, every man, woman, and child throughout the whole city was in an uproar. It went on for minutes.

Cojax ignored it all and instead fished Onar's Arc Blade out of the sand. He then presented Onar with the blade, placing it before him. Onar did not accept it. He shook his head, ashamed to pick it up.

Cojax then nodded to Onar, as he had while they were dueling, an explicit acknowledgment of the giant warrior's skill. This time, Onar returned the nod, as well as a crisp salute. With this Cojax Artino, Lord of the BloodBorne, left the arena.

THIRTY-EIGHT

Marcus played the conflict back again and again, studying Cojax's movements as he attacked, defended, and eventually conquered. His brother's skill was so beyond anything he had ever seen that he could not believe it. He slowed down the frame rate of the conflict, hoping to figure out exactly how his brother was doing this. Even at this speed, Cojax's movements blurred.

"I've never seen anything like it," Segundus replied.

"Could have been a trick of the cameras," Ion retorted. "The Numberless used to manipulate video all the time to convey any message they wanted."

"I was there in the room," Segundus answered, his voice filled with frustration. "It was no trick of the cameras."

"Then, he must have been working with Onar from the beginning," Marcus answered.

"You were with Cojax in the beginning, remember?" Segundus answered. "I imagine you would have noticed a big guy like Onar in the room at one of your early meetings."

Marcus fell silent as he completed the film again. Once finished, he played it again and then again.

Segundus shook his head. "If you keep up this pace, you'll be mad by the end of the day. Give it a rest. Your brother apparently has much more talent than we thought. It doesn't change anything. Our message is the same as it always has been—that our political party will offer the greatest freedom to the most amount of people. We stand to protect the disenfranchised and the broken, shield them from tyranny by giving them a voice."

Marcus did not answer. He restarted the film.

Segundus mumbled something about getting some sleep and left the room. Ion stayed but remained so quiet and motionless that Marcus thought he was alone.

It had been a disappointing day for the Populi Party. In the days that led up to the "Day of Titan," they had spent much of their energy criticizing the activity as a waste of time and resources. They manufactured some new ads that denounced the glorification of Titan, who was a Numberless and one of the key tyrants that ruled over them. The ads had been well received, and their support had even grown because of them.

Encouraged by this early success, they planned on staging their greatest and most dynamic political rallies yet throughout the whole city on the Day of Titan. While Cojax prepared food and banners for their festival, Marcus and his allies were overseeing the construction of platforms for their gatherings. They initially tried to rent the large and open public forums throughout the city, but the BloodBorne had already reserved those spaces for the day. It was not a significant problem; after all, most of their rallies were held in the streets anyway.

As the details of what Cojax and the BloodBorne were planning leaked out—especially at how enormously expensive all of it was going to be—Marcus felt sure that his brother had overstepped. He saw this as an opportunity to not only push the ideas of their party but undermine the efforts of the BloodBorne. If they could prevent the people from attending the festival, the BloodBorne would essentially gain nothing while at the same time bankrupting themselves. And then a rumor almost too good to be true reached Marcus' ears: Cojax was planning on challenging Onar to combat. Onar the self-proclaimed King, the man that slaughtered the three highest Validated as if they were nothing. Soon, all the major leaders of the Populi Party thought that the BloodBorne Faction would be broke and their leader broken by the end of the week.

On the morning of the day of the festival, the attendance at the first two rallies was poor. But this was to be expected since they started so early. As the next few demonstrations were set to begin, Marcus began to see the crowds of people that he was expecting. Except, they did not stop at the rallies, but continued on to the center of the city—towards the heart of the festival. Marcus did not believe it at first. His confusion turned to frustration that eventually boiled over into anger. Cojax had played to the baseness of the people, and they loved him for it. For the thousandth time, Marcus cursed his brother's name.

Marcus began mumbling something to himself.

Ion shifted in his chair. "What was that?"

Marcus turned, his face trying to sport a smile that looked more like a grimace. "Ion, I didn't know you were still here."

"Did you figure something out?"

"I think we've been looking at the wrong thing," Marcus said. "Do you have any footage of the crowds in the room?"

"We have a lot of footage of the crowds," Ion answered. "We recorded everything they broadcasted."

"Show me Jessica's face."

It took some time for Ion to sort through the footage, but he eventually found it.

"Sync up the time with this camera angle to the time that Cojax appears in the arena."

Ion did so only moments later. They watched Jessica's reaction as Cojax entered the arena.

"There," Marcus said. "Do you see it?"

Ion shook his head. "I see Jessica."

"She doesn't look anxious, does she?" Marcus asked.

"Actually, I think she looks very anxious," Ion answered.

Marcus instructed Ion to zoom in on other people in the BloodBorne Party. To Ion, each one seemed just as uneasy as Jessica did. Marcus, however, was not nearly as convinced and kept pointing at different faces, saying things like, "If they were really worried, why would they take a drink right now? Wouldn't they be more worried about losing their leader?"

Ion kept replying as directly as he could. "Maybe they were just thirsty."

"Can't you pull up the facial reading software and run the crowd of BloodBorne through it?" Marcus asked.

"The First Assembly has banned the use of that program," Ion replied. "You should know this; you were one of the individuals that spoke most passionately against its use."

Marcus nodded. "Yes, I know that, but this is more important. Did you save a copy of the program somewhere? Isn't there some way you can access it?"

"Are you saying you want me to break the very law that you voted in favor of?" Ion asked.

"We need to find out exactly what happened."

Ion shifted uncomfortably in his chair. "I did build a backdoor into the AC, just in case the Decamont had a way to invalidate everyone's user access somehow. But…"

"Just do it," Marcus replied.

"But I don't think…"

"Do it," Marcus roared.

Ion gulped, sliding himself to a computer console. Within seconds, he had the software and was pushing the footage through it. Inside a minute, Ion was looking at a chart of the collective emotion spectrums of everyone in the BloodBorne that was present at the conflict.

"What does all this mean?" Marcus asked.

"Most of them are showing signs of fear, trepidation, anxiety."

"You said most of them," Marcus answered. "Who isn't?"

Marcus honed in on the data, pulling up a few random faces in the BloodBorne crowd. Ion pointed them out. "These few are showing signs of excitement …and enjoyment."

"These two know something then."

Ion shook his head. "Maybe, but not likely. The software is not perfect and can sometimes misinterpret feelings of anxiety for excitement. Physiologically, those emotions affect someone in a very similar way."

"Who are these two people?"

Ion read off their names. Neither Marcus nor Ion recognized them. They were not widely known Validated, and according to their records, they were inconsequential.

Marcus shook his head in frustration. "No, this is nothing. Go back to the beginning where the conflict begins. Let's watch it again."

Either by mistake or by some good fortune, Ion happened to rewind the video to the part where Cojax forgot his helmet. Marcus was about to tell Ion to skip this part when he stopped himself.

Marcus began to speak his thoughts aloud. "He forgot his helmet. How could he do that? That's the last piece of equipment any seasoned Validated would forget. Linking shields is not nearly as effective without your helmet. How could he forget his helmet?" And then inspiration hit Marcus. "Ion, pull up two images of Cojax on separate screens: one where he is exiting without his helmet, and another when he is exiting with his helmet." For the next thirty minutes, they studied the two images carefully."

"There," Marcus said triumphantly.

Ion leaned forward. "His boot?"

"What's inside his boot," Marcus replied. "When Cojax leaves his dressing room the first time, he does not have a dagger in his boot. When he returns with his helmet on, however, you can just barely see the hilt of a dagger in his right boot."

"He might have placed that dagger in his boot," Ion said, "when he was retrieving his helmet."

"Or," Marcus replied quickly. "Cojax went inside to get his helmet, but someone else came out wearing it."

THIRTY-NINE

Marcus' mood went from bad to worse over the next week. The days after the festival proved more damning than the festival itself. Not only had Onar and all his followers pledged their unwavering loyalty to Cojax during the next assembly, but the Populi Party was beginning to hemorrhage supporters. The shift was not nearly as bad as it was for the Restorationists who were losing thousands of followers every day to the BloodBorne, but it did represent a tipping point had been reached.

Marcus spent much of his time trying to determine the exact point in which the BloodBorne had taken the lead. He turned into a recluse, stepping back from his duties as the Populi Consul. They still held Senate meetings with the same frequency as before, but Marcus had no heart to join them. He was exhausted by the endless debates and perpetual voting. Even the most straightforward and most obvious measures were often difficult to pass through simply because of their procedures and policies.

On the fifth day after the festival, Marcus Artino stared at himself in the mirror. They had fallen, but they were not beaten—not by a large margin. And Validated changed their support as often as the wind changes direction. *The combined force of the Restorationists and Populi Party could still overtake the BloodBorne. I just have to come up with a way to win over the Restorationist Party.* Using his ArmGuard, he requested an emergency meeting. Several of the Populi Party leaders resisted at first, voting to delay the meeting until that afternoon because it conflicted with several planned rallies. Marcus was willing to make the concession, since it would, at the very least, give him time to organize his thoughts.

Marcus called the meeting to order several hours later. He would have preferred to jump right into the heart of the matter, but their established procedure was to talk of ongoing issues first. Not long into it, the debating and voting began. Marcus was certainly not the only one affected by the BloodBorne's increased influence. Tempers were quick to flare; conflict was almost impossible to avoid. Finally, Marcus was given the floor, which he used to great effect.

"My brothers and sisters," Marcus began, "we are at a crossroads. A thousand years from now, as our descendants learn about our city, they will look to this point in our history as being the deciding factor of who we have become as a people. All of you are aware of the shift in support for Lord Cojax Artino of the BloodBorne. We have weeks, maybe even days, before he can consolidate enough support to rightfully claim control over the government. And then we will be at the mercy of a dictator; we will be at the mercy of my brother.

"We may have just taken a beating, but we are not beaten—not yet. Even now, I see a path to victory that will not only ensure our party's control but the survival of our people." Marcus paused, allowing his words to sink in.

"There are only three parties left: the Populi, the Restorationists, and the BloodBorne. Despite the BloodBorne surging in support, the combined support of the Restorationists and the Populi would be enough to gain control of the government.

"I know we've entreated them in the past, offered them all sorts of concessions in our new government, but they have stubbornly rejected any part of it. But our flaw has been that we've approached the leadership, not the people. Our party has always been one of grassroots. We need to be among the people, not among the leadership."

"What do you propose?" Cato asked.

Marcus looked towards the voice. Even though Cato had switched his support from the BloodBorne to the Populi Party, Marcus still did not trust him. Cato had been part of Cojax's inner circle, and yet, he had not provided very many details of their operation.

Marcus pushed his disgust of the man down and fiddled with his armguard, pulling up a 3D image of the city in the middle of the room. He hit another button on his ArmGuard, and the city divided into three colors: red for BloodBorne, blue for the Populi, and white for Restorationists. Marcus pointed towards the part of the city that was highlighted in white. "Some of the major Factions that support our cause are the Vixors, Cicones, Aemones, and Temmian, which are all based here." He indicated an area bordering the control of the Restorationists area. "All those Factions are effectively neighbors to the Restorationists. Since the AC fell, the Restorationists have only had two major concerns: One, a return to the AC, and two, an end to the violence that plagues their area of control. They have been made vulnerable because their leadership absolutely refuses to police their streets. They believe that if they start policing the streets, it will take them further away from the AC. So, I propose that we do it for them."

"You want to lead Populi forces into an area controlled by another party?" Segundus asked.

"Exactly," Marcus replied. "We would make it clear that we are there to stop the violence, not interfere in anything else. If we can stop the robbing, murdering, and looting, those in the Restorationist Party will have to see us as their allies. Even if their leadership condemns our actions, the people will see us as the ones who ended the violence."

"I don't know how that will play with the public perception," said a man named Hagnon. "If we occupy their streets, won't it appear that we are forcing our ideals down their throats?"

"We won't engage in any political discussion," Marcus replied. "We will simply be there as a sort of community watch."

"How long would we patrol their streets?" Cato asked. "And how many Validated are you proposing we deploy?"

"We'll stay as long as we're needed," Marcus answered. "As long as there is crime, we'll patrol the streets to protect their citizens. And I propose that we use thirty-percent of our forces. That would give us enough Validated to rotate on different schedules, so the duty of patrol doesn't become onerous."

"That's a tremendous use of our manpower," Segundus replied.

Marcus' felt his anger rise. He had never liked Segundus, even before he was elected to be the Consul of the Populi Party. He was arrogant and self-centered and never would get behind an idea unless he was the one to propose it. "Our forces do little every day. This would at least give them a purpose."

"Well," Hagnon said. "Your proposal has been heard and received. I propose that we set some time aside to debate the matter in its entirety. Moving Validated into another party's territory is a delicate matter, and we can't rush into it."

"I second that motion," Crantor said.

"Now that the motion has been seconded," Segundus said. "I'll open the floor to a vote. All in favor of a debate over the merits of Marcus' plan, raise your hand." The support was unanimous in favor of debate. Marcus was assigned the task of presenting the pros, while Hagnon was assigned the responsibility of the cons. The debate was set to take place in three days. Marcus made a motion for an injunction, asking the Senate to schedule the debate sooner because of the urgency of the situation. This was seconded by Ion and voted upon, only passing by a small margin. The debate was set to take place early the following morning.

Marcus prepared all that night as well as early the next day. He brought together all the recent reports of criminal activity that had occurred in the area controlled by the Restorationists. He was also able to find several incidents that had happened on the border between the Populi and the Restorationists, which seemed to support the idea that it was not exclusively the problem of the Restorationists, but also directly affecting the Populi Party. Ion came over to Marcus' apartment, and they brainstormed all of the possible flaws of the plan, including how to best assuage the Restorationists' concerns. Marcus and Ion took turns debating, first on one side of the issue and then the other.

Using his technical skill, Ion was able to plot several incidences of the violence starting from the fall of the AC to the present. It was slow at first and centralized in one main area, but quickly grew and spread. Whenever someone was murdered, a red dot hovered above the area; when someone was robbed or beaten, a yellow dot hovered above the area. They then compared and contrasted this to the Populi Party, which had seen a similar trend when the AC first fell. With the death of Sejanus, however, the Populi Party had voted upon and eventually instituted a temporary policing force. From that point on, all reports of violence almost completely disappeared. After that, the only incidents that occurred were in the area bordering the Restorationist Party.

Then, in an act of inspiration, Ion put together several pictures of all the Validated that had died during this time through senseless violence. The last image was that of Sejanus. Just below his image, it read, "All of these deaths could have been prevented."

Out of everything that he prepared and studied, Marcus spent most of his time perfecting his closing remarks. He used a rich rhetoric that mixed logic and emotion. By the time the sun rose the next morning, Marcus knew he was ready.

***

Marcus opened the debate, as was customary, outlining the general idea of his plan. His opponent then had an equal amount of time to point out flaws, problems, and details that may not have been well thought out. Marcus was then given even more time to address these new concerns indicated by Hagnon and propose solutions to these issues, all the while minimizing them so they appeared insignificant. Hagnon was given the same amount of time to exploit new flaws created by the solutions Marcus had suggested, all the while pointing out significant consequences that could result in these actions. A small recess was granted so that members of the Senate could speak to the debaters personally and provide insight or critique into their argument.

They then resumed where they left off. Marcus began proposing new ideas and solutions he had gathered from other members of the Senate. When they broke for lunch, Marcus, as well as several of his closest supporters, were confident that the voting would go in Marcus' favor. After lunch, it was time for closing remarks. Hagnon went first this time; Marcus followed soon after.

Marcus was only halfway through his impassioned closing remarks when a Senator from the Populi Party rushed in, her hands raised high in the air. The Senators were in an uproar at the unprecedented interruption, demanding an apology. The Senator ignored the request and instead utilized her ArmGuard to turn on a CityScreen that was situated on the wall.

At first, Marcus did not know what he was looking at. "What is this?"

The Senator responded with only two words. "Just watch."

The image was being broadcast by several HoverCams that were transmitting a live feed. It showed a BloodBorne Phalanx marching through the streets. Their ranks were disciplined and exact. The HoverCam panned out, revealing that instead of just one Phalanx marching, there were dozens throughout the city. At the head of one of the Phalanx formations marched Onar, his massive Numberless sword attached to his back.

Then Marcus began to realize what was happening, as did several of the other Senators. "Where?"

The Senator that had barged in took the HoverCams coordinates and overlaid them on the 3D image that Marcus had used during his presentation. The location was right in the middle of the Restorationist sector, right where crime was the greatest.

Marcus could not stop himself from whispering in disbelief. "They just did what we were debating on doing." It was far too coincidental for Cojax to have sent in his forces just as the Populi were discussing the merits of the idea. Marcus looked around the room, seeing some faces that were friends and others that were not far from being enemies. He knew then, as he never would have suspected before, that someone in the room had betrayed them all.

FORTY

Marcus was slow to answer the door, but answer he did. He knew who it was long before he reached the threshold. Cojax stood in the doorway. In his arms, he carried a metallic box. Behind him were twenty Validated, all who were not quite at attention but also not far from it. At the rear of the column, two Validated were patrolling the hallway, looking for any threats. Marcus also had bodyguards, but he had only four. All of which were now standing behind him.

The two brothers did not speak for a time, each one trying to gauge the mood of the other.

"Come to gloat, have you?" Marcus asked.

"May I come in?"

"No."

Cojax shifted uncomfortably, unsettled by the coldness in his brother's voice. "I brought you something."

Marcus took the box from his brother's arms and handed it to one of his bodyguards.

"Listen," Cojax said, "I don't want any of this to come between us."

Marcus felt a foul anger rising in his chest. "I have no problem with you winning. But I do take issue with how you do it: lies, deceits, intimidation, assassinations, using our deceased father to your political advantage. If even half of the things I've heard are true, you have dirtied and destroyed the name of BloodBorne for all time. Our father would have killed you himself had he known the villain you would become."

"Where do you get these accusations from?"

Marcus shook his head, looking at Cojax as if he was the greatest Dependent. "Even now, you pretend to be innocent. Even now, before your brother, who you have known your entire life, you will not admit the foul things you did to gain power."

"What are you talking about?" Cojax asked.

"Sejanus," Marcus replied.

Cojax shifted uncomfortably. "What about him?"

"Did you know about the plan to assassinate him?"

Cojax did not know how to answer.

"What about Deo's two followers? Did you know about them? Did you know that they would be butchered for doing nothing more than following their own beliefs? Is that how you will rule, with blood and terror?"

Cojax could not help but feel that this was a trap, that he was being recorded and that his brother was trying to solicit some sort of confession.

"I don't know anything about either of those unfortunate events," Cojax lied. "When I become the leader of the city, one of my first initiatives will be to appoint a special committee to investigate all murders and crimes that have occurred in the city since the fall of the AC."

"Initiatives?" Marcus asked. "Is that what you will call your unbreakable decrees?"

"My brother," Cojax said. "The conflict within our city is coming to a close, but the battle with the Decamont has yet to begin. I need people I can trust; people who have shown their brilliance as well as their political acumen. There is much to be done, and I need people I can count on."

Marcus looked at Cojax with disbelief. "Sejanus was more than just a friend; he was a visionary. A man so passionate and powerful that he inspired even the greatest Dependent to action. He was a far better man than you or I, governed by a moral sense of duty and civility. And you had that man removed because he had a different point of view."

Cojax again felt the urge to explain the situation, to explain that Adriana had acted without his blessing or his knowledge. He opened his mouth to speak, the words on the tip of his tongue, but then the nagging thought that Marcus was recording this whole conversation persisted. He would not be a fool and fall right into his brother's trap. If he explained the details surrounding Sejanus' assassination, they would be broadcast throughout the entire city by tomorrow.

Instead, Cojax decided to go on the offensive. "I don't know who murdered Sejanus, but I do know that the government you champion is destined to get us all killed. How long were you debating with your own party on the merits of sending in an army to the Restorationist sector? A few hours? The entire day? Perhaps even a few days? When I found out the need for protecting those in the Restorationist sector, I gave the order, and twenty minutes later, my forces were sweeping through the city. All the senseless deaths, such as Sejanus' assassination, will not be repeated. Do you think your government is the best to deal with an overpowering, stronger enemy? Do you think your party's indecision will lead us to victory?"

To this, Marcus had no reply. In truth, within the last few days, he had been thinking along similar lines. But he would not admit that now. Even if his government proved inefficient, it was undoubtedly more just. And it had checks and balances that would prevent the assassination and intimidation of political opponents. Had they been operating under the Populi government, Sejanus would still be alive.

This thought burned into Marcus' mind, giving him the reply that he lacked before. He took a half step forward, only inches away from his brother. "Do the Decamont even exist?"

"Of Course they exist," Cojax replied. "How can you even question that?"

"We have evidence that the Numberless were controlling the Roaches. Ion released those data files to us. We now know what happened to someone when they were Rifted. That was easy enough to find in the Numberless Information Network. But, the only person who knows anything about the Decamont is you. And if they did exist, where are they?"

"Our father told me about the Decamont."

"Just you?"

"Are you suggesting I made it up?"

"It would be the least of your crimes if you did, but not the most surprising."

Cojax frowned. There were thousands of people that knew about the Decamont. The entire city of Rome knew about them. Every Numberless that resided in Titan not only knew about them but were preparing to fight them. But, as Cojax opened his mouth to speak, he realized he could not tell that to his brother. At least not now.

Cojax sighed. "They will be here soon enough."

Marcus let out a scornful laugh. "Sejanus died to prevent a tyrant like you from taking power. And I will do the same if needed. I will not be subject to a ruler who pretends to make life or death decisions as if he is a god. The city might kneel before you, but I will not bow to a false king. Of this, I swear by the blood of my father."

Marcus shut the door a second later.

FORTY-ONE

Marcus called another emergency meeting. This time, however, he only selected those he most trusted. It was a much smaller number, but he could not take any chances. In the few days after he met with Cojax, the BloodBorne gained enough support to rightfully claim control of the government. Not long after this benchmark was reached, an announcement was sent out to all the leadership of the political parties that a First Assembly meeting would be held the next day. There was no mention of what the session would discuss, but it was evident to anyone that read it. Cojax was going to be proclaimed the Lord of Titan.

Marcus could not let this happen. If Cojax's actions in the last few months were a sample of how he was going to rule, Marcus just could not let this happen.

The meeting filled up quickly; all Senators were eager to find their seats. Marcus did not see the Senators filing in, however, since he was in a small, adjoining room that he had turned into his office. He did not know exactly what he was going to say, but he needed all of his skill of rhetoric if he was going to have any chance of succeeding. He breathed heavily, tension filling his chest. He needed something to distract him from his anxiety. As he looked around the room, he spotted the metallic box Cojax had given to him a few days before. His bodyguard had dutifully carried the box with him until Marcus instructed him to put it down on his desk. Now, a faint curiosity overcame him.

He opened the box, removed the plastic packaging, and stared at what he found. It was a robotic arm, specifically designed with Marcus' severed appendage in mind. He pulled it free and studied it. It was not hard to attach, as Marcus found out moments later. A brace tightened around his bicep as he slipped it over his severed arm, securing it into place. It was as comfortable as it was sleek, and Marcus could not help but marvel at the craftsmanship.

The arm, however, hung loosely at his side, ignoring any commands Marcus gave it. Then he began to feel a tingling sensation, as if hundreds of small needles started poking his severed limb. As the moments passed, he began to gain control over the metallic arm. It only allowed him gross motor skills at first, but the more the tingling persisted, the finer his control became. He rushed over to his desk, picked up a pen, and began writing. It was certainly not calligraphy, but it was still legible. He looked at the metal hand, opening and closing his fingers with ease, marveling at the innovation. He then blew on his fingertips, and he felt the sensation as if it were his own hand.

"Amazing," Marcus said. "But how did he did he manage this?" The answer seemed to hit him in a wave. "He must have found a machine to manufacture the arm in the Trinity—in the areas dedicated to the Numberless. But why did he wait so long to share this with me?" Marcus' initial elation turned to confusion and then anger. *Cojax held this back from me because he wanted to wait for the perfect time to bribe me with it. He let me go without an arm just so he could hang it over my head.*

He removed the metal limb, disgusted by it. He massaged the stump of his arm, making sure that there was no permanent effect.

Ion suddenly peeked inside the room. "All the Senators that you requested are present. We're ready to begin."

Marcus rubbed the stump of his arm for a few seconds longer before walking to the door, leaving the metallic arm behind. He went to the far end of the room, gingerly passing the Senators. This room had been given to them by the First Assembly, but they had rarely used it for debates or discussions. It was too small to accommodate all the Senators. The rectangle shape of the room also perturbed several of the Senators who complained that it made them feel unequal. Consequently, they typically used the same arena that was used by the First Assembly.

All eyes fell on Marcus as he stepped up to the podium in the front of the room. He raised his severed arm, as he typically did at the beginning of his speeches at political rallies. This was well received by the Senators, who cheered him on. After a while, silence fell. Marcus looked at each Senator in turn. "Brothers and sisters, we cannot let our city be enslaved by a king." The Senators echoed their approval. "And he must be stopped. I called this meeting today so we can come up with a final solution to this critical problem."

"What is there left to do?" said a tall, burly Validated.

"He has to die," said Cato.

The room fell silent at the suggestion, even Marcus seemed taken aback. He had not invited Cato to this meeting, so he was somewhat surprised to see that he was present.

"Is that what the true purpose of this meeting is?" Crantor asked. "To talk about assassination? He's a boy, nothing more."

Cato stood up, walking through the room as he spoke. "That boy had a hand in the murder of Diocles and Diotimus. That boy used Rifters to attack, mug, and assault hundreds of Validated in the Restorationist Party. I believe he sanctioned those attacks to add pressure to their leadership. When I was on the BloodBorne High Council, I saw that boy strip position and title from those who had shown him nothing but loyalty so that he could gain political advantage. Instead, he gave those positions to First Tiers, who, I remind you, had tried to kill him not days before. That boy was directly responsible for the murder of Sejanus. How much blood does Cojax have to have on his hands before you no longer see him as a boy?"

"Do you have proof of these things?" Hagnon asked.

"Nothing concrete," Cato replied. "Cojax is clever, of that there's no doubt. Much more clever than I gave him credit for. And so, he's covered his tracks, and now the trail has gone cold. But all of this he did, I remind you, before he was even our king. Imagine the horror he will bring upon all of us once he reigns as our supreme leader. We have to kill him before he becomes too much of a threat."

"I second the motion," said a pale looking Validated.

"He has to die," shouted another among the table.

"There are still plenty of Validated who would flock to our banners if we called," Crantor said. "Let's rally our forces and attack the BloodBorne."

This idea was met with cheers.

Marcus waited until the noise died before he shook his head. "That would cause a civil war, and we can't do that."

"I agree," Cato replied, still pacing the room. "Many lives would be lost, and we'd be just as culpable as the false king. No, Cojax's sins are his alone, and he must answer for them alone. We need a small, precise unit to strike quick and hard, sparing his bodyguards if possible."

"How many bodyguards does he have?" Segundus asked.

"Twenty during the day, but only ten at night," Cato answered.

"Then we kill him tonight," Segundus said.

The room erupted with cheers of acclamation.

"Death to the tyrant!"

"Where does he sleep?" Segundus asked.

"He changes his location every night, almost at random, but one of his bodyguards is loyal to me," Cato said with a smile. "We can be there in a matter of minutes. Cojax will be dead not long after that. There are twenty-three of us here. That gives us twenty-three blades to pierce his body."

The room erupted in cheers. A few began to chant, slowly at first, but gaining momentum as time passed. "Death to the tyrant! Death to the tyrant! Death to the tyrant!"

Marcus let the chanting go for several seconds before raising his good hand. "Brothers and sisters, we cannot have a king, that is true now, and it will be true tomorrow. Cojax will bring this people pain, terror, and bondage. But we cannot let ourselves be governed by our passions. I have another plan that—"

Suddenly, the room exploded. The floor and ceiling disappeared as bodies and debris were sent in every direction. The air became thick with smoke and flame. From up above, emergency lights were activated and a fog was deployed, putting out the fire. A warning siren hummed. Marcus had been blown back against the wall, his armor taking the majority of the punishment. He fell to the ground, gasping for breath. He coughed three times and rolled to his side. Smoke replaced his vision, forcing tears out of the corners of his eyes. Slowly, he pushed himself up, his one good hand shaking from the shock. Where the room once was, a crater now appeared. Marcus stood on the only portion of the room that still remained. He looked down through the web of cables and coils that poked out through random pieces of wall. He saw his friends in almost every direction that he looked—Ion, Glaphya, Marinus. All of them appeared to be dead. Their armor had protected most of their lower bodies, but their unhelmeted heads fell prey to the explosion. Marcus looked up, trying to make sense of what had happened. His head was spinning, unable to process the scene before him. He crumpled to the floor, throwing up a second later, losing the little food he had in him. He took a few minutes to gather himself before he stood up again, this time with a much clearer head. The explosion had not only claimed their room, but also several more rooms to his right. Gauging the distance from the damage, it appeared that the bomb had not been in their room, but in a room next to it. Then it dawned on him. The explosion had come from Marcus' office—the one he had been in just before the meeting had started.

Marcus looked at his stump of an arm and suddenly realized exactly what the bomb had been and where it was when it went off.

FORTY-TWO

"Lord Artino, something has happened," Adriana's voice came through Cojax's ArmGuard.

Jessica and Cojax had unintentionally fallen asleep in each other's arms as they laid down before the CityScreen in their apartment. Jessica was the first to respond, reaching for her Arc Blade that was now on the floor. She grabbed it and fastened it to her waist.

Cojax reached for his ArmGuard. "What's wrong? You alright?"

"I'm fine, but there's been an explosion in the Trinity," Adriana replied. "It happened at a Populi meeting. Ion sent me something. But now he's not responding. I think he might be…be gone."

"Was Marcus there?" Cojax asked.

"I think it was most of the Senators in the Populi Party. I'm being told that a few survived, but I don't know who. Cojax, I need to meet with you. I've got some footage to show you. This is important."

"Is Marcus alright?"

"I don't know, but this is more important than that. I have to meet with you now."

Cojax ignored the comment and cursed, grabbing his helmet and sword. As he moved, so did his bodyguards, who suddenly sprang into action, preparing to march. Cojax hailed Clandis a moment later, passing on the information about the explosion. "Assemble the BloodBorne High Council. And we need to activate the reserves to respond to the explosion. Instruct them to deploy to the area and help out with anything they can."

Cojax and Jessica were out the door not long after. Adriana hailed Cojax again on his ArmGuard. "Cojax, if you assemble the High Council, you can't be present. You need to lay low right now."

"What?" Cojax replied with a mixture of anger and confusion.

"You may be in danger," Adriana replied.

Cojax's pace slowed as he looked to Jessica. She only shook her head. He turned back to the ArmGuard. "What are you talking about?"

"Meet me at my apartment as soon as you can," Adriana replied. "Let the BloodBorne High Council convene in your absence. They'll handle the explosion just fine without you."

"Alright," Cojax responded. "I'll be there in a few minutes."

Jessica frowned. "I don't like this."

"What do you mean?" Cojax asked.

"A sudden explosion, and now Adriana wants to meet with you," Jessica replied.

"I ordered her to report to me directly," Cojax responded. "She's just following those orders. And we'll have our retinue of bodyguards."

"Then change the location," Jessica said. "If she has some urgent news, she could deliver it anywhere. Why do we need to specifically go to her apartment?"

"Probably because she doesn't know where we are staying right now."

"Please," Jessica said, "change the location to someplace that we know is safe. I still don't trust her."

"Alright," Cojax answered with a nod.

They took a private CargoLifter and headed towards Adriana's apartment. As they drew closer, Cojax changed the meet location to a vacant apartment that Cojax and Jessica would occasionally use.

Adriana did not object to the change of venue and appeared not long after. When she did arrive, Jessica insisted Adriana remove her weapons and be physically searched before being allowed to meet with Cojax.

Adriana looked bored by the time she stepped into the back room. When she saw Jessica present, however, her expression changed to annoyance. She was about to make a jibe at Jessica, but Cojax spoke first.

"You better have a good reason for this. I look weak as a leader if I convene the BloodBorne High Council and I don't even bother to show up."

"I've got a video that will change everything," Adriana said. "As you know, Cojax, Ion has been a...source of information for me." Jessica rolled her eyes, but Adriana pretended not to notice. "I have a recording of tonight's meeting—when they began to talk about your assassination in detail."

Jessica looked skeptical, Cojax curious. "Put it up on the CityScreen."

"Before I do," Adriana whispered, "you should know that one of your bodyguards is loyal to the Populi Party. I don't know which one, but we can't take any chances."

"Are you sure?" Cojax asked.

"The video will prove that and more," she responded. "But we need to get you away from your guards as quickly as possible."

"Blood and bile," Cojax swore.

"This video better be worth the trouble," Jessica grumbled.

Cojax grabbed his Arc Blade, using it to make a cut in one of the walls. He beveled the cut inwards so the piece of wall fell inside the room.

"Are your shields charged?" Cojax asked.

Jessica nodded. Adriana replied, "Of course."

One-by-one, they donned their helmets and leaped out of the building, falling seven stories downward. With three successive impacts, they hit the ground, cracking the concrete below. Jessica took the lead as they headed away from the building, down some service steps, and into the side of another building. They moved quickly, stepping into a hidden pathway that led them down to the Mahghetto. Not many knew of this path, as Jessica had cut it out herself. The path switched back and forth as it descended, but finally, they reached the Mahghetto. Initially, Jessica was going to head straight for the area with the Rifters. They would find loyal allies that could help them out with whatever needed to be done. Since Adriana was with them, however, she changed her mind. She instead headed towards the old BloodBorne section—the same area that all three of them utilized when they were Disciples.

"Feeling a little nostalgic, are we?" Adriana asked.

Jessica led them to one of the classrooms, which had a massive CityScreen at the front. All three of them removed their helmets as they studied their surroundings. Jessica nodded to the screen, her face not able to conceal her contempt. "What's this all-important message?"

Adriana powered up the CityScreen, linked her ArmGuard to it, and began playing the video. The video showed nothing but an empty room. The camera seemed to be situated on the chest of one of the Populi Senators because it jostled every time the wearer moved.

"Who's wearing the camera?" Cojax asked.

"Ion."

The video was crisp with detail and had excellent sound quality. As the minutes passed, Validated began entering the room. Cojax recognized all of them as being Senators from the Populi Party. As the room filled, Ion stood up, making awkward conversation as he tiptoed around a center table. He reached an adjoining office, peeked his head inside, and said, "All the Senators that you requested are present. We are ready to begin." With this, Ion turned around, taking a seat at the large table. Marcus exited the room not long after and took a position behind a thick podium at the far end of the room.

"Still not using the gift I gave him, I see," Cojax said.

Marcus' actual body was just outside the view of the camera, but his voice was unmistakable as he began a somber speech. "Brothers and sisters, we cannot let our city be enslaved by a king." The Senators echoed their approval. "And he must be stopped. I called this meeting today so we can come up with a final solution to this critical problem."

"What is there left to do?" said a tall, burly Validated who was just inside the camera view.

"He has to die," said an unseen individual. Cojax knew the voice well, knew that it belonged to Cato, his former adviser.

The room fell silent at the suggestion.

"Is that what the true purpose of this meeting is?" asked an unseen Senator. "To talk about assassination? He's a boy, nothing more."

Cato stood up and walked into view. As he spoke, he paced around the room, occasionally reappearing in the frame of the camera. "That boy had a hand in the murder of Diocles and Diotimus. That boy used Rifters to attack, mug, and assault hundreds of Validated in the Restorationist Party. I believe he sanctioned those attacks to add pressure to their leadership. When I was on the BloodBorne High Council, I saw that boy strip position and title from those who had shown him nothing but loyalty so that he could gain the political advantage. Instead, he gave those positions to First Tiers, who, I remind you, had tried to kill him not days before. That boy was directly responsible for the murder of Sejanus. How much blood does Cojax have to have on his hands before you no longer see him as a boy?"

"Do you have proof of these things?" asked a Senator.

"Nothing concrete," Cato replied. "Cojax is clever, of that there's no doubt. Much more clever than I gave him credit for. And so, he's covered his tracks, and now the trail has gone cold. But, all of this he did, I remind you, before he was even our king. Imagine the horror he will bring upon all of us once he reigns as our supreme leader. We have to kill him before he becomes too much of a threat."

"I second the motion," said an unseen Senator.

"He has to die," shouted another.

"There are still plenty of Validated who would flock to our banners if we called," said someone. "Let's rally our forces and attack the BloodBorne."

This idea was met with cheers.

Marcus waited until the noise died before he spoke. "That would cause a civil war, and we can't do that. Many lives would be lost, and we'd be just as culpable as the false king. No, Cojax's sins are his alone, and he must answer for them alone."

Cojax swallowed, his back going rigid. Even though he could not see him in the video, he knew it was his brother's voice. He let out a long breath that he did not even know he was holding.

"We need a small, precise unit to strike quick and hard, sparing his bodyguards if possible," said Cato.

"How many bodyguards does he have?" Segundus asked.

"Twenty during the day, but only ten at night," Cato answered.

"Then we kill him tonight," Segundus said.

The room erupted with cheers of acclamation.

"Death to the tyrant!"

"Where does he sleep?" Segundus asked.

"He changes his location every night, almost at random, but one of his bodyguards is loyal to me," Cato said. "We can be there in a matter of minutes. Cojax will be dead not long after that. There are twenty-three of us here. That gives us twenty-three blades to pierce his body."

The room in the video erupted in cheers.

Jessica stepped closer to Cojax, resting her arm on his lower back.

The Senators began to chant, quiet at first, but gaining volume as time passed. "Death to the tyrant! Death to the tyrant! Death to the tyrant!"

Cojax took a step closer to the CityScreen; the camera had shifted and was now pointing up towards a light above.

Marcus let the chanting go on for a time before calling for order. "Brothers and sisters, we cannot have a king. Cojax will bring this people nothing but pain. No offense intended Cato, but we only have one chance at killing my brother. If we deploy a strike force, there are too many variables that we cannot control. For example, what if one of us gets captured and they recognize it is someone from the Populi Party? I have another plan that is guaranteed to be successful. Ion has constructed a bomb so powerful that it will not only wipe out Cojax but all of the BloodBorne leadership as well."

"Where will you put this bomb?" Segundus asked.

"Right under the seats of the BloodBorne. And when they arrive for the First Assembly meeting—"

The camera jostled suddenly as Ion spoke up. "You said you were just going to blow up the First Assembly meeting room, not the BloodBorne. You said no one would get hurt."

"Quiet," Marcus replied. "The plan has changed. We now need to take out Cojax directly—anything less will not be enough."

"No," Ion said. "We can't do this."

"We can," Marcus growled, "and we will."

The audio cut out for a second before returning. Ion's voice was uncharacteristically strong. "I will not be part of this."

"Someone restrain him," Marcus said lazily.

Several Validated moved in, grabbing Ion around the wrists. The audio cut out as he fought back, kicking at some of the approaching Validated. But he was outnumbered and soon overwhelmed. The sound returned shortly thereafter.

Through the midst of the struggle, Ion's faint voice could be heard. "I'm sorry. I'm so sorry. I'm sorry." And then, the room exploded. A moment later, the video cut out.

Cojax looked to Jessica for support. He sat down, the weight of what he had just seen burdened him as nothing ever had before. He felt like he had aged ten years in the last ten minutes.

Adriana approached Cojax slowly, her voice sounding remorseful. "I'm sorry you had to see that."

"What happened?" Cojax asked.

"I've been trying to piece that together myself," Adriana replied. "I think when Ion realized what Marcus truly wanted to do with the bomb, he set it off remotely—either verbally or in some other way. It looks like they were keeping it in one of the adjoining rooms."

Cojax shook his head. His mind and body were so tired from this conflict that it felt like it had lasted years, not just months.

"My own brother," Cojax said finally. "My own brother would sooner have me murdered than take the throne. Where did all this hate come from? How did Ion send you this video if he was caught up in the explosion?"

"Ion was in the habit of streaming his armor feed to me whenever he attended a Senate meeting of the Populi," Adriana answered. "As soon as I heard about the explosion, I pulled up the latest footage, and I found the video I just showed you."

"How did they think they would get away with any of this?" Jessica asked.

"Marcus knew that Cojax would not be wearing his helmet during the First Assembly procedures," Adriana said. "He knew Cojax would not be nearly as cautious because he had already won."

"Last we spoke, he told me as much," Cojax answered. "He said that he would not bow to a false king. What a monumental waste of flesh. First, he abandons the BloodBorne and sides with the Populi Party, throwing his support to them just as soon as he can. Second, as a leader of his party, he blasts the city with ads that specifically and personally attack me. And then, to top it all off, when he doesn't get his way, he wants me dead."

Jessica rested her head on Cojax's shoulder.

Adriana stepped up to the other side of Cojax, placing a hand on the opposite shoulder.

"Perhaps it's best he died in the blast," Adriana answered.

"For his sake," Cojax answered, "I hope he did."

FORTY-THREE

BloodBorne Validated arrived long before any of the other parties, fanning out among the First Assembly room and checking every space for any possible threat. Once the room was secure, ten guards were posted at every principal entrance with several more assigned the job of roving through each stairwell and aisle. Decorations were hung up not long after, filling the First Assembly with the mark of the BloodBorne coupled with the Arc Blade of Titan. This was to be the new symbol of the Line of Cojax Artino, son of Titan, Lord of Titan.

Despite the explosion from the night before, this side of the Trinity was not affected and deemed fit for use. All other political parties began showing up early, their expressions serious and somber. The very last group to arrive was the Populi Party. Their shoulders sagged as if weighted, their brows creased into permanent furrows. They all wore their white togas but they were stained with ash, a sign that they had spent the night digging through the remains of the explosion instead of in their beds. Marcus was the last to arrive, carrying his shield, helmet, and dressed in his armor for battle. He alone did not wear a toga. He was not allowed to take his Arc Blade inside and instead left it in possession of some of the guards.

The arena was quieter than it had ever been, especially since the Populi Party was all so subdued.

Everyone found their seats, and then they waited. Minutes later, Onar entered, flanked by several influential members of the Saken Faction who were dressed in the colors of the BloodBorne. These took posts around two hastily constructed thrones that had been erected at the far end of the arena. The people waited another five minutes before Cojax arrived, flanked by a powerful array of warriors. They were all Numberless, warriors with skills so superior they far eclipsed everyone else in the room. As soon as Cojax entered, those in the political parties stood, most falling into lazy salutes.

Cojax had the Numberless dressed in the armor of a First Tier, so they would not be recognized for who they really were, but they were allowed to wield their dominating and unique weapons. Cojax himself kept his father's Arc Blade on his back, ready to be drawn if needed. At his side was Jessica, wearing an exquisite set of armor, freshly constructed by one of the machines still in the Mahghetto. It was a gift from Aias and was in the style of a Numberless. Her armor had to be custom made because she was so much smaller than all the other Validated. It was mostly white except for the gold lacing that zipped up the arms and through her shoulders. Flanking Jessica was a procession of Rifters, chief among them Aias. These warriors now had traded their charcoal "X's" for permanent metallic ones, clearly displaying their deep loyalty to Jessica. Finn and Orch followed, each sporting handsome grins. After Cojax's personal entourage, the BloodBorne High Council entered along with a host of Validated, counselors, and administrators. The BloodBorne Party soon filled over half the room.

Cojax and Jessica found their thrones, but they did not sit until all of the BloodBorne had arrived. When they did sit, the Validated followed suit, finding their seats among the stone benches.

Meloch, the Arbiter, looked to Cojax, who finally nodded, allowing the man to proceed. Meloch began speaking, his voice amplified by a microphone affixed to his armor. "On this Augustian 15, of the year 243, we gather as a people once divided but now united. The people have spoken, supporting Cojax Artino as the unquestioned Lord of Titan. All rights, powers, privileges are bestowed to Cojax Artino as being the sole and chief ruler of the city—"

"—I would like to pledge my loyalty personally," said a voice that filled the room. Cojax did not acknowledge the voice, although he recognized it immediately. He nodded to the Arbiter so he could proceed.

"As the power given to me, as one of three—"

"Are you not taking pledges of personal loyalty at this time?" Marcus asked. "I wish to come before you, bowing low, swearing fealty for you in this life and the next." He now stood up, his large frame singling him out among the crowd. Marcus began taking the steps two at a time as he approached the sandy arena below. Even though Marcus was almost on the opposite side of the arena, and clearly represented no danger to Cojax, two BloodBorne Validated stopped his approach, resting their hands on the hilts of their blades as they did.

Cojax shifted uncomfortably upon his throne. Those who had constructed the chair certainly made it ornate, but they completely forgot to think of comfort. He met eyes with his brother, who carried a shield but no sword, like a beaten Validated recently returned from battle. His face was black with ash, his eyes bloodshot and intense.

Orch leaned forward, glancing back at Marcus as he whispered in Cojax's ear. "Send him away. He only looks to make a scene. No one can blame you for having him escorted out of here."

Cojax shifted to the other side of his seat, away from the advice. Anger as rich and real as it was the night before still burned in his chest. He looked at his brother—the very man who attempted to assassinate him. The very man who would have finished him had Ion not proved so loyal. Cojax's anger would not allow him to send this man away.

Cojax gestured for Marcus to come forward.

Marcus obeyed, his chin high, his demeanor proud. He seemed to have purposely selected his most used and dirty armor in direct contrast to Cojax's ornate set.

Orch leaned forward, whispering under his breath. "Have him escorted out. His words will only hurt us." Cojax ignored the counsel completely.

When Marcus was halfway across the arena, he began to address the crowd around him. "I wish to swear my loyalty to our new King—my new King. No one is more surprised than I to hear those words leave my throat. My baby brother, freshly crossed over from the Mahghetto, is our new Lord and King."

"Make your point," Cojax said, his voice carrying through the arena, "if you have one to make."

Marcus laughed bitterly but then nodded quickly. "I would swear my loyalty to you in a heartbeat, had you, Cojax, obtained your throne in a manner that was befitting the office you now hold." He stepped forward, his voice breaking as he continued to speak. "I thought I knew you, brother. Now I see how you've stepped on the backs of those you have murdered to rise to your position. Diocles and Diotimus were killed by agents of the BloodBorne, as was Felix, Lucretia, and Sejanus. All of you have heard these rumors, most of you believe they are likely true, but no concrete evidence could be found. Under the command of my brother, the Restorationists were beaten, robbed, and murdered. Again, these were rumors that could not be substantiated."

"So, you come before my people with nothing more than rumors?" Cojax asked. "Are rumors and speculation now your standard of reason and logic?"

The room filled with scattered laughter.

"I do have evidence, but I wish to speak more of your crimes," Marcus replied, his voice falling to a lethal tone. "Cojax has hidden away the Rifters, utilizing them as leverage to exact his will. Where are the Rifters? Can anyone say? Are they as free as Cojax claims they are? And if so, why have none of them chosen to live on the surface? Cojax has fooled the Rifters as much as he has fooled us."

Cojax shifted uncomfortably in his chair. He nodded towards Aias' retinue of Rifters, all who carried the sign of the Aberration, but before he could speak, Marcus cut him off.

"And then, even though victory was already in your grasp, you could not help but kick down the Populi Party one last time. Cojax triggered a bomb yesterday that wiped out half of the Senators of the Populi Party—"

Cojax shot to his feet. "Is this another one of your rumors? Oh, the chain of lies you forge is even more than I could imagine. And yet again, you have no evidence. Tell me, brother, what was the purpose of last night's meeting? A meeting that was unscheduled and only attended by half of your Senators. What did you discuss?"

Marcus swallowed, losing momentum for half a moment. "We discussed—"

"You mean plotted," Cojax corrected, "an assassination attempt on my life. If we are being honest with each other, then tell me the truth. Did you plan an attempt on my life?"

Marcus lowered his head ever so slightly. He felt the muscles in his arms tense and then release. "It was discussed."

"And you would murder me?" Cojax replied. "You would plot to murder me over what? Rumors? I ask you, I ask all of you, is that the sort of city that we should build? Where we condemn a man to death based on rumors."

Marcus exploded into a rage. "I do have proof of your

treachery as well as your savagery. Onar, one of the greatest warriors in our city, was soundly beat by you in this very room." Marcus slowly turned around, gesturing to the crowd. "Do you not all remember this remarkable feat? I, too, was deceived. But this is only one lie among the whole host of lies he has pushed upon us. I know the skill of my brother, and what Cojax displayed was far beyond his capacity. I watched the video time and time again, trying to figure out what trick Cojax used to accomplish this great task. But then it dawned on me; it wasn't Cojax who was fighting at all. When he went to retrieve his helmet, another Validated wearing a matching set of armor returned. We couldn't see who this new Validated was because he now wore a helmet."

"Enough of these lies!" Cojax said.

"You asked for proof; here it is," Marcus replied, his voice taking on a mischievous tone. "If you beat Onar as soundly as you did before, then you should have no difficulty defeating me here and now. If you could defeat a master of the blade and one who was freshly recruited into the order of the Numberless, you should have no difficulty slicing down your one-handed brother."

Cojax's anger boiled red hot. "And if one of us is killed by the other, what will that prove?"

"That you should not be our Lord, that Onar was never really defeated by you, and that I, the eldest son of Titan, should take your place as King. I am duty-bound to these people, to those who have fallen in the Populi Party. And I challenge you, oh great King, to a fight to the death."

Cojax looked to the faces of the crowd, seeing doubt and consternation in many of them. Somehow, in a matter of minutes, Marcus had flipped the whole situation on its head. He had somehow given new life to old rumors—rumors that had no basis in reality. A few of the deaths he had known about, Adriana had been behind them, but he had not planned or approved of them. And as soon as he found out about them, he punished Adriana, stripping her of position and title. But he could not explain that and expect sympathy from the crowd around him. All that they would hear was that the BloodBorne had indeed been involved in the murders.

Marcus theatrically put his hand to his ear, waiting for his brother's response. "And now we see the true caliber of the King we were so eager to obey. Is this the one who would defend us against the Decamont?"

Cojax's eyes radiated the hatred in his body. One way or another, his brother wanted him dead, either with an explosion or at the end of his Arc Blade.

Jessica grabbed Cojax's arm. "Don't let him bait you. You are the Lord of Titan, and he's just embittered that his party lost."

"Jessica," Cojax said more harshly than he intended, "he tried to kill you, me, and everyone else in this room. If I let him live, then he'll just continue to plot against us. This ends now." With these words, he put on his helmet and stood, slowly pulling Titan's Arc Blade from his back. He then approached Finn, nodding to one of the Arc Blades at his friend's waist. Finn turned over the weapon without a moment of hesitation.

Armed with two blades, Cojax leaped into the air, crashing into the sandy arena thirty yards away, sending spirals of light up his legs. He stabbed both blades into the sand and removed his helmet. "Take a good look, brother. I will not have you thinking with your last few moments of life that you faced someone else in my place." With this, he lowered the helmet back on his head and retrieved his swords. "Retrieve your blade, Marcus. If you desire to rule this city so much, you'll have to kill me first."

FORTY-FOUR

Brother stood against brother, their steps short but even as they circled. They were beyond words, beyond reason. No Magister was appointed to oversee the match since this would be a bout to the death.

Marcus hesitated at first, unused to facing an opponent with two Arc Blades. Validated did not train with two swords, as it would have proved less effective against an oncoming wall of Roaches. But the Numberless did, and Cojax had been trained by one of the best. Cojax now took a wider stance, one blade forward, the other, larger blade further back, much different than a typical fighting stance.

Marcus rushed in, using his shield to hide his attacks until right before he delivered them. Light exploded from the conflict each time their weapons connected. Marcus hoped to end the duel quickly. The faster Cojax was defeated, the more sound Marcus' argument would appear. But Cojax proved light on his feet, and he would not be swallowed up by Marcus' flurry of attacks. The large man's swings were measured at first, testing his opponent's defense for weaknesses. But as none of his attacks succeeded, he grew more aggressive, picking up speed, but also opening himself up to counter attacks. They exchanged a mad series of blows that showed off both their skill and power. Cojax moved a little faster, however, catching his brother off guard as he sliced him across the chest.

The large man reeled back, recovering from the blade. He would not fall prey to his anger, as Onar had before. He attacked again, this time attempting a series of swings coupled with a quick side-to-side movement. Cojax saw it all coming as if it was scripted, blocking each attack while delivering his own counterstrike to Marcus' calf. But then the large man used his shield to swing high as his blade went low. Cojax misjudged the attack and ducked right into the Arc Blade. The impact was so powerful, he fell to his back.

Marcus capitalized on the situation, attacking with a brutal fury, catching his brother twice in the chest. Cojax rolled, but Marcus pursued, hitting him a third time in the back. Cojax swung wildly, almost clipping Marcus' helmet with his blade. This gave Cojax just enough time to find his feet.

The audience roared its approval.

Cojax breathed deep, the applause fueling his rage. He could not help but think that many of those within this city wanted him to fall—wanted to see Marcus' sword rip through his flesh and end his life. If Cojax did die, the political parties would continue, the endless debates would ensue, the indecision would become procedure and policy. And then the Decamont would arrive in force, leveling the city beneath an infinite army of Roaches. Cojax could not let that happen. He would not let that happen.

Marcus roared and lunged forward, hitting Cojax in the leg. At the same time, he took a blow to the chest. The large man went on the offense, attacking again and again, refusing to relent in his assault. Marcus was punished for each driving foray, his shields hemorrhaging light with each blow.

"So," Marcus said, "it seems you've been doing more than bedding the Aberration in your free time. Who has been teaching you?"

"Yield now, Marcus," Cojax replied, "and, I won't have you executed for treason."

"Treason!" Marcus yelled. "You dimmed Dependent. Did you mix up your sins with mine?"

Cojax frowned, his arms tightening with his rage. "Don't bore me with one of your pointless speeches. You can fool the Populi, but not me." This time Cojax attacked. As the conflict ensued, his mind drifted to his brother's actions, which had led them to this very moment. It was his brother that abandoned him as soon as they tore down the AC. It was his brother that fought against him at every turn, making him look the fool on more than one occasion. It was his brother who would take his life rather than admit defeat. Cojax's blades became a blur as his anger pulsed through him. Flashes of light shot through his armor, his rage now eclipsing all other thoughts. Marcus was hit in the leg and then the shoulder. A moment later, his chest flashed with light as Titan's Arc Blade was dragged across it.

Cojax continued to drive forward, delivering a series of quick, yet powerful attacks that pushed his opponent further back. Marcus tried to regain the initiative, but he was struck once in the arm and another time in the leg. Now that the onslaught of attacks poured in, Marcus was helpless to stop them. Cojax was now more beast than man as he became a sledgehammer and Marcus the chisel.

Cojax ducked under a swing, twisting to the ground and catching Marcus' leg. The large man fell to the ground and rolled, scrambling to get up. But Cojax did not charge in, as expected, as Marcus had done before. He would not capitalize on an opponent rolling around in the dirt. Instead, he walked slowly forward, sticking one blade in the sand and removing his helmet with his free hand. He retrieved his sword and continued on, taking his time with each step. Without his helmet, his shield would offer some protection but would do little if he was hit directly in the head.

"Do you still believe someone else fought in my place?" Cojax asked.

"How are you doing this?"

"If you would have never left my side," Cojax answered bitterly, "you would have already known."

"I will not serve a King!" Marcus yelled. "If you wish to build an empire of lies, you will have to use my dead body as your foundation." With this, the large man pushed forward, exhausting the very best of his training and swordsmanship. But it was not enough. He was not enough. Cojax responded in kind, his face more confident than ever, ripping his opponent's shields down piece by piece.

"Why?" Cojax pleaded. "How could you have let yourself become as you are now. Embittered. Broken."

In a desperate move, Marcus threw his shield and lunged forward, his blade aimed straight for Cojax's head. The attack would have gone clear through his skull had Cojax not moved at the last second. He blocked the shield with one blade, then ducked under Marcus' attack. Cojax grabbed Finn's sword with two hands and pulsed with all the energy he possessed. The Arc Blade exploded with white light just before it found flesh. It all happened so fast that the audience was unsure of what exactly had happened.

Then slowly, Marcus turned around, again facing his brother. Finn's blade had been buried into Marcus' chest down to the hilt. His movements became choppy, his breath short. He coughed once, sending blood dripping down the inside of his helmet. The large man grabbed the hilt that was in his chest, confused at what was happening. But that confusion turned to resolve.

"I...will...not be...your servant," Marcus coughed.

Marcus attacked one final time, but it was a weak effort at best. Cojax caught the blade and turned it on its owner, sinking it into Marcus' belly. The large man fell to his knees and then to his side, his blood turning the white sand into a crimson clay.

Cojax watched his brother fall, his eyes bitter, his cheeks taut. He then faced the crowd, slowly turning so they could all see his face. "Is this what you think will make our city stronger? To have one brother slay another." He waited for a response, but none came. "Marcus and I were as close as two brothers could ever be under the AC. He was more of a father to me than Titan ever was. But look at us now! Is that what you want for our people? For us to slowly pick at each other until there's nothing left?" Again, no answer.

"Our divisions have cost us too much already. We can't fight each other anymore—we can't be divided by political parties, Factions, or Tiers. We are one people, not many. We face a threat of incalculable power, a threat so great it has kept us as slaves these last two hundred years. If we are to defeat them, we cannot kill each other anymore!" Cojax let his words sink in, let the silence fall over the room. Several people in the audience looked down out of either reverence or shame.

Onar was the first to step forward, his massive frame drawing every eye in the room. In crisp fashion, he saluted and then dropped to a knee, bowing even lower to Cojax than was ever required for a Numberless. The room followed suit in waves, first the BloodBorne and then spreading out from there. Soon, every knee was bent and every head was bowed across the entire city.

Cojax still felt the rush of anger through his veins. He tried to take a deep breath, but rage prevented it. "Now rise, warriors of Titan, and pick up your blades. The Decamont assume we will stay here, safe behind our walls, isolated and trapped by the very city they built around us. But they are wrong. Rise you Validated of Titan, for we now go to meet the Decamont in battle."

FORTY-FIVE

Cojax felt numb. His fingers were still red, his armor still drenched in his brother's blood. When he removed his ArmGuards, his hands could not help but shake. He tightened his fists and released them in quick succession, trying to force stillness into his limbs. He sensed someone enter the room.

"Leave me," Cojax said tersely.

When the person did not leave immediately, Cojax turned, his rage rising in his chest. It was Jessica.

He turned his attention back to his hands. Jessica rushed forward, kneeling before Cojax and drawing his eyes to hers. Her eyes were a beautiful blue, although they were brimming with unfallen tears. They looked as they had only looked once before. That had been years ago, when she had first arrived at the city, wearing little more than rags. When he had first seen those eyes, although he did not know it at the time, they had just witnessed the death of her father. They had just witnessed the destruction of her people. They seemed so soft, so innocent and pure, that Cojax, like now, could not turn away from them. His anger began to wane. The tension slipped down his back and through his forearms.

Then tears began to fall, first down Jessica's face and then Cojax's. She pulled him into a deep embrace, which released a flood of emotions. He cried bitterly, at times gritting his teeth with so much fury that they hurt.

Neither one could say how much time passed, but as Cojax began to control his emotions, as his eyes could produce no more tears, his mind gave way to an endless stream of questions.

Cojax looked at Jessica again, recalling her eyes to his, asking her a simple but infinitely complicated question. "Why?"

Finally, Cojax's mind began to transition into something more rational. "Is he dead?"

"Yes," Jessica answered. "I had them preserve his body in the

Stasis Chambers so that he could be properly buried when the time is appropriate."

Cojax shook his head again. "Why did he force my hand?"

Jessica gave no answer, for there was no answer that could be given.

FORTY-SIX

The city of Titan turned from idolatry to industry overnight. Cojax expanded his BloodBorne Council to twenty-four members, many of whom had been his former opponents in rival political parties. For the first time in a long time, there was no debate when Cojax issued an order. The Council set to work quickly, and before noon, every Validated had been organized and assigned with rank and regiment. Cojax had insisted that the units not be arranged by previous Faction or Tier, but by a combination of skill levels and current Factions. Only Cojax's Vanguard, which consisted of only Numberless, were kept in a solid unit.

By the next morning, the entire city was training in the streets, as had been the practice of the BloodBorne. Everything had returned to being as busy as it had been the day the AC fell. Validated now walked through Titan with a collective purpose, eager to fulfill their new duties. Guard assignments were given, as well as patrolling duties in the Killing Field. Cojax assigned more Validated to the task than was needed, but he felt it was essential to involve as many as possible in the protection of the city.

Later that day, Cojax announced that he was sending emissaries to other cities to solicit their help. Not long after, Cojax reported that Rome had agreed to join their rebellion, as well as several Numberless from other critical cities. Of course, this was the city that Horace and Finn had forced into being their ally, but Cojax left that part out of the explanation. This was greeted with a chorus of cheers along all the streets of Titan.

Cojax formed a War Council that consisted of twenty-five members of the city of Rome, and twenty members from Titan, all of them Numberless, as previously agreed upon. Two days after Cojax had been conferred the Lord over all the city of Titan, he convened his War Council in the large room utilized by the BloodBorne. Also in attendance was Orch, Finn, Jessica, and Aias, who all surrounded

Cojax's chair as his personal advisors.

Cojax arrived late, as was now becoming protocol. All stood as he entered and saluted, bowing low as they did. Even the Numberless from Rome already seemed to revere and respect the Lord of Titan. Cojax sat down, giving leave to all the rest to do the same. The Lord looked to Clandis, who took this as a cue to begin the meeting. He was not an official member of the Council but had been assigned the task of being the Executive Secretary.

Clandis stood up, his voice reaching all those in the room. "We now convene the First War Council of the United Coalition of the Free Cities under the rule of Cojax Artino, Son of Titan, Lord of the city of Titan and Steward over the city of Rome. We recognize his authority in all things. We will begin this meeting with introductions of each of the members of the First War Council."

The Numberless then set about introducing themselves, some giving terse responses, others giving long, lengthy speeches. The Romans seemed much less verbose, except for Aeneas, who made a half dozen jokes during his introduction as well as told a few tales. Cojax studied them in turn, trying to gauge their potential merits as well as determine their level of support. The Numberless from Titan were easy to read, as most wore their emotions on their sleeves.

Cojax recognized several of the names of the Numberless that were now seated around his War Council: Marian, Horace, Seleukus, Alexander, and, unbelievably, the powerful and brilliant Achillian. Achillian was a legend, as evidenced by the hundreds of statues made from his image that were spread throughout Titan. These men and women were gods in their time. After introductions, Cojax allotted time to discuss strategy.

Onar spoke first. "By command of Lord Cojax Artino, we are currently assembling our armies and preparing them to march."

"And where will you take them?" asked Saturn, a small Numberless with an airy voice. "If you pull Validated from our cities, won't we be vulnerable to attack?"

Onar played with his ArmGuard, trying to call up a map into the center of the conference table. It took him several moments before the map appeared, a perfect depiction of the area surrounding Titan and Rome. "Our scouts do not detect the presence of the Decamont for five hundred miles around either of our two cities, perhaps even further. This allows us to roam the surrounding area, gaining what intelligence and supplies we can. We will also be able to detect any large approaching Decamont force."

"They can just whip down in their starships," Saturn returned, "and attack while our army is gallivanting around. I say we fortify our cities, preparing to repel a long siege."

Before Onar could answer, Orch spoke. "If we lock ourselves in, we do the enemy a favor. If we keep all of our forces in our cities, then they only have to worry about containing us at two points. We need to spread through the land, forcing them to divide their armies. If we mask our numbers, they'll be unable to ascertain the strength of each division, and they'll be forced to use caution even when they approach the smallest of units. It will compel them to place their ground troops and move forward in great numbers, clearing us out each step along the way. That will take time and give us more time to prepare."

Remus scoffed. "And what about their primary weapons on their Starships? Our Centuries won't stand a chance against an air assault from space if they're not protected by our city shields."

"Excellent point," said Seleukus, his words only slightly slurred. "Something that I've been working on since I first woke up. The technology, as I understand it, is not that complicated, especially since I've been able to study the generators in the Trinity. I've already been able to fabricate some small-scale shield generators."

"Interesting," said Saturn. "How large are these generators?"

"I believe I could fit one on a CargoLifter," Seleukus replied. "One large enough to generate a field a quarter of a mile. That will shield us from any air assaults, forcing our enemy to commit ground troops."

"How long before you can get these shield generators operational?" Cojax asked.

"Not long," Seleukus said. "I can get the first one operational in just a few days. Give me another two weeks, and I can streamline the process and produce as many as you want. The biggest problem will be creating a power source. We can retrofit another CargoLifter to act as a battery bank, but projecting a shield is energy intensive. The battery won't last long before it runs out completely."

"It could draw from the Validated," said Aeneas, "just as our city draws from its people to produce its shields." Cojax studied this man for a while, noting how similar he was to Horace in not only appearance but in mannerism as well.

"That will put a wee bit of a strain on the Validated that are deployed," Horace said. "The last thing we want is for our forces to have weakened shields just as the enemy is deploying its own forces."

Aeneas and Horace met eyes, each one sizing up the other. Aeneas smiled, obviously coming to the conclusion that he was definitely the better-looking version of the two. "Then, we compensate the energy drain by including enough forces in each unit so that they can rotate the duty of providing energy to the shield generator."

Horace frowned, obviously coming to the conclusion that he was not the better looking of the two. "Might work. Seleukus, how large would each unit have to be to make sure the shield generator could be perpetually powered?"

Seleukus punched some numbers on his ArmGuard. "I think our smallest force would have to be a hundred thousand or so. Of course, about thirty-three percent of them would not be able to engage the enemy as they would be needed to generate the energy for the shield."

"And of course," Horace said, his hands drifting for a pitcher of stock on the table that was not there, "we only have to activate the shields when the Decamont approach from the air. Any time before that would be a waste of energy, as well as could potentially limit our warrior's movements."

Saturn nodded, apparently satisfied with the answers.

Julia turned to Cojax. "So, where will you send our army? Will you attack other Roach encampments?"

Cojax shifted from one side to the other on his throne before speaking. "We will never win a war of attrition fighting against an enemy that has no number. If we stay in our cities, we are just creating the coffin in which we'll be buried. I do not doubt that the Decamont can deal with one rebellious city, or even two. But what about four or five? We do not march to fight the Decamont directly, but to liberate our brothers and sisters in other cities."

"You might make more enemies than friends," Julia said, her voice giving way to criticism. "Not all cities will welcome your presence, especially those who are fiercely loyal to the Decamont. And the more success we have, the more steps the enemy will take to ensure that the Numberless are absolutely loyal to the Decamont."

Cojax studied this woman with earnest. He had heard Finn's account of how she had threatened to remove his head with her blade. She seemed to be a complicated woman of rigid but varying degrees of moral principles. She was muscled and firm. Just by studying the hard lines under her eyes, Cojax could tell this woman had seen many trials as well as triumphs. The Numberless from Rome seemed to treat her with the same solemn respect that they showed Cojax.

"The Decamont will use our own people against us," Cojax replied. "That's something that's not only a possibility but an eventuality. But, until that happens, all the cities out there are vulnerable to our influence. Remember, the Validated in those places believe as we once did. That they are the sole survivors, and that no one else exists outside of their city."

"How will you approach these other cities?" Julia asked.

Cojax nodded to Onar, who took over the conversation as he explained the tactics of their upcoming campaign. Cojax was grateful for the reprieve. He had little desire to develop their tactics, much less explain them. His mind kept reverting to Marcus' last seconds on the sandy ground of the arena. There was no other choice, of that he had no doubt. Marcus had forced his hand, first when he attempted to assassinate Cojax with the bomb, and second when he challenged him to mortal combat. But it all seemed wrong, as if it was some surreal nightmare. Every time he thought of it, it created a queasy feeling that constricted his abdomen.

After Onar's explanation, suggestions and other proposals were made. Once a plan was finalized and approved, it was set forth and voted on by the First War Council of the United Coalition. Cojax could have weighed in on one side or the other, ensuring victory for that particular motion, but he did not. These Numberless were much more skilled practitioners of the art of war, and so, he set his pride aside, allowing them to fine-tune a comprehensive plan. Once the plan was formalized, Onar turned to Cojax, allowing him to nod a final approval. His thoughts once more turned back to the image of Marcus' bloody body as he lay in the sand.

FORTY-SEVEN

Cojax shifted uncomfortably on his throne. After a while, he gave up sitting entirely and started pacing back and forth next to the large conference table. After only a day of being Lord of the city, Cojax had his throne moved from the arena to the large conference room formerly utilized by the BloodBorne. It was certainly smaller than the arena, but more ornate, as it was once used by the Numberless. There were more spacious rooms, but he preferred this one over all the rest.

He was alone in the large room, save for ten guards—two that stood by the throne, two by the entrance, and the rest spread throughout in even intervals in the room. For some reason, Cojax felt more nervous about this meeting than anything else in the last few days.

His guest was late, as could be expected. Only he would be so bold as to keep a newly appointed Lord waiting. When he did arrive, Cojax's bodyguards tensed, their posture becoming rigid. He was allowed as far as the base of the conference table but no further—as protocol dictated. No unvetted Validated or Numberless could pass the threshold of the conference table without Cojax's explicit permission.

Cojax approached, his face devoid of emotion. When he reached the other side of the large room, he pulled out a chair. But instead of sitting on it, he sat on the part of the table that was exposed by the chair's absence. Cojax gestured to a chair across the table.

Brutus did not take it. Cojax studied his old friend in the bright light of the room. The Rift had not been kind. The iconic Rifter crisscross scars seemed to affect Brutus' face with more severe prejudice than it did many others. On top of that, a purple scar twisted up Brutus' cheek claiming one of his eyes. Cojax had been the one to give it to him. Brutus' clothes were so stained and dirty, it made it difficult to know precisely what the original color of the cloth had been.

Brutus seemed to be analyzing Cojax with the same level of scrutiny. The more he stared, the more his face twisted into a bitter grimace.

"So," Brutus growled, "am I supposed to bow before my new Lord?"

Cojax ignored the comment and instead smiled. "I've looked at the production levels before and after the AC fell. You've not only continued to maintain food production, but you've been able to improve upon it. As the numbers indicate, and by all accounts, you've done well in your respective command—better than anyone could have hoped. There have been no food shortages or delivery delays. Adriana has filled me in on how you've doubled your available space for crops and that you'll be harvesting those new plants soon."

Brutus shifted uncomfortably. "What do you want, Cojax?"

"To compliment you. You've taken what you've received and added to it."

Brutus' lower lip twitched.

Cojax shook his head, lowering his shoulders. "Guards, please leave me."

The warriors complied quickly, leaving the other two in the room alone.

"Bold move," Brutus replied.

"If you are to trust me again, I need to show my trust for you," Cojax said.

Brutus' body tensed. "I don't seek your confidence, nor do I want it."

Cojax shifted his weight on the table. "We need to start thinking about when we're going to tell the Rifters that they are now free."

"That's a bad idea."

"I've already figured out how we can compensate them for their time as well as where they can be housed. It will be crowded for a while, but we can start construction on new buildings."

"When?"

"In two weeks. That gives us time to iron out all the details."

"You can't stand to see me have even a little bit of authority, can you? You've taken everything from me. First my brother and then my eye. Now you want to steal the Rift."

"Why can't we leave the past in the past?" Cojax asked. "I don't want to take anything from you. I want to give you more. Forget about what happened in the Mahghetto. Join me and your brother as we fight against the Decamont."

Brutus exploded with rage. "What would you have me do? Put on a server's outfit and feed you grapes? Is that what you want? Just because you're now the Lord, you expect things to be better between us? Well, I'm beyond all of that rot. You're the embodiment of arrogance glossed over with pride. Now that you're more conceited than ever, you believe you can make amends?"

Cojax stood up, knocking over one of the chairs. "What good does this do any of us? What can I do to make you see I'm not your enemy? We were once friends, and I will gladly trade all of the ill will between us for our friendship again."

Brutus laughed. "Do you really believe you can just persuade me to trust you? Why do you suddenly have such an urgency to make amends with me? I've been in the Rift for months now—and where have you been? Throwing lavish parties until everyone on the surface promised to support you."

Cojax turned his back to Brutus. "I value true friendship."

"Are we having this conversation because you killed your own brother?" Brutus questioned, his voice rich with amusement.

Cojax stiffened.

Brutus grinned from ear to ear. "It is, isn't it? You wanted to make amends with me because, in some strange way, it will make you feel better about putting your brother in the dirt."

Cojax's rage flared. "Be careful what you say."

"Or what, you'll take my own blade from my hand and shove it into my stomach?" Brutus asked. "That is, after all, your signature move."

"You wouldn't understand what happened between Marcus and me. I was forced into that position. I didn't want it. He challenged me."

"Right," Brutus said. "Regardless, by the end of that conflict, you became a Lord, and he became food for the worms."

"I already warned you once, I won't do it again," Cojax roared. "I invited you here under the pretense of our friendship."

"You ordered me here!" Brutus retorted.

Cojax was now seething with anger. "You truly want to make me your enemy. Well, if you keep going down this path, you'll get your wish. But just know that I tried to choose something different."

Brutus laughed. "And then you'll deal with me as you do with all your other problems—through intimidation and death, of that, I have no doubt." He turned to go, his hands reaching for the door scanner. "For the life of me, I don't know what she sees in you. I would have betrayed you a dozen times before now, but somehow, you seem to have won her loyalty."

"Leave Jessica out of this," Cojax warned.

Brutus turned back around, his smile all but gone. "I wasn't speaking of Jessica." Then he disappeared through the large entry doors.

Cojax wanted to stop him, to try and knock some sense into his thick skull. He opened his mouth to speak, a command on the tip of his tongue. But, as Cojax knew, not even a Lord can command his subject's respect.

FORTY-EIGHT

It had been just over one week since Cojax had been pronounced Lord of Titan. Now the streets were lined with Validated in an impressive display of power and might. Cojax presided over them from a box situated at the largest city forum. As Cojax stepped up to the railing, a million Validated saluted in crisp fashion. The Lord of the City returned the salute, letting them stand at parade rest. Cojax wore a set of armor with intricate gold lines over a black background. On his head sat a golden crown, newly forged and richly designed with symbols of power. Jessica joined his side seconds later, waving to the spectators below. She wore armor of a similar style and design as well as a thinner, but just as ornate crown on her brow.

Cojax looked around at the massive crowd, his face stern but confident. "I am Cojax Artino, son of Titan, Liberator of Acadia, Lord of the City of Titan, Steward of the City of Rome. The Decamont have more warriors; they have more resources; they have greater weapons and technology. But with everything they have, they shall not have victory. For with all they have, they lack the greatest thing of all: a belief in their cause. No warrior, fresh or seasoned, will fight harder knowing that they not only fight for their freedom, but for the freedom of their people. Go forth with glory, and in the name of Titan, destroy them all!"

With this, the audience roared approval with deafening affirmation, beating their Arc Lances on the edge of their shields.

Cojax turned to Achillian, his commanding Omega, who gave the order to move out. This order was transmitted simultaneously to the ear of every Validated in formation. In absolute unison, the Validated began to march through the main road and towards the Northern Gate, where they were greeted with a concourse of fanfare and spectators. It was all for show, of course. As soon as they were out of the Northern Gate, they were picked up by hundreds of CargoLifters, HoverBuckets or ArcSpeeders. It took some time for the last Validated to march through the gate, but Cojax did not stop it prematurely. His people needed to see their strength.

Cojax turned to face Jessica, who frowned, despite her best efforts. They walked side-by-side until Jessica directed him into a small room. She kissed him on the lips before pulling him into a deep embrace. Cojax flushed red—his bodyguards had followed him into the cramped space and had witnessed the entire exchange. To Cojax, it felt odd to kiss in public, almost taboo. He gestured to the guards to wait outside.

After the guards left, Cojax turned his attention to Jessica. "What's wrong?"

Jessica looked up, her eyes pleading. "I already miss you, and you're not even gone. I know I'm being foolish."

Cojax played with a wisp of Jessica's blond hair, pulling it back behind her ear. "The army will have to move slowly, mostly because of the pace of the large Gouger cannons, and so I'll never be too far away."

"I want to be there with you—to stand by your side as you face them. If you are to die, I want to die with you—not hear about your death over the Comm hours after it has already happened."

"We talked about this," Cojax answered. "It was actually your idea that you stay here so you can keep the peace. We still have more enemies than we do friends—despite all the Factions swearing their loyalty. We need to keep control of the city. You command the Rifters—which is a substantial force. With you here as our Queen and the Rifters at your back, I can rest easy knowing that the people of Titan will stay unified."

"Perhaps," Jessica said, a mischievous smile on her face. "But I think you were a little too eager to latch on to the idea when I suggested it."

"It's more than that," Cojax answered quickly. "I need you to lead a special investigation into the explosion that killed the Populi leadership."

"I thought that matter was settled."

"I just don't…" Cojax hesitated.

"…Think your brother is capable of trying to kill you," Jessica finished.

Cojax nodded.

"Alright," Jessica responded. "I can get Rifters looking through the site as soon as tonight. I don't know anything about explosives, but I'm sure I can find someone who does."

"I might have found someone already," Cojax said as he turned to his armguard. "Send him in."

A moment later, a thin but proud man with proper features was ushered in. He wore no armor or sword, an uncommon sight in Titan. As soon as the man entered, he fell to his knees, ashamed to make eye contact with the Lord that stood before him.

Cojax rushed to his side, pulling the older man to his feet. "None of that from you."

Byron nervously glanced up, confusion in his eyes. "My Lord, I must apologize for my lack of…of faith."

Cojax shook his head. "I'm the one that owes you an apology. For my plan to work, you could not have known I had a chance at winning. I needed your opposition to make the conflict seem genuine. For that, I ask for your forgiveness."

Byron's lower lip trembled. He bowed low and saluted. When he had been summoned to see Cojax Artino, the new Lord of the City, he had been sure he was going to his death, or at least his imprisonment. He had abandoned Cojax, right when the boy needed his support the most, and he fully expected retribution.

But Cojax's words were so soft and genuine, Byron felt touched by their sincerity. When the older man spoke, he had a hard time keeping his voice even. "Of course, my Lord."

"My good friend, you proved all the more faithful because you were willing to tell me what others would not," Cojax answered. "That sort of loyalty seems to be rare in this city. I need you, Byron, more than ever. I'm surrounded by talented men and women who I don't know. Will you consider coming back?"

"Of course," Byron said quickly.

Cojax grinned and patted Byron on the shoulder.

"What do you need me to do?" Byron asked.

"First, I need you to stay here with Jessica and help her keep everything together. We made a lot of enemies climbing to the top, and I'm sure that in the absence of the army, some of them will see this as an opportunity. And second…the explosion. I need to know who was behind it."

"You don't believe it was Marcus?" Byron asked.

"Not sure. Can you work with Jessica to find out exactly what happened?"

"I'll get started right away," Byron replied, bowing low.

Cojax gestured to the door. "By all means."

Byron saluted and left.

Jessica nodded, her eyes sparkling in the low light of the room. She looked to the door as Byron left and then back to Cojax. "Hopefully, your conversation with Brutus went as smoothly as this."

Cojax shook his head. "He's more gone now than ever. His temper doesn't burn as hot as it did before—he didn't even try to kill me when I excused the guards—but now he seems twice as vindictive."

"Is he a threat?"

"Not as he is now. But it wouldn't hurt to keep an eye on him too."

Jessica traced Cojax's jawline with a finger. "And what else, mighty Lord, can I do for you while you are waging war?"

At that moment, Cojax loved her more than ever. She was such a complement of beauty and personality that it forced him to smile.

She smiled back. "Do you always just grin randomly when someone else is talking about war?"

"I want to marry you."

Jessica pulled her head back, confused by the words. "You mean like a Pairing?"

"No, I mean a real marriage, like how it used to be done. The way our people used to do it before Acadia, before our planet was destroyed by the Decamont. As soon as we get a chance, we'll get married."

Jessica gave a girlish grin; her face went slightly red as she pulled him into a passionate kiss.

After the kiss broke, Cojax waited expectantly. When Jessica did not answer, he finally prompted. "Is that a yes?"

Jessica laughed. "You silly boy, you haven't even asked me the question yet."

Cojax grinned. "Will you, Jessica Halworth, marry me?"

This time Jessica kissed Cojax with so much passion that it left him with little doubt of her answer.

FORTY-NINE

The army divided into three bodies, each one heading for a different city. Cojax led the largest force of four hundred thousand Validated as well as two thousand Numberless towards a city called Pincale. Since they were heading to the closest city, they took most of the slow-moving and heavily armored Gougers. The Validated traveled in flying craft in two parallel columns, with a train of supplies and Gougers winding through the middle. Horace had been placed in charge of one of the other armies, while Julia, the ProConsul of Rome, directed the other. Horace and Julia's armies were smaller but could move quicker in case they needed to return to the city.

Cojax rode in a CargoLifter that had been retrofitted as a command vehicle. The rear walls had been expanded to allow the addition of a projection table. The table updated and adjusted the map in real-time, highlighting each of their vehicle's positions and status. With him rode Finn, Orch, Onar, and three other Numberless of great renown.

Finn did his best to make jokes as they traveled, but it seemed lost on the stiff demeanors of the Numberless, who spent their time engaged in endless discussion over strategy. Eventually, Finn's attention turned to a meat platter in the kitchen area. Orch, on the other hand, fell asleep, appearing to have no worry in the world as they were possibly riding to their doom. Which left Cojax and Onar in the back, staring at the map projection.

Cojax shifted uncomfortably. The last time the two of them talked directly, it was in an arena. And at the time, Cojax had the sinking suspicion that Onar would have tried to kill him if given the chance. It did not seem the best start to a fruitful friendship. He opened his mouth to speak a few times but no words came out.

Finally, it was Onar who spoke in his grave, slow voice. "I am glad we are heading to battle."

Cojax nodded, unsure if that was the sort of statement that

one should nod to.

Onar continued. "For one that seems to talk endlessly on the CityScreens, you are rather subdued in person." The large man's deep voice and slow tone had a way of making the possible insult seem like nothing more than pleasant conversation.

Cojax looked to Onar for a second before he answered. "I have a lot on my mind."

"Tell me," Onar said.

Cojax grunted. "Do you want the long version—or the really long version?"

Onar laughed at this, even though it was not that funny. "I didn't know you had a sense of humor."

Cojax shook his head. "No, that's not me. Finn or Orch can make you laugh quicker than I can. Or Horace, for that matter. I don't feel much levity, especially now. I've pushed us in a direction that we won't be able to come back from if it ends poorly."

"Alea iacta est," Onar quoted. "Don't you know your Latin?"

"I know it, but I don't quote it," Cojax replied. "That was my brother's thing, not mine."

"Marcus? That was his name, wasn't it?"

Cojax's jaw went taut.

Onar bowed his head low, repeating the name. "Marcus." He paid his respect in the same way that he had done to the First Tiers after he slaughtered them.

"Why do you do that?" Cojax asked. "I've seen you do that before. What is that?"

"An old Saken tradition," Onar replied. "All life has value, even the lowest of rank. It breaks my heart to lose them before their time, and so I honor them for the sacrifice that they gave in death, whether it was by my hand or by someone else's. I honor them because I am better for crossing paths with them."

Cojax looked at the large man, intrigued by this unique philosophy. "So you pay tribute to your enemy?"

"They are no longer my enemy once they're dead, and with their death, I will be greater because of the challenge. My enemy's pursuit of my death would, therefore, give me strength. How can I hate those that make me stronger?"

Cojax scratched his chin, readjusting his initial assessment of the large man. He had thought Onar to be a bloodthirsty demon, who would cut through anyone and everyone for the mere pleasure of it. But the more the conversation progressed, the more he realized he had been wrong. Onar enjoyed killing as much as a painter who was forced to cut up a masterpiece painting. Even at the mention of the First Tiers that he had cut down, Onar became emotional, almost to the point where he could not continue to speak.

"What if someone attacked you and took everything from you for no reason?" Cojax asked. "And years later, you face that same enemy? Would you still honor them then?"

"He has still made me stronger, so of course."

"What if your best friend betrays you, selling you into slavery, taking away everything you have ever loved?" Cojax asked. "What if this same person deprives you of food, training, and the very basic human necessities?"

"In the moment I kill him, I would forgive and honor him."

"How do you know that?"

"Because," Onar said, "that is how I survived the Mahghetto."

"Then why do you serve me?" Cojax asked blankly.

"Because you are greater than me," Onar replied simply.

"And this doesn't make you angry?" Cojax answered. "Some might be embittered by the defeat. Some might even take an oath of vengeance."

"You defeated me," Onar answered in his typical, slow cadence, "which means I can still learn from you. If I seek vengeance, then I am succumbing to pride, because I would be assuming a false narrative that I am better than you. And then my ability to become better would end. Learning ceases when you believe you have the answer."

"So, you'll serve me until you feel confident you can defeat me?" Cojax answered.

"Until there is nothing that can be learned from you."

Cojax felt perplexed by this answer. "And then what?"

Onar shot Cojax a hard stare. "Then, I will be your equal."

"Well," Cojax answered. "I don't know how much you can learn from me."

"You're Lord of the City," Onar replied. "I think there is much I can learn from you."

"I am who I am because of the people that support me," Cojax answered quickly. "Aias, Byron, Jessica, Horace, Finn, Orch, Clandis, my father Titan, and so many more."

"And look," Onar said, a small smile on his face. "I'm already learning how to pretend to be humble."

Cojax was unsure if this was a joke or not. Onar said it with such a stern expression and conviction in his voice that it left little doubt that it was not. That is, until Onar broke into a loud, deep laugh, his voice carrying through the whole of the CargoLifter. Onar slapped Cojax on the back so hard that his armor actually lit up with light from the impact.

Cojax could not help but smile at the massive man's awkward humor.

"My Lord," said Antinium, one of the Numberless and the third in command of the expedition. "Our advance scouts are picking up some activity."

Cojax stood, a silly grin still on his face. His expression adjusted as he surveyed the map projection. Instantly, Cojax could see the change. A large force had assembled thirty miles north of their position. They were already deployed in battle lines that stretched for miles in either direction from their center. Despite himself, Cojax felt his heart leap, and his breath come up short.

"What are the scouts reporting?" Cojax asked. "Decamont forces?"

"It's a massive force, to be sure, but it doesn't appear that they are supported by the Decamont," Antinium replied. "It appears to be a standard Roach army—the same kind we've fought against for the last two hundred years."

"Were they deployed to stop our approach to the city?" Onar asked.

"Without a doubt," Antinium replied.

Finn joined the conversation, a plate of food in his hands. "Have you guys tried the seasoned roast beef, yet? It leaves a flavor in your mouth that just doesn't quit."

Antinium turned to Finn, a scathing rebuke on the tip of his tongue, but as he did so, he bumped hard into Finn's elbow, knocking free the plate he was holding. The roast that remained was cast into the map projection, landing right on the enemy's center.

All faces around the map stared at where the meat now lay. Just then, Orch appeared, stretching widely as he yawned. "Ooh, roast beef." Without another word, Orch picked up the beef from the enemy's center lines and swallowed it whole.

"You don't even know where that came from," Antinium said with some disbelief. "That could've been there for days for all you know."

"Absolutely delicious," Orch replied.

Finn smiled. "Yeah, I know, right?"

"Is that a Roach army blocking our path?" Orch asked.

"Undoubtedly," said Achillian, a Numberless who was rumored to be the most talented tactician ever born. He was second only to Cojax during this expedition. When Finn first met Achillian, he simply stared, as if he was watching some gallant hero on the CityScreens. Achillian was an absolute legend.

"What are our options?" Cojax asked.

"Well," Antinium replied. "They're utilizing a Roach army with limited air support. We can go around them. It will take some time, and they will pursue, but they won't be able to keep up."

"We then open our flank," Onar stated with his slow, deep voice. "And if there's another force coming at us from a different angle, it will be difficult to stay ahead of them."

"Precisely," Antinium said.

A shorter Numberless named Marian spoke next. "We can send out our skirmishers, drawing the Roaches into a battlefield of our choosing. It will take some days to tempt them out, but I've seen it done before."

"Will they go for that?" Orch asked.

"Most likely," Marian concluded.

"We could always do a full-on attack," Finn said.

The room fell silent as they all considered it.

Orch looked sternly at Finn, his eyes narrowed into fine slits. "You're speaking privileges have been revoked for the rest of the day."

"It could work," Achillian responded.

Orch nodded. "Alright, Finn, your ban of speaking has been lifted."

"They outnumber us ten to one," Marian responded. "They just need to hold us in the center long enough for the massive flanks to come in and surround us."

"It's the last thing they'd expect," Finn said.

"Alright, for real," Orch said, "you can't talk anymore for the rest of the trip."

Achillian stroked his chin. "It certainly is something they wouldn't expect."

Orch rolled his eyes. "Are you serious? You're considering that? Alright, Finn, you can speak again."

"What do you think, Antinium?" Achillian asked. "Look at these center lines. Don't they seem off to you? We have to remember that even though the Roaches are mindless, vicious creatures, their strategy is most likely being orchestrated by a Numberless in another city."

Antinium used his fingers to expand the area around the Roach center. From high above, the lines were certainly imposing, but as he zoomed in, the formations of Roaches seemed thin, as if they were spreading too few troops over too much land.

"It's a feint," Antinium pronounced.

"Perhaps they intend on us seeing it and are planning accordingly," Onar said.

Achillian studied it carefully, looking at the battle lines as they appeared, first one flank and then the other. Then he pointed at each side in turn. "They've put their greatest strength on the flanks. What do you say, Lord of the City? What is your impression of the field of battle?"

Achillian had quickly become accustomed to calling Cojax Lord of the City. He was not even sure if the powerful Numberless knew his real name. But Cojax took the question seriously as if it was some sort of test. He lowered his head until it was even with the map. "If we attack their center, I'm sure it won't be long before their lines break and they retreat, which will only compel our troops to pursue." Cojax used his finger to adjust the map until he found a natural elevation in the ground. "Can our sensors detect Roach activity here if they are below ground?"

"No," Marian responded.

Cojax turned the map and pointed. "My guess is that they have an army underground here. Their center will break, we will pursue, and then the real battle begins. Their two flanks will move in while the real strength of their army will appear. We'll be surrounded, outnumbered, and trapped. Our airships will be forced to the ground to prevent them from being shot down, and we'll be forced to cut our way free on foot or be destroyed."

Achillian nodded. "Very good. I do believe that is their strategy. But now that we know it, how do we counter it? Onar, what do you think?"

"We attack one of their flanks, concentrating all our forces there so they are quickly overwhelmed," Onar replied.

"Good," Achillian said, "but insufficient. As soon as we start heading for one of their flanks, they'll adjust accordingly, drawing back their army until we arrive at the spot that Cojax indicated. In essence, they'll know their plan is no good and will have time to adjust."

"Then we do attack their center," Cojax answered, "just like they want us to. That will let them believe that their plan is working, but as soon as they begin retreating, we push hard against one of their flanks. We can commit our fastest troops to hit the center hard and pursue for a time. Meanwhile, our most powerful force can head straight for their left flank."

"We should have enough time to smash that flank before the center and the other flank have time to react," Onar pronounced.

"I do believe that is our best approach," Achillian said. "Lord of the City, do you concur with this strategy?"

Cojax hesitated for a brief second, knowing that his decision could result in the deaths of hundreds if not thousands of Validated. He then nodded quickly. "Summon the Invictors for our War Council. We have a battle to prepare for."

FIFTY

As per Cojax's command, none of the debris and wreckage had been cleaned or cleared. Besides the bodies being removed, the scene was exactly how it was just after the explosion. Jessica had not seen the damage up close, and now that she did, she felt overwhelmed by it. Wires and bars crisscrossed the area at random intervals, like metallic roots in search of water. The bomb was undoubtedly well designed, as it had taken out four complete floors in almost an instant.

Byron was not far from Jessica. He was crouched over a dried pool of blood that formed a circular shape. By the direction of the stain, it seemed obvious where the body had once been.

Byron shook his head as he stood. "What a waste."

Jessica joined his side a moment later. "It certainly is. And all because they wanted the power that they were about to be denied."

"So, you think Marcus actually constructed a bomb?" Byron asked.

"I knew Marcus only briefly, but in that time, he made his feelings about having a king crystal clear. I didn't think he would go this far, but here we are—knee-deep in the wreckage. I don't know what Cojax hopes to find in all of this, but hopefully, he gets some comfort from it."

"Yes," Byron replied.

"How do we go about investigating the explosion?"

"I had the Rifters construct some sifting equipment that should be useful."

"Sifting equipment?"

"Yes," Byron said with a knowing smile. "Bombs create a tremendous amount of energy, pushing everything out and away from the epicenter of the explosion. They can shred material, they can rip it apart, but they can't destroy it. For that reason, explosions are much easier to investigate than say, a fire."

"What should we be looking for?"

"For the pieces of the bomb."

Jessica's eyebrows arched. "Are you serious?"

"The explosive material will be gone, but whatever the bomb was concealed in will still be here. It will be in shrapnel, of course, but we should be able to reconstruct it piece by piece."

"How will the sifting equipment help us?"

"We'll start with a large sifter, which will hold back any substantial pieces of debris. We'll take those pieces and compare them to known items that were in the room. If a material doesn't match up with anything that was known to be in the room at the time, then we set it aside. We'll do the same thing with smaller and smaller sifters, each time pulling out the material that should not have been there."

"What if they concealed the bomb using the same material as the walls or something?" Jessica asked.

"The Trinity was made by the Decamont, not us. The metal that the Trinity is comprised of is not something that we can produce. So, unless this bomb maker melted a portion of the Trinity wall down and used that material to construct the bomb casing, I think we should be able to eliminate most of the metal from the Trinity walls. Also, even if they did use the wall as the casing, the actual device itself, such as the ignition, the power source, and the receiver or timer, will still be around. Those are unique items that will most likely not have been in the room unless they belonged to the bomb."

"So, if, and I believe that's a big if, we can reconstruct the bomb, how will that help us figure out who did it?"

"Well," Byron replied. "That will give us a lot of clues about how the bomb maker went about his business. If we can figure out what sort of items were used to construct the bomb, and if we can figure out who might have had access to those specific components, we should be able to narrow down the list of suspects. We also need to make sure we don't contaminate the scene. Everyone should wear new boots and wash them before they enter or leave the area. I don't know what sort of forensics we will be capable of, but it's best to play it safe."

"How long is this going to take?" Jessica asked.

"I have no idea," Byron replied. "I've only read about this sort of thing, never participated in it. I assume it will take a while."

Jessica sighed deeply before she turned her attention to her

ArmGuard. She linked Comms with three hundred Rifters that she had specifically assigned to this task and began giving them instructions. They obeyed quickly, setting up decontamination stations at every major ingress into the scene of the explosion. Once decontaminated, the Rifters began utilizing Byron's sifters. As Jessica saw the process in motion, her heart fell. It seemed even slower than she had anticipated. All dirt and debris had to be shoveled through three sifters of increasingly smaller sizes. The items of interest had to be carefully collected and set aside. The debris was then sent to the next sifting station and the process repeated. The final sifter had openings so small that it would catch everything larger than ash and dirt. Everything of interest had to be carefully analyzed and studied until it could be determined if the item was likely to be present in the room or if it was unique and, consequently, could be part of the exploded device.

By the end of the day, Jessica was ash-covered and sore. That night she had several more sifters made, especially the smaller ones because they proved the most time-consuming. The next day, they set back to work, carefully sifting through the remains of the room.

Byron enjoyed the tedious process of analyzing each potential bomb component. Soon, he had a collection of promising pieces of metal. At noon, Byron called Jessica into a small room where he had set up shop. Byron held up a piece of wire as if it was the Golden Fleece.

Jessica's reaction must have been less than enthused because his face fell ever so slightly.

"What is it?" Jessica asked.

"This is part of our device," Byron said with childlike amusement. "This is a wire harness utilized in a very specific type of Blazer."

"Couldn't one of the Senators in the Populi Party been carrying a Blazer?"

"I've pulled footage from those that arrived at the meeting, and none of them were carrying a Blazer."

"You can pull footage?"

"Cojax has granted me complete access to all available footage."

"Why not just pull the footage from the actual room to see what…you know…exploded?"

"That footage doesn't exist anymore," Byron said. "Someone had the foresight to eliminate recording capabilities of the room. I imagine this is something they did early on to prevent other political parties from spying on them."

"What about the footage from the Senator's that were wearing armor?"

"None of them were recording at the time of the explosion."

"Ion's armor was recording."

"Yes, you mentioned that. But, so far, I've been unable to find any record of it."

"So, Adriana is lying," Jessica stated hopefully.

"Perhaps," Byron replied, "but we can't be sure. From what I understand, Ion was a genius when it came to computers. He might have just programmed his armor so it didn't leave a trace on the Acadian System when it was recording."

Jessica looked at the wire harness with new interest. "So, this was part of a Blazer?"

"Not only that," Byron said with more enthusiasm. "This type of Blazer is not commonly used, nor is it regularly assigned to a Validated. This is part of a Star Blazer, one of the most destructive and yet portable weapons we have. It can generate a short-range beam of light that is two feet tall and one foot wide. The light will cut through anything and everything until it runs out of charge. The greatest drawback is its power usage, which is why it's rarely used in the field. This is the same sort of cannon that is mounted on our Gougers. The Gougers, of course, have a battery bank, so the drain is not nearly as damning."

"Do you think it was just a Star Blazer that somehow malfunctioned?"

"No," Byron replied. "The Star Blazer is tremendously powerful but well designed. It wouldn't malfunction on its own. But, if someone re-engineered it, it's possible that the energy could have been trapped long enough for it to create an explosion instead of a beam. But this is Decamont technology. I doubt there are any in our city that have taken the time to study it, let alone understand it."

"Do you think the Decamont could have planted a bomb in the city?" Jessica asked.

"Perhaps, but not likely," Byron replied. "The simple logistics of a Decamont soldier infiltrating and planting a bomb in the city seems impossible. Besides, why would they target the Populi Party and not Cojax? That would've made more sense. But the other possibility seems just as unlikely. Whoever constructed this device not only understood Decamont tech, but they knew how to manipulate it without getting themselves blown up in the process."

"Titan understood Decamont tech."

"What do you mean?"

"Well," Jessica said slowly. "Titan severed our city from Decamont control without sacrificing our power infrastructure. So that means he must have understood Decamont technology, at least in part."

"Excellent point," Byron said. "But then, Titan also had years to study and examine the problem until he was able to understand it. Whereas, our bomber only had a few months, maybe even less. Perhaps, that's enough time, but I doubt it. We understand so little about how our armor and weapons function that the bomber would have to be starting from scratch."

Jessica used both her hands to push her hair out of her face. "Well, at least it gives us something to work with."

"Also, I've had all the ArmGuards of the deceased Senators gathered and analyzed. Most of them are password-protected, but I have a friend that is working on hacking them. Perhaps the bomber sent something to someone just before or after the explosion."

"So, you don't believe Ion set it off?" Jessica asked.

Byron shrugged. "I don't think we know enough, even for a guess."

"Weren't there a few survivors too?" Jessica asked.

"Three survived, including Marcus. I've tried to interview the other two, but they have refused to speak to me."

"Alright," Jessica replied. "I'll get back to sifting. Hopefully, we can just find a handwritten confession from the bomber somewhere in the debris."

Byron smiled. "It'd make it a lot easier if you did."

FIFTY-ONE

Cojax walked among the Roach corpses, their bodies still looked intimidating even after they were dead. He now stood at the point where the most vicious fighting took place. The smell of ash and blood dominated his senses. He was surrounded by a host of Validated who were still finishing off the remnants of the enemy army. To his side stood Onar, Marian, and Achillian. Orch and Finn had long since left to join the hunt for the retreating enemy.

It had been a decisive victory, one that worked out almost exactly as they had planned. After engaging the enemy's center, the Roaches broke, retreating almost to the exact spot Cojax had indicated. They then turned their attention to the left flank and met them with tremendous fury at the very place where they now stood. The Roaches were as numerous as the sand, but they proved inadequate to deal with the force of Numberless that Cojax sent against them. The Numberless were unstoppable and sliced through thousands of Reevers in a matter of minutes. All order and rank soon broke among the Roaches allowing them to be cornered and cut down with little resistance. By the time the Roaches' right flank reached Cojax's lines, his Validated were more than ready for them. They assaulted this force with their heavy Gouger guns, ripping them apart as they tried to bridge the distance between them and the Validated. The Roach flank soon crumbled into chaos and the wholesale slaughter of the enemy had begun.

They would have suffered minimal losses during the battle, but the mobile unit that had first attacked the enemy's center was surprised by the sudden emergence of several Diggers and the Roaches they were carrying. They took a defensive position, trading their mobility for security. They formed Phalanxes and met the enemy head-on. They were holding their own, but then the main contingent of Roach forces from the centerline regrouped and charged. The battle would have turned into an execution had Achillian and Onar not responded, bringing with them their own set of elite warriors in several CargoLifters. Luckily, the Roaches had been too distracted by the enemies in front of them to concern themselves with shooting down the aircraft. Cojax had seen some footage of Onar crashing down on the enemy instead of waiting for the CargoLifter to land. Onar was a savage among the Roaches, each swing from his blade cutting a dozen of the creatures down. Even Achillian was not as effective as Onar when it came to the sheer destruction of the vile creatures. Cojax made a mental note to assign a Numberless to train Onar in one-on-one combat. With some additional training, Onar would be unstoppable.

But as the rush of battle faded from Cojax's body, he could not help but think of the Validated that had fallen. *Fifty-five thousand three hundred and four.* Even though it was declared a decisive victory by all accounts, Cojax wondered if the price was far too high. In comparison, the Roach casualties were estimated to be in the millions. What's more, they had either killed or captured thirty-thousand Damnattii that had been trying to flee.

"Any word from Horace or Julia?" Cojax asked.

Achillian nodded. "Horace has just begun to engage a Roach army a little smaller than the one we faced. And Julia has been plagued with a squad of Damnattii saboteurs and snipers that have slowed her progress."

"Is Horace requesting more support?"

"Not yet, Lord of the City, but I've ordered ten of our Decurians to standby in case he does."

"Why do you think Julia's forces faced no army?"

Achillian shook his head. "If I had to guess, I'd say that they are consolidating their forces. And when they do finally come against us, it will be with an endless tide of black carapace."

"It will be a battle for the ages," Onar whispered.

"This small conflict is more of a distraction than the real fight," Achillian replied. "A sacrifice that they made willingly to slow us down, but it is in vain, since you've sent a large contingent of the army ahead. They should be reaching the city within minutes."

Cojax looked to his Omegas. "Remove the armor and bury the dead."

"That will..." Marian began, "...take some time. We'll have to split our forces, leaving either force vulnerable in the meantime."

"Request additional support from Titan," Cojax answered.

Marian looked to Achillian and then back to Cojax. "That will leave the city vulnerable."

"Do as he commands," Achillian ordered.

"Yes, sir," Marian replied. "It will be done." She saluted and disappeared, speaking through the Comm on her ArmGuard not long after.

Cojax sighed in frustration.

Achillian stepped up to Cojax, examining a series of SataniKahn bodies that were hacked down in a row. "What's on your mind, Lord of the City?"

"How do you deal with such a loss? Over fifty-five thousand."

Achillian took his time to answer, carefully measuring his words. "Everyone deals with it differently."

"And you?"

"Just don't let them die in vain."

***

Cojax wore his best armor, Titan's sword strapped to his back. On his brow, he wore his golden crown. He now stood in the center of the Killing Field in front of the city of Pincale, just out of range of small arms fire. Behind him and to the right stood Orch with his Blazer, Finn with his Arc Lance, and the massive figure of Onar; to his left was Achillian, Marian, and Antinium. Directly behind them were two thousand Numberless, mostly from the city of Rome, all in crisp battle formation. Around these elite warriors, and forming a half-circle around the whole of the city, stood the bulk of their army.

The city walls of Pincale were brimming with Validated, all of which had gathered to see the army before their gates. Besides the city wall being black, instead of grey, and the Validated wearing armor modeled after the people of Rome, it appeared to be very similar to Titan.

They stood in the sun for thirty minutes before the gates opened, and a host of Numberless exited to meet them. They approached Cojax at a slow and steady gait. There were only thirty, but they were armed for war—their shields up, their weapons drawn. It was all for show of course, probably more for the people in their own city than anything else. When they were about fifty yards out, the main body of Numberless halted, and only three continued on.

The Pincale Numberless were imposing, one was almost as big as Onar. Cojax saluted in crisp fashion as they approached, but he did not bow, something he had decided in advance not to do.

The Numberless saluted in turn and bowed, more out of tradition than respect.

"Who are you? And what are you doing here?"

Cojax waited for a moment before speaking. "I am Cojax Artino, Lord of Titan, Steward of the City of Rome, Leader of the United Coalition of the Free Cities. We have rebelled against the Decamont. We have won our freedom. And we seek to free all people from under their oppression."

"Well, boy," a thin, narrowed face Numberless replied. "You best take your army and keep moving. No one here is suffering from their oppression."

Cojax felt anger ripple through his body, but he pushed it back down. "I wonder if everyone in your city would feel the same way if they knew the truth."

"They know enough."

"Which is nothing," Cojax retorted. "We are here to let them know the truth—to let them know that there is another way."

"To serve a boy who thinks himself a king," the Numberless asserted.

"I am the Leader of the United Coalition of the Free Cities. We fight for freedom, not to subjugate your people."

"Listen, boy, we know who you are, and we know what you offer," the Numberless replied.

"Call him boy one more time," Onar roared, "and you will die."

"Is that how you intend to rule us? With promises of freedom to our faces but a sword at our backs?" the Numberless replied.

Onar stepped forward, but Cojax raised a hand to stop him. The large man obeyed as quickly as he received the order.

Cojax stepped forward. "I've spent months trying to convince men and women who were more stubborn than you. I've watched my people suffer because of inaction and indecision. I am Lord of Titan, a title that was not given to me, but one that I earned. Weigh your next words carefully, for if they are not more reasonable than your first, they shall be your last. If you don't listen to reason, I will follow through with my plan, and turn every last Validated in your own city against you. Your people have seen my armies, and they already suspect your treachery. You won't be able to explain away how the Roaches suddenly disappeared from your borders and a people like their own suddenly appeared. You won't be able to explain how their sensors pick up everything except for the army that now stands before them. I have already destroyed the Roach army you sent against me; do not push me to destroy your city."

The Numberless shifted uncomfortably, looking at his two companions in turn.

Cojax's mind flashed to the fifty-five thousand dead Validated that now lay in an empty field not far from Pincale. This image forced anger into his words. "I already have enough blood on my hands today; do not force me to add to it."

"I am Tithinus, ProConsul of the city of Pincale," answered the Numberless. "And we need time to discuss this as an Infinite Council. I can't make a policy that would affect the whole city by myself."

"No?"

"No."

"I can't give you any more time," Cojax answered, "because I don't have any more time to give. The Decamont are coming. You can either tell the people the truth, or I will do it for you. Of course, if I have to do it, I won't be casting you in a very pretty light. Either way, by the end of the day, I will rule your city. And if you don't do it now, as you stand, then you will be the first casualty that falls."

Tithinus' voice shook as he spoke. "But you raised a banner of truce. You wouldn't violate a banner of truce. You have to honor the codes of war."

"And if I was at war with you," Cojax answered. "That would mean something. Patch into the entire city Comm system. Tell them the truth. Tell them that you were just as deceived as they, but now that you know, you have chosen to rebel against the Decamont."

"But what if the other Numberless disagree with me? What if they just as quickly get on the Comms and refute every word I said?"

"They can't refute," Cojax said with frustration, "what the people can see with their own eyes. Even if I left you now, never to return, your people would never be able to forget what they've seen today. You'd face questions and complaints—so many you couldn't make them all go away. At best, your control of the situation is fragile; at worst, it's nonexistent. I will ask you one last time to broadcast this message to all of your people."

The Numberless swallowed, his mind spinning with possible options. He finally tightened his jaw and elevated his chin. "We are not some rabble you can bully into doing your will. We will not bow to a boy, who—"

Cojax stepped aside as his entourage surged forward. A brief struggle ensued, but soon, the Numberless from Pincale were laid low, their armor depleted of its charge, their bodies cast aside.

"You want us to engage the Numberless?" Onar asked. "They've started to fall back to the city."

"Let them go," Cojax said, "if we cut them down, there will be no one the people of Pincale can blame for being lied to all these years. Deploy the CityScreens."

This command was already anticipated and quickly followed. Several dozen CargoLifters went airborne, large CityScreens hanging from their decks.

With the tone of a god, Cojax's face and voice were broadcast on the CityScreens that hung from the CargoLifters. "I am Cojax Artino, Lord of Titan, Steward of the City of Rome, Leader of the United Coalition of the Free Cities. I live in a city not far from here. And I, like you, was lied to my entire life. Your city is not the only city, as our presence now proves." At this time, one of the CargoLifters was hit with some scattered and poorly aimed Blazer fire. Several of the Pincale Gougers pivoted and locked on to the CargoLifters. After some hesitation, they began to fire upon the airborne vehicles. What should have been an easy shot with the large Gouger guns went horribly wide, missing by a good margin. It seemed the people of Pincale were receiving orders from their Numberless, but that they were not eager to carry them out.

"But there's so much more that you haven't been told," Cojax said. "What you haven't been told is that we are under the secret rule and reign of the Decamont, a people I now fight against. Not all, but some of your Numberless are agents of the Decamont, whose sole mission has been to keep you from the truth—to keep you in chains that you never even knew existed." This was somewhat of an exaggeration, since it was not *some* of the Numberless who were agents of the Decamont, but in truth, *all* Numberless really were. Cojax had resisted the urge to blame them all, however, since doing so would destroy any possibility of them joining the rebellion. Not long after Cojax began, all attempts to shoot down the CargoLifters ceased.

Cojax spoke long and in detail about how some of the Numberless were actually the ones who commanded the Roach armies that were a constant plague to their city. He talked about where one goes when they are Rifted, how they are treated, and about the high cost all of them had to pay under Decamont rule. He spoke about how the Damnattii were also a people, much like humans, who were forced into a conflict that they did not want. He spoke of the losses he had faced under the old Acadian Code—Hadrian, his mother, his brothers, and sisters. And then Cojax spoke of how the rebellion began—with Jessica, a young girl from the Killing Field entering the city of Acadia. This story ended with the sacrifice of Titan, his father, who was the first Numberless to rebel.

"But this information I give you today," Cojax said, his voice breaking ever so slightly, "comes with a price." He paused before continuing, pushing all emotion out of his tone. "In order to come to your city, we had to chop through a Roach army that blocked our path. Fifty-five thousand of your brothers and sisters now lie dead so that you can have the knowledge I just shared. We are not here to conquer you, but to liberate you from our common enemy—"

Just then, the gate to the city opened at a painfully slow pace. They waited to see if something or someone was going to come out. As the minutes passed, Cojax realized that no one was going to come out, but that it was an invitation to come in.

Onar stepped up to Cojax, his voice low. "Could be a trap."

"Most likely," Marian replied.

"The people of the city will not go along with the Numberless," Cojax answered. "Not now, not ever again. If it's a trap, it's one that only a handful of Numberless have set."

"I will go with a few of my warriors," Antinium replied. "We'll figure out what's going on."

Cojax shook his head. "No, if we expect them to trust us, we need to show a little trust first. We march into the city with banners raised and weapons sheathed. If we are to be liberators and not conquerors, we have to act the part." Cojax looked to Achillian for support.

Achillian laughed, slapping Cojax on the back. "Well, you heard the Lord of the City, prepare to march."

The command was obeyed within seconds, creating a large column that fell in behind Cojax and his small entourage. It was sometime before they closed the distance between their position and the city gate, all the while Cojax could feel his rapid pulse in his ears.

Cojax studied the gate as they approached. It was identical in every way to the gates in Titan, except it was black. Along the wall, stood hundreds of Validated, all peering down with a solemn, quiet air. As Cojax walked through the city gate, he resisted the urge to look around, and instead, fixed his gaze on those that stood to greet him. The street was lined with Validated, all of whom were on their knees, their hands on their chests in a crisp salute.

Cojax made his way deeper into the city where a group of thirty Numberless stood. Their weapons were not drawn, but their expressions were also not submissive. When he reached the Numberless, Cojax saluted and met each of their gazes in turn.

Nothing happened for some time. For a horrible instant, Cojax began to feel that this was indeed a trap. That he, in his arrogance, had just forfeited his life as well as the lives of his command staff.

But then the Numberless saluted. And then they kneeled.

It was at that point that Cojax realized that his image was being filmed and broadcast throughout the entire city on the large Pincale CityScreens. The leading Pincale Numberless removed his blade from his back, offering it to Cojax in a gesture of humility and servitude.

"My Lord," the Numberless whispered, "the city is yours."

FIFTY-TWO

Orch and Finn made themselves comfortable in the large amphitheater. It was very much like the First Assembly arena, except the floor was metal, not sand. Orch and Finn were enjoying a spread of food fit for a Numberless. In place of stock, the people from Pincale had a drink called wine. Finn immediately preferred it over stock, but not by much.

As they were finishing their meal, their stomachs groaning from the effort, Cojax walked in. Upon seeing him, Finn stood and saluted, bowing low.

Orch laughed. "He left his guards in the hallway, boy. There's no one else around. No need to inflate Cojax's ego any more than we have to. He's still the same boy I used to pick on in the Mahghetto."

Finn ignored the comment. "How did the negotiations go?"

"Better than expected," Cojax answered. "We were able to severe the connection with the Decamont and keep their power running, which was one of their largest concerns. After that, it was more a discussion of logistics than a demand of concessions. They've taken oaths to serve me as long as we are at war with the Decamont. Five of the Numberless are to be added to our Senate, bringing the total Senators up to fifty."

"That's great news."

"But it won't stay at fifty for long," Cojax said with a smile. "Horace has also been able to win over the city of Oreaus, and they have agreed to many of the same terms."

"It seems our revolution is beginning to spread," Orch said.

"We can go from city to city and free every one of them," Finn added.

"The Decamont will make it more difficult each city we go to," Orch replied. "They won't give up that easily."

"But with the support of four cities," Finn replied, "there won't be much they can do to stop us. Especially now that the Numberless are starting to get behind our cause."

"Every time a city joins our rebellion," Cojax said, "we become a bigger problem that the Decamont cannot afford to ignore. But there are over three thousand cities like ours, and we only have the support of four."

"Yeah, but they were preparing to deal with the rebellion of one city, and now they have three others," Finn replied. "I think that if we keep freeing enough cities, they'll never have enough time to assemble a sufficient amount of Roaches to stop us."

"What about Julia?" Orch asked.

"She's had," Cojax said, measuring his words, "less success. They've surrounded the city and broadcast their message, but for some reason, they haven't been able to take control of it yet. The Decamont have adjusted, either by warning the people that Julia was going to arrive, or tricking them in some other way."

"Is she going to siege the city?" Orch asked.

Cojax shook his head. "No, we can't win friends if we leave a trail of blood everywhere we go. We'll give it some time. Hopefully, the people in the city will begin to rebel. We'll need all of the Validated we can get before the Decamont arrive. That's why I'm here."

"And here I thought you just wanted to check up on your old friends," Orch replied.

"I need people I can trust to scout the edge of our borders," Cojax said. "People that won't embellish or underestimate the enemy's forces. Achillian and Antinium believe that when the Decamont come, it will be from the North."

"Just when I'm starting to get used to the catered food," Orch said, "you want to send us to the border."

"I trust you two more than anyone else here," Cojax answered. "I need valuable intel from the ground. It might be months, or it might be days before they approach, but as soon as they do. I need to know. I'll be sending you up with a Decurian."

Finn straightened up a little. "Ten thousand Validated? I've never commanded anything except for our little group in the Mahghetto, and that was only for a few weeks."

Orch laughed. "You'll be in the detachment, not commanding it."

"Actually," Cojax said, "I was hoping you would command it,

Orch."

"Nah," Orch replied. "I'm good. I'll go, but I'm not taking command."

"What?" Finn asked. "Why not? I'd give anything for the chance."

"More responsibility means more liability," Orch replied. "If I'm in charge, I'd feel guilty when I inevitably break the rules."

"Or, you could just follow the rules," Finn suggested.

Orch laughed. "Just when I think you don't have any sense of humor, you go and say something like that."

"Have you ever commanded before?"

Orch sighed. "I was an Invictor before I began teaching at the Mahghetto."

"What?" Finn replied, his voice portraying his skepticism. "Since when did they lower the standards enough to allow a Second Tier the position of Invictor?"

Orch was about to respond with an insult that would have made the other two blush, but another person walked into the large room, their face shrouded by a helmet.

Cojax turned the direction that both Finn and Orch were now looking. He placed his hand on the hilt of his blade, a motion that was becoming second nature, but then the Validated removed their helmet.

Adriana stepped forward, wearing a set of red armor that spidered with white lines. As she approached, Cojax noticed the ornate design of this new type of armor.

The woman saluted and bowed. Cojax returned the salute.

"What's with all of this formality when we're alone with Cojax," Orch growled. "Don't you guys remember that this is the same guy that was just about Rifted out of your Mahghetto?"

"That is a good point," Finn said.

"One that I will endeavor to remember," Adriana replied with a generous smile.

Cojax was somewhat relieved to see Adriana in a good mood. Last time she and Cojax had spoken, their conversation was tense and heated. He approached, his arms spread wide, and gave her a warm embrace. Finn did the same, although he took his time letting go. Orch did not stand and instead gave the girl a wink before he turned his attention back to his food.

"What brings you to the city of Pincale?" Finn asked eagerly.

She smiled playfully. "Do I need a reason to come visit you?"

Finn turned as red as Adriana's armor.

"But you're not the only reason, love," Adriana said. "The Lord Cojax gave me a task, and I'm here to tell him about the progress."

"You completed the armor?"

Adriana rubbed her hands down her sides. "Do you like it?"

Finn leaned forward.

Cojax nodded. "Is it better?"

"We get the same protection as before, except at only a fourth of the energy use," Adriana replied. "Also, energy transfers to weapons are twice as smooth, making them almost twice as powerful."

"Impressive."

"Would you like to touch it?" Adriana asked with a wicked smile.

Cojax straightened up. "Not necessary. How many of these sets of armor have you made?"

"Twenty thousand so far," Adriana replied. "I've been custom making them for each of the Numberless, which has been a process in itself. When wearing a complete set of armor, each Numberless will be like an army."

"Excellent work," Cojax said.

"I wouldn't mind touching it," Finn added.

Cojax ignored the comment and continued. "When can you get the armor out to the Numberless?"

"Already done," Adriana replied. "The Numberless in this city are the last to receive their armor."

"Excellent."

Adriana stepped forward, her eyes becoming vulnerable for a moment. "Now, do you mind if I have a word with you alone?"

"Alone?" Cojax asked. "Yeah, it shouldn't be a problem."

Finn's shoulders slumped. His usual smile disappeared. "Alone? Do you want me to go then?"

"That is the kind of alone I'd prefer," Adriana replied.

Finn sighed. "Alright, I'll be in the hallway."

Adriana turned to Orch.

Orch was still hovering over his food, one of his feet kicked up on a seat in front of him. "What? Me too? I won't be a bother."

Cojax gestured to the door with his head.

Orch obeyed, but slowly, and with a grunt so long and loud, it could have been mistaken for a war cry.

When Orch disappeared, Adriana looked down, studying the floor as if it was a unique piece of art. It took a while before she looked up again, but when she did, there were tears in her eyes.

"What's wrong?" Cojax asked.

She wiped the corner of her eyes, shaking her head with anger. "I'm sorry. I told myself I wasn't going to do that."

"What's wrong?" Cojax repeated.

Adriana waited until her voice was steady. "Once, when I was a girl, there was a boy who stole my affection. We started as enemies, competitors in The Games. Whatever I did well, he always sought to do better. But he never did. Competition turned to friendship, which finally turned to affection. I think he thought he liked me more than I him, but that was only because I hid my true feelings, as I have always done. He was my first kiss—he was my first love. We hid all of this from our parents—as this was all strictly forbidden under the Acadian Code."

"What was his name?"

"Calamis."

"Strong name."

Adriana began walking around the room, slowly circling Cojax. "And he was a good man, but he didn't have talent. Kindness, goodness, empathy—these are attributes in the city of Acadia that were not only to be avoided, but they could also get you killed. I learned that from Calamis. For as Calamis entered the Mahghetto, he never returned. They took a boy so pure and kind, and they let him be consumed by the Magisters."

"I'm sorry to hear that."

"I was then, but I'm glad of it now," Adriana replied. "Calamis was older than me and entered the Mahghetto years before I did. When I realized he would never return, I also realized that I was not good enough. I put everything I had into becoming physically and mentally better, but it was never enough. I wasn't enough. I knew that if I didn't change, I would soon disappear forever as soon as I entered the Mahghetto. I did have one talent that most others didn't possess. The ability to judge, change, and manipulate those around me. I then honed and developed this skill by reading hundreds of books on the human psyche, body language, and persuasion, all of which had been readily available in our intellectual archives. I began to implement these tools on those around me, achieving small changes at first but getting much greater success as time progressed. By the time you met me in the Mahghetto, I had become the creature I am today."

"And you've proven your talent again and again in this respect."

"And I thought I'd be better for it," Adriana said, her eyes again filling with unfallen tears. "But the thing I had to become to survive, the one thing that I'm truly good at, is the one thing that seems to push you away the most."

"I'm not pushing you away."

"I love you, Cojax," Adriana said. "If that surprises you, you have no idea what it does to me. I have always prided myself on my ability to change my emotions as someone changes their clothes. But I cannot change this."

Cojax swallowed hard, trying to fathom what he was hearing.

Adriana stepped forward. "You don't need to say anything, but I cannot live much longer without you knowing how I truly feel. This is something I didn't recognize until you removed me from the BloodBorne High Council. I missed seeing you every day. I missed your confidence; I missed your passion. There are many people in this world, but so few who stand out from the rest."

"Adriana…I…I…"

Adriana stepped forward, placing her lips against his. She kissed him with all the passion that she possessed, raking her hands through his hair. For the briefest moment, Cojax found himself kissing back. But then that moment passed, and his lips turned cold and distant.

Adriana let the kiss end and instead pulled herself into a long embrace in Cojax's arms. He patted her back as her body began to shake with small, sharp sobs.

"I love Jessica," Cojax said. "I will always love her. But I don't want to lose you or your friendship. It was wrong for me to remove you from the BloodBorne High Council, especially after all you've done. We need your abilities now more than ever."

Adriana tried to speak but nodded instead.

"Will you accept my apology and take a seat back on the

Council? I can't grant you a seat at this very moment, as there are now new procedures that govern how that's done, but I will as soon as I return to Titan."

Adriana pulled herself deeper into Cojax's embrace. She did not care to be on the Council or to hear his apology or to hear how much she was needed. She wanted him more than any of those things. But she found that she could not say any of that, as her throat hurt too much to speak.

FIFTY-THREE

The War Council convened in a large room in the city of Pincale. Only half of the Numberless were present, while the rest were projections. Cojax presided over the meeting. He sat upon an imposing throne at the far end of the room. Despite all the Validated bowing before him, he felt alone. Orch and Finn had been sent to the borderlands; Adriana was stationed in Titan; Horace, Clandis, and Seleukus were busy restoring order in the city of Oreaus. Byron and Jessica were investigating the bomb that had taken out much of the Populi leadership. Besides Onar and his retinue of bodyguards, he hardly recognized anyone who was physically present in the room.

After the formalities and introductions finished, Horace took the floor, explaining in detail how they had seized the city with little bloodshed. The Validated had been willing, but the Numberless were resistant, but eventually, they caved to the pressure. Horace also spent some time complimenting Adriana's new armor, claiming that one unit of Numberless equipped with this armor cut through the entire main line of Roaches.

Next, Julia spoke. She had not engaged a Roach army on the way to Delphi, but there were a mix of Damnattii saboteurs and snipers that plagued her column every step of the way. Consequently, she arrived much later than Cojax or Horace. The Validated of Delphi were slow to rebel, however, giving time for their Numberless to reaffirm their control. It would have all been in vain, but the Decamont, as soon as they realized they were losing public support, remotely destroyed all the power capabilities of Delphi. With no power, they had no city shields and could not produce or deliver food. In this vulnerable state, the city of Delphi, under a banner of truce, surrendered the city to Julia.

"And what of the people?" Cojax asked.

"They are optimistic, but concerned," Julia answered. "Without city shields, they won't stand a chance against a Decamont air assault.

And without the ability to produce food, they'll be driven to starvation."

"We need to move the people to another city," Cojax said.

"Ten million people?" a Numberless whispered. "Where can we put that many?"

"And how will we feed them?" asked another.

"What city is the closest?" Cojax asked.

Julia nodded towards Cojax, her hologram projection making her look slightly blue. "Titan is the closest city, but the city won't be able to handle a doubling of its population."

"True," Cojax answered, "but we only need to worry about two things right now: first, getting those people into a city where they are safe, and second, transporting all available resources from that city to another. Once we get everyone to the city of Titan, we'll separate and transport them to other cities from there. We'll also use Titan as a staging place for food, weapons, and any other supplies we can remove from Delphi."

Julia raised a hand, still unaccustomed to speaking without being called upon. "I believe some of the Validated will resist leaving their city."

"It's what their Lord commands," Onar said.

"Even still," Julia said, "they might resist relocation."

Cojax sighed. "Any suggestions?"

"We can't allow any of them to stay," Aeneas said. "If we do, it will encourage even more to stay. They have to either go voluntarily, or they will be forced to move."

"I believe I have some information that can motivate them," said Ajax. "The Decamont are coming. Our scouts caught visual of a massive army just north of our borderlands. An endless force composed of Roach and Damnattii soldiers alike. Their ranks are bolstered by air support in vessels that I've never seen before."

Cojax had already received this information directly from Finn and Orch, but he had not been able to share it yet. His chest tightened as he heard the news again. It seemed that much more real now that he heard it for a second time.

"What's more," Ajax said, "is that my scouts had stayed behind the advancing army, just to see if they were leaving their supply lines unguarded. Unfortunately, it turns out that the army they were observing was an advanced unit and only a small part of the assaulting forces. What followed, as they said, was a force so strong that it didn't seem to have an end on the horizon."

Cojax shifted in his seat. He had not heard about the advance of this second, more massive army.

"The advancing Decamont army is slow, but thorough and wiping out everything in its path. My scouts know of at least two human villages that were completely obliterated."

"Can our sensors pick them up?" Horace asked.

"Sometimes," Ajax responded. "I know that we've got people working on adjusting the sensors so they can pick up the Decamont forces, but it isn't completely successful yet."

"I will assign some of the brightest minds to the task," Julia offered.

"How many more villages are in the path of the Decamont?" Cojax asked.

All eyes turned to their Lord.

Ajax looked confused at the question. He finally turned to his ArmGuard and pulled up the information. "There are two, my Lord."

"And how far are they from the Decamont army?" Cojax asked.

"Hours away, maybe less," Ajax answered.

"Divert some of your scouting parties to rescue the human villagers," Cojax said. "Take them to Rome. That should be the closest city."

"My Lord," Ajax said, "I've already pulled my main scouting forces further south than the villages. If they went back, they might run into the advanced scouts of the Decamont. We'd be putting at risk the lives of some of my best Validated. Not to mention, we would only be doing it to save a few hundred villagers."

Cojax shifted in his throne, considering the advice. "What's the primary vehicle used by your scouting forces?"

"Speeders or Lancers," Ajax answered. "There are a few Screamers and UniLifters."

Cojax took some time to gather his thoughts before he stood, addressing all in the room. "There are two sides to this conflict: humans on one side, the Decamont on the other. We have to treat those villagers as if they are the most valuable Validated we possess. Just because they offer little tactical value, does not mean they have no value. This entire revolution was started by one of those villagers. We can't ever forget that. We can't forget where we come from or who we must protect. Deploy your Speeders and rescue all you can before the area is occupied by the enemy. Hopefully, they won't anticipate this move and won't plan for it."

Ajax saluted and bowed. "It will be done, my Lord."

FIFTY-FOUR

Finn hated the orders, despite knowing exactly who gave them. It had Cojax written all over it. Orch seemed to read his thoughts as he opened a Comm-Link with Finn.

"Looks like your old buddy is still looking out for you! I'm sure these suicide orders come straight from the top."

Finn frowned but did not answer. Undoubtedly, Cojax had ordered them to rescue the human villagers. The only benefit was that he could finally push his Speeder to its full capabilities. It hummed as it moved, always staying between four and six feet above the ground.

"Easy there, string bean!" Orch said. "You won't get a medal for killing yourself before you even reach the battle."

"Hah!" Finn laughed. "I'm sorry if the dust I'm kicking up is making it hard for your ego to breath."

Orch did not need another prompting. He wrenched the accelerator, pulling up next to Finn. They separated for a moment to weave around a tree but then regrouped, Orch pushing his Speeder so hard it whined in protest. He took the lead, but only for a while. Although Finn had only the most basic training with the ArcSpeeder, he had always been a quick study. After banking left and right, ripping over a river and a sand barge, he landed with a thump just in front of Orch.

"Ah," Orch said, "so the string bean has some skill."

"What is it with you and Horace always calling me string bean?"

Orch dropped back, pumped the throttle, and twisted the Speeder to the side, slipping through two trees that were so close they were almost touching. Orch retook the lead. "Would you prefer we called you something else?"

"I'd prefer you'd recognize my skill and take that into consideration next time you generate a nickname for me."

"Alright then, Kid-tastic. What name do you prefer?"

"Certainly not Kid-tastic. What about Blade or Hunter?"

"Blade Hunter?" Orch asked. "That would suggest you hunt down other people's blades. And what do you do when you find them?"

"Not Blade Hunter," Finn replied. "Blade or Hunter…." He stopped short as he hit the next ridge. Immediately, he slowed his engine, turning sideways as he did. Orch pulled up next to him. No explanation for the sudden stop was needed.

There was a wall of Roaches in the distance as wide as the horizon. Finn swallowed hard as he magnified the vision on his helmet, scanning the endless ranks of the creatures. SataniKahns were as numerous as the rocks beneath their ArcSpeeders. He saw all the creatures he had ever seen on the battlefield and more: Reevers of all classes and shapes; Sliders; Ankle Biters; Spine Rollers; Skewers flying high above; Ultain Deer; Hellhounds; Skillians; Spinners; several different sizes and strains of SataniKahns, including Lancers, Boilers, Leapers, Blue Veins, and Beserkers; and Damnattii in their armor, war tanks, and heavy machinery. They were accompanied by dozens of sleek flying vessels of various sizes that were shaped like elongated spheres. At multiple points along the ships, there were docking bays, lethal gun placements, and robust engines. One vessel was much larger than the rest, stretching on for a mile from front to back. This ship was flatter than many of the vessels and sleeker in design. It appeared to truly have been crafted with space travel in mind.

Finn pulled his helmet off. "Have you ever seen anything like that?"

Orch also removed his helmet and stepped off his Speeder. "Nobody has ever seen anything like that." He then turned his attention to his ArmGuard. "All units, be advised we have enemy inbound from the following coordinates. Finish moving out villagers and fall back to location Alpha."

Just then, a beam of light flew past, hitting and splitting a large boulder behind them. With no pause, Orch drew his Blazer from his back and unloaded at the assailant, a Damnattii who was approximately two hundred yards away. The first shot split the unarmored enemy in two. Another Damnattii opened fire, forcing Finn and Orch to take cover behind some boulders.

"Get out of here," Orch replied.

Finn shouldered his rifle, firing several times before removing the head of another attacker below. "I'm not going to abandon you."

"I'll catch up—"

Orch's words were interrupted by a thunderous crash. The large boulder that had been split by the first shot fired at them, cracked where it had been struck and rolled, crushing Orch's Speeder as it did. The boulder rolled for another few feet until it got stuck between several rocks and a large tree. The Speeder's shield preserved most of it, but the unprotected engine in the back crushed under the heavy weight.

"Wow," Finn said, a smile on his face. "That's unfortunate."

"Looks like we'll have to double up."

Finn frowned. "I guess I could make room for you."

Thirty seconds later, they were whipping through the wind in the opposite direction.

"How is it that you're driving again?" Finn asked through his helmet. "You were the one that parked your vehicle right in the path of a massive boulder."

Orch did not have time to respond before they could hear screeching from up above. Finn looked up to see the source of the noise. Three of the sleek aircraft vessels now passed them in earnest. These were small, only slightly bigger than the Speeder that they road on.

"Scout ships," Orch said over the Comm.

"Don't worry," Finn answered. "They passed us."

Moments later, the ships turned back around, heading right towards them. Then they began to unleash a torrent of fire at the Speeder below. Everything they hit exploded from the impact, littering the air with rock and debris.

"You still have your Blazer?" Orch yelled.

"Yeah," Finn said.

"Do I really have to tell you what to do with it?"

Finn slowly unholstered his Blazer, careful not to let go of Orch's waist for more than a second at a time. "This is exactly why I should have driven, oh great Master of the Blazer. You could have really done something with your Blazer that might have impressed someone."

Orch was about to respond, but Finn's Blazer fire cut him off. The shots were wild and misplaced; sometimes going so wide, Orch was confused at what exactly Finn was shooting at.

"Use my shoulder to prop the Blazer on," Orch instructed. "And aim ahead of what you are shooting at. Follow your shot."

With the next shot, by some odd luck, Finn clipped the back of one of the flying ships. The vessel was shielded, so it was not a killing blow, but the force of the impact sent it down and to one side, lining it perfectly with a large tree trunk. The tree exploded into shards of wood and branches that rained down. The ship lost momentum and hit the ground, bouncing twice before it began to roll.

"See what happens when you listen to my advice?" Orch asked.

"I didn't use your advice to take that shot," Finn replied.

"What are you talking about," Orch replied. "I told you my advice, and the next shot, you made a perfect hit."

"You don't get to take credit for the hit just because you were saying something that I definitely ignored right before I fired. Just because I told you that you need to drive faster, doesn't mean I get to take credit for us surviving."

The other two vessels came in again, strafing the ground. This time Orch was struck right in the arm, sending him and the Speeder pitching to the right. The force of the impact would have completely blown him off the Speeder had Finn not been there to counteract the effect.

"You're welcome," Finn said.

"If you're fishing for a thank you," Orch replied. "Why don't you shoot down those other two ships first?"

"They're all over the place," Finn replied. "I can't get a clear shot. Those things are shielded anyway. I got lucky with the first one; I doubt it will happen twice."

Orch suddenly slowed the Speeder down, letting it come to a stop.

"What are you doing?" Finn asked. "You can't stop now."

Orch did not respond as he unlatched his Blazer from his back and then used a rock to post up his weapon. Orch had parked in a bald spot of the forest, on a patch of yellow grass that made their Speeder stick out like it was being broadcast on a CityScreen.

Then the first ship came in, laying down a trail of fire straight for them. Finn dove behind a cluster of rocks, but Orch held his position. From his Blazer, a ball of energy shot out, hitting the ship head-on. In a flash, Orch fired again; this second projectile was needle-thin, no bigger than the width of a pinky. This, too, hit the cockpit straight on. At first, Finn thought this second projectile had no effect, as the ship did not shake on impact, nor did it adjust its course. But then the ship started to tilt to the side more and more until it whipped into the ground.

Orch twisted around to see the second vessel coming from the opposite direction. Two more shots and this ship came crashing to the ground as well. Finn was glad he still wore his helmet because he did not want Orch to see the admiration in his eyes.

Orch latched his Blazer back onto his back and gestured for Finn to take the driver seat. Finn's movements were a little slow as he was still thinking about the fantastic Blazer work Orch had just put on display.

"Not bad," Finn said, "but it's a lot harder shooting from a moving Speeder."

Orch laughed.

Finn started the Speeder turning it towards location Alpha.

"Orch," a Validated said over the Comm. "What's your status? We heard some fire not far from our position."

Orch responded quickly. "Nothing we couldn't handle. Did everyone get out of the village?"

"Yes, sir," the Validated replied. "We had to subdue a few of the locals, but we're en route to location Alpha now. We'll meet you there."

"Don't wait for us," Orch replied. "We're going to take the scenic route." He linked his Comm with Finn. "Kid-tastic, turn the Speeder back around. I just got an idea. Let's give Cojax a present he won't soon forget."

FIFTY-FIVE

Cojax studied the crafts from different angles, pretending to be more pleased than he really was. "Why is there mud all over them? There's more mud than ship here."

"It seems like old boy Cojax isn't so impressed with our new gift," Orch said as he nodded towards Finn.

"Oh," Cojax replied quickly, "I'm impressed...."

"We had two of them to tow back," Finn supplied, "and even though they hovered above the ground, they kept bumping into each other and then into the mud. We had to move quickly to keep ahead of additional Decamont scouts. Luckily a couple of CargoLifters showed up and took them off our hands before we had to drag them too far."

They were standing near one of the massive gates of the city of Delphi, in an open area once designated for gathering warriors as they prepared to defend themselves against an onslaught of Roaches. The parade grounds were empty except for Finn, Orch, Cojax, and two small escorts. Mud dripped down from one of the ships and plopped onto the polished concrete.

"So, can they still fly?" Cojax asked.

Orch unfolded his arms and nodded towards several Validated at the edge of the grounds. "I guess it's time to find out." Two Validated and an unarmored Damnattii stepped forward. Cojax frowned, surprised he had not noticed the Damnattii sooner. The creature was hunched; its clothes were well made but oil-stained. All four of its hands rubbed together anxiously, as if its survival depended on the next few minutes.

Finn stepped up, his face fixed with a stern expression. "You maintain these things?"

The Damnattii was confused by the two large mud piles in front of him. "I'm no gardener, if that's what you mean."

"Don't play dim with me," Finn said.

The Damnattii straightened up, his hands shaking. "I can maintain ships, but as far as these piles of mud, I think you'd be better suited to find a gardener."

"Those are ships," Finn said sternly.

One of the Damnattii's hands reached up and patted the sweat on its brow. "That's like no ship I've ever seen. Does it run on dirt clods?"

Finn puffed out his chest. He opened his mouth to speak, but Orch cut him off. "Let me have a shot at this, string bean." He stepped in front of Finn, addressing the Damnattii directly. "I've been told you volunteered to help us in our revolution."

"Yes," the Damnattii replied, "but that was before I knew you were trying to turn a pile of mud into a flying craft."

"Why would you want to help us?"

"Because you're not the Decamont."

"That's it?"

The Damnattii looked down, shifting on his feet as he did. "I have my reasons."

"Well," Orch said, "we picked up two Decamont ships, and none of us here have any idea how they work."

The Damnattii looked at the mounds of mud with new interest, taking two steps forward. "What? Are those Screamers? How did you get a set of Screamers?" He walked forward until he was only feet away from the muddy exterior. He placed a grubby hand on the side of one of the ships, gingerly scrubbing at the mud. "By the Holy Creed of Handel, you've got a set of Screamers. How is this possible? These things are shielded. By what genius maneuver did you take these vessels from the sky?"

"See," Orch said to Cojax. "That's the sort of reaction I expected you to have." He stepped up to the Damnattii, patting him on the shoulder. "Well, my new friend, I took them both out of the sky with a Blazer."

"By the brows of the Elders, you shot them down with a Blazer?"

"Have you worked on these before?" Cojax asked in earnest. "Can you repair them?"

The Damnattii wiped the mud off his hands and looked to Orch. "I've worked on them, but it's been a few years. Several of them crashed near our underground city, and I was ordered to recover them and see what went wrong."

"Can you get them working?" Finn asked.

The Damnattii studied Finn in earnest—he did not seem fond of the boy. "Depends on what is wrong with them, but most likely. The ships are complicated, but they have an onboard system that can pretty much diagnose any major problem. From there, it's all about finding or fabricating the right parts and putting them together."

"And once you understand the vessel," Cojax asked, "could you make more of them?"

The Damnattii rubbed his head again, smearing some mud along his cheek. "Well, that would be a task, wouldn't it? With enough time, and with the right people, yeah, I bet I could."

"How much time?" Cojax asked.

"Ohhhh," the Damnattii said, pausing for effect, "it would depend on several factors. But, and I'm just guessing here, maybe after a few years of study, with a little luck, we could reverse engineer the thing."

"A few years?" Finn said.

"Yeah, string bean," the Damnattii said with a growl, "this isn't exactly as easy as coming up with a recipe after trying someone's soup."

Cojax's shoulders fell. He let out a long, deep breath. "Well, then, only two ships won't do us much good."

"Can you at least teach us how to fly them?" Finn asked.

Orch shot Finn an annoyed look.

"What?" Finn asked. "We might as well have a little fun while we can."

"I can teach you," the Damnattii replied. "They aren't much different than your UniLifters. I'll have to hack their access code, but that shouldn't be too hard."

"Why were there Damnattii inside, not Decamont warriors?" Cojax asked.

The Damnattii laughed. "The Decamont don't put themselves in harm's way. They use other species to carry out their dirty work."

"Have you seen one before?" Finn asked.

"From a distance, yeah, but they were in armor so I don't know what they look like," replied the Damnattii. "And I have no idea how great of warriors they are—nobody does. But the real threat comes from the HIECs. That's what should keep you up at night. These ships are fast, shielded, and well-armed, but they are nothing compared to a HIEC."

"Hike?" Finn asked.

"It's pronounced hey-k, string bean," the Damnattii snapped.

"What's a HIEC?" Cojax asked.

"A High-Intensity Energy Cannon," the Damnattii replied. "They're equipped on every Decamont ship capable of intergalactic travel, and I've heard they've got one coming this way."

"What does it do?" Orch asked.

"It produces a beam of light so powerful it will burn through even the strongest of your Phalanx formations in an instant," the Damnattii replied. "If they decide to deploy that to the field of battle, they will decimate your ranks in a matter of minutes."

"That's the massive ship we saw," Finn said to Orch.

"If?" Cojax asked. "Why wouldn't they deploy that as soon as they showed up?"

"Because," the Damnattii replied, "that ship, known as the Perdition, holds the Crine, and they aren't going to put him at risk unless absolutely necessary."

"So," Orch said, his voice taking on an annoyed tone. "What you're saying is that unless we were kicking their butts, they wouldn't deploy the Perdition. But if they did, it would mean almost certain defeat?"

"Yeah, that's it," the Damnattii said.

"How can we take them out?" Cojax asked.

The Damnattii shook its head. "The ship is heavily shielded, so any external attack would prove ineffective. You'd have to shoot at the ship until its shields broke, but unless you had an Equalizer or a HIEC of your own, I don't think you would have enough firepower. The other way is to destroy it from the inside."

"From the inside?" Finn asked.

"Like placing explosives on the cannons?" Orch asked. "We don't have anything like that."

"You don't," the Damnattii said, "but the Numberless sure do. I used to rig up explosive for them all the time when they needed to level a building."

"Can you rig something up?"

"Of course," the Damnattii replied, "but, those explosives won't do anything unless they're placed inside the ship right next to the base of the HIEC. And you're not going to get into the Perdition unless you've got some way to take out their shields. And the only way you'd even have a chance at taking out their shields is if you had your own HIEC or something better."

"So, in sum," Finn said. "We're dead."

Orch frowned. "Of course it's going to sound bad if you say it like that."

Finn fixed a smile on his face. "We're dead."

"Nope still sounds as bad," Orch replied. "What do you think, Cojax?"

Cojax did not respond; he was too busy picking at the mud on the side of the ship. After taking a chunk of the muck off, he studied it as if it were an intricate piece of jewelry.

"Cojax?" Orch asked.

"I may have an idea that involves us not dying."

FIFTY-SIX

The final battle plan was proposed, debated upon, adjusted, and approved. It would not be a battle of half-measures. Every available Validated above the age of sixteen was called to take up arms, either in protecting the cities or on the battlefield. Between five cities, they were able to field an army of twelve million Validated and twenty thousand Numberless.

Achillian presented most of the strategy, which took several hours as various Numberless added to the discussion. Then Cojax spoke of the potential threat of the HIECs. This news was received with some trepidation until he proposed his plan on dealing with them. The plan was well received—except for the part when Cojax volunteered to put himself in danger on behalf of the mission. The room split with argument, but Cojax would not have it. If he expected his people to risk their lives for him, he had to be willing to do the same for his people.

After the plan was approved, they briefed all twelve million warriors at the same time. More specific briefs were to follow with several of the units, but for most of the Validated, the initial brief would be sufficient. Most of Cojax's forces had already deployed to the base of a mountain known as the Wedge. This point had been the topic of some discussion during the War Council. If the Decamont wanted to, they could deploy a force around the mountain to keep them pinned down while sending another detachment to attack the weakened and more vulnerable cities. Some of the Council proposed that their defenses should be set up at a city instead of on the Wedge, but then the debate of which city would be most advantageous ensued. By the end of it, the voting lines were split evenly down the middle.

The decision was left up to Cojax alone. He chose to fortify the base of the mountain. Not only was Wedge Mountain evenly spaced between the cities, but it was also directly in the path of the Decamont forces. It was a gamble, but Cojax felt confident that the

Decamont would not allow a free-standing army of Validated running around in the world. If they did bypass the rebels, Cojax figured, he could always use his army to flank the enemy as they attacked a city.

But for once, Cojax's mind was not on the coming day or battle plans. His chest constricted with nausea and his breath came in short gasps, but it was not out of fear of what tomorrow may bring.

When Jessica arrived, dressed in her most elegant formal attire, Cojax felt he lost his breath altogether. Never had he seen anything more beautiful. Her blond hair was unbound, her face bright and cheerful. He kissed her as soon as he saw her, and she kissed him back. It had only been two weeks since he had last seen her, and that was far too long.

Cojax led them to a small personal office formerly utilized by one of the Numberless of the city of Delphi. Aias, Byron, Horace, Finn, Seleukus, Achillian, Onar, and Orch were already waiting. They each saluted in turn, grinning at the happy couple.

Horace presided over the ceremony, missing more words than he remembered. It was short and sweet. At the end of the service, Cojax slipped a ring on Jessica's finger, taking an oath to always aid and protect her. Jessica did the same, repeating the oath. Then they kissed, the union now official. They had recorded the ceremony but were not planning on broadcasting it until after the battle. The wedding in itself was controversial, as it had been strictly prohibited under the AC. During that time, they had been assigned partners in what was known as a "Pairing." Usually, the pairs did not know each other before the arrangement, and love was rarely, if ever, part of the equation. They needed a solid victory before broadcasting their new Lord's deviation from standard practice.

Cojax took Jessica's hand in his, and they retreated to the spacious room where Cojax was living. It was a massive space, easily twice the size of a standard Validated apartment. It had a fully furnished living room, kitchen, and three bedrooms. The ceilings were vaulted as well as lined with pillars, in the classical Ionic style.

Jessica turned around, taking in the opulence of the room. "You could pretty much fit every house of my old village in here."

"Well," Cojax said with a wink, "let's give it a few days before we invite all of them up here."

Jessica smiled, pulled back into the moment. "I can't believe we're married."

"I can't believe you said yes," Cojax answered.

Jessica stepped closer, rubbing her hands up and down Cojax's arms. She kissed him, enjoying the sweet taste of his lips. "I was on the fence, I really was."

"What pushed you over the edge?"

"The fact that Finn said no to my proposal, and I didn't want to die alone."

Cojax laughed at that, picturing Jessica and Finn together. He shook his head. "You'd make a horrible couple."

"What makes you say that?"

He kissed her on the neck. "Because we make such a great couple."

"That answer doesn't make any sense," Jessica replied.

Cojax kissed the other side of her neck. "I love you. That, to me, makes all the sense in the world." He kissed her again, taking care to caress her hair.

Jessica pulled back. "Wait, wait. Before we get... well... preoccupied. I've got something to share with you. I didn't think this was something I should share over the Comm since...well, I don't think it's something everyone should know just yet."

"And what's that?" Cojax said, still lost in her eyes.

"I'm serious, Cojax. This is important."

He straightened up and tried not to smile.

"Let me show you," Jessica said. "That will go a lot further than my explanation." She fiddled with her ArmGuard, pulling up several pictures she had recently taken. She then pushed the images to a CityScreen hanging from the wall. "This is the device that contained the explosive."

"What?" Cojax said, still in a daze.

"Remember the explosion in the Trinity that killed half of the Populi Party leadership? Well, this is what the device looked like."

Cojax studied the picture, unable to pick out anything remarkable. "What is it?"

Jessica switched to another picture, this one taken from above. The device was made from a unique metal that now had been shredded into long strips. Despite the damage, from the new angle, it became clear as to what it was. "It's a metal arm."

All levity left Cojax's face as he stepped closer to the image. "I've seen that arm before."

"Where?"

"I was the one that gave it to Marcus."

"What?"

"I gave it to him a few nights before the explosion. I was hoping to make amends?"

"Where did you get it from?"

"Adriana."

"Do you think she planted the explosive?"

Cojax did not answer for a long time. "Maybe. Or maybe Marcus knew that an arm that I gave him would not appear suspicious if it was turned into a bomb. Marcus could have engaged me in conversation, found some reason to return the arm to me, leave in sudden haste, and set off the explosion. Since I gave it to him, it wouldn't have raised my suspicions."

"That's possible. But Byron was able to figure out the power source of the device, and he believes that it was triggered and powered by the person wearing the arm—much like how our bodies charge our armor. So, it would be a suicide mission for whoever was wearing that arm. I think it's more likely that it was already a bomb when you gave it to Marcus."

"That's because you don't like Adriana."

Jessica clenched her teeth. "For good reason too. I also found something else. Aias and I were able to access Ion's ArmGuard. The odd thing was that no messages were sent to or from Ion that day. All the days before had messages, but on that one day, there were none. Don't you remember that Adriana said that Ion had sent the video transmission to her around the time of the explosion? Well, according to his log, he didn't send anything."

"Well, if he was regularly sending out and receiving messages every day up to the day the explosion occurred, isn't it more likely that the messages that day had been deleted?"

"It's possible," Jessica replied. "But who would've deleted them? Ion? Even if he had survived the explosion, does it seem to make sense that he would spend his last dying moments deleting the messages he sent and received that day?"

"It doesn't seem likely," Cojax agreed. He stood up, walking to the far end of the room, staring out a large glass window that overlooked the city. The city was a nest of activity as CargoLifters and HoverBuckets zoomed back and forth, transporting people and cargo in preparation for the coming conflict. Despite the city looking very similar to Titan, besides the more abundant use of Pyramid shapes and Obliques, this place felt strange to Cojax. The people and customs were different; even many of their swear words were odd. He had enjoyed his time here, but now he wanted to return to Titan, to confront Adriana with these new revelations.

"She won't admit anything," Cojax said.

Jessica approached from behind, hugging Cojax as he stood at the window. "I'm sorry I brought this up now. I contemplated not saying anything until after the battle. I just had been working on it, and it was on my mind."

Cojax's countenance had changed. Once again, the weight of his mantel seemed to rest on his shoulders, making him stand tall and tense. "I'm glad you did. Although I don't know exactly what it means. Adriana would have done anything for our political party to win. In large part, we did win because of her political savvy, but I can't imagine her attempting to kill my brother. What about the video we saw?"

"I don't have access to it," Jessica replied, "I haven't been able to study it."

"Well," Cojax answered, "we need to take steps just in case Adriana really did construct the bomb."

"I'll head off to Titan tonight," Jessica replied, "and call upon the Rifters. As long as that rat is not hiding somewhere, we should be able to find and detain Adriana quickly."

"And once you have her in custody, you'll have to find the video that she showed us. We'll have to study it until we can determine whether it's been manipulated or not. I've warned her so many times already about this. If she is responsible, I will have her executed."

"I agree."

"But don't kill her before we have all the facts," Cojax said.

Jessica grinned. "Who? Me? I'd never."

"A lot seems to indicate that she was involved, but we can't be sure just yet," Cojax replied.

"Why would she want to blow up the Populi Party?" Jessica asked.

"She was romantically involved with Ion right up to the time of the explosion," Cojax said. "He was her main source of information for the Populi Party. Perhaps, Ion leaked to her that the Populi Party was becoming so desperate that they would consider an assassination attempt. So, she planted a bomb, just in case their words turned into actions. Either way, we'll have no idea until we find out if that video she showed us is genuine or not." Cojax felt his anger rising, his hands involuntarily turning into fists. "There better be a good explanation behind all of this."

Jessica pulled Cojax's chin towards her until their eyes met. "I have no idea how long it will take to determine the authenticity of the video, but Adriana will be locked up the whole time. Perhaps, by the time you see her next, she'll be much more willing to talk."

"I'm so sick of her lies," Cojax said in exasperation. "Why is she constantly going behind my back?"

"I can hardly wait to see the expression on her face as I escort her to one of the holding cells, regardless of her guilt." It was meant to be a jest, but Cojax did not laugh. His expression was still stern, so different than what it was only minutes before. Jessica kissed him and pulled back to see his reaction. She kissed him again and again, each time it seemed to draw tension from his body.

Jessica sighed, "I'll head out right now." She turned to go but Cojax held her hand fast. "Wait…wait…Adriana isn't going anywhere. If she did do it, she did it so we could win—and we did. So, her plot has run its course. Please stay. There's no point in rushing off right now."

She folded back into his embrace, kissing him softly on the lips. Then she reached down, grabbed his hand, and kissed it. She guided him along through the living room, pulling him into the bedroom.

"I love you, Cojax, and I always will," Jessica said, as she slowly began to unbutton her formal attire.

FIFTY-SEVEN

In the early hours of the morning, the Roach army appeared, their numbers seemingly endless as they spilled over the land, filling every available inch at their approach. The Validated stood at attention, their rows perfect, lined up in thousands of tight, phalanx formations. The Numberless were separated into two primary groups: one positioned at the centerlines, another higher up the hill surrounding their heavy equipment. The mountain peak allowed the Titans a height advantage, and they used it to great effect by deploying all of their Gouger guns at the highest elevation. They entrenched the cannons into the mountain, allowing them greater shot accuracy as well as protection. These would act as heavy turrets to soften the approaching enemy.

Achillian commanded the field of battle. He stood before a large conference table that held a real-time projection of the surrounding area. The sensors had been adjusted so that they were finally able to pick up the advancing Roach army in its entirety. The War Council surrounded the projection, all of them silent as the massive army approached. It was so large that the army spilled off the edge of the map. Even after zooming out, the Roach army was still off the board. Someone zoomed the projection back in—it was less intimidating that way.

The Numberless were absolutely imposing in their sleek, new red armor. They could feel the power ripple through their bodies each time they moved. The Validated from Titan, who were all armored in black with bronze highlights, were assigned to the left side of the formation; next to them were the Delphins, who had a mix of white armor with red highlights; next to them were the Oreaians, who were fond of large blue and white banners that complemented their armor; next to them were the Numberless, endowed in power in their elite, red armor; next to them were the Pincalians, who were armored in green and gray; and finally, on the opposite flank, were the Romans, who wore polished metallic armor that shimmered in the sun.

Achillian had positioned them in an old and relatively unused checkerboard configuration, which would allow each Phalanx to withdraw when their shields were weak and another unit to advance into their place.

"I suggest we deploy the shields," Marian said. "We're vulnerable by air until we do."

"Remember the plan," Achillian said. "There's a chance they don't even know about our shield generators, so let's not play that card until they force us to."

"And what if they've brought Diggers?" Antinium asked. "They can just as easily attack us from the ground as they can from the air without our shields."

"Our sensors should pick them up if they do, giving us just enough time to react," Achillian replied. "Besides, the bedrock of the mountain would make it difficult for any Digger to make any progress."

Moments later, a light flashed on the projection. Antinium pointed at it with his index finger. "The first Roaches have reached the range of our long-distance artillery."

"Hold fire," Achillian replied. "We want to separate the first ranks of Roaches from their supporting units in the back."

Marian swallowed. "Yes, sir."

The Roaches stopped their march, waiting for the rest of their army to file in. They were in range and just sitting there, perfect targets for their long-range artillery.

Marian sighed long and hard.

Achillian smiled. "I'll bet my blade that within moments after their initial wave hits our ranks, you'll change your mind."

"Sir," Marian said. "I didn't say anything."

"You said enough," Achillian replied.

Marian smiled. "I apologize."

It was not long before the Roaches began their advance. Row after row of Reevers poured out into the field of battle; their sleek, quick bodies made lethal with multiple rows of serrated teeth. The creatures went manic, leaping forward in a massive arrow-shaped assault. The ground thundered as they ran, trampling every blade of grass and bush in their path.

"Sir," Marian prompted.

"Wait," Achillian replied.

As the Reevers drew nearer, they sounded like thousands of pairs of rusty scissors being opened and closed in quick succession. They quickly made their way across the field, pouring down into the lower parts of elevation and then rising again like a pack of wolves.

"Fire upon all creatures at these coordinates," Achillian whispered.

Moments later, the Gougers unleased hell on their enemy in a blinding display of power. About halfway back in the Reevers' ranks, the ground exploded into dirt and debris. The thick Reever shells were no match for the Gougers, which took chunks out of their bodies with each impact. The barrage of fire hindered their movement, substantially slowing their rank and file to a crawl. As Achillian predicted, this separated the first wave of Reevers from their companions, effectively diminishing their advantage of numbers by delaying the approach of the second wave.

Achillian smiled. Marian frowned.

***

Julia had never seen anything like this, not in all her time in Rome or as a Numberless. She had never seen Roaches charge with so much bloodlust or collective fury. She knew well how Roaches were controlled—by releasing pollen in the air that turned on their aggression and savage nature. There were an array of pollens used to work up these creatures to battle—depending on how you wanted them to react. But these creatures had been turned absolutely demonic. They began to make a croaking noise from their throats that she had never heard before.

For a second, she felt fear—a real palpable terror that tightened her chest and blurred her vision. She knew they would be able to handle the first wave of Roaches, and then the one after that, and the one after that. *But for how long?* She pushed down her fear and replaced it with her intense anger.

"Link shields," she ordered. The Numberless obeyed, some

more slowly than others. This had been discussed beforehand and was somewhat of a sensitive issue for many of the Numberless, who preferred to fight as individuals rather than in a Phalanx formation. But Julia would not give on the issue. She was not about to underestimate an enemy that had kept them slaves for over two hundred years.

"Blazers," Julia ordered. "Open fire."

The Numberless responded quickly, laying down a thick layer of projectiles. The Blazers were more of a nuisance than a real threat to the thickly shelled Reevers, but it slowed their charge just the same. The creatures were only a hundred yards away now. All, Phalanx formations had opened fire, filling the killing field with a blinding light.

Julia swallowed. When they were sixty yards away, she ordered Arc Lances to be drawn—something that many would criticize as being premature. This caution, however, proved fortuitous. At thirty yards away, the creatures began leaping towards the Numberless in a way never before seen.

Julia skewered a Roach through the head and pushed it off with her boot. The creature still writhed in aggression, trying to snap at her feet. She stabbed the beast again and again, and still, it clung to life. It was not until she drove her spear deep into the creature's chest before it finally died. She did not have time to contemplate the persistent vitality of the animal before the wave of Roaches exploded against their shields.

Carapace met blade, spilling Roach wax across the ground.

Julia skewered another creature, and then a third, the bodies began to mound at the feet of the Numberless. More creatures poured in, filling in whatever gaps they could find and snapping at whomever they could reach. As the bodies piled, the Roaches began to launch themselves into the middle of the Numberless ranks, where they were dispatched quickly at first, but as more and more appeared, it began to be difficult to keep up with the assault. As the Roach bodies turned lifeless, they slipped to the ground, no longer upheld by the shared shields of the Numberless. The sheer number was overwhelming. With each move of Julia's wrist, she put another one of the creatures to the ground. Killing them was not the issue as much as trying to avoid being overwhelmed by the mounds of dead creatures.

Julia looked around, seeing her unit beginning to be cocooned by the bodies of the fallen Reevers. This was known as being "buried," but it rarely happened, and never this quickly. It was usually something that happened to an inexperienced unit that was too timid to advance. But they were only seconds into the combat, and they were being buried by carapace.

She reached down for her anger, finding it in an instant. She pulsed a command to her soldiers to prepare to leap forward. Convention would have dictated that she should pull back, instead of forward, allowing the creatures to expedite their own deaths, but she had a feeling she should push on. She would not fall into a routine that would be predictable to the Decamont.

She pulsed the command to surge forward, and instantly, the rear line of Numberless leaped through the air, landing in front of Julia and on top of the mound of bodies. The Numberless were vulnerable since they were on unstable footing. Julia pulsed again, commanding the next line to leap forward. These Numberless came down hard, cutting through the Reevers as if they were made of water.

She pushed her unit hard into the enemy ranks, forcing them past the battle line and into a slow-paced charge. When Julia ended up in the rear, and as she was leaping into the first row, she happened to glimpse at the units to her right. The Numberless were holding their ground, some of them backing up to prevent themselves from being buried under carapace. But most of the Validated, either because of some sense of bravado or inexperience, were not advancing or retreating. These units looked more like a small hill of live Roaches than they did a Phalanx.

"*Fools,*" Julia thought. "*The weight of the creatures will tax their shields until they are broken.*" When Julia landed, she pulled back, having another take her place. She then conveyed to the other Numberless units what was happening to the Validated Phalanxes at the front. She did not wait for a response, nor did she expect one.

There was no pulse assigned for the maneuver Julia was about order, so she had to explain it over the Comm. "The front lines of Validated are being buried. We've got to give them some reprieve from the onslaught of Roaches; otherwise, they'll soon be crushed. We'll create a single line shield wall, only one person in the first row. That will enable us to stretch out along the battlefield and divert the Reevers from the other Phalanxes."

"Move," Julia ordered. This was not, in itself, a complicated maneuver, but it was unique and rarely practiced. And in her experience, in the heat of battle, even the simplest of movements can sometimes prove the most difficult. But the Numberless proved their Tier, using their new armor and skill with the blade to cut past the Roaches. One by one, Julia's formation began to stretch out across the battlefield until it was one thin line. Their shields were still linked, but the effect was abated owing to the distance. This long line effectively cut off the Roaches charge, but now the entire force that was previously attacking multiple units focused their complete attention on the line of Numberless.

When the bodies began to collect, Julia ordered the Numberless forward, not back. They cut through the masses of Roaches, spraying wax across the land and driving the creatures into the ground. The Numberless were unstoppable, even in their thin, fragile-looking formation. Julia pushed her Numberless forward and forward, robbing the momentum of the Roaches' charge.

This gave the Validated units behind them enough time to finish the Reevers that were burying them as well as push forward and reform battle lines, leaving behind the dead Roaches. Despite her actions, at least twenty different Phalanxes of Validated had broken, turning those units into a bath of blood and bodies.

As Julia cut through a large Reever, the battlefield opened up. Achillian's delayed firing of the Gougers had worked, breaking up the Reevers assault into many waves instead of one. Now that Julia had broken through the first assault, the subsequent groups were much easier to cut down. The creatures crashed against the Numberless in small ineffectual groups of a dozen or so. It was not long before the Reevers were pulling back.

A disjointed but raucous cheer erupted from the humans.

Julia scanned the horizon, whispering to herself as she did. "It can't be that easy." The remaining Reevers continued to retreat, disappearing into the ranks of Roaches.

Then a mass of SataniKahns appeared in such rank and file as never to have been seen. Usually, when these massive creatures were deployed to the field, they were in groups of two or three for each Phalanx. But now, as Julia looked up, she could see nothing but a wall of carapace and pincers. They moved in row after row in numbers she had never dreamed of.

Julia swallowed hard. "Fall back to the battle line and reform ranks." She allowed her troops to pass her by as she still stared at the coming onslaught. "I hope that boy knows what he's doing."

FIFTY-EIGHT

Jessica moved with purpose through the large apartment building. Flanked by twenty heavily-armed Rifters as well as Aias, she felt confident that this would be a simple operation. When she reached Adriana's apartment, she knocked once, twice, three times. No answer.

Jessica donned her helmet. "I guess she's a little shy today."

"Please don't enjoy this as much as I know you're going to," Aias replied. He also placed his helmet on and drew his blade.

The next second, Jessica synced all of her energy to her right foot just as she kicked the door. The door exploded inwards, the handle sticking into the far wall. Jessica and Aias went first, followed by their entourage. She stayed in the main room, waiting for confirmation that Adriana was detained. The apartment was not dirty, but it was cluttered with scattered food trays and pieces of underwear.

Jessica could not help herself. As she waited, her mind began to conjure up potential insults. She was so convinced that Adriana was hiding somewhere in the apartment, she did not hear when one of the Rifters reported that the apartment was empty.

The Rifter repeated what he had said.

"What?" Jessica asked.

"My Queen, the apartment is empty. No one is here."

Jessica frowned. She had just thought of a cutting insult that she was sure to forget when they finally found the snake. "Alright, ten of you post up here, I'll be heading down to the Rift to see if she's locking lips with Brutus. Repair the door the best you can. Probably best she doesn't know we're looking for her until we have her. Report to me as soon as you have her apprehended or you catch sight of her."

The Rifter saluted and assigned ten others to stay in the apartment.

"I don't like this," Aias replied.

"She's always running around," Jessica replied, "always trying to screw someone else in one way or the other. We'll find her."

"Just in case," Aias said. "Why don't we request additional Rifters?"

"Fine by me," Jessica replied. "Maybe we should get all the Rifters to standby for now, at least until she's apprehended."

"Good idea," Aias whispered. He then put all the Rifters on standby as well as ordering another twenty to meet them at one of the entrances that led to the Rift. She thought that twenty was a little excessive; after all, they did not want to make this a public affair. But Jessica did not say anything.

When they met up with the additional Rifters, they descended into the Rift, first visiting Brutus' quarters and then the armor fabricators that Adriana had set up. They did not find Brutus or Adriana at either location.

As they approached the armor fabricators, Aias slowed down to scrutinize them. No one seemed to be running the machines, as he had expected. His Rifters had been the ones utilized to transfer the machines from the Mahghetto to here. But, despite the many offers from Aias, Adriana refused any help to set them up.

"Aias," Jessica said. "Someone might have tipped her off. We've got to find her before she can cause any more trouble."

"Get to the Main Control Room," Aias replied. "Give me some time to look at these machines. There should be people here running them. I want to find out why no one is."

"Why does that matter now?" Jessica said, her voice betraying the fear she felt. "I'd hate to leave you here and find out later that Brutus showed up with his thugs."

"I'm more than a match for Brutus and his thugs, but something isn't right. I'll request another twenty Rifters to meet me here while I look this over. Get to the Control Room and make sure she doesn't have access to it. I can't imagine she could do any damage, it all has multiple levels of security, and she doesn't have the access codes to any of them."

Jessica disappeared, flanked by thirty Rifters. The Rift became silent as they left, and it would be that way for another five minutes before the Rifters Aias requested would arrive.

Aias stepped around the first armor fabricator. The lights indicating that it was receiving power and functioning correctly were on, but it appeared that the device had been assembled in the wrong order. The device was ten sections in length, and each one was about four feet long and five feet tall. There was a design etched onto the outside that should have been seamless had it all been hooked together correctly. The first two sections were connected properly, but every one after that was in a different order. At one point, the incorrect sequence created a gap in the device that was covered up with a rubbery putty.

"How could that possibly hold the machine together?" Aias commented. From the little he knew about how these machines functioned, they required a tremendous amount of heat and pressure.

Aias drew out his Arc Blade, cutting free one of the service panels. It was a tight fit, but he was able to squeeze inside. What greeted him turned his stomach. There was not even an attempt to reconnect the sections properly. The only thing that appeared to have power running to it was at the front of the machine. Aias tugged on the cord, and the light power indicator that had been visible from the outside fell to the floor.

"That's just a light bulb they rigged up to make it look like it was on," Aias pronounced. His mind worked on the problem, pushing it to a final conclusion. "She never made any elite armor." This confused him since he remembered seeing multiple Numberless wearing some of the advanced armor. "But if she never made it, where did it come from?" His mind started considering the implications of this new revelation. He closed his eyes as he followed all the evidence to its logical conclusion. He felt a mix of fear, trepidation, and finally, anger.

Aias tried to open a Comm with Orch. But there was no answer. He tried to reach Finn and Cojax, but still, there was nothing. "We've been cut out."

Aias opened a Comm with Jessica. "We've been fooled, Jessica. We've got to get out of the city."

When Jessica responded, he sighed in relief. "We've just arrived at the Control Room. What did you say about the city?"

"Jessica, we've got to leave the city now!"

Jessica was about to ask for clarification, but she was distracted by the sudden appearance of a Validated in the Control Room dressed in red armor.

***

"What are you doing here?" Jessica asked.

For the first time in a long time, Brutus' smile was genuine. "I rule this city now, have you not heard?" The large youth was dressed in blood-red armor—the same type Adriana had manufactured for the Numberless. Except this one had black highlights instead of white. Brutus was armed for war—two swords at his side and a Blazer on his back.

Jessica tried to reach Aias on the Comm, but it was not working. She now understood what Aias was saying.

"Don't do this, Brutus," Jessica warned. "Cojax sees you as family. Even though you don't get along, he would never betray you."

At this, Brutus laughed. "He already did betray me. And if he thinks of me as family, then I'd hate to see how he deals with his enemies."

"We outnumber you," Jessica growled. "Put down your weapons, or we'll cut you down. I won't ask again."

The threat fell flat as Validated began to appear behind Brutus, all of them wearing the same blood-red armor with the black highlights. Another Validated appeared who was also not wearing his helmet. His face had been so severely burned on one side that his right ear and hair had completely disappeared under scar tissue. Despite the disfiguration, Jessica instantly recognized the man.

"Cato?" Jessica asked, disbelief in her voice. "You're alive? How did you survive the explosion? Whatever you're planning, don't do this now. Our people are fighting the Decamont as we speak, and we can't afford to be divided. We can't do this now. Once we have victory, you can go your separate way, but don't do this now. Not when we are so close."

"Unfortunately," Cato replied. "We can't do this later. Order your Rifters to put down their blades."

Jessica gritted her teeth, pulling out her Blazer and donning her helmet. "I would sooner fall on my sword than be taken captive by a bunch of traitors."

FIFTY-NINE

Achillian stared at the line of SataniKahns. Never had they seen a show of such power, and brute strength. The creatures began to rumble forward, transported by dozens of their spindly legs. They moved as a collective unit, so different than any other time he had seen in the past. These creatures worked together, not independently.

"Concentrate all fire at the SataniKahns on the left and right flank," Achillian commanded. "The Numberless should be able to hold their own in the middle."

The next moment the Gougers erupted with light as they opened fire on the creatures. This annoyed the SataniKahns, more than anything, slowing their movement but never stopping them. But they were too many, and the Gougers too weak.

Achillian swallowed. "We've got to slow their charge. If we don't, they'll break through the front lines, allowing the rest of their army time to swarm in."

Marian shook her head. "How? The Gougers hardly do anything to them. Even if we could slow a few of them down, it would not be enough to stop their momentum."

Antinium looked closely at the advancing enemy on the large projection map. "I knew they would have SataniKahns, but not like this. No one could have planned on this. They'll smash into the Phalanx formations, one after another. And once they do, they'll let the Reevers finish what's left."

Achillian stepped closer to the battlefield, his eyes focused on the mostly flat field that lay between their army and the Roaches. "Aim the Gougers at the ground directly in front of the charging SataniKahns."

"You want us to shoot the ground?" Marian asked.

"Exactly," Achillian responded.

Marian and Antinium exchanged looks. Finally, Antinium nodded, conveying the orders on his ArmGuard. The Gougers changed their point of aim, now striking the ground instead of the heavy carapace. As soon as the order was obeyed, dirt erupted like geysers, leaving burning pockmarks behind. For a small instant, the SataniKahns disappeared in the debris as it was sent skyward. As they pushed through, the Gougers adjusted their aim, always staying just a few yards in front of the assaulting SataniKahns.

The Gougers lived up to their name, cutting into the earth at random intervals, turning the ground into uneven splits in the land. The intense fire of the Gougers, coupled with the blinding dust cloud that was created, proved effective.

"It's working," Antinium whispered as he stared at the map projection. He turned to Achillian, repeating what he said before. "It's work—"

Then he was cut off as fire exploded from the enemy's ranks. The Damnattii had opened fire with their massive, assault cannons. While the Titans were focused on the SataniKahns' charge, they neglected to notice the Damnattii moving their heavy cannon into range. Now beams of light as thick as a Validated's chest ripped through the Gougers, depleting their limited shields. One of the guns exploded as its shields succumbed to the fire. A piece of shrapnel whipped in the wind, striking Achillian in the shoulder.

"Raise shields," Antinium yelled over the roaring fire.

"No," Achillian said. "Divert some of the Gougers to return fire at the cannons; the rest keep their fire on the SataniKahns."

"Sir," Marian said. "Those Validated in the Gougers won't last long under that kind of enemy fire. A Gouger shield is nothing compared to the shields the Damnattii are using."

Achillian whipped around. "And what do you think will happen if we ease our fire on the SataniKahns? Thousands may die in the Gougers, but hundreds of thousands will die if they can't slow down those SataniKahns."

Marian clenched her jaw. "Sir, if we don't raise our shields, it won't be long before they've destroyed all of our Gougers. And at that point, they'll turn their fire onto our Phalanxes. We have no other option."

"There's always another option," Achillian said with a smile. "Antinium, you are in command until I return. Do not—under any circumstances—raise the shield until our main objective is met. All of this will be for naught if you do. Do you understand?"

Antinium nodded. "Yes, sir."

"And have the Phalanxes hold their positions. I don't want those fools to be inspired by our stupidity."

This time, Antinium saluted and bowed, finally realizing what Achillian was planning. "Yes, sir." Despite his realization, he could not help but ask, in hopes that he had guessed wrong. "What do you intend to do?"

"Even the odds," Achillian said. The powerful man placed his helmet on his head and linked Comms with four thousand reserve Numberless that were the elite guard of the shield generator. These had been the most powerful warriors of their day and age, each one a legend in their own right. They were seasoned and battle-tested. And now with swords in their hands, and with their new elite armor on their chests, they mounted Speeders and headed for the front line, Achillian at their head. The Speeders maneuvered quickly through the ranks of the Phalanxes, like a river flowing past rocks that poked out of the water. Achillian split the ranks, sending half to the north, the other half to the south.

No orders were needed, as each Numberless knew what they had to do. They formed a single line, two thousand on one flank, another two thousand on the other. Achillian stood fast, slowly drawing his blade from his back. They were now dwarfed by the stampeding SataniKahns, only moments away from impact.

Achillian linked his Comm to all the Numberless on the battlefield. "Titan sacrificed his life to give us freedom; we now make that sacrifice to keep it."

Achillian lowered himself into a fighting stance, both hands on his blade. As the SataniKahns were within thirty yards, Achillian ordered his Numberless to surge forward. The creatures were caught off guard. Numberless collided with SataniKahns in a horrific explosion of light and blood.

Achillian skewered a beast in the head, but the creature refused to die. It used a dozen of its dagger-like legs to stab at the Numberless. Achillian drove his sword down the beast, slicing it from throat to thorax, leaving a mess of thick carapace and blood behind. Once the Numberless hit the ground, the SataniKahn lurched forward, its massive pincers aimed for his head. He ducked under the first set of pincers and sliced clear through the next. The creature roared in frustration. It went in again, this time successfully striking Achillian with a long spindly appendage.

Achillian returned his own attack, slicing low and high, cutting limbs and shell with each swing. He finished the creature with a final thrust to it's now exposed heart. The beast lurched sideways, colliding into another SataniKahn who was battling two Numberless at once. Achillian moved to the next creature, and then the next, each falling as one domino after another. As the battle continued, however, Achillian's elite group of Numberless began to shrink. He could see them fall through his peripheral vision, see a glimpse of their bodies before they disappeared beneath claw and carapace. And still, they pushed on, facing unavoidable death. Creature and Numberless fell to the ground in turn, never to find their feet again.

Achillian sliced the next SataniKahn's chest wide open and jumped inside, ripping the lungs out as he cut himself free and exited out the back. As he landed, he realized that he was the last of his elite Numberless. He now faced a sea of Reevers and Spinners. They went for him with a frantic thrill, several dozen leaping in great arks in an attempt to crush him underneath. He cut several of them in mid-flight, but then was caught off guard as one snapped at his chest, sending light pulsing through his armor. He returned the favor, cutting the creature in two. Body after body fell before the epic warrior. Slowly, the warrior's shields were drained as the occasional mandible landed its mark.

Finally, a claw pierced flesh, sending the warrior pitching to one side. Despite his shields being gone, his weapons bloody, he held his ground. He was last seen sinking his gigantic sword into the chest of a massive SataniKahn. The creature bellowed as it collapsed to the ground, crushing Achillian underneath.

Antinium's computer informed him that he was now the Omega in charge of all battlefield decisions. He bowed low, a final honor for the fallen Numberless. When he raised his head again, his eyes met a surprised Marian.

"He did it. He not only slowed their advance, he stopped it completely."

Antinium slowly nodded. "Yes, he did. Order all units to stand their ground—and shift the focus of any of the remaining Gougers towards their heavy artillery."

"Yes, sir."

Antinium shook his head. Achillian had been his mentor when he had first become a Numberless. It was through his words that he learned about the Decamont. *And now he lies dead because of them.* He unsheathed his sword and tightened his hand around the grip, swearing vengeance.

Achillian's charge had confused and delayed the enemy, taking all momentum out of their ranks. The SataniKahns tried to recover, pushing up and over the massive corpses of their fellow-creatures, but there was not enough time to make up the momentum they had lost. When they did reach the ranks of the Validated, they met fresh warriors who had just rotated to the front line. The giant creatures' attack was separated and disjointed, attacking in ones or twos. The Validated handled them with a vengeance, putting them down by the hundreds. The smaller Roaches funneled in, attacking with a fury. The Validated were more cautious this time, careful to avoid being buried.

The battle continued for what seemed like hours in deadlock, each side unwilling to yield to the other. The Roaches certainly had greater numbers, but the Validated had the superior skill and position. It seemed the Decamont had decided to simply try and overwhelm the human forces with a constant deluge of creatures. Achillian's formation, however, proved all the more genius as it enabled Antinium to rotate his front lines as they were taking too much damage. If the battle continued like this, however, it would only be a matter of time before they were slowly chipped away into defeat. There were simply too many Roaches. But it would take a long time, perhaps days, maybe even a few weeks.

Then a sudden sonic boom sounded over the field of battle as a Decamont warship appeared far above.

"Looks like somebody's a little lit," Marian said. "Maybe Cojax knows what he's doing after all."

The Decamont warship was massive, stretching a good distance across the entire battlefield. It was shaped like a gigantic oval with large square sections for weapon emplacements. No sooner had it appeared before it released thousands of warships into the sky.

"That's it," Antinium said. "That's what we've been waiting for. Raise the shield."

The shield appeared a second later, just in time to intercept several massive beams of light fired from the HIECs on the Decamont ship.

"Cutting it a little close, don't you think?" Marian asked.

SIXTY

"And why didn't I get a set of fancy, red armor?" Finn asked.

"Because you're not a Numberless," Onar replied.

"Cojax isn't a Numberless," Finn retorted. "And he's got one."

"It doesn't work if you're not a Nova, I think," Cojax replied.

"Why didn't Onar get one then?" Finn asked.

"Some men are bigger than others," Onar said with a juvenile laugh. "The fabricator couldn't make one big enough. They'd first need to make a bigger machine."

"I got one," Horace added.

"No gloating," Orch hissed.

They were cramped into the bellies of the two Decamont warships that Orch had shot from the sky a few days before. Over their armor, they wore Decamont pilot uniforms: a red and brown jumpsuit with various mechanical attachments. Cojax and Orch wore the only actual pilot suits that they recovered, while the rest wore the best approximation that could be fabricated in such a short time. This had been one of Cojax's more uncertain plans, to be sure. But when he told his closest friends of what he intended to do, none of them backed away. Finn, however, did make it clear that he wanted a statue made in his honor if they succeeded.

In order to fit all of them and their gear in the bellies of the ships, they had to remove all of the vehicle's firepower, making them a little less than "completely vulnerable," as Orch had put it. Despite making these adjustments, Finn barely fit. His face was now flush against Horace's backside.

Onar and Cojax flew in one, while Orch, Horace, and Finn in the other. They had spent the last few days learning how to operate the ships. They were very similar to the UniLifters, and so learning to pilot them took no time at all. Orch controlled one; Cojax the other.

Cojax swallowed hard as he listened to the Comms. All they could do was wait. And with each word he heard, waiting became more and more of a burden. They were stuck several miles to the south, far outside the field of battle, as well as out of the range of the human's energy shield, which had not yet been engaged. They were in a large grass field that covered them almost entirely except for their metallic tops. The time passed in strange intervals, sometimes it seemed to go by fast, as when the Decamont began to first approach, other times it slowed. Cojax raked his hands through his hair again and again, his heart pounding with tremendous force.

"Either you have lice," Onar said with a deep growl, "or there's something wrong."

"If we don't do this right, there's no telling how many of our people will die," Cojax replied. "Everything we've done up to this point depends on the outcome of this battle—and the outcome of the battle depends on us."

"Cojax, you've done more for your people than anyone," Onar replied. "You have united your city under one banner; you have revealed the truth to several more cities; you have climbed from the Tenth Tier to become the Lord of our great city. If there was ever a chance we could succeed, it would be now. If there ever was a chance that we could earn our freedom, it will be with this battle."

Cojax nodded slowly. "I hope you're right." He turned his attention back to the Comms. He took a deep breath, trying to calm his nerves as the battle progressed. As panicked reports came in from different commanding officers, it was easy to get caught up in the moment. He felt fear, first for his army, then for himself. He closed his eyes, pushing his emotions to the side. It usually worked. This time it did not. His chest felt as tight as a drum. He forced himself to take deep, indulgent breaths, inhaling through his nose and out his mouth. The only thing that gave him some respite was Achillian's clear, concise voice over the Comm. The great commander's tone seemed to have a calming effect on the whole army.

That is who should be the Lord of the City, Cojax thought. *A warrior without peer, a leader without equal. If Achillian was awake when Titan was alive, would he have chosen Achillian to lead the city? Or would that have still fallen to me? Would Achillian have fought against the rebellion, or would he have sided with it?*

When Achillian, that god-like warrior, fell on the field of battle, Cojax felt as if the ground had disappeared from beneath his feet. The

SataniKahn charge had been slowed, but it had come at a terrible price. Cojax felt a raw, unkindled rage replace all of his emotions. It was a long time before Antinium finally said the words that Cojax was anticipating. "That's it. That's what we've been waiting for. Raise the shield."

Cojax cued up his Comm, his body now filled with resolve. "Falcon One, engage the enemy in formation Delta. I repeat, all units in Falcon One, engage the enemy in formation Delta."

With this command, several thousand CargoLifters and HoverBuckets, located thirty miles to the southeast of Wedge Mountain, fired up their engines and emerged out of the large prairie grass. As they hit a cruising altitude, they sped off towards the large Decamont ship that had appeared out of nowhere. As soon as the human craft had emerged, the Decamont main vessel responded in kind, deploying hundreds of their own aircraft. The human aircraft outnumbered the smaller Decamont ships by twenty to one, which gave Cojax the slightest hope. The Decamont air forces split in two, half staying behind to protect the sizeable Decamont ship, the rest speeding off to engage the appearance of this new flying threat.

Cojax studied the formation of the human air force on his ArmGuard. As they began to cruise towards the enemy, their ranks slowly began to form into a set of bull horns that stretched for a mile in either direction from their center. Despite the distance, both sides closed the gap quickly until they were almost directly above Cojax and his small band.

The Decamont ships changed shape as they approached, their hulls adapting from their sleek design to something more apt for close combat. Cojax could identify at least three different types of Decamont vessels, all, no doubt, with varying capabilities and functions. As the sleek vehicles flew towards their quarry, they formed into the shape of a spear, only a few feet gap between each ship. The humans were the first to fire, opening up a torrent of projectiles all at once. Each time a Decamont vessel was hit, it glowed with light as its shields absorbed the attack.

Then both sides collided, and the Decamont finally opened fire, tearing through the lightly armored human ships. The Decamont formation broke into groups of three and spread out. As quickly as they engaged, CargoLifters and HoverBuckets began to fall from the sky, crashing in giant plumes of smoke and debris. The human ships were slow-moving and barely shielded, making them easy prey. It was a wholesale slaughter.

Cojax pounded the side of the ship, his voice betraying his rage. "Unit X, open fire on the Decamont! Take those Rifters down." This order was obeyed after a small delay. Unit X had been a concealed ground force of Gougers, Crushers, and Rollers staged so they could support Falcon One. They had used experimental and untested technology to shield themselves from the enemy scanners, and for now, it seemed to have worked. But they had not planned on engaging until the Decamont had committed more forces to the combat. That all changed as Cojax saw how ineffective Falcon One proved to be against the enemy.

The ground lit up with light as Unit X opened fire. The Crushers, large tanks with thick armor and an independent shield generator, proved the most valuable. They were not only able to deliver punishment but take it as well. The tanks were too heavy to fly and relatively slow compared to the CargoLifters, but they proved apt at taking down the enemy ships. The air battle devolved into chaos as all semblance of rank and order utterly disappeared. Human ships continued to fall to the earth, but now Decamont ships were beginning to fall just as fast.

The Decamont were forced to change their tactics, splitting their ranks again, half targeting the ground forces as the other half continued to stay with the airborne enemy. The skirmish seemed even for a while, both sides continuing to lose vessels in the hundreds, making the land burn from the wreckage. Then for the first time since the air battle began, the human forces appeared to be gaining the upper hand. While the CargoLifters and HoverBuckets distracted the Decamont, the ground forces continued to knock the enemy out of the sky. Minutes slipped by as the air battle intensified, and soon it became evident to anyone watching that the Decamont had been outmaneuvered and outgunned.

"Looks like we've got them on the run!" Finn shouted over the Comm. "Wipe them out of the sky!"

Cojax grinned.

But they were not the only ones to notice the change in the battle. Thousands of small enemy ships began to pour out of the main

Decamont vessel. They soon had a force that was double the size of the humans' and yet it kept on growing, blotting out the sun from Cojax's eyes, like an ominous cloud of death. These new reinforcements headed straight towards Falcon One and Unit X in a formation so tight it appeared to be one solid vessel.

Cojax shook his head in disbelief. Orch gave voice to Cojax's thoughts. "They have no chance against a force like that."

"Falcon One, pull back!" Cojax ordered over the Comm. "Get out of there."

Since Falcon One did not respond, Cojax repeated the order. "This is Cojax Artino, Lord of Titan. Falcon One, pull your ships back. You face a force you can't hope to defeat."

"It's no use raising them on the Comm," said a familiar voice over the radio. "As soon as I saw that new force appear, I cut you out of our communications. Being a Numberless still has some benefits."

"Seleukus?"

"Yes, my Lord,"

"If I am your Lord, then you must obey my command."

"At the risk of sounding insolent," Seleukus replied, "we've got one chance to win this battle. And if we're going to get you where you need to go, Falcon One can't go running now. The only chance you have is in the confusion that my forces can create. I'll be sure to say hello to your father when I see him."

"Pull your forces back now," Cojax yelled. "Regroup to position Beta."

But there was no response. Instead of pulling back, the human air force began to push forward, aiming themselves directly for the enemy's center.

"Get them out of there!" Cojax yelled.

Onar rested a hand on Cojax's shoulder, his expression stoic. "This is his part to play. He's right. If we hope to succeed, we need all the chaos he can provide."

Cojax turned his attention back to Unit X, which began to focus its fire on the oncoming swarm of enemy craft. It proved effective, ripping into their ranks as smoothly as an Arc Blade cuts through water.

"There's still time to get them out of there," Cojax pleaded.

"No," Onar replied. "The battle has called for them, and they have shown the courage to answer. Do not let their sacrifice be in vain."

Cojax swallowed hard.

"We have to move, my Lord," Onar said in his low, bellowing voice.

Cojax hesitated for ten more indulgent seconds, his eyes fixed on the oncoming enemy. When he turned his attention back to his ship, he felt a rage stronger than he ever had before. He engaged the drive in his Decamont vessel, pushing it up into the air. A second later, he increased the throttle, aiming the vessel directly at the Perdition—the main Decamont ship. Orch was quick to follow, mimicking Cojax's movements.

"Get the smoke ready," Cojax said to Onar.

Onar shifted uncomfortably in the small cabin until he could reach and activate the canister of smoke on cue. "It's ready."

"Pull back," Orch ordered over the Comm. "Our ship will take the lead. You're too valuable to send first."

Cojax's anger burned hotter as Orch mentioned the words "too valuable." This deepened his resolve. Everywhere Cojax looked, he could see fires burning from the wreckage of ships below. He turned his attention to the large Decamont vessel, unable to stomach the losses that were splayed out before him. He pushed his ship to half of its maximum speed, making the ground blur beneath them. At this pace, it was not long before they were able to make out the fine details of the Perdition, including the twelve HIECs that were concentrating powerful beams of light at the human shield below. It made such a powerful impact that Cojax was sure he would have been blinded by it had he not been wearing his helmet. At this rate, there was no telling how long the human shield would last.

"Cojax," Orch said, his voice much calmer. "Let us take the lead. If this doesn't work, there's no point in both of our ships being shot down."

"If this doesn't work," Cojax replied, "then there's no point to anything else."

They began passing Decamont vessels going the opposite direction. None of them seemed to take any notice of Cojax and Orch's ships. Even if one of the other Decamont ships tried to hail them over the Comm, it would be unsuccessful. They had purposely damaged the Comm system to stop the Decamont from requesting any information.

Cojax began maneuvering the ship as if it was barely staying aloft. As part of their ruse, their two ships had been made to look as if they had sustained significant damage.

"You're flying too predictably," Orch said.

"What?" Cojax asked.

"You look like you're flying badly on purpose."

"I am flying badly on purpose."

"You have to fly with more jolts, as if you have to fight with the machine to stay in the air."

Cojax tried to apply the advice, occasionally twitching his vessel to the left.

"Better," Orch replied. "We should have had Finn fly that one. He can't help but fly badly."

Despite himself, Cojax smiled. "Alright, I'm kicking off our smoke. Pull back a little so it doesn't look like we're in a formation."

"I hope this works," Finn said.

"It's going be a very short ride if it doesn't," Orch answered.

"Alright, when we get into the docking bay," Cojax said, "I'm going to land as far back as I can. The further back we land, the closer we'll be to those cannons."

The next second, a contrail of black smoke began bleeding from the tail of their vessel. He continued his jolting pattern as he headed straight for the docking bay. As he drew closer, two small Light Cannons turned Cojax's direction, locking their sights onto his ship.

Cojax stiffened. He was sure that they were trying to reach him over the Decamont communication system. He just hoped that his ship would relay back that his Comms were down.

As two more larger cannons locked onto Cojax's ship, this suddenly seemed like a terrible idea. At any moment, the Decamont could open fire, killing Cojax and Onar before they even realized they were dead. The guns continued to track their vessel as they approached the docking bay.

This is not going to work, Cojax thought. *This is a horrible idea.* But just then, the cannons whipped away from them, tracking something else in the distance.

He looked to Onar and nodded. Cojax flew his craft through

the large bay doors, slowing down substantially as it passed through some sort of thick energy field. Cojax was in awe at what he saw as they came out on the other side. The Decamont were nothing if not orderly. There were thousands of ships in the bay, most of them stacked on dozens of racks in front of them that spread from floor to roof. The ships were being unloaded by a beam of light that would levitate each one and place it on a track below.

It was only then that Cojax realized that he had already passed his designated landing pad. At that location in particular, there were several other severely damaged aircraft as well as crew members that were running from burned-out vessels. These ships were slowly being picked up by another beam of light and loaded onto a rack that seemed to be designated for them.

"I think you should have landed back there," Onar said.

"Yeah, I'll remember that next time I get the chance to fly a ship into the enemy's docking bay," Cojax replied.

"Can you loop back around?" Onar asked.

"I think it's better if I just keep pushing forward. Maybe they'll think I just lost complete control of the ship."

Onar shook his head but did not answer. They continued to fly deeper into the vessel, passing between two of the large racks that held the aircraft. They were most definitely not supposed to fly this way. The rack was expansive and replete with ships like their own, but there was barely enough room to fly between them. When the rack ended, they entered another bay that was filled with larger, more impressive ships that seemed more suited for space travel. Only two of these ships fit on each one of the racks.

Then their ship jolted to a stop.

"What was that?" Onar asked.

In answer to his question, a device whirled to the front of their ship and cast a blue light over the cab.

"That's not good," Cojax answered.

"Try accelerating through."

Cojax shook his head. "Won't that look suspicious?"

Onar shrugged. "We can't just stay here."

Cojax linked his Comms with Orch, Horace, and Finn. "Are you through yet? We just got stopped by one of their machines."

"Yeah, we're through," Orch said.

"But I think we passed our landing pad," Finn added.

"We don't know that yet," Orch contested.

"Please tell me that this ride will be over soon," Horace said. "I think I'd prefer surrender over having to endure these two another minute."

Cojax and Onar's ship suddenly started moving, being pulled by the blue beam of light. They were being relocated to one of the far bays.

Cojax frowned. "I can't control the ship anymore. They've somehow locked us out."

Onar nodded towards a landing pad a few hundred yards in front of them. There were two dozen fully armored Damnattii soldiers lined up and waiting. "I think that's where we're going."

"Blood and bile," Cojax hissed. He then opened his Comm to Finn, Orch, and Horace. "We've got a reception party waiting for us. I don't know how this will turn out. You might want to find a different spot to land."

Their ship moved quickly through the air until it was placed onto the landing pad. Automatically, the Decamont vessel deployed some kind of landing gear, which was something that Cojax had no idea how to activate.

Cojax secured his sword on his back. "Well, this plan turned to rot pretty quickly. You ready?"

"Yes."

Cojax opened the cockpit, letting it slowly slide back. He stepped out, quickly nodding to the Damnattii warriors in front of him. The Damnattii were confused by what they were seeing. Cojax still wore the Damnattii pilot suit, but it was unpowered and ill-fitting. It was loose in places and tight in others. Besides that, the sleeves for his third and fourth arms hung loosely from his sides. Cojax did not draw his blade and instead fell to all fours, pretending he was short of breath. Five seconds passed. And then ten.

One of the Damnattii stepped forward. "Take off your helmet. Stand and report."

Cojax's helmet was the one article that could not be disguised very well. The Damnattii helmet had to be cut in pieces and then fastened to the outside of Cojax's helmet. It looked awkward in parts, where his Validated armor clearly was visible underneath.

"Onar," Cojax whispered over the Comm. "Where are you? I thought you said you were ready."

"I'm stuck," Onar replied.

Cojax began to tug on his helmet, pretending that it simply would not come off. "They aren't going to believe this act for long. Get out here."

"I can't even get my blade out," Onar responded.

"Hurry up, you large mammoth," Cojax whispered.

"Take off your helmet," the Damnattii warrior repeated. "Do it now, or we kill you."

Cojax pretended to try and remove it again. "It's stuck—"

Just then, a small ship crashed right into twelve of the Damnattii on the landing pad, barely missing Cojax. The ship skidded to a stop, completely crushing four of the creatures under its weight.

Cojax grabbed his blade, slicing the leading Damnattii warrior across the chest. Light exploded from the blow as the creature's shields reacted to the attack. The beast responded in kind, quickly drawing his own thin blade. The Damnattii had skill but lacked any power. With three more swings, the creature was dead, split in two.

From the wreckage of the fallen ship, Orch, Finn, and Horace jumped out, cutting down Damnattii as soon as they emerged. The Damnattii were brave, but their shields did not compare to the warriors they now faced. Within moments, all the Damnattii were dead or dying.

Orch turned to Cojax. "Where's Onar?"

"He's still inside my ship," Cojax answered.

"What?" Horace bellowed with a laugh. "Is he too scared to come out?"

"I'm stuck in here," Onar growled. "Now, get me out so I can show you all how a true warrior deals death in battle."

Horace laughed. "Finn, turn off the ship. I don't want its shields interfering with me as a cut through this thing." Once the ship was powered down, and the shields were off, Horace made quick work of the ship, freeing Onar moments later.

"You owe me a pitcher of stock," Horace said.

"I'll pay you back on the field of battle," Onar replied.

"Save my life or don't," Horace answered, "I'll still expect a pitcher of stock from you."

"Come on," Cojax said. "We better get moving before they

send more Damnattii after us."

Finn pointed to something above them. "Too late."

On another platform a hundred yards away and two stories up, Damnattii warriors were beginning to congregate, their weapons drawn.

"What are they waiting for?" Finn asked.

"Let's not stick around to find out," Cojax answered. "Come on."

Cojax led the way, slicing through a pair of doors. He went down a hallway, sprinting at full speed, his friends not far behind. In his haste, he ran headlong into two armored Damnattii, who carried their helmets at their side. Before the creatures knew what was happening, Cojax, with a rage still boiling in his veins, raised his blade to eye level and dispatched them instantly.

"Who put you in a bad mood?" Orch asked.

In preparation for the battle, they had taken some time studying recorded footage of the Perdition and were able to determine the exact distance from the docking bays to the beginning of the HIECs. They could not determine the exact route they needed to take, but they did know how far they would have to travel.

They ran on and on, cutting through doors and walls alike. Occasionally they ran headlong into an unsuspecting warrior, and each time, Cojax ended them with a vengeance. After they made it to the other end of the docking bay, they ran into six Damnattii, all of which had blades drawn and shields raised. These ones had been prepared to receive them. They spread out, taking one down after another.

"Finally," Horace said with a mock bow. "Onar got a kill. I was afraid he was using a rubber sword."

Onar growled.

"Orch, how about giving the Decamont something to worry about besides chasing us?" Cojax said.

"Hopefully, we're far enough away from the ships," Finn added.

Orch nodded. "Only one way to find out." He fiddled with something on his ArmGuard, hitting in the correct access codes until a green button appeared on the interface. He looked up to Cojax. "You ready?"

"Do it," Cojax answered.

"Just how strong are the bombs we put on those ships?" Finn

asked.

"I have no idea," Orch responded. And then he hit the button. Instantly the two vessels that they had landed into the docking bay exploded into fiery debris, shredding everything around them. A deafening noise followed, shaking the walls and floors.

Orch looked to Cojax, who looked to Finn. Finn uneasily glanced at the pack he wore, which was filled with the same type of explosives that they had just set off.

"Blood and bile, that probably shook half the ship," Horace said.

"Must have been all that methane you stored up in our shared cockpit," Finn retorted.

SIXTY-ONE

They continued on, running into small enforcement or repair crews that were heading in the opposite direction. They cut them down, whether they were looking to fight or not. The creatures simply could not stand against three Novas, a Master of the Blazer, and…Finn, who took up the rear guard. According to the information they were able to ascertain from their Damnattii captives, any assault on the Perdition would recall soldiers to the upper deck, where the vital functions of the ship were located. This proved true and they met little resistance.

After a quarter-hour, they reached their primary objective, the base of several of the High-Intensity Energy Cannons.

"Horace, Orch, cover the main entrance," Cojax ordered. "As soon as they figure out what we're doing, I'm sure they'll come for us in force. Onar, Finn, on me."

Cojax tentatively tried slicing the door, but it sparked as soon as his blade touched it. "It's shielded. Finn, do your stuff."

Finn stepped forward, removing a small device from his pack. He placed it next to the access panel, hit several buttons, and waited. It was a minute before the door synced, and the energy shield went down. Cojax cut off the lock and stepped inside.

The inside of the cannon room was massive, more cathedral than compartment. Several catwalks zipped back and forth, allowing workers to access and maintain the enormous weapon. Below the catwalk was open-air, giving them a perfect vantage point of the entire battlefield. The two opposing forces were easily distinguished between the orderly ranks of the humans and the disorder of the Roaches. The battle line stretched on for miles, disappearing out of view because of the spray of light that impacted the top of the human's shields. The human center still held—that's were where the Numberless stood. The rest of the lines seemed to be slowly overtaken by the endless stream of Roaches. The left flank in particular seemed to be faring poorly, as several of the Phalanxes had been crushed. The front line now resembled a "U."

Cojax picked up his pace, reaching a control compartment not long after. Finn again had to use his device to take down a shield that protected the hardware inside. This time it only took thirty seconds. Once inside, Cojax exposed a series of wires and controls. He removed a small device and clamped it over a display screen. The wiring for the cannon was very similar to the control room in the Trinity. Cojax had not only hoped that this would be true but had counted on it. The Trinity had been Decamont technology after all.

Cojax linked Comms with Antinium, who was labeled as the new commanding Omega. He did not have time to ask for updates on the battle. "We've synced the device to the first cannon. Get them doing their stuff."

Cojax did not have time to ask for updates on the battle. "We've synced the device to the first cannon. Get them doing their stuff."

"Yes, my Lord," Antinium replied.

The little device that Cojax had put on the display suddenly whirred to life with flashes of lights. This had been similar to the device that Titan himself used to sever the controls with the Decamont. They had replicated the design and used it to protect multiple cities from power loss. Now they planned on using it to severe the Decamont's connection with the HIECs.

"First one done," Cojax said. "Eleven more to go."

***

"Why do you prefer the Blazer to the Arc Blade?" Horace asked Orch.

Orch shrugged. "I'm better at it, I guess."

"Are you any good with a blade?"

"I can hold my own."

Horace shook his head. "What are they teaching this new generation where they would prefer to use a Blazer over a blade. I don't think you could persuade me to drop my ax no matter how good I was with the Blazer."

Orch was about to reply with a cutting insult when his ArmGuard caught his attention. He had set it up to scan for nearby enemies, and now a massive blob appeared, far larger than any force they had faced so far. He tapped the screen, hoping it was a mistake of the scan. The blob continued to approach, its size getting bigger by the moment.

"Well," Orch replied. "Looks like you'll get your chance to see just how effective I am with the Blazer."

"How many?"

"Looks like…well…all of them," Orch replied.

Horace's laugh was cut short as the enemy arrived. Row after row appeared of heavily armored Damnattii. With blade and shield in hands, the fighting force filled the entire expanse of the large hallway.

Horace stepped back, his massive ax at the ready. "Step into the HIEC room. Maybe we can lock the door from the other side."

Orch went first, followed by Horace. They shut the door, fiddled with the controls, trying to lock it. The door tried to comply, but Cojax had severed the lock as he gained entry. A second after that, it opened of its own accord.

"Well," Orch whispered. "It was worth a shot."

"Make sure you watch our backs," Horace ordered. The next second, the creatures were pushing their way through the entrance. Horace cut down one then another, his powerful ax completely annihilating their shields with only one direct hit. He spared a glance at Orch, "They aren't linking their shields together."

"They can't," Orch replied. "It's too cramped in here."

The next Damnattii raised a blade as he pushed through, but Horace hit it hard, splitting it in two with the first swing. He finished the Damnattii with the next. All the while, Orch laid cover fire, slowing the movement as well as softening the shields of the Damnattii with a volley of precision.

"We can hold them like this all day," Horace said.

But then the shield surrounding their compartment was shut off. The Damnattii stopped their charge through the door and instead began cutting their own, separate entrances. Each time a hole appeared, Orch fired his Blazer, punishing some Damnattii with a powerful beam. Before too long, however, there were three additional doors to the one that already existed. Four opponents appeared, and

Horace took them all on, delivering crushing blows with his ax as Orch kept the others occupied with his Blazer. Four Damnattii fell, and then another eight. Still, the creatures pushed through, their determination making up for their weaker shields.

Horace took a hit to the side and another to his back. He turned around, repaying the attacker in kind, crushing them beneath his boot. More doors began to appear off to their left and their right. As they opened up, they revealed a row of opponents behind each one. Before long, they were surrounded by at least fifteen new openings.

Orch frowned and drew his blade with his left hand. He then hailed Cojax on the Comm. "You need to pick up the pace."

***

"Will do," Cojax responded to the transmission. He then turned to Finn and Onar. "How many do we have left?"

"We've only done four so far," Finn replied.

"We're going to have to divide up and just blow up the rest. Horace and Orch are getting overwhelmed."

Finn nodded and opened up his pack, handing out the explosives to no one in particular. "You think these are strong enough to take out each gun?"

"They were the same type we left in the cargo bay," Cojax answered. "And they seemed to work pretty well back there."

"Yeah, but we had a lot more in the ships."

"We just need to disable them, not destroy them. Just attach them to the cable leading into the cannon. That should stop their power flow."

Cojax ran one direction, Onar and Finn, another. Within the next two minutes, he had attached two of the explosives to the lower part of the cannon, right where the main power cable fed into the large device. When he was setting the third, Antinium's voice came over the Comm. "We've hacked three of the four cannons you linked. The fourth one is proving more difficult. I think they might have caught on to what we're doing."

"Can you just severe the Decamont connection to that last

cannon?" Cojax asked.

"I believe so."

Cojax placed a third explosive. "Just lock them out—we'll have to make do with what we have."

"Yes, sir."

As Cojax placed the fourth explosive, he checked in with Finn and Onar. Finn had completed his task, Onar was still two behind.

"I'll help him out," Finn said over the Comm.

"As soon as you do," Cojax answered, "find some shelter and get down." Cojax switched Comms to Antinium. "How are the lines holding up?"

Antinium did not respond for a while. "The center is holding. The flanks, however, are being pressed inward. They sent everything into our lines, holding nothing in reserve. They've smashed through the first six rows of Validated Phalanxes. If something doesn't change, both my flanks are going to be overwhelmed by the onslaught."

"Alright," Cojax answered. "Hold on."

"Cojax," Finn said over the Comm, "we've placed the last two. Blow it."

Cojax turned and ran down one of the catwalks, pulling up the correct interface on his ArmGuard. He ducked behind a metallic wall, his hand hovering over the initiation button. "I hope this works." The next second, the ship rocked as the explosives went off, completely obliterating everything in the area. Metal shot every direction, sticking into the wall that he was hiding behind. As Cojax peered around the edge, he was enthralled by the destruction left behind. One of the cannons screeched and tipped. The next second, it separated completely, colliding into the shield below.

Cojax opened a Comm with Antinium. "Now, drop the shield and take over the cannons."

***

Antinium turned to Marian. "Drop the shields. Take control of the cannons. And fire at all preselected targets."

"Yes, sir," Marian replied.

The shield dropped the next second, and three of the High-Intensity Energy Cannons from above came alive. Instead of beaming down on the humans, they turned and fired, aiming at multiple Roach targets that had previously been assigned. One large beam strafed the SataniKahns on the right flank, turning them into a mess of flesh. This action was complemented by another cannon on the left side. The SataniKahns' thick armor protected them from being completely killed, but the beam ripped off all their limbs and pincers, making them nothing more than lumps of living flesh. The cannons continued to weave back and forth among the Roach lines, leaving nothing behind except ash and black blood.

The third cannon was aimed at the heavy Decamont artillery that had been set up on a far ridge. The large beam of light ripped into the assigned targets, leaving nothing but destruction in its wake. Each artillery gun the beam touched exploded into flames.

Antinium looked on with awe, as did the other Numberless around him. Within seconds the dynamics of the battlefield had changed. The Roach lines were driven back, their forces stunned by the devastation. The Decamont heavy artillery was all but destroyed. The SataniKahns were limbless and close to being lifeless.

For thirty-five seconds, the humans completely controlled three of the Decamont's most potent weapons to great effect. After trying in vain to re-establish the connection, the Decamont finally decided to shut off power completely to the HIECs. The cannons, powered down, their beams of destruction disappearing.

The battlefield went silent, all fighting ceased. In those thirty-five seconds, the Roach army had lost the initiative. Smoke billowed from the field of battle, curving up with wicked slants along the scorched trails made by the HIECs.

Then the death rattle began from somewhere among the Validated. More joined in until the noise was so deafening, it could be heard for miles. No order was given; no order was needed. The Validated now pushed their advantage, driving the enemy back.

Antinium grabbed his helmet and his sword, as did the Numberless around him. He linked his Comms with every Validated under his control. "Kill them all."

Julia ordered her Numberless to sever the shield link. This allowed the Numberless to fight on their own, spreading out among the creatures to expedite their death. They surged forward in a powerful tide of destruction. All creatures before them died. The entire human line now pushed forward into the enemy, eager to avenge those who had fallen. Nothing was held in reserve, and no quarter would be given. Antinium led the charge into the enemy's ranks. The creatures died by the thousands as Arc Blade pierced carapace.

***

Horace had to step back to prevent himself from being overwhelmed. He sent one after another to their death, but they kept coming, dripping out of the walls in a constant, unremitting wave. Horace was taking hit after hit, each one sucking the power out of his armor. If it were not for the specialized armor that Adriana had crafted for him, he was sure his shields would have succumbed long before. The body count grew and grew, making mounds of the Damnattii.

Then the Damnattii changed their strategy, positioning several warriors with Blazers at the entrances who fired down on Horace and Orch. This would have brought Horace down had Orch not been at his side, picking off the snipers as soon as they found a roost. Horace's shields now glowed almost constantly, as blades or Blazers struck him at odd angles. A large Damnattii with four blades, one in each arm, took to the field. The new warrior proved too much for Horace. He was able to deliver one final blow with his ax before his shields gave out, sending the large man to the floor and out of breath.

Before the Damnattii could land the killing blow, Orch stepped between them. He now used his Arc Blade and Blazer in concert. Softening the Damnattii before he stuck them with his blade. "Horace, get out of here!"

Horace rolled to his side and pulled himself to his feet. His exhaustion made it difficult to stand, but he was not going to run. Just then, a tremendous explosion occurred, sending the unshielded door behind them pitching forwards. The floor and walls trembled and shook. A horrific screech filled the air.

Horace peeked inside the cannon room and could hardly believe what he was seeing. The catwalks had all but disappeared, giving him a perfect view of the battlefield below. The High-Intensity Energy Cannons were no longer firing at the Titans but at the ranks of Roaches.

"That boy did it," Horace whispered. "I can't believe it worked." He stepped sideways, slumping to the ground. There was nowhere else to go—the catwalks were now gone, and they were entirely surrounded by the Damnattii.

Orch moved at a pace and with a skill that was beyond his Tier. He kept the creatures at bay with the Blazer and would use the Arc Blade if they drew too close. But his attacks lacked the power and potency of a Numberless. Soon, Orch was backed up to Horace's feet. The next second, his Blazer was cut in two by the large Damnattii with four Blades. Orch's shields now took the punishment he had avoided for so long, glowing with light each time he was struck. Without a Blazer to keep the enemy back, he would not last long.

Then a blade erupted out of the large Damnattii's chest, killing the creature instantly. Onar now stood where the creature was before. Behind him were the bodies of dozens of Damnattii he had cut through to reach Orch and Horace. Onar roared like a beast, casting several of the Damnattii to the side. Others charged in, but Onar palmed one of the warrior's skulls and used him to batter several of the others.

Orch fell to the ground, sliding next to Horace. "There's something purely bestial about the way Onar fights."

This point was accented as the massive warrior cleaved the heads of four Damnattii in one swing.

Horace nodded sagely. "Complete savage. Although I hope he doesn't think that this gets him out of the stock he owes me."

Finn and Cojax showed up not long after, finishing off the remaining Damnattii. The compartment was riddled with the dead, completely covering the floor in blood and body. Cojax reached Horace's side and removed his helmet. "Are you alright?"

"Not a scratch on me," Horace said. "Thanks to Orch's Blazer and ballet training."

"Ballet?" Finn asked.

"Come on, old man," Orch said. "We need you to stay alive."

"We did it," Cojax pronounced. "The High-Intensity Energy Cannons decimated the Roaches. Our people are now charging the enemy. We've won."

Horace laughed. "Well, then, let's get out of here and find someone to share the good news with."

"Cojax."

Cojax looked around, trying to find the source of the voice.

"Cojax."

"I think that voice is coming from somewhere on the ship," Finn suggested.

Then a screen appeared on the wall. Cojax stepped forward, studying it carefully. There was a single person on the display, her face highlighted by a dim light. He had no idea where she was, but, judging by the background, he was sure she was not on the ship.

"Adriana?" Cojax asked.

She stepped forward, her face filling the screen. "Yes, Cojax. It's me."

"Can you see me?" Cojax asked.

"Yes," she replied."I want to explain why I've done what I've done."

Cojax swallowed. "What are you talking about?"

Adriana looked off the screen, nodding to someone in the distance. "Do it."

Cojax felt his heart sink. He did not know exactly what was going on, but dread filled his chest. He could hear sudden explosions ripping through the air, hundreds of them at first, then thousands. The noise grew as did their consistency.

"What's happening?" Cojax did not wait for an answer. Instead, he turned his back on the screen, following the noise. It took him to the entrance to the High-Intensity Energy Cannons. Below he could see his army—the army he had forged from discontent and disorder. Their ranks were being ravaged by massive explosion after explosion.

Cojax turned back to the screen, his voice breaking. "Stop whatever you're doing. Adriana, we've won the battle. Adriana, what are you doing?"

"They are the Numberless," Adriana said, her eyes filling with tears. "Their armor was as good as I promised, but with one additional element I didn't mention. At a push of a button, I can, and I just did, turn their suits of Static Armor into explosive devices. Your greatest weapon now has become your greatest threat. It's over, Cojax.

Surrender to the Decamont, and I may be able to convince them to keep you here with me."

Cojax approached the screen, placing a hand on a wall to steady himself. "Adriana, stop what you are doing. We've won." He closed his eyes in anguish, trying to control his rage. He suddenly punched the wall, leaving a fist-sized dent behind. "Stop it!"

Adriana shook her head. "It's already done."

Cojax removed his helmet and stepped closer to the screen, revealing two tears that were pooling on his chin. "How can you betray us? How can you betray me?" The explosions continued down below, each one was as a blade to his back.

Despite the tears on Adriana's face, her voice continued on without fluctuation. "You were so passionate about your rebellion, you never considered the one question that you should have. You found out how the Decamont kept us as slaves, but you never asked why. Did you really think that an advanced civilization, which is governed by rules and regulations, decided to pick on humans for no apparent reason? Well, Cojax, there is a reason, as I have found out. And weighing their needs with ours, I've realized that we are in the wrong."

"What have you done?"

"I've brokered a peace treaty with the Decamont," Adriana answered as she wiped away her tears. "In exchange for a victory today, and in destroying the rebellion, they have agreed to leave our planet for good. The only thing they will be taking from here is the one thing they have wanted since the beginning—the Numberless. They will remove the Numberless, and we will be given our planet back."

"Why do they need the Numberless?"

"Because there are things in space that are more dangerous than Roaches. Expand your mind and consider everything you know. The Decamont spent the last two hundred years on our planet forging a sword in the form of the Numberless. I knew you would never agree to give it to them, and I knew that they would never stop trying to take it back."

Cojax felt his anger rise. "You can't trust them."

"Yes, I can," Adriana replied. "I hope one day you will see it how I see it. I hope one day you will forgive me."

"And my armor?" Cojax asked. "Did you plant a bomb on me as well?"

Adriana shook her head. "They need you alive, Cojax. I need you alive. Surrender to them, and I will make sure you walk away from all of this."

Cojax unsheathed his sword and sliced the screen, splitting the wall wide with three massive gashes. He fell to his knees and let out a bestial howl.

Orch came up to his side, resting two hands on his shoulders. "My Lord, we've got to get you out of here. They can't claim victory if they don't have you."

SIXTY-TWO

The Rifters fell one by one. They were no match for the better-equipped warriors. Brutus was a beast, taking more time with his kills and enjoying the way the blood flowed from his victims.

Jessica brought her Blazer up to her shoulder, unloading a torrent of shots into her opponents. When her bodyguards were cut down to five, she fought with her Arc Blade. Brutus hit her across the head, and then across the chest, sapping her energy with each blow. She struck back, but it did little against the elite armor. Brutus kicked her in the chest, sending her into the far wall. Her shields powered down, and exhaustion overcame her. She fell to her knees, the wind knocked out of her chest. She pulled her helmet off. She would not hide from Brutus, not even if she now faced death.

The last bodyguard was killed and sent to the ground.

"You have no honor," Jessica said, her voice laced with venom.

"Be careful," Brutus teased. "I was ordered to bring you in alive, but I have been known to break orders from time to time."

"You Rifting Dependent," Jessica yelled. "Just because you don't measure up to Cojax, you have to betray your people—your own brother. Are you still so jealous of him? Why can't you—"

Brutus backhanded her, sending her knocking into the wall. The blow took barely any effort from him, but it felt like she had been hit by a sledgehammer.

"Bind her and bring her to the Queen," Brutus said. "She still has an important role to play." Once Jessica was secured, Brutus led the way out of the Control Room and down the hall. He was about to lead them into an elevator when he stopped in his tracks.

Aias stood between Brutus and the elevator, an army of Rifters behind him. "Let the Queen go."

Brutus laughed. "There is only one Queen now, and the Aberration is not her, nor was she ever."

Aias turned to his Rifters. "Protect the Queen!"

The Rifters charged in like a pack of wolves, easily outnumbering their opponents. The black mixed with the red in a chaotic struggle. Explosions of light were seen everywhere, as Blazers were fired and Arc Blades found their marks. Cato fell back from the main lines and fiddled with his ArmGuard. Within a minute, thousands more Validated in their blood-red armor appeared, attacking the Rifters in earnest. The conflict spread into the streets, throughout the front entrance of the Trinity, and along the stairs to the Control Room. The building was scorched with Blazer burns and slashes from Arc Blades.

Cato stood next to Brutus, one hand around the cuffed arm of Jessica. "We need to get out of here."

Brutus laughed. "They can't stand against us—not with our armor."

"Even still," Cato said. "Where did Aias go?"

In answer to his question, a blade struck him in the back, pitching him forward. Brutus turned around. The wall behind him had been cut open to make a door. Aias stepped through the doorway, his Arc Blade burning bright. He attacked Brutus with a manic frenzy, pushing the giant warrior back. Cato recovered quickly and caught Aias with a horrific blow to the head, sending him smashing into a wall.

Aias used the wall and leaped forward, hitting both Brutus and Cato with one horrific swing.

"You fight better than a Rifter should," Cato said.

"I allowed myself to be Rifted so I could bring down this city," Aias replied. "And now you two have undone everything."

"We will achieve so much more now that the boy king has fallen," Cato replied. "For the first time in over two hundred years, our people will be free."

Aias attacked, not giving his quarry much time to react. He moved quickly, proving his skill with the blade. He defended attacks against Cato while returning his own against Brutus. Brutus only laughed each time he was hit, absolutely confident in his new elite armor.

Aias found himself being driven further back by his opponents. He ducked and dodged, but received three blows in quick succession. He kept trying to maneuver around Brutus, so he was directly in front of Cato. The tactic worked for only a few seconds at a time before they adjusted and attacked in a coordinated effort.

Then, Aias' persistence won out, breaking Brutus' shields as well as removing the boy's right leg from his body. Brutus yelled as he fell to the ground, his hands reaching for his now stump. Aias' attack came at a cost, however. Cato stepped forward and, in a show of power, drove his Arc Blade clear through Aias' chest. He had stabbed with so much force it left Aias skewered against the wall.

Cato removed Aias' helmet, a smile spread over his face. "Come now. Did you really believe that a Rifter such as yourself could beat someone in the First Tier? You just proved my point."

Aias smiled. He coughed up some blood, but his smile persisted.

"Are you happy to die?" Cato asked.

"I'm happy…I succeeded," Aias replied.

In a panic, Cato suddenly glanced around the room, unable to find what he was looking for. He turned his attention back to Aias, pulling him close. "Where is she?"

Aias laughed, spraying blood on Cato's face. Cato roared and sent a pulse through his blade just as he separated Aias' head from his body.

"Cato, help me," Brutus pleaded.

Cato rolled his eyes as he turned his back on the large boy. He then linked his Comms with all of the Validated under his command. "The Aberration has escaped. Find her and bring her to me."

***

Within moments of Aias' appearance, two Rifters had grabbed Jessica, pulling her through the makeshift door. One Rifter threw her on his shoulder while the other guarded the entrance. Two of the red armored Validated pursued, cutting down the first Rifter. As the other Rifter ran, more pursuers joined the hunt.

A red armored Validated leaped for the Rifter, barely missing him by a finger's length. The Rifter jumped up and over another attacker, never breaking stride. Jessica's body was tossed back and forth as he carried her at a full sprint—his pursuers not far behind. He met up with another group of Rifters, who were just finishing off three red-armored Validated. He tossed Jessica onto the shoulder of one of them, yelling in a deep voice, "Protect the Queen." With this, he charged back into the pursuers, slowing them for a few seconds before his blood was added to the ground.

This new Rifter broke from the engagement and ran, leaving all of them behind. She ran hard and fast until she reached a window. She leaped out, cradling Jessica's body in her hands as she landed several stories below. For a brief moment, as Jessica fell through the air, she could see the streets split in conflict between black and red armor. The entire city seemed caught up in the violence.

The Rifter that was carrying Jessica was shot in the side, sending her pitching in the opposite direction. Jessica rolled across the ground and found her feet, just in time to see the Rifter who had been carrying her, stabbed in the back by a thick blade. The Rifter slumped over as the blade pinned her to the ground.

Jessica reached out a hand for the fallen girl, but she was pulled back by several others. She fought against their grips, reaching for a sword, but she was powerless as she was carted off by a mix of Rifters. They took her into the belly of the city. Several times she was passed on to another group, and each time, the same words were repeated, "Protect the Queen."

When they reached the Rift, she found a suit of armor waiting for her. It was the first she had ever received, the one that she had used in the Mahghetto. She changed quickly and sheathed a new, unfamiliar sword at her waist.

"Gather Aias' War Council," Jessica ordered.

"Yes, my Queen," replied one of the Rifters.

"They might have made the first move, but we will be sure to make the last," Jessica announced. "Gather what's left of our forces in the Rift. Now is the time that we take back our city!" This was received with a tremendous cheer.

"It's too late," said a voice from across the room.

Jessica turned. She was more surprised than angry at the interruption. "Who said that?"

Byron stepped forward into the low light, dressed in armor that was already bloody from conflict. "My Queen, this is a battle we cannot win. We've got to pull back our forces from the streets."

"We have to win," Jessica replied with more venom than she intended. "Our forces are out there right now, and they depend on us keeping this city safe until they return."

Byron pressed a button on his ArmGuard and then pushed the footage to Jessica's ArmGuard. She accepted the feed and looked down, studying it in earnest. It was a camera view of the street above. Byron began to change to different cameras, but each one showed the same thing. Those in the red armor were not only winning, they seemed unstoppable. The streets were filled with dead or dying Rifters. Jessica felt a lump in her throat as each camera view flashed before her eyes.

Byron stepped forward, resting a hand on Jessica's shoulder. "They have planned this for weeks. We can't hope to scrabble together some counterattack that will turn the tide of battle."

"We can't just give up on the city," Jessica said.

"It doesn't matter if we lose this battle, as long as we never lose sight of winning the war," Byron said. "Pull back the remaining Rifters to the Rift. Seal off any known entrance and hold them off until we can get our people safely away from the city."

Jessica turned around, her mind caught up in thought. She felt so many emotions at once, she did not know which to give into. Byron was right. She knew it. So did everyone else in the room. The city had been lost, and there was nothing she could do to change it.

Jessica turned back around, latching onto her anger so her voice would not shake. "Do as Byron instructs. Pull back the Rifters and block all entrances. Prepare our people to head out from the Rift. But… we will not leave empty-handed. They may have taken the city, but we will take something much more valuable."

"What do you mean, my Queen?" Byron asked.

"While they were distracted by the glory of taking the city, they neglected to remember that it's in the Rift where we keep our food. Load our vehicles down with all the provisions you can. And whatever supplies we can't carry, light it on fire. Let's see how long Queen Adriana's rule lasts when all they have left to eat is dirt and ash. Once that's done, we evacuate our people."

SIXTY-THREE

Cojax shook each time one of the explosions went off. They were far fewer now. Even at this height, he could tell that the tide of battle had once again shifted in favor of the Decamont. With the explosions, the Roaches had rallied, releasing everything they had left. They swarmed in like a black tide of carapace. Most of the Phalanxes had broken up now, severely damaged by the explosions. After only a short time, only the far-right flank stood whole, owing to the lack of Numberless in their ranks when the explosions started.

But they would not last for long. Now that the human shield was down, the Decamont air force attacked, raining down fire from the sky and strafing the formations below. To the credit of the Validated forces, they kept their order and discipline, several of them transitioning to Blazers to deal with the threat from above.

Cojax turned away, sickened by the sight.

"Come here, boyou," Horace said. Cojax knelt next to his old mentor and friend. "I'm proud to serve you, my Lord. And I'm sorry I was not enough, that we were not enough."

Cojax felt tears at the corners of his eyes. "It is I that failed you. It was I that decided that we should make our stand at the Wedge."

"You can't blame yourself for this," Horace insisted. "That emotional garbage will only wear you down and make you useless. Listen, boyou, and let these words ring in your ears for years to come: Titan would be proud of the man you have become. He was right about you. He was right to pick you above all else. I didn't see it before, but I'd be blind if I didn't see it now. You care more for these people than you do for yourself. You are a balance between strength and wisdom. And, because of that, you will be the one to free our people."

The tears flowed freely from both Horace and Cojax's faces now. The Numberless continued, his voice breaking as he spoke. "You've got to get out of here and continue our fight."

"Only with you at my side," Cojax replied.

Horace laughed. "You'll need a distraction if you're going to get off this ship in one piece."

"Your shields are gone. What can you do?"

Horace smiled. "I can surrender."

"Surrender?"

Horace knocked his fist against his armor. "I wear a bomb strapped to my chest, just as all the Numberless did down there."

"Why didn't it go off?"

"It will," Horace replied. "But my shields have been down, and so it has not received the signal to explode." Then the old man smiled, his eyes sparkling with mischief. "Adriana asked us to surrender, and I feel inclined to comply."

Cojax shook his head.

"Go, boyou," Horace said. "I'll remove the chest plate for now, which should stop the charge, but I can't keep it off forever. I'll give you ten minutes before I put it back on—hopefully, that will give you enough time to get off this ship."

Orch grabbed Cojax's shoulder. "Come on. He's right. After we hijacked their guns, there's no way they would let us just leave."

"Goodbye, boyou," Horace said, his hands falling into a sincere salute. "Remember this day—let it burn into your mind. Let the memory of all those who fell today scar your flesh until it forms you into who you need to become. Become the blade of our people."

Onar helped Horace remove his chest plate. While the large man busied himself with the task, Horace handed Onar his large war ax. "Take good care of her. Her name is Lucretia."

Onar bowed low, taking the weapon with his right hand.

Once his chest plate was removed, Horace gestured to the door. "Now get out of here."

They all paid their respects to Horace in turn and left the room. Cojax was the last to leave. He glanced back. The image of Horace sitting on the floor, surrounded by the bodies of all who had opposed him, would be forever burned into his memory.

Minutes later, more Damnattii appeared. Horace found his feet and stood, slipping on his chest plate as he did. He stumbled forward, his hands raised in surrender. His mechanical leg was powered in the same way as his armor and it also had no charge. Now it was stiff and rigid like rigor mortis had set in.

Horace raised his hands. "I am Cojax Artino, son of Titan, Liberator of Acadia, Lord of the City of Titan, Steward to the cities of Rome, Delphi, Pincale, and Oreaus, and Leader of the United Coalition of the Free Cities. I am he who led the rebellion in the heart of this land. Allow me to speak to your leader, for I am the voice of my people, and my people wish to surrender."

SIXTY-FOUR

Before the rubble from the battle had been cleared, before the bodies were cold in the streets and the blood had been cleaned, Adriana had ordered the construction of a new throne room. It would be a grand monument to her reign, lined with pillars that were faced with marble and precious stones. The floor would be replaced with an elaborate tile, imported from Pincale, which was known for that type of work. Behind the pillars, lining the walls, she planned on commissioning a series of statues that reflected all the best traits that her people possessed.

She now stood in the largest building that was closest to the Trinity. This, along with three other surrounding buildings, would be converted into her palace. Adriana walked the length of the bottom floor, imagining the changes to the room. With the benches gone, the space would be much more open. *Perhaps I can even remove most of the walls,* Adriana mused.

She reached the other end of the hall, eyeing one side and then the other. *This will be where my throne will sit.* Ever since she saw Cojax's simple but functional throne, she began designing her own. It would not be too ostentatious, but it would demand attention. It would be elegant, but not soft. She'd planned setting it atop a series of five steps, each one representing two of the Tiers and made of progressively finer material, starting with concrete and ending with gold.

The far door opened and two red armored validated entered, each one holding a side of Cojax's throne. They stopped in their tracks, unsure if they should approach Adriana or not. She nodded slightly, giving the two Validated leave to enter. They obeyed quickly, spanning the distance with their awkward burden. They placed it on the ground, but it was too far back. Adriana had them move it more forward, but then it was left of center. Again, the Validated moved the throne.

When she was satisfied, they left as quickly as they came. Adriana looked forward to studying the throne, rubbing her hands down the slick, polished wood. It was well crafted, no one could deny that, but it was also forgettable. Among a thousand chairs, no one would remember this one, much like the Lord that once sat upon it.

Adriana frowned as her thoughts turned to Cojax. She had all but warned him that this would happen. *What a stubborn boy. What a fool.* Her mind flashed to his face—his handsome features, his well-intentioned eyes. She had tried everything she could possibly do to keep him here with her, but on this, the Decamont insisted. Unbidden anger appeared, tightening her grip on one of the armrests of the throne. The wood cracked, but it did not break. *Why would he not listen to me? I was the one that brought him the throne. I was the one that united our people under his banner.*

A tear slipped passed her chin, striking the floor. She did not realize she had been crying until that moment. She wiped her face, replacing her remorse with resolve. "Well, if I can't have you, Cojax, I will help myself to your throne." She circled the chair once, picking out all the flaws, and slowly sat down. This throne would do for now.

The door opened and four Validated entered. They were in a heated debate, as evidenced by the tone of their voices.

"How can you even accuse me of that?" Cato hissed. "It was your task to eliminate the Rifters. You had been given the vast majority of our forces, had you not?"

Tidas looked affronted. "But it was your task to cut the head off the snake, but she still lives. And who do you think commanded them to rob us blind?"

Adriana sighed. She wanted to be alone. She had given these Validated prestige and power, and already, they were bickering like children.

Brutus pushed passed the other two, his hands gripping a pair of metal make-shift crutches. "Get out of my way, you Rifters." He made for Adriana at a quick pace. Despite being mostly cauterized, the new stub of a leg still dripped blood, which showed up brightly on the light-colored floor.

Adriana's mood shifted from introspection to annoyance.

"Adriana," Brutus called, "the Rifters removed one of my legs. Where are you hiding the mechanical limbs?"

"Ask her then," Tidas roared. "Ask her if she agrees with you that it was my fault."

"You prideful Tier Setter," Cato retorted. "If you can't do a job right, then at least give someone else the control over the army so they can do your task for you."

Tidas reached for his blade at his side, but before he could draw it, Adriana interrupted them.

"Enough. I will not listen to all of you whine."

"But they sliced off my leg—" Brutus began.

"And I will slice off your head," Adriana roared, "if you can't keep your rotting tongue in check. And you two, what are you arguing about?"

"He let Jessica escape," Tidas reported. "Both of them did."

"Says the man whose job it was to secure the perimeter," Cato replied coldly. "If she broke out of the perimeter, that clearly falls on you."

"Let her go," Adriana cooed. "We've taken their city, and slaughtered most of their Rifters. The rebellion has been crushed, and we have an alliance with the Decamont. If she didn't die during her escape, she will soon."

"They torched our food supply," Tidas announced.

Adriana's body twitched ever so slightly. "What?"

"It's gone," Tidas said. "What they didn't steal for themselves, they set ablaze as they left the city. We were able to stop the spread of the fires and salvage some of it, but most of it was destroyed."

Adriana drummed her fingers on her throne, her expression unreadable.

"If I may, my Queen," said Cato.

Adriana frowned. This man was nothing if not arrogant. Everyone else always seemed to buy this man's false modesty, but not her.

Cato stepped forward, a snake-like smile across his lips. "You now control all of the cities that were part of the rebellion. They've accepted you as their Queen, at least for now. We can split their resources among ourselves. With the casualties from the battle, there will be far fewer mouths to feed."

Tidas clenched his jaw. "Watch your tongue when you speak of the fallen."

Cato ignored the comment and pressed on. "I would suggest, oh great Queen, that you consolidate your power as quickly as possible.

The other cities recognize your authority, for now, but if they don't see proof of it, they'll slip from your control."

Adriana now regretted letting the older man speak. "I've already got a plan in motion. Stop worrying."

Cato bowed. Tidas rolled his eyes.

"My Queen," said the fourth Validated, who until this time had remained silent.

Adriana sighed before gesturing for the woman to proceed.

The Validated took a step forward. "Jessica must be killed. We need to hunt her down and put her in the dirt." Her voice was similar to Adriana's but slightly more cryptic and lethal.

Adriana laughed. "She's as good as destroyed. She can't have more than a few thousand followers left at most."

"I would estimate her numbers are closer to fifty-thousand."

"Fifty-thousand Rifters hardly represents a threat."

"She represents another choice."

Adriana stood up from her throne, her voice just as hostile. "Another choice to what!"

"To you," the Validated replied. "Now, quit acting like a child and play your role as a Queen. Consolidate your power, acquire resources from the other cities, and hunt down the Aberration."

Adriana stared down this masked Validated, anger apparent in her flushed features. "Leave us."

"But I'm bleeding out—" Brutus began.

"Leave!" Adriana replied.

They responded slowly, but they did respond, and within a minute, only Adriana and the fourth Validated remained. She began softly, but her voice rose with each step she took forward. "You might have had some good ideas, but I had just as many. And everything you thought of depended on me pulling it off. I didn't rise from the lowest Tier to become Queen just so I can be lectured by my sister!

"Besides, you were her greatest spy—you were number Seven, remember? How is it that she learned more from you than you learned from her? Your one task was to make sure she couldn't do the thing she just did."

"I brought you the throne, so don't you dare try to blame me for the actions of the Aberration."

"You're right, Alexandria, of course," Adriana said sweetly.

"You did bring me the throne, but our position of power is tentative at best. You will not speak to me again like that—especially in front of others. Otherwise, I will have your body impregnated with Roach larvae just as they are beginning to hatch. And I will watch with a smile on my face as they slowly consume your body."

The Validated removed her helmet. Her features were identical to Adriana in almost every aspect. The only difference was a scar that stretched from the woman's right eyebrow to the back of the head. Whatever had caused the wound had left one of her eyes off-color and claimed her right ear. "Don't be soft—not now. Not ever again."

Adriana let out a low sigh. "I'm not soft."

"Then wipe the tear trails from your cheeks and hunt down the Aberration."

SIXTY-FIVE

The Damnattii took some time communicating with an unseen authority. They finally searched Horace for any weapons and then cuffed him behind his back. They escorted him to an elevator that first went up several floors and then shifted in a horizontal direction, speeding through the center of the ship.

Horace glanced at his two closest guards. "Not much for conversation, are you? Well, excuse my ignorance, but which one of your four arms does the wiping?"

One of the guards shifted uncomfortably; the other one cracked a slight smile.

"At least one of you has a sense of humor," Horace said. "I was afraid this ride would be nothing but awkward silence and subtle coughs." Horace turned to the Damnattii who had cracked the smile. He was larger than the others, his armor much more battle-worn. "What's your name?"

The Damnattii looked around, before leaning forward. "TannerX."

"It's a pleasure to me you," Horace replied. "I'd shake your hand, but you still haven't answered my question as to which hand does the wiping."

"We don't shake hands," TannerX replied. "We touch our chin and bow." The Damnattii demonstrated with the greatest of reverence.

"You honor me," Horace replied.

The elevator stopped and the doors opened. Horace was led out and pointed down a long, ornate hallway. Metallic pillars stretched up high above, each one had intricate designs cut into them. His escort grew and grew until he was surrounded by a small army. They then entered a massive room that stretched into an extensive series of steps. On the highest step was a gigantic throne. Horace thought it was a bit much, even for a supremely powerful alien race. On top of a throne sat a figure almost as towering as Onar.

For the first time in two hundred years, a human was able to see one of the Decamont in person. It was a powerful looking creature with rigid horns that ran up and down its lower forearm and back. Its skin was more bone than flesh. It had four eyes, two centered in the face like a human's and two more above that. The head was smooth as if it wore a bandanna of bone. Its mouth and jawline looked normal, but its teeth were sharper. It wore an ornate set of armor that glowed with light and power—in a way very similar to a Numberless and yet somehow grander. Horace did not notice it at first, but the creature's forearms moved, revealing a set of pincers beneath, almost like that of a praying mantis. Its legs were armored, and so it was difficult to tell exactly what they looked like.

"You must be the guy in charge," Horace said.

A Damnattii struck Horace in the leg, bringing him to his knees. "Do not speak unless the Crine speaks to you first."

Horace nodded. "Well, that one is on you. You had all this time to tell me while we walked up here and you failed to mention anything."

They sat there for a good two minutes before the Crine stood up, seemingly just as curious about Horace as Horace was of him. It seemed he had never seen a human in person. "Oh, little child, how the mighty are fallen in battle. Your army has been destroyed, your kingdom has dissolved, your people have—"

Horace felt his breastplate charging back up. "—Listen, I'd love to chat, but we're all about to die."

"Silence—"

The room exploded with such fury that the control room above and below disappeared completely in ash, blood, and debris.

***

The ship suddenly shook with a tremendous force. It was much stronger than any of the explosions from before. The hallway became a mix of lights and sirens.

Cojax knew his friend was gone, but he could not think of that now. He pushed on, leading the group back to the large cargo bay. His mind was numb, his fighting reckless. Between the four of them, there was nothing that could stand in their way. And hardly anything tried. The lights and sirens seemed to change everyone's priorities, and now the creatures seemed more keen to get out than to keep them in. When they reached the cargo bay, ships were streaming out of the entrance in large swarms.

Orch pointed to an unoccupied ship not too far away. They reached it just as a group of Damnattii did. The four made short work of the creatures.

"Keep the pilot alive," Cojax ordered.

This was obeyed, but just barely, as Onar's massive ax had been posed to strike. As they entered the ship, Cojax was very much glad he had the foresight to preserve the pilot. The ship's navigation systems were much different than any of them had seen before. Fortunately, the Damnattii was just as eager to survive as they were. The Damnattii entered a passcode into the ship's interface, which then allowed him to fire up the engines and release the clamps holding the craft in place. He steered the ship out of the docking bay without much prompting.

Cojax looked out a rear window, and it was like seeing the massive ship for the first time. The shields were gone, as was the ship's ability to control itself. It was slowly spiraling down to the ground, something they had not noticed until they had left it. Not long after, the ship lost its ability to maintain altitude, and it crashed into the mountains below in a terrific wave of smoke and debris. Anything below, whether it was Roach or human, now became buried in endless amounts of metal and machine. The impact sent a concussive wave towards them, picking up dirt and rocks as it did.

"Where do we go?" Orch asked.

Before anyone of them could answer, their ship shook. It was only a slight tremor, but then it shook again.

"What's happening?" Finn asked.

"We're being fired upon," the Damnattii responded. He gestured to a 3D projection on the control panel that showed they were being followed by three larger ships.

Suddenly the Comm system came alive. "Land your ship."

"How did they know we were on this ship?" Finn asked.

All eyes turned to the Damnattii, who looked down. "I took an oath to serve my Crine. I cannot break that vow even now." Onar picked up the creature, his hands almost bigger than its head. The massive warrior planned on simply squeezing the beast until it snapped in half.

"No, don't' kill him," Cojax said. He stepped back away from the situation, looking at the massive Decamont ship that was now a pile of wreckage. He knew what he must do, but he did not like the taste of it on his tongue. After the vessel shook three more times, Cojax turned around, "You'll need him to pilot the ship out of here."

Orch turned to Finn. "Grab your Blazer. Maybe we can open a window and lay down some suppressive fire. Cojax, try to find out if there are weapons on this rig."

"This is a transport vessel," the Damnattii replied. "There are no weapons, and even if there were, we are being chased by Ravens—the Elite ships of the Crine. Those ships belong to the Revelator, and so, there is—."

"—Nobody asked you, four arms," Orch replied.

Finn whipped the Blazer off his back, inspecting it briefly for any damage. Orch did the same. They began to head for the rear of the ship when Cojax stopped them.

"No," he said simply.

Orch turned around, confusion on his face. "You have a better plan?"

"I plan to turn myself in."

"What?" Finn asked. "What are you talking about? You know better than anyone that you don't have to simply accept your situation. We can get ourselves out of this."

Cojax shook his head. "We're flying in a cargo ship—unarmed and outnumbered. We try to outrun them, they'll shoot us down. We try to fight them on the ground, they'll overwhelm and eventually overrun us."

"We've faced bad odds before."

"They want me," Cojax answered. "If I don't surrender, they will exterminate every Validated they run into until I'm captured."

"What are you saying?" Orch asked.

"They only want me," Cojax replied.

"I repeat, land the ship," a voice said over the Comm.

"And I won't let them have you," Finn said quickly.

"It's not your choice," Cojax replied sternly.

"You can take your title and throw it into the Rift," Finn said.

"I'm not going to let them take you."

"Enough!" Cojax roared. "I've lost too many friends for one day; I can't bear to lose anymore." He then pulled the Damnattii out of Onar's grasp and gestured to the controls. "Land the ship."

Onar looked confused. Orch and Finn exchanged perplexed looks.

Cojax positioned himself in front of the Comm system. "This is Cojax Artino, Son of Titan, Lord of the City of Titan. We will land our ship, and I will surrender, but I need an oath that everyone else here is allowed to leave unharmed."

A sharp, crisp voice answered, one that was so different than anything any of them had ever heard before. "I only seek Cojax Artino, son of Titan. The rest are not my concern."

"What are you doing?" Finn asked.

Cojax shook his head. "It's the only way."

"If this is to be your end," Onar bellowed, "then let it be ours as well. It will be a glorious end."

Cojax looked at the massive warrior. They hardly knew each other, and yet, Onar had been nothing but loyal. Now the giant warrior was willing to give his life simply to prove that loyalty.

Cojax shook his head. "Our people are still out there. Jessica is still out there. You must do what I cannot. Find them. Protect them. Find her. Protect her."

"Wait, wait," Finn said. "Are you serious?"

"If we all die here and now," Cojax replied, "no one will know what we have done this day. Our story must continue, and you three are the ones that will not only protect our people but remind them of what we have accomplished. How many of our people have ever been able to take out a Decamont flagship? And yet, not far from here, we've smashed one against the earth. Your task is still ahead of you, but mine ends here."

Finn shook his head, his eyes filling with tears. "No, I will not lose another friend. I'll die before I let them take you. You are my brother. I cannot lose you."

Cojax felt tears in his own eyes begin to form. He embraced Finn, his oldest and most faithful friend. Never had he doubted his friendship—not in the Mahghetto, not when they started the revolution, and not even now when he faced certain death. He pulled back from the embrace and looked at his friend. "Find Jessica and protect her. You must do what I cannot." He then embraced Orch and Onar in turn.

The ship landed so smoothly they hardly even noticed.

"What if it's a trap," Orch asked, "and they shoot us down as soon as they have you?"

Cojax stepped back to the main entrance. "I will not drop my blade until you are free from here. So, if that is their plan, they will pay dearly with their blood." He operated the door, letting it fall open. "Remember Horace's words. Remember what was done this day. And one day, our people will win their freedom."

Finn stepped forward, but Orch stopped him.

"We can't just let him go out there alone," Finn said.

"That's exactly what we have to do," Orch replied.

Cojax saluted and stepped out into the sun. He placed his helmet on his head and raised his blade, the one that Titan once carried. The three Decamont ships had landed in a semi-circle around his own ship. In the air, two dozen more hovered above, ready for the order to continue the attack. Already, elite Damnattii warriors had deployed into orderly, boxy formations.

From the midst of their impressive ranks, a creature Cojax had never seen before stepped forward. It wore ornate armor that looked more like it was carved than forged. The beast had two blades at his side, but he did not draw them. "Drop your sword."

"Let them go," Cojax replied.

The Decamont stepped forward, his armor seemingly projecting a yellow glow. He was taller than the Damnattii, but not quite as tall as a human. The Decamont warrior spoke into his ArmGuard. He then turned his attention to Cojax. "Is he the one?"

Adriana's voice came through the Comm. "That's him. That's Cojax Artino. I'd recognize his build and armor anywhere."

The Decamont nodded slowly. "Your friends are free to go."

Cojax linked Comms with those inside the ship. "Get out of here as fast as you can. I'll make sure they stay true to their word."

The cargo ship lifted off the ground—Cojax could almost hear Finn's adamant protests—but eventually, its engines revved up and sped off into the distance. He kept his Comm line open while they disappeared from sight.

"Drop your blade," the Decamont demanded again.

"Not until they're far enough away."

The Decamont slumped his shoulders. "I don't care about them."

"But I do."

They waited another fifteen minutes, Cojax communicating with his friends the whole way. It seemed the Decamont had been true to his word and did not have them followed.

Cojax dropped his blade to the ground.

"Remove your helmet," the Decamont commanded.

Cojax complied.

The Decamont was surprised by what he saw. The features appeared so young, far too young to be the leader of the rebellion. The Decamont turned back to his ArmGuard, now sensing that he had been deceived. "Are you sure this is him?"

"Yes," Adriana's voice replied. "That's Cojax. Don't let his age fool you. He's a dangerous mix of passion and luck."

With this, the Decamont stepped forward, dropping a set of energy shackles to the ground. "I am Bracks the Revelator, commander of the forces you faced on the field of battle. I give you my word that while you are under my care, no harm will come to you. Remove your armor and place the shackles on your wrists."

Cojax complied with the order. The Decamont turned away, a show of giving him some privacy, but none of the Damnattii did. He was given white clothing that had a silver Placard that sat just over the right pectoral. He shivered as the Placard settled over his body. It was identical to the one that he wore on his armor in the Mahghetto.

"Follow me," the Decamont gestured to the largest of the three ships.

"Where are you taking me?"

The Decamont looked at Cojax appraisingly. He seemed to be considering how to best answer. He finally spoke, the pincers on his forearms opening and closing as he did. "We go to my ship in orbit—the Charron."

A Note from the Author

Sterling enjoys hearing from his readers. If you have any comments, thoughts, critiques, questions, and/or just want to say hello, please email him at isbnwriter@gmail.com. It may take some time for a response, but he tries to answer each email personally.

Also, if you enjoyed this novel and want to see more written by Sterling, please take the time to leave a review on Amazon. Your comments and support help out tremendously.

Other Books Written by Sterling Nixon

Historical Fiction:
Gladiators of the Naumachia

Post-Apocalyptic Fiction:
Seven Days
Rising Storm (To Be Released)

Dystopia Fiction:
Acadia
Titan
Charron (To Be Released)

Young Adult Fiction:
Nickle Brickle'Bee: In the Heart of EarthWorks (To Be Released)
Nickle Brickle'Bee: In the Halls of Alberdeen (To Be Released)

Made in the USA
San Bernardino, CA
20 May 2020

71963914R00256